I0825362

ISLAND OF GHOSTS AND DREAMS

ALSO BY CHRISTOPHER COSMOS

Once We Were Here

Young Conquerors

The Rise

ISLAND of GHOSTS and DREAMS

A NOVEL

CHRISTOPHER COSMOS

PEGASUS BOOKS
NEW YORK LONDON

For those who don't run.

ISLAND OF GHOSTS AND DREAMS

Pegasus Books, Ltd.
148 West 37th Street, 13th Floor
New York, NY 10018

First Pegasus Books cloth edition March 2026

Interior design by Maria Fernandez

Library of Congress Cataloging-in-Publication Data is available.

ISBN: 979-8-89710-056-9

10 9 8 7 6 5 4 3 2 1

Printed in the United States of America
Distributed by Simon & Schuster
www.pegasusbooks.com

THE ESCAPE

APRIL 23, 1941

I raise my eyes and look up towards the bright and fractured light. The explosions have shaken the ground and sky and thrown me from my feet and the place I stood only moments before. I land heavily in the dirt where displaced earth falls around me in uneven and staccato waves. As the churned and burnt soil returns back to where it once rested, I squint through the haze of unnatural precipitation, holding my hand up to shield my view, and this is what I see: the soldiers I travelled with from Thermopylae are all dead, bodies lying between and amongst the rocks of the mountain we've defended, and the young Greek resistance fighters we met along the way are in retreat, heading farther up the mountain to run south across the rest of the Attic Peninsula and on towards Athens. I'm the only British soldier that's left. I'm the only one from my entire company that's still alive. The women and children we saved from the orphanage have gone ahead of us, to try to get to Athens, to Piraeus, and the sea, to be able to evacuate to the islands, or Africa, somewhere that's still safe and free, and we've stayed behind to fight the Germans to give them time. We've done that now; we've fought the Germans that march south, and delayed them, so it's our turn to try to get to Athens. As I rise from the ground where I've been thrown by the force of the explosions, that's the only thought I have, the only one that's still left. Rise. Rise. We have to go.

I stand.

I wobble on unsteady feet as I look north and west, towards the advancing Germans, coming up the mountain through the swirling storm of dust they've created.

Then I turn and begin to run south.

My legs work slowly at first, but after a few paces they start to stretch and loosen, and I begin to sprint along with the young Greek fighters. We run to the top of the pass we've defended as the air around us explodes with bullets and mortars. The ground shakes even more, and the young, dark-haired, dark-eyed Greek that runs next to me falls. He must have tripped, I think, but when I glance down, I see that he didn't trip at all, and it was more than that. There's blood on his shirt, near his stomach. I'm about to reach down to help him but his friend comes first, the one who used to talk around the campfire in the moments that were silent and full of fear and doubt, and who told me in accented English his name was Costa. So I turn back towards the Germans, instead, and raise my rifle and fire blindly into the dust and swirling wind where I know they march. I'm trying to help hold the pass just a little bit longer, to give Costa and his friend more time to stand, and keep going, but Costa holds his friend's head in his lap and I realize I'm not giving them time to stand, but for something else, instead.

I hear words.

I hear passionate and important words with deep and labored breaths in-between, and they come from the soldier that Costa's holding, the one that's dying in his friend's lap in these wild hills north of the city and the sea.

Promise me.

Raise him to honor his grandfather.

It's beautiful, it's all beautiful.

I hear the words, and I feel them, too.

I feel what these two have gone through together, and endured, and what they've fought for and what they still fight for—what all in this country still fight for—and it's why we need to keep going.

So, after a moment, we do.

It's hard to leave him there.

It's hard to leave him with empty eyes staring up at the clear, blue, and endless sky, but we have to, and there are only two of them now, only two Greek fighters left out of all that stood with me and fought against evil under the warm and late spring sun. We start to run again, together, faster, then I hear one more bullet and as soon as I do, there's a searing pain in my thigh and I fall in another shower of dust and dirt that powders my face and rushes into my throat and lungs to choke me.

The Greeks whip their heads around.

They stop running and come back to me.

They try to pick me up, to help me back to my feet, but I shake my head.

"*Oxi*," I tell them. "No."

It's one of the only words I've learned in the weeks I've been in this country, and when I say it, they understand: they still have to get to Athens before the Germans, and they won't be able to do that if they have to wait for me, if they have to travel with someone who's been injured and can't run.

They look at each other.

"Go," I tell them and hope they can see in my eyes that I want them to, that my word is more than just a word, that it's a prayer, too, and a wish.

There's another moment.

Then they nod, each in turn.

"May God watch over you," the taller one says, in thicker and more-accented English.

"Thank you," the second answers, the one I'd seen cradle the head of his friend who has just died. "*Efcharisto*."

There's one more moment, and one more look.

Then they turn and begin to run again.

Like Pheidippides, I whisper, barely even a whisper, more breath than words that pass between my lips as they sprint into the distance, quickly over hills and grass and dirt, on and towards the ancient city and capital.

After they're gone, I turn and look around.

I have a pistol with only two rounds, so that won't be much use in defense, and there's nowhere to hide, really, but the sun is beginning to set and soon the light will be gone, and it'll be night. I see a small grove of low bushes. I make a decision based on fading light and last chances and crawl towards it. The land here is dry and dusty—too dry and dusty, on this part of the peninsula—and dirt cakes to my legs, arms, and face as I crawl, and I let it. I let it come and stay wherever it will on my skin to help disguise me, to make me and my body part of the earth and this peninsula, too.

I get to the bushes.

I look behind me, where I just was.

The Germans are cresting the mountain pass, cautiously coming to the top and then peering over to the other side, the southern side, where I am, looking behind rocks, around trees, searching for any place more resistance could be hiding to continue to shoot at them as they advance.

But there's no more resistance left.

There's only me.

I pull myself into the bushes.

I position the branches and leaves so they partially cover my body, then reach down to my leg and look at the wound that's there. The bullet passed through the flesh of my upper thigh, tearing muscle, and blood has seeped out and through the cloth of my military-issue pants. I know what I need to do. I grab onto my leg. I take a deep breath and even though the pain is excruciating, beyond anything I've ever felt in my life and infinitely more painful than the bullet itself, I squeeze my leg as hard as I can so more blood comes. When it does, I put my hands into the blood, then reach up and smear it in uneven streaks across my face, chest, arms, nearly every inch of my body so that it's everywhere on me, and then I lay still.

I don't move.

I stay like this in the same spot, in the same way, and I close my eyes so I don't see them.

I can hear them, though.

They keep walking, down the mountain, coming very carefully.

They get closer.

Soon I can feel the ground rumble from their tanks and hear the soldiers that walk alongside and in front of the tanks speaking, shouting, answering each other in foreign words I don't understand and a language I wish I'd never heard. I smell gas and oil, too, as they get closer. This might sound strange, but I can smell evil, as well, amongst the smell of everything else. I can feel it. It comes with them.

A soldier walks near me. I hold my breath.

His leather boots crunch on small rocks as I silently compose a prayer in my mind that he continues, that he doesn't stop at the grove here where I hide. But he does. He comes even closer and then I feel him directly above me, looking down. This is it, I realize. I make a quick calculation. I still have my pistol resting in my outstretched hand, on my palm, and I could bring it up and get one shot off and still have one bullet left after that, so if I'm to die, I could still kill one of them and bring one with me. That's it, I think. That's what I'll do. It will be my death, but it will be one of theirs, also, and just before I go to make my move, I feel the pistol gently taken from my palm and so I remain as I am. My eye cracks ever so slightly and I see a young German soldier—probably no more than eighteen years old, by my guess, one that doesn't need to shave yet—and he looks at the pistol he's just found. He opens the chamber and sees the two bullets that are in it. He nods once, satisfied apparently, then closes the chamber and reaches back down again. I can feel my body tense. I don't want it to, but it does. He wipes the blood that's on the handle back onto my uniform, then stands and tucks the pistol into his belt and turns to jog back towards the tanks and other Germans.

I wait until he's away, until he's far enough away.

Then I finally exhale.

In the distance, the sun sinks even further until it's almost gone, and I watch from the bushes with slitted eyes as the Germans continue on and into the distance, light and color reflecting off them as they head farther south, closer and closer to Athens with each step they take, with each revolution of the tracks on their tanks. The sun finally leaves altogether, and sets, and with it the warmth leaves, too; it gets very cold this time of year when the sun's gone, so I shiver now, also, and I wait.

I need to be sure.

When I am, I stand again.

The muscles in my injured leg have begun to tighten and lock, and any way I try to move the leg is incredibly painful, but it will have to be, and I will have to endure the pain if I want to leave, and if I want to live.

I do.

I do want to live. I *need* to.

I try to think beyond the throbbing in my leg as the soldiers that just passed will now make it to Athens before I ever could, even if I wasn't injured, and soon this entire area where I stand will be controlled by Germans, so I have to find another way. I think back to the map I studied while I sat in the bright Egyptian sun at Alexandria and waited for the ship that would bring me and the rest of the British troops here. The Germans will have taken Chalcis already, I know, so I'll go south of Chalcis and find somewhere smaller, somewhere they don't care about and won't conquer until later, after they take Athens. I rip a piece of uniform—a strip of cloth from around the hem of my shirt, near the waist—and I tie it above my thigh. I pull firmly on the fabric to cinch the knot as tightly as I can, and the bleeding stops, or at least slows to something manageable and I begin to drag myself through night and darkness. I say drag because that's what I have to do with my leg, to make it obey the commands from my body it can't obey on its own. I have to reach the coast before the sun comes, so I pull myself and limp through the entire night and am nearly there when light starts to peek above the hills in front of me. It rises higher in the sky, and exposes me again, to any enemies that might come or be near.

It's a chance I'll have to take.

I keep going, faster now, as fast as I can.

Fresh blood starts to come but I ignore it, then smell salt on the breeze, and that's how I know I'm close. I crest the last hill in front of me and then do more than smell the sea, because I see it now, too, calm and spread before me to the east. I see a small house near where sea meets land, and I begin to walk towards it. As soon as I'm there, even though the sun has only just begun to rise, a man emerges with a rifle pointed at me and I quickly raise my hands into the air. My uniform is bloody and torn, but it's still what it is, and belongs to the nation it belongs to, and he sees that and recognizes who I fight for and that I'm a friend.

"British," I say to him. "*Anglia*."

He lowers the rifle.

"*Nai*," he says, nodding. "*Kalo*."

"*Nai*," I repeat, also nodding, then see his wife and two young children come to the doorway behind him. He notices my leg and gestures because he knows I need help, but I shake my head again to tell him no, *oxi*, there's no time. "I need a boat," I say instead. "*Skafos*."

"*Skafos*?" he asks, eyebrows raised now.

"*Nai*," I nod.

He waits for a moment, then looks back at his wife and motions for her to stay with the children. He starts to walk. I follow after him. We go down a rocky path and he goes slowly, in front of me, so I can keep up. I soon see another house in the distance, one that's nearly the same size and shape as his house.

"*Skafos*," he says, and I look to where he's pointing.

There's a dock below us that extends into the sea and a small fishing boat tied at the end of it, bobbing gently in the soft waves.

"Doesn't he need it?" I ask.

"*Aftos einai nekros*," he responds, shaking his head.

I know what the man has told me even without knowing the words, and I still want to pay him or somebody for the boat rather than just take it, but I can't, as the only thing of value I have is the ring I wear on the second finger of my right hand—the ring I've worn and never taken off for a day in my life, not since I turned sixteen—and I'd rather die than give it away.

I stand there and look back at him.

This is his friend he's talking about, I know, and whose boat he's giving me, probably his lifelong and childhood friend, and I finally nod, slightly.

So does he.

"God bless you," he says in heavy, accented English.

Then without any more words, he turns and begins back up towards his family.

I go in the other direction, and down towards the boat.

I soon get there and to the dock, quickly untie the boat, toss the rope inside, then climb over the edge myself and to where I can sit on the wooden bench and take the oars that rest against the sides. I use one of them to reach out and push off from the dock. I begin to float out, into the Aegean, through the silent and calm morning that is of course anything but those things. I spin the boat so my back is to the south, the direction I need to travel, then dip the oars into the salty, wine-dark, and ancient sea, and I begin to pull.

It's not very long until the storm comes.

I keep the land to my left, the still-rising sun to my right, and follow closely along the coast, as closely as I dare. As the sun begins to climb even higher and warmth begins to return, the coast narrows to a point, then ends altogether, and I sail past it and continue between intermittent islands of all shapes and sizes and whose names I don't know. I wonder what they are. I wonder what their histories have been, and what they've seen, and what stories live there. I sail around and past them, not sure what I'd find if I stopped, as most don't look inhabited, and I need to get to Crete; it's the southernmost and largest of all the Greek islands and where the Greek government and royal family have fled, and where they'll set up another government and continue to fight, and I'll join them there, and I will, too.

I pass by more islands, and more time passes, also, as I dip the oars and pull them through water, then soon it becomes dark.

The sun sets in the distance in a way I've never quite seen before, a majestic spectacle of burnt oranges and soft yellows, juxtaposed against the clear azure of the water and craggy pieces of land, then once the light is gone, I follow the stars.

The temperature drops even more.

Even for this time of year, it seems unnaturally cold, and I can feel the pressure begin to change in the air, all around me.

The wind picks up.

And then, after the wind comes, so too does the rain.

Based on the calculations I've made of how long the journey from Attica to Crete should take, I must be close, I think—somewhere south of Santorini, and north of Irakleio, my destination—but I'm not close enough to reach Irakleio before the full brunt of the storm gets to me. The wind begins to whip even more and waves get bigger. The swells are small at first, then larger, and that's when the wind begins to change, too; it's swirled for the last few minutes, but then starts to blow uniformly, in the same direction, and it blows west. I'm confused by this because west is the direction in which weather usually *comes*, not goes, but there's been nothing normal or natural about any of this, not anything that's happened over the last months of war and death and men killing men, all in the name of power, prejudices, and lies. And that's why I'm here, after all, isn't it? That's why I'm here and it's what we're fighting against. I don't know how long the storm lasts, but it seems to go on forever, and so does the rest of the dark and cold night; wind and swells only increase as it drags on, and waves crash over the side of the boat and fill my mouth with salt and foam and water.

Then as the waves and wind increase, even more, the boat starts to fill.

It's small at first, just a little bit of water, then there's more.

One of the oars is ripped away by a wave, then soon the other is, too.

I cup my hands together.

I try to scoop as much water from the boat as I can, but it's no use, there's too much, and the waves only get bigger, crashing over the edge with more strength and determination and frequency. I shiver violently, freezing in the cold Greek night but there's nothing else to do but try because the alternative is death.

How far am I from Crete?

How far am I from land, from any of the islands, even one I'm *not* trying to reach?

It's dark so I can't see anything, but I sit higher, then stand to try to see further, too, over the waves, and that's then when the biggest one comes—the biggest wave yet—and I lose my balance and the boat starts to tip and then flip and I'm thrown from it as it's launched up into the air on the back of the great wave and I plunge down into the cold and dark water. I hold my breath then quickly push myself back to the surface and I get there in just enough time to see the boat coming back down again and straight towards me and where I tread water. It strikes me squarely on top of the head, and as it does, my arms go limp, and I feel water rush into my nose and mouth and it burns, and so does the top of my head, and I slip back beneath the waves.

I push myself to the surface again.

I gasp for air between the swells and reach and feel my hair and find blood there, a great deal of blood, then I look for the boat but it's been pushed away by current and wind and never-ending waves. I try to fight for a moment and swim towards it, but it's too far and only getting sucked farther and farther from where I swim, and I need to conserve energy. I look around. Another wave comes and washes over me and I clear the salt and water from my eyes, and spit as much from my mouth as I can. I look around and still don't see any land, not anywhere that I look. Is this it? Is this the end? Will I be lost here, and forgotten, my body never seen or found or brought back to England, or will my fate be something else, and something different?

I'm determined for it to be something different.

So I start to swim.

I pull myself in the direction I think is south, and even though I'm a strong swimmer, I soon begin to tire. I'm losing blood from the wound on my head and my mouth fills with more water, and my nose does, too. Soon my limbs don't respond like they normally do; first it's my arms, then my legs. My whole body seems to relax. I don't want it to, but it does. I try to lift my head. I try to lift my eyes to see over the waves and towards the horizon, to see if there's any land there, and even more water rushes into my mouth. I reach for my hand. I feel my ring. It's still there, on the second finger, as it should be. At least that's something that won't be broken; at least, if nothing else, that's a promise that will be kept, even if there are no others that will be fulfilled. I look at the bright and cold moon above and try to whisper another prayer, a prayer to any God, ancient or modern, that might be watching or listening, but before I finish and last words come, there's more water. There's more water, everywhere, all around me, rushing between my lips and then filling my lungs. I splutter and choke as I lose consciousness and finally succumb and begin to descend into the sea.

The last thing I taste is salt.

The last thing I see, above me, is light.

1

APRIL 25, 1941

I walk along the familiar road from Chania that heads west from the city. It hugs the rugged northern coast of the great southern island of Greece, and once I'm outside the city and beyond the ancient Venetian walls, I go past the place where sea meets rock until there's sand, I round a sharp bend to where the water either laps or crashes against more rock, depending on the season, then when the rock turns to sand once more, that's where I find his body. I stop walking and look towards where it's washed onto the beach, squinting my eyes, making sure this is really what I'm seeing. It is. Is he alive or dead? I don't know but I can tell it's a man based on the size of the body and military uniform he's wearing, even though it's ripped, torn, and drenched with water. I look around. There's no one else on the road. There's no one else that can help, so I pick up the hem of my skirt and start to run down and towards him. The beach of Chryssi Akti is shaped into a crescent and there are only gentle waves that lap against the sand here as the beach is shielded from any larger ones by the small island that's only a half kilometer into the sea and creates a natural barrier. I leave the path and when I reach the body, and see it even closer, I see the man doesn't wear a Greek uniform, like I was expecting, but the uniform of a British soldier. It's one I see often as there are British everywhere on Crete, quartered in the Old Town of Chania, here in the west, and they've been here for some months now; they've come from North Africa and are constantly shuttled between Chania and Souda Bay, a few kilometers east of the city, over the low and soft hills of the Akrotiri Peninsula, with Souda Bay being the largest and deepest harbor in the Mediterranean so also where much of the British fleet is now docked.

The British have garrisoned and held our ports and cities so the Greek soldiers of the Cretan 5th Division could go to the mainland to fight the Italians and Germans who came and invaded after the Greek victory over the Italians, which was the first Allied victory of the entire war. And it was Greece, and our Cretan soldiers, with my husband amongst them, who helped bring that victory. I received Demetrios's last letter just two weeks ago. Every time I walk this road I look north, across the soft waves and past the small island, hoping to see a boat or any sign of him coming home. I haven't seen anything yet, but I still look, every time I pass, and still hope, because I know one day he will.

I roll the soldier over, and when I do, I see his chest move.

He's breathing.

It's soft and shallow and labored, the type of breathing that feels like it could give out at any moment, but it hasn't, at least not yet. I shake him to try to get him to return to consciousness, but his eyes don't open. Then I see the wound on his leg and blood that's stained his trousers and hasn't washed away. Or, perhaps it has, but more has come since he's washed ashore. How long has he been here? I shake him even harder and when he doesn't respond,

I gently slap him on the cheek, to try to get him to return to this world, but nothing seems to work.

I look around again.

There's still no one else on the small, winding road that leads west and away from Chania, then up towards the mountains and my village, and I can't carry or move him on my own. It's risky to leave him in this state, but if he's going to have a chance, it's the only way, so I grab him underneath his arms and strain the muscles in my chest to pull him farther up onto the sand and away from the cold sea that's been softly lapping against his body.

I turn back towards the path.

I look behind me, once more, at his pale skin, wet hair, and still-closed eyes.

Then I take a deep breath, pull the length of my skirt up to my knees again, and begin to run.

It's not long until I come to the olive groves.

Our village is in a valley between two hills, just south of Chania, and a little west, on the way towards the high-peaked mountains called the White Mountains because of how long snow stays crested and bright on their greatest heights, and even when the snow finally melts in late summer, there's limestone underneath which is white also, so the mountains always seem to look the same, no matter the season or time. But before you get to the mountains, and the valley between them, where we live, there are rows of olives that the family I've married into has owned and tended since before any on this island can remember. That's where I find the boys. Our farm has both olives and sheep, and since all the young men we'd hired previously to help are now fighting on the mainland, it's fallen to me and Demetrios's two younger brothers, Ikaros and Tasos, just fifteen and thirteen, to keep the farm running and bring our wares to sell in the *agora* at Chania. When Demetrios first left more than six months ago, I started going to the olives alone because Tasos, his youngest brother, wasn't yet tall enough to reach the branches, even with a ladder, or carry the buckets of water. But Tasos has grown a great deal in the last months, as boys do when they're young, so he can reach the lowest branches to help prune now. He's grown wider in the shoulders and arms, too, and is strong enough to carry the buckets, so I've been going to the fields above our village with the sheep to graze, which I prefer, and leaving the boys to take care of the trees that are closer to the coast and city, where it's warmer, and where the olives grow better in the hot sun on the north-and-east-facing slopes, dusted by the salt carried to them on the breeze from the Sea of Crete.

When I see them, I call out.

"*Ikaros!*" I shout, as I keep running. "*Tasos!*"

They hear my voice and when they see me, hurrying towards where they stand on ladders with shears in their hands, heads and bodies amongst the branches they're trimming, they jump down with concern in their eyes and when I reach them, I tell them what's happened, and what I've found. As soon as they hear, the trees are immediately forgotten. Ikaros and Tasos both were too young to go to the mainland when the young men of this island were volunteering to fight, but they're still old enough to *wish* they'd been allowed to and do their part to help defend our country from those that would come once again and try to take it from us.

Especially Ikaros.

He was only fifteen when Demetrios and the others left, but he's nearly sixteen now, just a few months shy of his birthday, and he's devoured every single letter that Demetrios has sent to me; he's pored over maps of mountains near the northern border, drawn lines by candlelight representing troops and movements, studied strategy and logistics and battles along with listening to every radio broadcast from both Athens and the BBC. Now, in front of me, he runs to the donkey that carries the buckets of water slung over its back—a bucket on each side of the animal, connected by a piece of thick rope to balance them—and tosses the buckets from the donkey and to the ground.

"Let's go," he says.

All three of us turn and run towards Chryssi Akti, pulling the donkey behind, and when we get to the beach, I see the soldier hasn't moved. No one else has come, either. We run to where he lays on the sand, where I pulled him from the sea and waves, and when we get to him, I take him under one shoulder, Tasos takes him under the other, and Ikaros grabs his feet. We lift and spin his body so he's face down, then lift him again, higher this time, and drape him across the donkey's back. The donkey is used to carrying dozens of buckets of water and olives that together weigh more than one British *palikari*, so it's not an unexpected or too-heavy burden for the animal as we quickly start back up the path again, and towards the village. I think about taking him to Chania, and the British garrison that's there, but it's too far; our village, and the doctor that lives near us, is much closer.

"Do you think he was in the war?" I hear and turn to see Ikaros looking at me.

His brother is looking at me, too, and I glance at the soldier's wounded head, his leg, the bullet-sized hole that's there in his uniform and the blood still on the fabric that's around it.

"I don't know," I tell them, but without conviction.

Because the truth is obvious: of course he was in the war.

"How do you think he got separated?"

It's Tasos that asks this time.

I turn and look at him, as we keep walking.

"I don't know," I tell him. "But I'm not sure how much time he has, so if we want to find out, run ahead and make sure Doctor Papadakis is ready and then maybe you'll be able to ask him yourself."

Tasos looks at me for another moment.

Then he nods and starts to sprint up the path.

I watch for a moment, his young and skinny legs expertly picking their way between small rocks and not seeming to tire at all—not when there's a task at hand as important as this—and as he heads into the distance, I turn and look behind us for a moment. I look at the beach, then out at the sea: at the gentle and familiar waves and small island that's there. I think of the last time I was there, on the island. I also think of the first time I was, both of which were with my husband, and memorable, but for different reasons, and then I look at the waves again and I know what they've brought to us, and I wonder, what else will they bring? What else *could* they bring? Where is the fighting now that it's no longer in the north, and what has happened in Greece to bring this man to our shores? Where is Demetrios in all this? If a British *palikari* was able to cross the Aegean, then what about my husband, a Greek *palikari*? Will he be able to cross, too, and in the same way? And what about the others, all the other brave men who have left to go and fight? Will they also return? Will the sea also bring them back, back to us, back to this ancient and beautiful island where we've made our homes for more generations than can be counted? They say that Knossos, in the eastern part of Crete, is the oldest city in all of Europe, and while I don't know if that's true, or if it's typical Greek embellishment and storytelling, I know what I believe, and what I hope, and what I've prayed for. I normally only pray at night, right before I close my eyes for the day, but I now let myself whisper one more prayer, and I whisper it in the light. I pray for my husband. I pray for him, and our future, and our island. Then when the prayer's finished, I turn back to Ikaros, who walks steadily next to me, and the foreign soldier that we carry back towards our ancient village and the doctor that's there that might be able to save his lost and brave life.

When we arrive, people have come from their houses to get a glimpse of this strange man that's been brought to their village. They've all heard what's happened on the mainland, of course, with Athens falling to the Nazis and now they wonder, the same as I do, what will be next: will the Germans come here, to Crete, or will they stop at the capital and leave the islands alone? The entire village has been able to talk of nothing else for the last days and weeks but now, with the arrival of this soldier, the future seems to have finally intruded into our lives in a way we haven't been able to imagine yet or comprehend.

Eyes follow us as we go.

We hurry down uneven cobblestone streets—Ikaros, myself, and the donkey, with the soldier draped across its back—then finally come to our house at the northern edge of both the village and valley, with the white-capped peaks in front of us and just a little farther south.

Doctor Papadakis is waiting at the door.

Tasos stands next to him, and Giannis and Angeliki are there, too, Demetrios's parents and my mother and father-in-law. The doctor comes forward when he sees we've arrived, and so do Giannis and Tasos, and they help me and Ikaros pull the soldier from the donkey's back and carry him into the house. It's a large house where we live, in comparison to the others in the village, with a living room, kitchen, and three small bedrooms. We take him to the smallest of the bedrooms, which Tasos and Ikaros normally share, and gently lay him down on Ikaros's twin bed where Doctor Papadakis starts to examine and see if he might be able to save a life this morning.

"There's a wound," I say, as I point. "On his leg."

"Has he been shot?" Tasos asks, his eyes wide.

I look at Giannis and Angeliki and they push the two boys towards the door, and when they're gone, I turn back to the doctor.

"Do you think he'll live?" I ask.

"It looks like he's lost a lot of blood, but the saltwater probably helped, at least a little."

"What does that mean?"

"It means there's likely no infection, so we'll sew him up, do everything we can, then the rest will be with God and we'll see if he wakes in a day or two."

"And if he doesn't?"

"Then he'll starve and die."

I stand there for another moment, looking at the doctor.

Then I nod, understanding.

I go back out of the room as he begins his work, through the house and outside again to where Giannis and Angeliki wait with Tasos and Ikaros, under the shade of the great olive trees that grow here, too, with tall and pointed cypress scattered around and between them.

All four of them turn and look as I come to stand in front of them.

We're silent for a moment, all of us, each with our own thoughts.

Then Angeliki speaks, softly and carefully.

"We heard on the radio while you were in the city that the king's gone to a village near Knossos, and the government's on its way here."

"*Here?*" I ask, frowning. "What do you mean?"

"To Chania."

"They must think it's safe here, then," I say, and speak a little louder than I normally would to make sure the boys hear, too, and they do.

Tasos smiles.

Ikaros frowns.

"What about Demetrios?" he asks, the question that's been on all our minds, the one I've only dared whisper when no one else is listening, when no one else is there to hear or remember except the wind and gnarled trunks and ancient branches of the olives that we tend.

"There wasn't any mention of our troops," Angeliki says to her middle son, then swallows.

That's why she's spoken softly, and we can't go down that path.

"I'll take the boys to my parents," I say instead, because their bedroom is now being occupied by the British *palikari*, and Giannis nods, then Angeliki, and after a moment, the boys do, too, both at the same time.

We turn and we go, and bring the donkey with us.

We walk through the rest of the village and towards the farm where I grew up, which is not far beyond the last of the buildings, just a little bit farther south, through the valley and away from the main part of town. The sun's beginning to set and shadows reach down and crisscross in shapes and patterns across our path. As we get closer to the farm, the wind picks up and brings with it a strong scent of cinnamon. There's almond, too, that I smell on the breeze along with the cinnamon, and I know that means Mana is baking *paximathia*. My mother's the best cook in the village, a gift that somehow hasn't passed to me, and the secret ingredient in her *paximathia* that gives away what she's making is always the extra cinnamon. The boys smell the cookies, too, but I take them to the barn first, on the far side of the house and near the fields. They put the donkey back into his stall and pour him a cup of grain, exactly as my father has shown and taught them, then Tasos takes the bridle off the donkey's head and hangs it on a nail. I show the boys where they can sleep. The barn is where our sheep are kept at night, in addition to the donkey, and I show them where there are blankets and the small cot from when I was their age and decided I wanted a room of my own and moved out of the house and to here, with the animals, after Demetrios had finished building it, so many summers ago. We weren't married then, but it's how we met, or at least how we first began to spend time together because everyone in our village knows everyone else and it was during that time building this barn that we began to fall in love, before we even really knew what that was, or what it was that we were feeling.

Ikaros takes the blankets and puts them on the cot and offers the now-made bed to his younger brother before he pushes two bales of hay together on the other side of the barn. He drapes a different sheet over the bales to protect himself from the sharp edges of the straw, then pulls a thinner blanket over top of the sheet, and it's ready, also.

"If it gets too cold out here, there are more blankets in the house," I tell them.

They hear me but don't answer because blankets and sheets and the chill from the mountains are the absolute furthest thing from their minds.

We leave the barn.

The boys run ahead of me and are inside the house by the time I get there and to the kitchen, and they already have their hands full of *paximathia* that have just finished baking in the stone oven in the corner of the room. Mana's standing next to them and smiling and giving them more, as soon as they finish what they already have. She looks up when I come in and smiles at me, but then sees my eyes. She knows something's happened, that something's wrong, and can tell because she's my mother and so she's me, too.

"What is it?" she asks.

"Nothing," I shake my head. "Baba's still up in the fields?"

"He'll be back soon. What's wrong?"

"Maria found a *palikari*," Tasos answers for me, still chewing his cookie while reaching for another. "A British one. We brought him here and he's in our room now with Dr. Papadakis."

"No more cookies until you've had dinner," I tell them, and Tasos just smiles, my words meaningless because they know my mother will enforce no such rule. She wouldn't do the same with me, even when I was their age, but the boys? She can't say no to the boys who are closer to grandchildren to her than children, just the same as they're closer to children to me than brothers, and she treats them that way, also, just the same as I do.

"A British *palikari*?" she asks, turning back to me.

"He was down on the beach. He must have washed ashore."

"From where?"

"I don't know," I say, then try to change the subject again. "I set the boys up in the barn with my old cot and blankets. Baba will see it when he gets back."

"They can stay here in your old room. We could bring the cot in from the barn for Tasos, and Ikaros could have your bed."

"We like it outside," Ikaros says quickly.

My mother looks at him, then both of them.

She recognizes they're young boys who are almost young men, or at least one of them is almost a young man, and they want the independence the barn would give. They probably even need it, too. "Alright," Mana finally nods. "As long as you promise to come to the house for every meal."

They smile.

Of course they will.

Mana points up the hill and towards the fields where we take the sheep for the fresh grass that grows higher in the mountains. "Why don't you go help Baba bring the sheep down for the night. He'll be glad to see you," she says to the boys, then they each grab another *paximathia* and run out of the house and towards the fields to find Baba.

"They seem to be handling it well," Mana says, once they're gone.

"They're young."

"You're young, too."

"Maybe."

"Maybe? You are. Trust me, *Maria-mou*, you are. Now what is this they're saying about a British *palikari* you found?"

"He's in a coma and hasn't regained consciousness, so we don't know any more than that, and won't until he wakes up."

"Does Dr. Papadakis think he will?"

"I don't know. He says he might, but if he doesn't soon, then he'll starve and die."

"And you haven't heard anything from Demetrios?"

"I asked Ione and Kore before I left, and Cassia when I was in Chania, and no one's heard anything from anyone in the 5th for over a month. Not a single letter or telegram."

She's silent.

We're both silent.

Ione and Kore are a few years older than I am and married to Stelios and Elias who also left our village with Demetrios, and Cassia is my best friend from when we were both very young; she's moved to Chania and works in one of the *kafeneios* there now and is who I stay with when I go to the city to sell our goods and remain for the night before coming home. She sees many soldiers there that she waits on, and brings coffee and sweets to, and I know a great many of them write to her, also. She's always been the most good-looking of all the girls who grew up here in our village, and perhaps maybe all of Western Crete and Chania, too, and she always has men and soldiers writing to her, and often more than one.

"Let me know if they're too much," I say to Mana as I walk towards the door.

"It's good to have their voices here, their young voices. And you know how much Baba loves having them around. Do you want to stay for dinner, too, Maria? Let me cook for you."

"I'm going to get back and see how he's doing."

"Who?"

"The *palikari*."

We look at each other one more time, me by the door, Mana by the stone oven, then she nods. "Of course," she says, then nods once more, and so do I before I walk out and start back up towards the village and the house where I live with my husband and his parents. Theirs is the largest house in our village, and Demetrios and I live in a section that's separated from the main part, which is why we moved there rather than the farm where I grew up, where everything's cramped and my childhood bedroom is separated from my parents' by a paper-thin wall and a few pieces of stone and wood. Wealth on this island is measured in olives and sheep, and Demetrios's family has an abundance of both; the groves north of the village, on the path to Chania, are the largest in all Western Crete and have been in their family for generations, and it's the wealth from those olives that they used to buy the sheep we keep at our farm. My father was a shepherd, the same as his father before him, and when Demetrios's family bought their sheep near Irakleio, and brought them to Chania, it was my father they hired to tend and keep them. The only problem was our barn wouldn't hold all the sheep that they bought, so they sent their oldest son down to help build a new one that was larger and would hold every last one of the large flock they'd purchased.

I think back to that summer.

I smile when I do.

Demetrios was fifteen and I was fourteen, both younger than Ikaros is now, and it feels strange to think of it that way. I knew Demetrios before he came to work on the barn but only in the way you know someone who you nod to when you pass them on the street and say hello and goodbye and good evening and how's the weather. But that summer I really got to know him. I brought him lunches that Mana made, sat and ate with him, and learned how funny he was as we spent the warmest and hottest months together there, at the barn, under the Cretan sun. He would smile at me. He would look at me and smile in a way that no one ever had before, much less someone my age, and then even after the barn was raised and finished and he no longer came to work, he said he missed Mana's cooking and lunches she prepared so I'd still find him and we'd take the lunch she'd make for us up into the hills and we'd eat together. We would sit high above our village and look out, licking leftover honey and cheese from the *sfakianes pites* we'd have for dessert from our fingers, looking out together over our village, the olive groves and pastures and rolling hills, looking out and all the way to the great sea. We'd look out over everything. I once thought those days would last forever. My mother used to smile as she'd give me whatever she'd cooked, wrapped in old newspaper and placed into a basket always with her famous *sfakianes pites*, which she knew were Demetrios's favorite, and of course she also knew what was happening before I did. I think our parents always do, and they especially do here, on our island, where families are all such large and important and inescapable parts of who we are and remain that way for the entirety of our lives.

He wanted to be a builder.

And he was, at least before the war.

We got married when he was twenty and I was nineteen, which was six years ago, and he built the addition onto his parents' house that we moved into together and is where we lived until seven months ago when the Italians woke the Greek prime minister in the middle of the night and gave him the ultimatum of either letting their soldiers occupy Greece, without a fight, or it would be war.

Oxi. No.

That's the single word our prime minister allegedly said, at least according to the folklore that's sprung up around the event, but whether he actually said *oxi* or something else, what's undeniable is it's the word the whole country has resoundingly and continually repeated since the ultimatum was issued then rejected. It's also, since that morning, been war. We've been isolated from the actual fighting here in the South Aegean, the southernmost of all the Greek islands and nearly halfway to Africa, but even though we've been isolated, we haven't been spared.

I keep walking.

The sun's almost completely gone as I arrive back, the last remnants of disappearing yellows and oranges spread across the tops of olives and cypress near the house. I walk in to see Giannis and

Angeliki at the dining table. There's a small glass of *raki* in front of Giannis, and Angeliki has a cup of *malotira*, Greek mountain tea, made from the plants that grow wild in these hills. This is their afternoon ritual, something they've done every day since I've known them, and they both look up when I return.

"Any change?" I ask.

"Nothing," Angeliki tells me. "Doctor Papadakis left a few minutes ago."

"I wondered if we should take him to the barracks, and to their own doctors there," Giannis says. "But he didn't think moving him would be good."

I pause for a moment.

"We'll take him when he wakes up," I finally say, with more hope than I feel.

Then I leave the kitchen and go to the bedroom where he still sleeps.

They watch as I walk in to look down at the *palikari* on the small twin bed. His chest still gently rises and falls, just like when I found him. I see sweat that's started to bead on his skin, and I know that means a fever has begun, even though the doctor said an infection was unlikely, so I take a cloth and dip it into the water that's still there and gently dab it on his forehead, wiping away the sweat, trying to cool him down. I look at his eyes. They're closed, staring at nothing at all. I wonder, what have those eyes seen? Have they seen the same things that Demetrios's eyes have seen, and do they know if my husband will be coming back to me, to our island, the same way that this soldier has come?

I wonder.

I usually only pray for Demetrios once a day, as I've said, and as I've already done, on my way back to the village, but today I decide not to listen to what I've promised and make an exception as I bow my head and pray once more. I think of the last thing he said to me, before he left.

When I'm gone, don't look for me in the sunsets, look for me in the sea.

I've looked, Demetrios.

I've looked, my love, I've looked every single day . . .

But still you haven't returned.

2

APRIL 26, 1941

The next morning, I wake early before the sun and rise from my bed while it's still dark. Once I'm dressed, I go to the main part of the house and peek into Ikaros and Tasos's bedroom to see the *palikari* still breathing, and that he's made it through the night. His chest is still rising and falling in weak and unsteady rhythms, and there's no sweat on his forehead anymore so it seems his fever must be less, too. I know Giannis and Angeliki will take care of him when they wake, and Doctor Papadakis will be back soon, and can do more for him than I can, so I grab one of Demetrios's jackets, wrap it around my shoulders, and leave. It's still very cold in the morning this time of year and the grass that grows around the path I take north is damp from the night and clings to my ankles as I walk through fields of flowers, and that's what I smell. This is the time of year when they first begin to bloom—the small blue ones, with the white dot in the middle that only grow here, on Crete—and the herbs are all beginning to rise as well, wild and untamed; the *thymari*, the *thentrolivano*, and the *faskomilo*. I can smell their fresh and ubiquitous scent as I continue to walk, mixing with the familiar and more intimate one in the jacket, the scent that belongs to my husband. I soon come to the farm. When I get close, the smell of flowers, herbs, and Demetrios begins to mix with the smell of Mana's cooking, as she's already awake in the kitchen making breakfast. But I go to the barn first. I go past the sheep, who are awake and waiting to be let out, and towards where I used to sleep and Ikaros and Tasos have each now made their beds. When I get there, though, I pause. I see Tasos, on the cot, still asleep, but the bales that Ikaros pushed together and threw the sheet over to make his own bed are empty.

I frown, then bend down and shake Tasos.

"Hmmm," he says, mumbling, not yet awake.

"Where's your brother?"

"What?" he asks, rubbing his eyes.

"Where's Ikaros?"

He blinks as he looks up at me, then turns to the empty bed next to him.

"I had to go to the bathroom," I hear from behind us.

I turn to see Ikaros walking into the barn, already dressed and ready for the day.

He goes past the sheep, too, and towards the donkey, where he pours another cup of grain into the trough, and the donkey starts to eat.

"Did the *palikari* wake up?" Tasos asks me.

"Not yet," I tell them.

They take that in, both of them.

Then as the donkey finishes, Ikaros picks the bridle from its place on the wall and puts it around the donkey's head and tightens it. Tasos goes from his bed to the buckets connected by rope and drapes them across the donkey's back, then grabs the shears and pruners they'll need for the olives and puts them in one of the buckets. There's a saying in Crete that if you water your trees, you're begging them to give you olives, but if you prune them, you're ordering them to. This is the skill they've learned and which is in their blood. They were taught by their parents and older brother, and they were taught by me, too, who was also taught by Giannis, Angeliki, and Demetrios.

I smile at them.

They smile back at me.

We leave the barn together and as we walk out and into the darkness of the morning that hasn't yet arrived, Mana comes from the house carrying two knapsacks of food, and Baba follows behind, pulling on a thick jacket not unlike the one I wear and tying a red-checkered cloth at his neck to act as a scarf and keep the exposed skin there warm. Mana hands one of the sacks to Ikaros, as Tasos leads the donkey behind him, then the other to me, for Baba and myself up in the mountains.

"*Efcharisto*," I tell her, as I do every morning, and the boys do, too.

"Of course," she smiles, then kisses Ikaros and Tasos on the top of their heads, and she turns and kisses me as well. She kisses Baba last, and his kiss lasts a little longer than ours, before she heads back into the house to start planning what she'll make for dinner.

It's her life.

It was her mother's life, also, and her mother before that.

Will it be mine?

Ikaros and Tasos start to head north.

They walk down the path, leading the donkey behind them, on their way to the olives that are away from the mountains and towards the sea. Baba and I will go in the opposite direction. We turn and walk to the enclosure next to the barn where the sheep wait. He opens the gate and stands on one side of it. I stand on the other. This is something we've done more times than I can count—since I was just a little girl—and the sheep start to come. We point them south, as we also always do, and when they go in that direction, we start to walk after them, heading onward and up towards the great, white, and familiar mountains that stand tall and proud in the distance.

There are three different fields we use for grazing, and today we go to the highest one, the one farthest south. We rotate fields so the sheep don't eat in the same place every day and the grass has a chance to start growing back before it's eaten again. We sit on a rock together and eat fresh *bougatsa* that Mana's packed for breakfast, as in front of us the sun begins to rise and bring light again, light that reaches now and touches everything; the mountains behind us, the sea in front, and the village in the valley below.

It touches us, too.

We eat in silence.

Near us, the sheep eat, also, though not silently, ripping, chewing, swallowing, and making noises as they move to new spots with fresh and longer grass, and we watch them.

Then I feel Baba watching me.

"What are you thinking?" he asks.

My thoughts go to yesterday and how I wondered if the war would come and touch us on this island. Now, as I look around me, I realize the thoughts were naïve because it already has. In fact, I realize, war has always been here. As I mentioned, the oldest city in Europe is at Knossos, and with the oldest city comes the most wars; we're the land of Ikaros, who flew high in our sky and above our sea; we're the land of Theseus and Minos, and their Minotaur;

we're the land and people who've fought Romans, Byzantines, Venetians, Muwallads, and Turks. Now we fight Italians again, and more besides, because we fight Germans this time, as well. We've fought against all those invaders, sometimes won, sometimes lost, but even then, when we lost and were conquered, we weren't ever, not really; we were never actually conquered here because we never stopped fighting. Have we ever? Our island has been someone else's more often than it's been ours, but we're still here, and we still fight for our families and who we are, no matter the odds, no matter the conditions, no matter the war or invader who comes. We fight because it's our blood.

"Nothing," I finally tell Baba.

He laughs.

"Nothing, in all that time? You have to have been thinking something," he says, then smiles, all the way to his eyes. "Because that was a long time to wait for just . . . nothing."

I gather my thoughts.

I look at the light in front of us as it grows, spreads, becomes even more.

"When does it end?" I finally ask him, still staring down at our village, our valley, and all the light.

"It doesn't," he says, knowing exactly what I'm talking about and feeling.

"So what do we do?"

"The same we've always done, which is the best that we can," he says, very slowly. "We wake up, each day, and simply do the best we can, and as we know how, and in-between . . . in-between, there might even be some moments that become more than that."

"More than what?" I ask.

But he doesn't answer.

He turns back to the sheep and mountains, and looks out across the valley towards the sea, and he's silent.

I sit there another moment, then I turn and look out, as well.

When the sun starts to go down, we gather the sheep and lead them from the upper field and back to the barn. When we get there, we see Ikaros and Tasos haven't returned yet from the olives, so we close and lock the gate behind us, then head to the house. When we go inside, I see that Mana's not there. That's strange. She must've gone to the village to get something she needed for dinner. Baba sits down and pours himself a small glass of *raki* and offers one to me, too, but I shake my head and tell him I should get back up to the other house.

"Are you sure?" he asks.

I smile and kiss him on the head as I tell him to wait for Mana and the boys, and that I'll see him tomorrow, and then I leave. I walk alone up the path and through the village to Giannis and Angeliki's, nodding and smiling at those that walk in the other direction, noticing the sadness and sympathy I see in their eyes when they pass me. I get to the house and go inside. I don't see either Giannis or Angeliki, but there's a pot hanging over an open fire and I look inside and see that Angeliki's making soup; the lentils are what give away the type of soup, that it's *fakes*, along with the slowly simmering tomatoes, vegetables, and spices. Perhaps Angeliki went into town, too, for something else she needed for the *fakes*, and maybe even went with Mana. Perhaps that's it, and they went together?

I don't know.

I reach for the ladle that hangs by the fire and dip it into the soup, then bring it up to my lips to taste it. The broth needs a little more salt and spice, but that can be added later, as the carrots, potatoes, and onions continue to soften with the lentils and tomatoes, and the broth reduces until it's the desired consistency to be served with a drizzle of our olive oil and a dash of white vinegar. I bring the ladle to my mouth once more, about to taste again, and that's when I hear the voice, coming from behind me and the other side of the room.

"Where am I?" I hear.

Then I turn to see the British *palikari* standing there, in the doorway to the bedroom and framed by the dying light, with his bright blue eyes that have so many questions in them, and are finally open again, and staring back at me.

3

APRIL 27, 1941

The first thing I ask is his name, and he tells me it's William. We sit in his room together as morning light spills across the pillow where he's rested, and I watch as he looks at me: the night before, when he'd first woken, he was unsteady on his feet and wounded leg, in particular, which wobbled as he stood in the doorway. I'm sure the hunger didn't help either, so as soon as I'd seen him, I remembered Dr. Papadakis's words—*he'll survive if he wakes up before he starves*—so I'd gone to the still-boiling pot of soup, taken the ladle, and put some of the broth into a bowl. He ate quickly, perhaps too quickly, as much as I've ever seen someone eat in one sitting, then as soon as he was done, held his stomach with one hand and went back to the bed and immediately lay down and went to sleep again.

He only asked one question before he did, the same as the first question.

"Where am I?" he'd breathed softly, his eyes still closed.

"You're safe," I'd told him, in English, in his own words, which I first began to learn from the American films we used to go to as a family on Friday nights in Chania, before the war.

"Safe where?"

I waited for a moment, looking down at him as his chest gently rose and fell.

"*Kriti*," I'd said.

And then he'd slept.

He wakes now, though, sometime just before noon.

I've waited in the bedroom as he's rested and as soon as he opens his eyes again, he tries to stand, but I stop him, so we just sit there and look at each other. I've already sent Tasos for Doctor Papadakis, and soon they arrive, and come to the room together, with Giannis, Angeliki, and Ikaros following after them. The doctor goes to William and asks about how he feels as he examines him. The doctor checks his eyes and ears, touches around his stomach and abdomen, and seems satisfied with what he finds. He tells William to eat slowly from now on, to let his body adjust to food after going without it for so long, and tells him to stay off his injured leg as much as possible, too, to give the muscle time to heal and sew itself back together. The more he stays off the leg now, Papadakis tells him, and us, the better chance he'll have to eventually be able to walk without a pronounced limp. William nods, understanding. Giannis reaches for some coins to pay the doctor, but he shakes his head, refusing the money.

"Just keep fighting," he says in English, and to William.

"We have to pay you something," Giannis insists, in Greek.

"He can pay me in dead Germans," Papadakis answers, still in English.

William understands. He nods again.

"I will," he says.

"*Bravo*," Papadakis answers.

Once the doctor leaves, William goes to get up, and I go forward to help, and Ikaros does, too. We support him under his arms as he limps out of the bedroom to sit at the table near the kitchen where Angeliki puts more soup in a bowl and sets it in front of him. It's lunch time and the soup is the same *fakes* he had the night before, but he doesn't care. He looks up at her, sees her smile, her kind Greek eyes.

"Thank you," he says. "*Efcharisto*."

"*Parakalo*," she tells him. "I know it's the same as you had yesterday, but the doctor said another meal of soup would be good."

"It's perfect," he tells her.

We watch him, we all watch as he eats, but he doesn't care about that, either.

When he's finished, he starts to stand again, and I go to help, but Giannis puts his hand out and gently stops me.

I look at him.

"He needs a bath," Giannis says in Greek. "Let the boys take him."

"What?" William asks, looking back and forth between us, not understanding the words or what we're saying.

"Bath," Giannis says in English now.

"Where?"

"The boys will show you," Giannis tells him, then Tasos and Ikaros come forward as their father's asked and help William from where he sits and to the door, one boy holding each shoulder so he doesn't put too much weight on the injured leg. I follow behind and when we walk outside, I see news must have traveled, as there are many in the village trying to inconspicuously walk by our house, very clear they've heard about this foreigner who has arrived in our village.

"What?" Giannis calls to them, holding his arms wide. "You've all seen a British *palikari* before. This island is full of them!"

"I heard on the radio that Athens fell this morning," Vassilis the baker says, his eyes on William now. "Is that true? Is that where you've come from?"

"They were close to Athens when I left," William tells him. "I don't know more than that."

"When did you leave?"

"A few days ago."

"Are the Germans coming here next?"

The question comes from Chrisoula, my friend Ione's mother.

William turns to look at her.

"I don't know," he tells her.

"What about our soldiers? What about the 5th?"

This time it's Elena who speaks, a woman closer to Mana's age and married to Anteros the cobbler, and they have a son that's also fighting on the mainland.

"I really don't know," William tells her. "I'm sorry, I wish I did."

"Have you seen any of them?"

"I was with Greek soldiers on the way from Delphi to Athens, but they weren't from Crete."

"Where were they from?"

"A town called Agria, outside Volos."

"What happened to them?"

William opens his mouth, then he stops.

No words come and I see emotion as it begins to rise in his face, his features, and especially his eyes.

His mouth stays open.

I look at Angeliki and all the others, knowing this is exactly what I and so many others have feared, and then Giannis comes forward. "He needs a bath," Giannis tells them all. "He doesn't need to try to answer questions he doesn't have answers to," Giannis waves them away, then nods to his two youngest sons, and they walk again, supporting William between them. They head into the distance towards the river that comes from the White Mountains, and as they do, the crowd begins to disperse with many dark looks between them about the news this British *palikari* has brought to our village, which really isn't any news at all, and thus the worst type.

"It'll be alright," Angeliki says, quietly, once everyone's gone, as she turns to look at Giannis and take his hand.

"No, it won't," he says, and for the first time I hear anger in his voice.

"What do you mean?"

"All our men are on the mainland, and whether they're alive or dead, if the Germans come here, there'll be no one to defend us. There will be no one on this island at all."

"The British are here. The Australians are with them, and the New Zealanders, too."

"Yes, but for how long?"

"Until our men return home, as they promised."

"Promises in war mean nothing. When it's the fate of our island, or the fate of the world, what do you think they'll choose? The world. Every time, *Angeliki-mou*, it's the world that they'll choose."

"Perhaps the Germans won't come here."

"The government and king are here now," Giannis says. "They'll come."

"It's an island. How will they get here?"

He stays looking at Angeliki for a moment, then turns to look back to me.

"The boys can take care of the *palikari* today," Giannis finally says. "The olives will be fine without them for an afternoon."

"I can stay and help, also."

"Your father will still need you," Giannis says, then walks past me and into the house.

Once he's gone, I stand with Angeliki, and it's just the two of us now.

"I know it's hard," she finally says. "It's hard for me, too. But maybe it will help get your mind off it. That's what the breeze up there does, you know. The breeze and the caves and the flowers up there in the mountains."

"What about you?"

"I'm too old to climb the mountain, so now I just have to settle for watching others climb, and drinking the tea they bring me," she says, then forces a smile before putting her hand on my cheek, just as my own mother would, and finally turning and following her husband back into the house.

What have I learned today?

What has the British *palikari* told us, and how has it changed things?

It hasn't.

I've learned nothing, and all his words have done are made things more real by taking everything I've feared but haven't dared whisper and saying it out loud, which somehow seems to have given it more power, because words always make things more real. There are still miracles, though. If I know anything, it's that there are still miracles in this world, so with nothing else left besides faith and hope and a dream not yet shattered, I turn and start to walk south once again, towards the mountains and fields and uncertain future I know will now soon come.

After I join Baba above the village and help him bring the sheep back down, I see once again the boys haven't returned to the barn for the night. After we put the sheep into their enclosure and close the gate, Baba asks if I want to stay for dinner. I'm about to answer and that's when Mana comes from the house carrying a large plate of *moussaka* and says Angeliki has invited all of us up, and that we're all going. I turn to look at Baba who just smiles and shrugs because it wasn't a question, and he learned long ago not to argue with such things. So the three of us turn and leave the farm together, and start to head up towards the house.

When we get close, I see Tasos and Ikaros at the table outside.

They sit under one of the olive trees, and William sits next to them; he looks clean now and dressed as a Cretan man here in the mountains and village would be dressed, with black trousers, a colored sash around his waist, and a loose-fitting white shirt. I recognize the clothes as some of Giannis's from when he was younger and his body was shaped and built more like William's is now. Underneath the clothes I see William's skin has been scrubbed, his northern skin that sees less sun and is more pale than ours, and I see his hair has been washed, too, and where before it had hung loose and unkempt on his brow and in front of his eyes, it's now pulled straight back. He's eating marinated olives with Ikaros and Tasos. They pick pits and stems from between their lips as they chew and talk, then strangely, I watch as they don't throw the pits or stems away, but rather place them on the table in front of them. Mana and Baba go past me into the house to bring the *moussaka* to Angeliki, and when they're gone, I walk closer to the table where William sits with the two boys. I begin to hear their words. I can also see what they've been doing with the pits and stems:

they have them arranged in front of them on the table in the shape of Greece. Well, the Greek peninsula, at least—the whole of the mainland—and I can tell the boys have asked William at least one thousand questions already. He patiently listens and responds and they hang on every word he speaks, especially Ikaros, as William explains how he came to Greece from Alexandria, where he'd been fighting before this, and they know Alexandria because of the proximity to Crete and how many Greeks live there. He'd sailed to Piraeus first, he tells them, pointing at the makeshift map they've created, before quickly being shipped north to Thessaloniki by train with the rest of his company. William tells them about the fighting at the Metaxas Line, near Thessaloniki, and how they were eventually broken when the Germans made it behind the line, and how they retreated south to Thermopylae.

"The Hot Gates?" Ikaros asks, his eyes wide.

"Yes, the same," William nods, acknowledging the history that occurred three thousand years before: the last stand of Leonidas, the *basileus* of Sparta, and his three hundred *palikari* who fought and died with him, battling against the Persian invaders from the East. He tells them how he retreated with the rest of his company even farther south, after they were broken at the Hot Gates, and how they still fought. He picks specks of *rigani* used to season the olives with the tips of his fingers and puts the pieces of herb between the pits and stems to illustrate the path they took, the cities along the way, and the battles and skirmishes to try to delay their enemies. I hear him tell the boys of Delphi, the great oracle high in the mountains, a place they've never been and only heard about in books and stories, then he tells them of the end of his journey, too. He tells them about the wound to his leg when the Germans finally caught them, and the Greeks he fought with from Agria and Volos, and their final race to Athens, and his to the coast, and the boat that brought him here and to our shores.

"How many of your company survived?" Ikaros asks.

William looks back at them.

He's silent, and they understand.

"What will happen next?" it's Tasos that asks this time.

William looks at the boys again, and then, very strangely, he turns.

He moves his head and eyes so that he now looks straight at me, where I stand under the cypress, and it's as if he actually knew I was there this whole time, listening to them.

Did he know?

How could he?

"We'll fight," William says, his eyes still meeting mine. "We'll fight again, and we'll keep fighting, until one day, and hopefully one day very soon . . . we won't have to fight anymore, and we'll all come home."

Tasos nods, agreeing with him.

So does Ikaros, slowly.

I notice he says *come*, not *go*.

He says it for me, I realize. And perhaps he says it for them, too.

Angeliki calls from the house and the moment's gone as the boys then stand and go to help both their mother and mine carry dinner to the table. When they do, William's alone so I walk forward until I'm to him and where he sits. When I'm close, I see his injured leg held at an angle to keep it straight, rather than bent, and I see there are two carved sticks next to him, as well; improvised crutches.

They're worn.

They've been used, and I recognize them, of course.

He sees me looking at them.

"It was Tasos's idea," he explains. "He told me how Demetrios broke his leg a few summers ago when he fell off the roof of a house he was building, and he carved these from some olive branches so he could still move around."

I look at them for a moment longer, remembering that summer.

"Oak," I tell him.

"What?"

"They aren't made of olive. He carved them from an oak tree, and he didn't fall off a roof, either."

"No?" William raises his eyebrows. "I think that's what Tasos said."

"It's what Demetrios told his mother."

William smiles when he hears that, understanding.

"Of course," he says, a man who was once a boy, too, and surely has his own secrets, as well.

And what are they?

What are his secrets?

I sit at the table across from him.

"You all speak English so well," he says. "Even the young ones."

"Did you expect something different?"

"I don't know. I don't speak Greek."

"The other British *palikari* in Chania and at Souda were surprised when they heard us, too. Perhaps you think us barbarians here on our southern island?"

"I'm sure that's not it," he laughs. "Where did you learn?"

"Everywhere," I tell him, then smile, so he knows I'm joking and I watch as he smiles, too, then glances down, ever so slightly, and touches the ring that he wears. It must belong to his family. It must be important, and whatever else it might be or is, it's also the only thing he's brought here; it's the only thing he's brought through blood and death and salt and sea.

"The boys told me I was staying in their room," he says as he looks back up and meets my eyes again. "I'm happy to move. I don't want to displace them."

"They're boys."

"So?"

"They're happier outside, and in the barn."

"Why?"

"You're one, too, so don't you know?"

Adventure.

The reason, of course, is because of adventure and the unknown and the complete and utter lack of rules where there are no walls.

We stay there for another moment and I hear them in the kitchen, finishing making dinner.

"I want to apologize."

"For what?"

"Earlier, with the crutches. They told me your husband . . ." he pauses, swallowing. "They told me that Demetrios was fighting on the mainland."

"He is. Why would you need to apologize for that?"

He opens his mouth and is about to say more, but words don't come, then before any do, Giannis and Baba walk from the house carrying jugs of fresh spring water and Giannis sits at one end of the table, Baba at the other, and Angeliki follows after. She walks with Mana and the boys who carry plates and bowls with every available hand, and I see Mana holding the *moussaka* she made, while Angeliki and Tasos carry heaping plates of *dakos* and *horiatiki* and *tzatziki,* and Ikaros is next to them with two large jugs of dark red wine. They set the plates and jugs spaced across the wooden table, then the boys pour wine into cups, and put them in front of each person. Mana and Angeliki uncover the bowls and through the steam that rises I see even more food: there's *kleftiko,* but also *paidakia*, both flavored with *lemoni* and sprinkled with more fresh *rigani* grown less than twenty paces from where we all sit; there are *sfakianes pites*, but also *klitsounia*, from the wood-fired oven next to the house that can bake anything to flawless perfection, a combination of smoke and heat that's been perfected over the course of many generations; and along with the *tzatziki*, there's also chilled and cool *tirokafteri*, whipped fresh and spiced with the same *lemoni* and *rigani* used for the *paidakia*, and fresh bread for dipping and wiping and soaking it all. We normally reserve lamb for special occasions, and I can tell by the look on William's face he recognizes this, too, when he sees it, especially since we have it prepared two different ways, just to make sure one of them is how he'll like it. It's tradition in our family that the youngest always helps serve, so Tasos holds the bowls and dishes as Mana and Angeliki put the food from them onto each of our plates.

They come to William first, our guest.

"Thank you," he says, as they pile food in front of him, and we can all hear the deep and sincere gratitude in his voice. "Thank you so very much, it's so kind of you."

"Of course," Giannis says.

"*Philoxenia*," Baba adds, in his thicker-accented English.

"What?" William asks.

"It can be the first Greek word you learn here, on our island, because it's something that's everywhere in *Kriti*," Baba smiles, then says it again. "*Philoxenia*."

"What does it mean?"

"It's hard to explain," he says, and everyone nods, knowing the truth in what Baba's saying.

"Can someone give me a clue?" William looks around.

Everyone looks at each other, then they all look at me.

"It means . . . *this*," I say, trying to explain.

"I don't understand."

"There's no English translation, but it means this, what we're doing here. Hospitality. Honoring both friends and strangers alike."

"It sounds like I washed up on the right island."

"If you want to eat well, you most definitely did," Baba laughs.

"So if that's how you treat strangers, then how do you treat family?"

"As more than that."

He pauses, looking back at me.

"*Philo-xenia*," he tries to sound out the word.

"*Philoxenia*," Baba says again, in his thick accent.

"*Philox-enia*." William tries once more, with the wrong emphasis, still saying the word with only two syllables instead of four.

"*Phi-lox-en-ia*," Tasos sounds it out for him, enunciating each syllable.

"*Phi-lox-en-ia*," William repeats, determined to get it right. "Was that close?"

"Close enough."

"I'll practice," he says as he ruffles Tasos's hair like an older brother would do.

They all smile, but I don't.

Tasos has a brother.

He has an older brother that should be here in the place where William sits, but he's gone, and will he return?

Odysseus did, even after twenty years.

Will Demetrios?

When dinner ends, Ikaros and Tasos are about to stand to clear dishes and bring them inside, their job after a meal, but Giannis motions for them to stay. They leave the plates and leftover food on the table as Giannis goes into the house himself. After a moment, he comes back, and he's holding a bottle of clear liquid and eight glasses, which he places around the table in front of each guest, as well as a small bowl of honey. He pours the clear liquid into the glasses with a little bit less in Ikaros's than the others, and a little bit less in Tasos's than he put in Ikaros's.

"What is it?" William asks, bringing the glass to his nose, smelling.

"*Raki*," Giannis tells him.

After he's done pouring, he takes the pot of honey and puts two tablespoons into Tasos's and gives it a quick stir, then puts one tablespoon in Ikaros's and does the same. Ikaros frowns as he does this, but Giannis ignores his son's teenage scowl and goes back to his place at the head of the table.

He raises his glass.

So do all the rest of us.

"*Stin yeia mas*," Giannis says. "To our health."

"*Stin yeia mas*," we all repeat, even William, pronouncing the words correctly.

"He normally just says *yasou*," Tasos smiles at our guest.

"Well, that sounds easier," William smiles back at him, and even Giannis smiles now, maybe his first smile since his oldest son left.

We all drink.

I watch William over the top of my glass as he brings the *raki* to his lips and sips, then the unexpected look that comes as it does to all foreigners. It's a drink that's made from the press residue of the grapes used for winemaking, which is then distilled over heat and stored in barrels until the fermentation is complete, and becomes alcohol, and it's served after every meal. William swallows heavily then takes another sip, because everyone else does, still making a slight face as he sips smaller and with more caution, but less surprise now, and less fire in his throat as he gets used to the strength and taste. Next to him, Baba takes a pipe from his pocket and begins to pack the bowl with loose tobacco. Giannis reaches inside his jacket and takes two pipes, one he keeps for himself, and a spare that he passes down the table to William. When Baba's pinched enough leaf from the pouch he carries, he passes the pouch to Ikaros, who then passes it to Tasos, who passes it to me. I hold it out for William, who sits next to me, and meet his eyes again as he swallows once more, the taste of the *raki* still in his throat and burning, I'm sure.

"Do you know how?" I ask, nodding towards the tobacco.

"I used to pack my father's pipe for him every night, until I was old enough to have one of my own."

He almost smiles again.

But then something stops him and his lips; something stops them from turning all the way up.

"What's the matter?" I ask.

"Nothing," he says too quickly, so I know there is, then takes the pouch and pinches out the exact amount he'll need before passing it on to Giannis on the other side of him who does the same. I watch as Giannis reaches back into his jacket for a match that he strikes against the box, to light the tobacco in the pipe, before passing the matches to William, who does the same, then back down the table and to Baba.

"So," Giannis says, as smoke from the three pipes begins to rise and create a cloud above us, near the olives, gathering around the tops of them. "Tomorrow you'll go to Chania."

"Yes," William nods.

"When you do, I need you to tell them something, the rest of the British that are there in Chania and Souda. Something they can tell the others farther east, too, in Rethymno, and Irakleio."

"Giannis," Angeliki says, warning in her voice.

"What?" he asks, turning to her.

She subtly nods towards the boys, and towards me, also.

"They're old enough," Giannis says.

"They're children."

"Yes, but they're still old enough, whether we want them to be or not, because this war is going to come, one way or the other, no matter how old they are, and their age won't stop that. It's just a matter of how soon now. It's already come for their brother. It'll come for us now, too. I wish they had more time, of course I do. I wish *we* had more time, all of us, but sometimes the world takes that from us. And that's what the world has done again now."

"We don't know the Germans will be able to get here, this far into the sea," William begins, sitting up in his chair. "With just their boats, and not enough large transportation—"

"They'll get here," Giannis says, cutting him off.

"It'll be a logistical nightmare. They'll have to—"

"They've said those same things about everything else in this war, yet the Germans still found a way. That's who they are. That's what they will do once again. There is no doubt, or question."

William looks back at Giannis.

Then he nods, very small.

"You're right," he says, after a moment. "And you've been very kind to a stranger that would sit at your table and begin to try to tell you otherwise."

"We're just speaking, as we should, but when you go back, when Maria and the boys take you down to Chania, tell them what you've seen here in the mountains and in our village," Giannis says to him, with great emotion now. "Tell them *who* you've seen. My son went to fight so the rest of your people could stay here and not fight. So have so many others, just like my Demetrios, from all the villages on this island. Make sure they remember us. Make sure they remember what we've given, and what they've promised.

Make sure they remember *all* of us, even here, high in the hills, where they can't see and don't have to look if they don't want to, if they want to try to forget."

William looks back at Giannis.

"They'll remember," he tells him, and us.

"I hope so," Giannis answers. "But sometimes in war decisions become hard, and that's when people need to be reminded. Our time here is very short. Honor, courage, family, and what we do for others. Those are the things that last, William, even after us, even after the very last of us. Do you understand?"

"I think so."

"Listen to an older man, which you will be one day, too."

"I understand."

"And you'll tell them?"

"*Philoxenia*," he says, pronouncing the word correctly this time. "I'll tell them, and I'll show them."

Giannis looks back at him.

I do, too.

We all sit and there's silence while the temperature begins to drop as the sun disappears in the distance behind the mountains. Giannis finally nods, having said what he's needed to say, and instead of more words he pours another *raki* for William and the rest of us as we start to talk of other things and pull our jackets closer. There are smiles and laughter now, but how much more will there be? How many more moments like this will we have, in the coming days, weeks, months, and perhaps even years, with drinks and laughter and smoke rising and gathering into a cloud above us and the olives? The pipes burn until the tobacco is gone, then I stand and help Mana and Angeliki gather dishes along with Tasos and Ikaros, although Ikaros does so begrudgingly, thinking he's getting too old for such things. What he doesn't realize is that

Angeliki will never let him be too old until he has a house and wife of his own, so we all bring dishes into the house to clean and put back away, and when we're done, I kiss Mana and Baba on the cheek and they leave with the boys, who I kiss on the cheek, also. Once they leave, Giannis and Angeliki go to their room for the night, too, so I'm alone in the house. William has stayed outside at the table, seemingly impervious to the chill that's come. Is it because he's British, and used to it, or because he's a soldier? There's the first hint of moonlight and he has another glass of *raki* that Giannis left him, along with the bottle, so I'll leave him there with his thoughts and the moonlight.

I go to my room.

I change into the gown I wear at night, then lay in my bed and try to sleep, under the thick fur blanket I use in the winter and I do, at first. I sleep because I was up early, but only for an hour or two, then I just lay there in the bed where I used to lay in the moonlight with the one that I love.

I remember.

I remember what it used to be like, and could be again, if only he'd just return.

If.

I stand.

I pull warmer clothes over the lighter gown, then go to get some water from where we keep it next to the sink. As I drink, I glance towards William's room and the door that's still open. I walk over and quietly peek inside and see the bed is still made, also, so I turn and look outside and that's when I see him at the table. He's exactly where we left him, after dinner, the moon still high above and bottle of *raki* on the table next to his hand and the glass he drinks from.

I hesitate, just for a moment.

I know going back to bed is what I should do, but in this case, curiosity bests reason, as perhaps it always should, so I turn and walk outside with my water. I begin to go towards him, through night and mist and the smell of *thymari* that grows wild, something I've always seemed to smell more at night and in moonlight. He doesn't hear or notice. I pass the cypress and olives, and when I get closer still, I see him looking down at his hand, next to the *raki*, spinning the engraved ring he wears on his finger back and forth, back and forth, deep and lost in what must be far away and important thoughts.

"It's late," I finally say.

His whole body seems to tense as he spins towards where I stand behind him, between him and the house, then he relaxes when he sees it's just me and the moonlight and nothing else.

"Sorry," I tell him. "I didn't mean to scare you."

"It's alright."

I go to the table and sit next to him and sip water from my glass as he raises his own glass and takes another sip of the *raki*. He doesn't make a face as he drinks anymore. He must be getting used to the taste.

"It's come a long way with you," I say.

"What has?" he asks.

I nod to his hand, where he wears the ring.

He glances at my eyes, then moves his hand and puts it in the pocket of his trousers so it's out of sight, and he's silent for a moment.

"What were you thinking about?" I finally ask.

"When?" he answers.

"When I first came out."

I think he won't answer, at first, like he hasn't about the ring he wears, and that he'll hide that part of him, too.

But then I'm surprised when he does.

"I was thinking about the Greeks I travelled with," he finally tells me.

"Which Greeks?"

"The ones I met on the road from Delphi to Athens. Only we didn't get there."

"Why?"

"Because we stopped at a monastery."

"Which one?"

"I don't know, somewhere in Attica. I'm not sure the name. There were Jewish children there. The nun gave them to us to take to Athens, so the Germans wouldn't find them, and that's ultimately why we weren't able to get there and why we had to stop and fight. We didn't make it. The children did, though. The children did because we stopped and fought and that's why the Greeks died."

"That sounds . . . very noble."

"I wouldn't have."

"You wouldn't have what?"

"I wouldn't have stopped," he says, then finally looks up and meets my eyes. "That's what I was thinking about, when you came out. If it was up to me, I wouldn't have stopped, and I wouldn't have brought the children with us."

"But you're here," I tell him.

"Yes," he nods, looking down again.

"You're alive."

"I am. But as the Greeks we travelled with showed me, there are different ways of living, aren't there?"

More silence hangs between us.

Now it's my turn to answer, when he thinks I won't.

"Then how fortunate are we that every moment we're here is another chance to turn it all around."

"Yes," he nods.

"*Nai*," I nod, too.

His face has shadows across it and no more words come, from either of us, so we just sit there; we both just sit there in the night and under the light of the moon, between the tall cypress and olives, and we smell them, too, the mist and dampness making the scent of the leaves more pungent, more close, more immediate and consuming, as if it's packed into every spare inch of our nostrils.

It's a lot.

It's too much, perhaps.

"We should probably go back in," I tell him.

"You're right," I see him swallow. "We probably should."

We sit for a moment longer, then I stand, and he does, too, and I see it's difficult for him, something still painful on his injured leg that's only just begun healing. I help him back to the house, even though he has the wooden crutches from Demetrios, and when we get there, he turns and looks at me, next to him. I no longer smell the *thymari*. I only smell him, and for some reason he seems to smell of both pine and leather, and I don't know why.

"I'm sure he'll come back," he finally says, looking deep into my eyes.

"Who?"

"Your husband."

"No, you're not."

"Then I *hope* he will."

"I hope so, too."

"It's not nothing."

"What?"

"Hope."

"No," I nod my head, agreeing. "It isn't. It most certainly isn't."

And for some reason, after hearing his words, I feel better than I have in days.

We stand there and look at each other for another moment, then he motions that he can go the rest of the way on his own. He's just about to go inside, to his bedroom, carefully making his way across the rest of the space with only his crutches, but there's one more thing first.

"You know, in Greece, that means you're married," I tell him, as I nod to his hand and the ring he wears.

"What? It's on my right hand."

"That's where we wear our wedding rings."

"Really?"

"Yes."

"Why?"

"I don't know, we just do."

"Maybe I am."

"Maybe you're what?"

"Married."

I look back at him, and he looks down at his hand for a moment, flexing it back and forth before letting it hang down again at his side. He doesn't say anything further and instead just shuffles across the living room and towards his bedroom on the other side. He goes inside and closes the door behind him, and once he does, I hear the soft noise of more shuffling and then him laying down on the bed.

I go to my own room and close the door behind me.

I go to my bed and take off my warmer clothes so I'm just in my gown again, and careful to not make any noise as I lay down myself.

I have so many questions.

I try to put them out of my mind, though, and as far from me as I can possibly put them, because if I know anything, it's that the future is not yet now, though it will be shortly, and we'll need to be ready. I haven't been certain of much in recent days and months, but of that I am.

The future will be soon.

And it will be here, on our ancient and peaceless island.

4

APRIL 28, 1941

The next day, I wake before the sun again and go down to the farm to get the donkey ready. William can't walk to Chania on his own, so he'll ride, and the boys and I will go, too, to show him the way and then bring the donkey back. I could do it on my own, but the boys insist on coming, because they want to ask William more questions and my parents insist I let them, so I'm not on my own when I return. I've done the walk more times than I can count, by myself, nearly every time I've gone to Chania in the last year, and even as recently as two days ago.

But things are different now.

When I get to the farm, I see that Ikaros is already awake and dressed, sitting on the pushed-together bales that make his bed. He's fed the donkey, has the bridle on him, and when he sees me, he gently shakes Tasos awake, too. After his younger brother gets up and dressed, we go back to the house. When we get there, I see William outside with Giannis and Angeliki, and I see he's still dressed the way he was yesterday, in Giannis's old clothes. They wait for us as the sun rises, and when we get to them, the goodbyes begin: Angeliki kisses William on both cheeks, while Giannis shakes his hand firmly and they nod at each other as men do, and William expresses his gratitude with the elegance of language the British are known for, then it's time. He hands the makeshift crutches back to Angeliki, limps to the donkey, and the boys go to help him up onto the animal's back. The sun rises higher as they push him, and once he's there, on the donkey, he turns to look back down at us, all of us gathered, one more time.

There's one last nod. Then we start to walk.

As we begin our journey, he must see me looking at his clothes.

"Giannis told me to keep them," he explains. "Angeliki was going to try to sew my uniform back together, but it was too torn."

"And bloody, also, I'd imagine."

"Yes," he nods. "That, too."

Tasos leads the donkey, with Ikaros next to him, and I'm a few paces behind as we continue through the village and it's no surprise that everyone looks as we pass, because what a strange sight we must make; the women in the streets stop talking when they see us, and the men at the *kafeneios* hold their *kolomboi* still instead of spinning them. Two boys walking, a woman next to them, and a British *palikari* dressed as a Cretan on the back of a donkey. I can't help but smile. We continue past the village and follow the road as it heads down the valley and away from the mountains. I look next to me again and see William's hand, his right hand, and I frown when I see his ring is no longer there on his finger.

"I can't be giving the women of Crete the wrong impression, can I?" he says, when he notices my eyes.

I look up at him. I see he's smiling again now.

He holds out his other hand, and shows me it's there, on the ring finger of his left hand.

"No," I say, then smile in return. "Of course not."

We continue through the hills.

We walk in silence, getting closer to the coast, but before we get there and he leaves us, there's one more thing.

"The movies," I tell him.

"Excuse me?" he frowns, not understanding.

"You asked once how we speak English so well," I tell him. "The answer is a little bit of everything: newspapers, books, visitors we meet in the city, but it's mostly the movies. There's a theater in Chania, near the Old Town, or just south of it, actually. It closed when the war began and both the owner and projectionist were sent to the mainland to fight, but before it closed, we used to go every Friday night as a family, since before I can remember."

"So taught by Clark Gable and Gary Cooper, then?"

"Mixed with a dash of Barbara Stanwyck and Bette Davis."

"Good to know," he says, and we keep going. "Good to know," he says again, as he looks ahead, still smiling, every step now bringing us closer to Chania and the fast-approaching future.

We arrive in Chania around midday.

We come from the west, heading towards the harbor, and at first I think it must be a strange sight, like it was in our village; a wounded British soldier on the back of a donkey, dressed the way he's dressed, with Ikaros and Tasos in front, leading them, and me walking behind, but then I think about the times we're living in and this city that has seen so much in the last months, and I realize it's not a strange sight at all. We pass the ancient *kastro* on our right, built by the Italians several centuries earlier, high and tall above the *limani* and the city. I see William look up at it and I tell him the castle was built to fend off attacks from Hayreddin Barbarossa and other Turkish pirates, and there are similar *kastros* in Rethymno and Irakleio that were built for the same reason. I point to the harbor and lighthouse that are across from us, on the other side of the calm water, and he takes that in, as well as the Yali Tzamisi Mosque next to it, with several small domes and a single tall minaret, reaching up towards the sky and the clouds. It looks out of place here. We've still kept it, though, as we've kept all mosques in our cities, even after the Turks were driven from here, which wasn't that long ago, only during the lifetime of my father. William is surprised by this, but I tell him Crete didn't become independent when Greece became independent, but rather was occupied for another seventy years after, and wasn't reunited with Greece until 1908 or 1913, depending who you ask, and it happened right here, in Chania.

We keep walking as he takes that in.

We continue around the western side of the harbor, and we see how busy the *limani* is now. There are the usual *kaiki* bobbing gently in the water, belonging to the fishermen that fish this coast and sea, but there are also other Greek boats, too; military ones, and British boats also, arriving from the mainland or farther east in Crete and unloading passengers and cargo and the path along the harbor is filled to the point of it being hard to move between all the people, so I lead us up the side of the *kastro* and towards the Old Town instead. The streets are more narrow in the Old Town, reminiscent of what Venice must look like, I assume, and the narrow streets are filled with shops, vendors, restaurants, and small *kafeneios* with tables spilling onto streets and men sitting at them sipping drinks and spinning *kolomboi* and letting them *clack clack* against each other in their palms. The men are dressed differently here. In our village and all the rest of the villages on the island, the men have thick mustaches and wear black trousers with colorful cummerbunds and loose-fitting white shirts, like William's wearing, and oftentimes a vest, too. Here in the city, though, the men are clean-shaven and they wear square and ill-fitting suits of various muted and dull colors. Some of these men are from here, I can tell. Some are only visiting. They all try to look and feel modern, though, even though they live and work in an ancient city, a city of history, a city of great stories and great lives, and I tell William some of the stories of our city as we walk. I point at the buildings around us and tell him how this Old Town was originally built by the Venetians, during their time ruling the city, the same as they built the *kastro* and the lighthouse near the *limani,* and I show him examples of the Venetian architecture in the shuttered windows with small balconies that span only the length of the windows. Then I point to what the Greeks built: the windows that have the balconies underneath them that are larger, and span across the entire building and multiple windows together. Then after I show him that, I show him what the Turks did, too, when they eventually conquered this city, and the buildings and windows they made that have no balconies at all.

"What did the Turks have against balconies?" William asks, frowning.

"They're Turks," I tell him. "Who knows what they like, or why they do what they do."

He smiles. We keep walking.

We wind and twist through more alleys and streets, the walls and cold stone close enough to touch, on either side, if we reached our arms in either direction, then right before we come to the great fountain in the middle of the city, at the place where the two roads that border the *limani* meet, that's when I hear Tasos shout.

"*Cassia!*" he yells.

And he starts to run towards the fountain.

He drops the reins when he starts to run, so Ikaros picks them up, and my eyes follow Tasos to my friend standing there and I also see she's talking to a soldier dressed in the same British uniform William was dressed in when I first found him. The British soldier turns and sees us and the boy that runs towards Cassia and quickly says his goodbyes to her, then continues on into the newer part of the city, the part built by the Turks that's south and east of the Old Town, and also where the British have set up their headquarters. When he's gone, Cassia turns to Tasos and scoops him into a big hug when he reaches her, then we get to her, too, and she hugs Ikaros next, then looks past him, and to me. "You told me he'd grown, but this much, *Maria-mou*? He's taller than I am!" she says, holding Ikaros at arm's length and looking him up and down.

"Don't feel left out. He's taller than me, too."

"He's turned into a man in a week!"

Ikaros blushes as we talk about him this way, color rising in his cheeks as Cassia then looks past him, also, and to the donkey and William sitting on its back, looking down at her.

"And who is this?" she asks.

"We're bringing him to their headquarters."

Cassia looks back at William for another moment, at his clear blue eyes and the blond hair that hangs on his forehead, then she nods. "I guess we better get him there, then," she says, then turns and heads east and south, in the same direction the British soldier she was speaking with just went.

We follow after her.

"How many soldiers are at Souda now?" Ikaros asks, keeping up and walking next to her, matching the strides of her long legs, the way people walk here in the city, faster than they do in the villages.

"I don't know. How would I know that?"

"You see them, don't you?"

"Yes, but I don't count. There's a lot. And there are a lot of boats, too."

"How many?"

"I don't know."

"More than a thousand?"

"Why don't you ask them when we get there?"

Cassia smiles and so do I as we round the corner and come to the town hall the British have turned into their administrative building over the course of the last weeks. But there's more activity here now, even more than a couple of days ago when I was last in the city. Soldiers outside the building load food and supplies into the back of roofless lorries, parked in the streets that are wider here in this newer part of the city, and some of the British soldiers look up when they see the fair-skinned, blue-eyed man that rides towards them on the donkey, dressed like a Cretan. When we get to them, Ikaros and Tasos go to help William down and he winces in pain as his injured leg touches the ground. Then when the pain's gone, he nods his thanks to the boys and hops over towards where the other soldiers look back at him, taking a break from their work to inspect this new *palikari* and, I'm sure, wonder who he is and where he's been and what he's doing here now, too.

I watch from a distance, with Cassia and the boys next to me.

"Where did you find him?" Cassia asks again, still watching.

"Chryssi Akti."

She turns and looks back at me now, curiously, with raised eyes.

"That does sound like a long story."

I don't answer.

I continue to watch as William speaks with the soldiers, then hobbles past them and towards another man nearer the town hall. This must be an officer, I realize. They exchange more words before

William salutes and starts to limp back towards us. He stops at one of the roofless lorries and reaches into the bed as two of the other soldiers come and try to stop him, but he spins and yells at them with such conviction they back away and leave him alone. He loads something I can't see into a military bag, then hobbles the rest of the way back until he stands in front of us again.

He faces us, all of us. We face him.

His eyes seem a little bit brighter now. Am I imagining it, or is it just a trick of the light?

"I don't know what to say," he begins, "because whatever words I might have, I know they're not enough."

"It's alright."

"You saved my life," he says, turning so his eyes meet mine, and only mine now. "If you hadn't found me, I would have died."

"So save someone else's life in return, and if we all do that, then soon maybe this will be over."

He reaches out.

He hands me the duffel he's taken from the lorry.

"Don't open it until you're back in the village," he tells us. "They're sending me to Souda, which is where their medics are, for my leg, so when I go, take this home with you and don't let anyone know you have it. Do you understand? Don't show it to anyone between here and the village, or once you return, until you need it."

"What's in—" I begin, but he cuts me off.

"Just promise me," he says, meeting my eyes. "Don't open it until you're back, and keep it hidden."

"Alright," I say, and nod, too, as I reach for it.

It's heavy.

That's the first thing I feel, when I take it, but I don't ask any more as I sling the strap over my shoulder and feel whatever's inside shift and move. Then he turns to the boys. He tells them to take care of their mother and father, and ruffles Tasos's hair again, like he did at dinner last night, but perhaps recognizes who Ikaros wants to be or thinks he is, so instead of ruffling his hair, he holds out his hand and Ikaros slowly takes it and nods, the same as my father did, and as men do, and William nods, also, as if they're both warriors and one's not and only just a boy.

William seems to understand him.

It's of course because William was a boy once, too, and perhaps a boy too eager to become a man, the same as Ikaros is now.

There's one more look, between all of us.

My eyes, his eyes, one last time.

Then he turns and hobbles back towards the nearest lorry and pulls himself into the back of it with several other British soldiers. The engine starts and he raises his hand. We all raise our hands in return, even Cassia. The lorry begins to drive down the road that heads east and out of town, towards the five-kilometer route that goes over the hills of the Akrotiri Peninsula and down to the bay on the other side, where the British have made their main camp next to the deep harbor where they've anchored their entire fleet.

We watch as they go.

We watch until they're nearly out of sight, on the road that turns and begins to climb, and then soon they are.

Silence.

We each stand with our own thoughts, our own deep and important thoughts and concerns as something seems to have ended, and also something seems to have begun, a new phase of this and our lives and history, all at the same time.

"What do you think will happen to him?" Tasos asks, breaking the silence.

"I don't know," I say, and my words are soft, I realize, even as I speak them.

"Can you stay the night again?" Cassia asks.

"Not with them," I nod to the boys.

"Why can't we stay?" Tasos asks.

"We have to get back," Ikaros answers, and I look at him curiously because I'm surprised he feels this way and doesn't want to stay in the city, too, like his brother does.

"Just for lunch, then?" Cassia raises her eyebrows. "You can't walk back on empty stomachs."

I look from Tasos to Ikaros, and Ikaros seems to be alright with this, so I nod.

"Alright," I say. "Just for lunch."

Tasos yells and runs back towards the *limani* and the Old Town, where he knows Cassia's apartment is, and Ikaros starts to walk after him more calmly, as I'm sure he thinks someone who's older and not a boy anymore should do. But then he forgets, just for a moment, and he starts to run, too, as I adjust the bag on my shoulder and follow after both of them, along with my oldest and best friend.

"What do you think is in it?"

"I don't know."

"What does it feel like?"

"I have no idea."

"So open it!"

"He said not to, until we're back."

"So, what, you've never broken a promise before?"

The duffel is on the floor between us in her apartment, and I give Cassia a look and she laughs as we both then glance back down at the plates and leftover lunch she made: the grilled *lavraki* she bought near the *limani* on the way back, the simple *horiatiki* we have at every meal, and some fresh bread from the bakery a few blocks over, owned by a man named Fotis. We clean up the remains of our lunch then move out to the small balcony where we look down and watch all the commotion near the docks. Cassia has a new apartment that's on the fourth floor of a bright and blue-painted building on the west side of the *limani*, with a spectacular view of the sea and lighthouse, and all the boats coming and going in the harbor. And that's where Ikaros and Tasos have gone, to watch and be amongst the soldiers and fishermen and their hurried work and preparations for war.

"So . . . is he single?" Cassia asks, lighting a cigarette.

"I don't know," I tell her. "He had a ring on his right hand when he arrived. I told him what that meant here in Greece, and the next day he switched it to his left."

"So he's single, and he's handsome, too. Maybe I'll see him again here in town."

"If he comes back to town."

"Trust me," Cassia says. "They all come back to town."

"What does that mean?"

"They're men. Whether they're here or there, and no matter how buttoned-up and mannered they might seem, they're still men, and can't stay in their camp when the sun goes down."

"Why?"

"Because there are no women there, *Maria-mou*."

"You could move to London with him," I tease her. "You could live with him in the rain and under the clouds there with no sun."

"I think I could like London. The prams and clothes and all of the tea. Is that where he's from?"

"I don't know."

"Really?"

"I didn't ask."

"Why not?"

"I don't know, I—"

"You what?"

"Nothing," I say, then pause. "I should have, there just . . . wasn't time, I guess."

She takes another puff of her cigarette and exhales smoke into the air above us.

"Can you imagine me with a blue-eyed child?" she asks, through the smoke.

"I can't imagine you with children at all," I tell her, and she playfully slaps my arm and we both laugh.

"I need someone to bury me."

"Oh, is that it?" I raise my eyebrows.

"Perhaps more than that, too. But not yet. I'm having too much fun to have children yet."

"Of course you are. You always are."

"Don't you want to stay the night? I've started a new job at a club and I could take you. The boys would love it."

"I'm sure they would. But we do need to get back."

"Of course," she nods.

I narrow my eyes and squint, trying to look closer below.

"Who's that?" I ask.

She follows my eyes then sees what I see: amidst all the chaos on the docks and British soldiers loading and unloading all sorts of things, there's an older man with a balding head and small eyes robed in the outfit of a priest. Only it's not exactly like the Orthodox priests here in Greece; he's dressed in clothes that are slightly different, and he looks different, too.

"That's Father Angelo," Cassia tells me.

"An *Italian*?" I ask, hearing his name, and frown, because aren't the Italians who we're fighting against?

"Yes," she nods. "He's Catholic, too, and a cardinal."

"How do you know him?"

"I know everyone that comes to Chania."

"What's he doing here?"

"The thing that priests always do, I suppose. Saving lives. Or at least trying to."

"What do you mean?"

"They're Jews," she tells me, and I look even closer and see that he's helping people out of a boat that's just docked: there are men and women, boys and girls, grandparents, families of all shapes and sizes and he takes hands and helps them from the boat and up onto the stone.

"I don't understand. Aren't the Germans coming here next?"

"Yes, or at least that's what everyone thinks," Cassia exhales again from her cigarette. "And so when they do, all they'll find are simple Greek villagers, like all the rest of the Greek villagers that are here. Father Angelo's been working with Archbishop Vasilios to have baptism certificates printed for every single one of them that shows up."

"And everyone here knows this?"

"Of course. And when the Germans come, if they take the city, no one will say a single thing or give them up. Everyone will loudly tell the Germans that these are all our brothers and sisters who have lived here with us for their entire lives, and are Orthodox, and go to church every Sunday."

I keep looking down as I take that in.

I watch Ikaros and Tasos as they talk to some of the British soldiers because there are no Greek soldiers, who are all still on the mainland, and the boys watch in awe and with wide eyes as the British unload a massive, large-barreled howitzer via pulley and crane, lifting it from a cargo ship then swinging it out and onto the level surface of the docks.

"There sure are a lot of them."

"Who?"

"Soldiers."

"This is the new capital of Greece."

"Surely the capital will be Irakleio, right? That's where the royal family is and government has gone."

"Yes, for now. But Irakleio is large, and exposed, so they'll all soon come here."

"How do you know?"

"Do you see him?"

"Who?"

"*Him*," Cassia says as she finishes her cigarette and puts it out, then points farther down the *limani* towards a different group of soldiers and there's one in particular that stands out because he's taller than the others, with a thin build and thick glasses, and doesn't wear a uniform at all, but a light-colored suit with a wide-brimmed straw hat.

"Who is it?"

"James Roosevelt."

"An American?"

"Not just any American, Maria. He's the son of Franklin Roosevelt, the American president."

"The *president*?" I ask, then look even closer.

"The very same."

"And he told you that?"

"Yes."

"Why?"

"He comes to the club you don't want to go to, and he comes every night."

"Like the soldier by the fountain?"

"Who?"

"The one we saw you with, when we first arrived."

"Yes," she smiles. "Like Henry, too."

"So what's he doing here?"

"Henry? He's a soldier."

"No, the president's son."

"That's the big question, isn't it? That's the one that everyone, including Henry, has been asking since young Mr. Roosevelt arrived. So far, he hasn't said anything. He's just been here and watched and observed as preparations are made."

"And it's Henry who told you about Irakleio, and the government?"

"It's an open secret among the British."

"So not very secret at all, then."

"No," she smiles. "Perhaps not. But still secret from the Germans, I'd hope."

"We should get going, if we want to get back before dark."

We both hear the words from behind us and turn to see Ikaros standing in the doorway.

He must have come up while we were talking, and we didn't hear him come in.

"Where's your brother?" I ask.

"Still down with the soldiers."

Cassia and I both stand.

"I'm sure there'll be news soon," she tells me.

"*Efcharisto, Cassia-mou.*"

"I'll send word if I hear anything at all."

I pick up the bag again that William gave me and sling it over my shoulder, then head to the door.

"Do you want me to carry it?" Ikaros asks.

"It's alright," I tell him.

He hugs Cassia, and so do I, then as she waits in her doorway, we take the stairs back down and out of her building and to the harbor. When we get there, I look at the water that's been churned by all the boats of various shapes and sizes that are docked. More and more boats keep coming, from the horizon, from the distance, past the lighthouse and into the calm waters here, just like I hope Demetrios will do one of these days soon. I wish I had Cassia's optimism. I hope, and I pray, but with each passing day more and more doubt and fear creeps into my soul.

I look farther down the *limani*.

Tasos is near the mosque where men carry priceless artifacts and statues that must belong to the Archaeological Museum to store there, in the mosque, and he stands with the British soldiers and the American that Cassia told me is James Roosevelt. When Tasos sees me looking, he must let the soldiers know he has to leave, or something close to that, because the British nod and smile and hand him a tin of chocolates and the American reaches into his pocket and hands him something, too, which I can't see, then Tasos comes running towards us.

I look back at the soldiers.

The British return to their task and the boat they're unloading, moving our treasures into the mosque for safekeeping, but the American stays looking after Tasos as he runs towards us. My eyes meet his, and he smiles at me, also, and tips his wide-brimmed hat before he turns and walks in the other direction, towards the newer part of the city, where the streets are wider, and the place all foreign men and women here have claimed as their own.

"Ready?" Ikaros asks.

I turn to Tasos.

"What did he give you?"

Tasos opens his palm and shows us.

A pair of fighter wings with an American flag between them.

"They all loved I could speak English," he explains. "They said most kids they've met can't."

"That's because they're not you," I smile.

"They don't watch enough movies."

"I'm sure they do. They love movies in America. They just need to watch some Greek ones, too."

He smiles at that, and I run my hand through his hair as we collect the donkey from where I've tied him to a brass ring near Cassia's building, then start back the same way we came, through the Old Town and small, narrow streets, and past the *kafeneios* on either side with the men at the tables spinning and catching their *kolomboi*. We get close to the *kastro* and see the *limani* again, with all the boats there, and more that are coming, too, from the distance, and then soon the city is behind us. We go past the place where there's sand, to the place where there's rock, then come to sand again and the beach where I found William. We don't stop, though. We keep going, keep walking, on and up the familiar path, past our groves of olives, then farther and towards the village we call home.

卐

When we return, the sun hasn't yet fully sunk behind the White Mountains, so Tasos and Ikaros quickly change and run down to swim in the river before dinner while there's still some light and warmth. Once they're gone, I go to my room and sit on my bed and set the bag I've been carrying down at my feet, and look at it as it rests there.

I think of William again.

What will happen to him?

What will happen to us, all of us, and what will it mean for this island?

I reach down and unzip the bag, then slowly pull it open.

I look at what's inside, and when I do, I realize that William knows, too, and that's why he's sent this with us, back to our home, small and unimportant as this village is to the British, as there is precious little still left on this island of what he's given us, and which is surely why the other soldiers tried to stop him.

But they couldn't.

Above us, I hear raindrops begin to fall, speckled on the roof.

"Well?" I hear, and look up to see Giannis in the doorway.

"What is it?" Angeliki asks from her place next to her husband.

I open the bag wider and show them.

I show them the rifles, pistols, and ammunition that are there, as well as grenades, a first aid kit, and even a few knives and bayonets to fit onto the ends of the rifles.

They don't seem to be surprised when they see this.

Giannis comes over and sits next to me.

Angeliki sighs and goes back to the kitchen, her head down and happiness gone, as rain comes even harder now. We sit there together for another moment, Giannis and I, then he finally stands and takes the bag and goes to the doorway. I let him. I don't ask what he's doing, because I already know; this isn't the first war that's come to these hills, and these aren't the first enemies that will arrive on our shores and think they can conquer us, so this is a house that has hidden weapons before. It will now once again. I know that's where he takes the great gift we've been given, to tuck and hide in the place where they won't be found until they're needed, the same as his father has done, and his father before him, and his father before that, all the way back until before any that are alive can remember and the time is almost here now; the time is almost here where we will all once again have to fight for our mountains, our sea, our homes, and our island.

This island where we were born.

This island we won't ever leave.

5

MAY 19, 1941

As much of the rest of Crete has continued to prepare for a German invasion by sea, life goes on in the village, almost as usual, and I leave the sheep to be tended by Baba and go to help the boys with the olives. It's the time of year to paint the trunks with a mixture of slaked lime and water that protects them from the insects that are about to hatch as it gets warmer. It's a task that seems pointless with what's going to come, but we do it anyway. April is a month of mixed weather in Chania; some days are hot and feel like summer, while others are cold and many layers are needed to protect from the wind and chill, but May is when summer finally comes and it's hot every day and it's under that hot May sun that we work. Tasos makes the mixture and brings it to me and Ikaros in wooden buckets, and we dip brushes into it and paint it onto the trunks. Tasos then takes the buckets when they start to empty back to where he keeps the lime and water, makes more, brings it back to us again, and we repeat this for weeks until nearly all the trunks are painted bright white. Just as we're almost finished, with only a few more rows of trees to go in the lowest part of the groves—the part nearest the coast and sea and city—that's when everything changes again.

Our first sign an attack is imminent arrives the day before, though.

We'd all heard that King George and the rest of the Greek royal family were now staying near the British base at Souda Bay; they'd fled Athens and the mainland when it fell to the Germans, but thought it important for morale they didn't flee Greece entirely, so they'd come south to Crete with the rest of the government and first gone to a villa outside of Irakleio, near the ancient city of Knossos, but then, as the threat of invasion became more imminent, and just as Cassia had told me they would, they came west to be as close to the strongest British garrison as possible.

Now, though, they'd left even Souda Bay, and started to move again.

I'm not sure where else on the island I would have expected them to go, but I certainly didn't expect them to come to our village. Or, well, the village next to ours, at least. The valley our village sits in is long and narrow, and at the opposite end there's another village, named Elaionas, one that's slightly larger than ours, and that's where the royal family arrives.

We hear rumors first.

Then after the rumors, we see them with our own eyes.

The wealthiest family in Elaionas is named Magarakis, and they haven't gotten along with our family, or any in our village, for more generations than can be counted. And not getting along is perhaps an understatement. Giannis and Anastasios Magarakis hate each other. So did their fathers before that, and their fathers before them. Most think it's just two families vying for control of the same valley, resources, and wealth, but it's more: it's a feud that's ancient, and a feud that's timeless, just like the land where it lives. It's a feud that people write famous stories about and some say goes back ten generations to when someone in Giannis's family called the Magarakis clan Turks because there were rumors that the Magarakis family had willingly sent their first-born sons to be Janissaries when the order was formed. Becoming a Janissary itself wasn't frowned upon, as so many on our island and other Greek islands had been abducted and forced to join their order. The rumor and accusation, though, was the Magarakis boys had volunteered and gone *willingly* to work and fight for the Turks. There were many that did such a thing in exchange for the education it brought and positions of power and influence at court in Constantinople. The truth is, though, it was hundreds of years ago and no one really knows the truth, whether the Magarakis family sent their children, or if they were taken. It's essentially a six-hundred-year-old rumor that only took one offhand comment to start a blood-feud that's lasted since, and been sustained by the intermittent burning of olive groves, stealing of sheep, and many other things up until the present day. Even though the feud has continued to last, after we hear the rumors then see the caravan of soldiers and vehicles winding their way up the road towards Elaionas, on the far side of the valley, on *their* side of the valley, we go to pay our respects, anyway, and get a glimpse of the royals and hear any news they or any who travel with them might have.

We walk to Elaionas together, the whole village.

We take the narrow path that winds the length of the valley, then soon get there and see all the villagers, waiting to greet the caravan that's coming, and we arrive just before they do. We stand next to the other Cretans, though a little apart from them, and I see Giannis look back at Anastasios Magarakis who is across the crowd with his three young sons, two teenaged daughters, and his wife, who's named Lydia.

Giannis and Anastasios stare at each other.

They don't nod, don't speak, don't do anything except just stare.

The royal caravan soon reaches the village and when it does, the two men finally turn their attention to the distinguished and important visitors. As the cars and lorries pull to a stop, the door to the first vehicle opens and the driver gets out to open the passenger door behind him. When he does, I see a leg first, then a jacket, and finally an arm and face, as the man exits the car and stands in front of us, and that's when we all see for the first time, in the flesh, the man who must be King George II of the Hellenes. He's tall and slender, just like the pictures in the newspapers, and balding in his middle age with skin more pale than ours or that I would have thought, and a narrow face with sunken eyes. I wonder if this is how he always looks, or if he only now does because of what he's gone through in the last days, weeks, months, what we've all gone through, these great and perilous times. After the king is out of the car, he turns and reaches a hand to help a woman behind him who we all know is not his old wife, his Romanian cousin Elisabeth, who he had been married to and who divorced him some years ago, while still childless, and long before the war started; the woman he's now with is tall and slender, and quite beautiful, also, I see, and when she speaks, I hear a familiar accent and realize she's British, too, just like William.

Anastasios Magarakis goes forward.

He introduces himself, as he bows to the king, as well as the woman at his side who he calls Mrs. Jones (*Missus*, I realize he says, not *Miss*). Then behind them, the door to another car opens and we all recognize Emmanouil Tsouderos, the new prime minister of Greece. Ioannis Metaxas had been the prime minister who'd said the proud *"Oxi!"* to the Italians, but shortly after he had died, under mysterious circumstances, and been succeeded by Alexander Koryzis, the former governor of the Bank of Greece. But as German troops reached Athens, Koryzis shot himself in the head rather than flee or be captured, so Tsouderos was chosen to be the next head of government even as that very same government fled from Athens to Irakleio.

And now, here they are, in our valley.

The people go to him.

They crowd around and shake Tsouderos's hand, and I watch as my father goes with them and he does, too, and I stand behind my father and smile when Tsouderos gets to me. He was chosen to be prime minister because he's from Rethymno, not many kilometers to the east, and he was chosen because the government had to flee and come here and they wanted to be sure of their reception. On Crete, there isn't much sentiment or sympathy for the royal family, as the government and political party the king supported was at odds with the government and party of Eleftherios Venizelos, the favorite son of our island, and our most famous politician, who had been the leader of the Greek opposition.

But that was before, during peacetime.

Now there's a great war, and in war, such things are put aside.

The king and his family may not have been favorites here, but he's still king, and he's now among us; he's in our mountains, and on our island, so we'll do him honor, as we do to all who come to visit.

Philoxenia.

I look at Tasos next to me, at his wide eyes.

It's a day he'll remember, I know, for all the rest of his life: the day he saw the king of Greece.

Then I look at Ikaros, next to him.

There's a look on Ikaros's face that's hard to read as it isn't the wide-eyed wonder of his brother.

What is it?

What's the look that's there?

In front of us, Anastasios Magarakis shows the king into his house, along with Mrs. Jones, and valets follow behind, carrying luggage. We take everything in, after they go inside and disappear, because I know this will be a moment. Even as it's happening, I know this will be talked about for years and generations in this valley, about how king and prime minister came to our village and stayed the night. They won't stay longer than that, as they're of course on their way somewhere else, but they're here now, and they're our guests.

Or, at least, they're Anastasios Magarakis's guests.

I turn back towards the soldiers.

I look past the rest of the officials and cabinet members who have gotten out of cars, too, and to where the British escorting them are getting out of their own vehicles. I scan faces, eyes and cheeks under helmets, and I find I'm looking for one soldier in particular, hoping he might be there amongst them.

He's not.

I do, however, recognize one of them.

It's the young, thin, and already-balding American that Cassia told me is James Roosevelt, the son of the American president.

He sees me looking at him and walks over.

"From the docks, right?" he asks.

"Yes," I say, looking back and nodding, taking in this strange American accent I've only heard on the radio and in movies, not ever in real life, and from a flesh and blood person in front of me.

"I'm James."

"I know."

"Word travels fast, I guess," he smiles.

"It may seem like a large island, but it really isn't," I tell him, then nod towards all the others, the entire caravan he's travelled with. "Where are you going?"

"A place called Agios Roumeli, they tell me, which is near Samaria, I think," he says, then waves towards the peaks of the White Mountains behind us and to the south. "We're to leave our vehicles here and take donkeys the rest of the way over the mountains, or at least something along those lines."

"The *king*? On a donkey?"

"Not even the Germans would expect it, right?"

"So it's happening, then," I say, very quietly.

"Yes," he nods, knowing what I mean, exactly what I mean. "I'm afraid that it is."

"When?"

"We don't know exactly, but it'll be soon. It'll be very soon now."

"Why are you here?"

"Because we need to get the king and government to safety before—"

"No," I shake my head, cutting him off. "Why are *you* here."

He pauses as I look back at him and I'm surprised.

I'm surprised I've asked such a forward and blunt question, and also that I've cut off his words, but it is Greece, after all, and being forthright and honest is a cultural inevitability, and we'd been speaking so casually the words just came.

He's not offended.

"Strictly speaking, I'm not," he says.

"Not what?"

"Here."

"What do you mean?"

"America's neutral in this war."

"But it soon won't be?"

"I certainly hope that's the case. My father faces an incredible amount of political pressure to not intervene, to not send our men to fight in what his opponents have deemed someone else's war."

"*No foreign entanglements.*"

I remember the slogan from the newsreels that play before the movies.

"That's right," he smiles and nods. "That's what many of them think, and the signs they plant in their yards."

"And what do you think?"

"What do I think about what?"

"This war. What else?"

A pause.

The soldiers keep walking around us, carrying things into the large Magarakis house for the king, Mrs. Jones, and the government, as the villagers begin to show the others that travel with them into smaller houses where they'll board them and they'll be able to stay and sleep for the night.

Philoxenia.

There it is again.

"I believe," James Roosevelt finally tells me, very slowly, picking his words carefully, "just as my father believes, that evil shouldn't not be fought simply because of the distance from us or number of borders between us and that evil. He believes, and I believe, too, that it's our duty and moral obligation to fight evil both *whenever* and *wherever* it's seen, regardless of politics or whatever other excuse the ignorant might design and speak to each other in darkness to try not to do their part, and sometimes even actually convince themselves that they're right."

"And that's controversial in your country?"

"Unfortunately it is. Unfortunately, it's the most controversial topic and subject in our *entire* country right now, and there will be an election soon, too, in just a few months."

"This issue will be important in your election."

"Yes," he nods. "It will perhaps be the only issue."

"You still haven't answered why you're here."

"Because election or not, I'm reporting back to my father what I've seen, and to assure all the governments that fight against the evil we should be fighting against, also, to hold out for just a little bit longer because he's doing everything in his power to join this fight, and hopes we soon will."

"And you?"

"What about me?"

"What do you think? What do you hope?"

"I'm not a politician."

"What does that mean?"

"It means if it were up to me, we'd be here already, politics and all the rest of it be damned and we'd blow the Germans, Italians, Japanese, and all the rest of them right back to where they came from, just the same as we did twenty years ago, and then none of this would be happening at all. It likely wouldn't even have started."

"Are all Americans like you?"

"Some. Not enough, unfortunately."

Giannis sees me and comes towards us.

He looks at James across from me, and the American sticks out his hand.

"James," he says.

"Giannis," my father-in-law answers as they shake, and the younger man smiles at him.

"Good to meet you."

But Giannis doesn't answer, he just turns back to me.

"It's time to go."

I look at him, then nod.

I turn back to James and there's one more moment, then James nods, too. "Good luck," he says, then leaves and goes back to the vehicles and his task of unloading and settling in to the house where he'll stay. When he does, I turn and join Giannis, my father, and the rest of the family as we start back along the valley, towards our own village in the distance.

We go a few paces, but then I stop.

I turn back to where we've just left, and the men that are still there, and one in particular, the one I've just spoken with.

"Mr. Roosevelt!" I say, loud enough so he'll be able to hear me.

He looks up from his task amongst the soldiers, from unloading his things from the vehicles they'll leave here in Elaionas before they take donkeys the rest of the way across the mountains; he's just another one of them, just another soldier, along with all the others, which is how they must do things in America and part of what it must mean to be American.

"Yes?" he asks, eyebrows raised.

I wait one more moment, for eyes to gather, and look at us.

"Thank you," I tell him.

"No," he shakes his head. "It's of course very kind of you, the sentiment, but misguided."

"How is it misguided?"

"Because unless I'm very wrong, based on all I've seen here these past weeks, I think it's the rest of us who will be thanking you, perhaps many times over, before all this is over."

I understand what he means.

The Greeks on the mainland have done their part, and now it's time for us to do ours, too, whether the world sees us or not.

But the world *does* see us, doesn't it?

That's why he's here, and why his father has sent him in secret.

It's the last I'll see him, or speak to him, I know.

Baba looks at me, his eyebrows raised now, also.

"Mr. Roosevelt?" he asks.

"It's a long story," I say, and see Giannis looking, too, and wondering now about the man he's just met, so I tell them about who he is and why he's come to our small Cretan village, and when I do, I see a small glimmer of hope, in both their eyes, the first I've seen in much too long a time.

When we arrive back at our village, the others that walked with us begin to disperse and go back to their houses. My parents return to the farm, but before they do, I see something: it's Ione, who now wears the all-black of a widow. Once she puts on the black, she'll wear it the rest of her life, and when my eyes find hers, I can read her look, the accusation that's there. She thinks me a fool and naïve because I have not lost hope. After a moment longer, she leaves, and I shake my head and go in the other direction, to the stone house where Giannis and Angeliki have already returned, and Ikaros and Tasos have moved back into their room.

I sit at the dining table with Giannis and Angeliki.

We're silent.

Next to me, Giannis pours a *raki* and Angeliki has her *malotira*, which she sips slowly. I drink nothing, even though I sit with them, and as I do, my eyes keep returning to the loose boards in the kitchen and the hole dug deep into the earth under the house where Giannis hid the weapons that William gave me to bring back to the village. It's an ancient hole, an eternal hiding place. Who built it, or when? I don't know. We're an island that's been occupied by so many; not conquered, but *occupied*, so this hiding place has seen weapons before: broadswords and arrows to fight the Romans, knives and spears to fight the Venetians, curved sabers to fight against the Ottomans with their own weapons, and pistols, too, that came later. And now, finally, here are British rifles and bullets that will be used to kill Germans that will come.

How will they come?

The seas are still controlled by the British, so perhaps that will buy us more time.

Giannis doesn't seem to think so, but regardless of what he thinks, and how the Germans get here, this is the decision and promise that I make: I will not wear the black. Why has this small thing affected me so much? I don't know, but I do know that no matter what happens, I'll not wear the black, not ever, even though they all think me a widow already, which is a near certainty, after the amount of time that's now passed. I will refuse. A life for me is ending. Perhaps it already has ended, some time ago, and it's not Demetrios's life, or anyone else's, because it's mine, and it's a specific type of life: the life of being second, being spoken over at dinner, being left to walk behind, being asked to make lunch and dinner and do nothing else besides these things, to only read about deeds and great things or watch them in movies, rather than participate in them myself and only be allowed to take a place after all others have taken theirs.

That will end now.

I will not wear what they tell me I have to wear, even if Demetrios never returns.

I have nothing left; no husband, no children, no future to think of.

So what is there to lose?

Nothing, absolutely nothing. What freedom.

I know my family will support me in this, but will the world?

No.

The world will do what it always does when it's presented with change, and reject it, but I still don't care and will never become what they want me to; instead, I will be something else.

"Can I talk to you?"

I hear Ikaros's voice and look up from where my eyes have been staring at the floorboards with these thoughts steaming through my head like a freight train. Giannis looks up, too, and so does Angeliki. Tasos is still in the room they share, so it's just the four of us, and there's change in my eyes, I know, and when I look at Ikaros, I recognize the same thing in his eyes, also.

"What is it?" Giannis asks, looking back at his middle son.

"I love Kyriaki Magarakis," Ikaros tells us, speaking very slowly. "I've loved her for a long time now, I love her more than anything else in this world, so I've asked her to marry me, and she's said yes."

6

MAY 20, 1941

Looking back, I should have recognized it.

I should have seen the signs when he wasn't in his bed, when he wanted to return early from Chania, and not spend the night in the city, the look in his eyes when we were in Elaionas and lack of interest in the royal family or soldiers or any of the rest because, of course, there was something else he was interested in and it was something that had taken over his body; it was something that had taken over his mind, and most importantly, most blessed of all, it of course had taken over his soul, too.

I'm jealous.

I think back to when I first met Demetrios, and what it felt like, all the stolen nights and fluorescent moments when colors seemed brighter, the world seemed both bigger and smaller at the same time, because the world felt the way our hearts felt when they were together. I miss the uncertainty, the obsession of thought, the always-occupied space and place in my life for the all-consuming fire of both fulfilled and unfulfilled passion that's left to burn, burn, burn.

And while I might be jealous, I'm glad, too.

I'm so happy for him that he's found this, as we all should in our lives, at least once.

Giannis and Angeliki don't feel the same.

They're from a different time that believes love is something that's made, not found, and it's a parent's job to pick a husband or wife for their child and once that match is made, that's when love will eventually be fashioned. Surely Anastasios Magarakis feels the same way, Giannis says, so how could this possibly work?

I don't know.

I hope it does, though.

I hope it does for Ikaros, in the same way it did for me and his brother.

After Ikaros tells us his intentions, we all decide to go to sleep as it's something best sorted in the morning, when everyone is fresher and thinking clearly. But as it turns out, there isn't time. I'm not sure Giannis sleeps at all, and when I wake before the sun and come from my room, I see Giannis at the table outside the house with a mug of *malotira,* and I make one for myself and go sit next to him. In front of us and over the mountains, the sun begins to rise and a new day comes. We don't talk. I just sit there and he reaches out and puts his hand on mine, and that's how we stay until eventually Angeliki comes to the table, also with a cup of tea, then the three of us sit there. We sit in silence for a few more moments until Ikaros walks from the house and sits next to us, too.

He has no tea.

He never drinks it, unless Angeliki forces him.

"I won't change my mind," he finally says, breaking the silence and looking across where I sit to meet his father's eyes.

Giannis is silent. Then he finally nods.

"I know you won't," he says, softly.

"How?"

"Because you're my son."

"So you'll give us your blessing?"

Giannis opens his mouth, but before any words come, that's when we first hear them.

The noise comes from the distance, and from the north.

We all pause and turn towards it.

We look away from the mountains and where we had been looking before, and it takes a moment until we realize what it is we're hearing: the soft buzzing of planes. We sit there for a moment more, then Tasos rushes from the house, too, because he's heard the noise and then sees the planes, and we all wait in silence, one last moment of peace, as a family, until finally Tasos speaks.

"Maybe they're British," he says, the innocence of a child.

"They're not British," Giannis answers.

"Just like you said," I turn from the sky, and look at him. "They didn't come in boats at all."

Next to us, Ikaros turns and runs into the house.

He's only gone a matter of seconds, though, before rushing back out with an Enfield bolt-action rifle and a handful of bullets from the duffel that William gave to me and Giannis hid under the floorboards. He swings it over his shoulder in a single fluid motion, and keeps running.

"*Ikaros*!" Angeliki calls.

But he doesn't listen.

He takes the small, narrow path to the east, away from our village and towards the other, and it's of course no secret now as to where he's going, and why.

"*IKAROS!*" Angeliki calls again, louder.

But he's too far away now.

Giannis watches his middle child as he continues to run, and I look at Giannis, and for the first time in my life, I see a tear on his cheek. He doesn't wipe it away. He doesn't say anything, either, he just walks towards the house and I follow after him. So does Tasos. After a moment, Angeliki does, as well. We're almost to the door when I see my parents hurrying up the path from the farm, then they're to us, also, and we don't speak because what words could we possibly say? We all just go inside and Giannis crosses to the hole under the kitchen that's now no longer covered and the duffel inside it. Ikaros only took one rifle, but Giannis reaches down and pulls the whole bag out before reaching inside. He finds another Enfield bolt-action—the standard rifle of the Commonwealth and all British soldiers—and hands it to Baba, then another that he takes for himself, and he finally takes one more and without even a moment's hesitation hands it to Tasos.

Tasos looks down at the large weapon in his young hands.

"*Giannis*," Angeliki whispers.

But he ignores her and gives two grenades to Baba and keeps three for himself, which he tucks away into the loose pockets of his black trousers, then is about to walk to his bedroom, but before he goes, I stop him.

"What?" he asks, looking back and meeting my eyes.

"What about me?"

"They won't hurt you if you're not armed."

"Do you really believe that?"

He stays looking at me for another moment, then I reach down and find a rifle myself, and one for Angeliki, too, that I pass to her, and my mother also, and they take them from me as Giannis watches us.

Who I used to be is dead. This is who I'm going to be now.

Giannis doesn't say anything.

He just watches what I do, then when the weapons have been passed to my two mothers, he goes to his bedroom and comes back carrying five Cretan daggers. These are daggers that are larger than normal knives, made with carved handles of animal bone or horn, and a silver blade with a slight curve up at the end, at the very tip. Their history in Crete is long and part of our culture and heritage, with making them a skill passed from father to son. Giannis has been making them since he was a boy. He showed Demetrios how to make them, also, and the dagger they'd made together with the handle of goat horn carved with the history of their family on it had travelled with Demetrios and the 5th to the mainland. The presence of the daggers and blades on this island is ancestral and ubiquitous and now, more than just being worn for culture, history, posterity, and tradition, now . . . they'll finally be used once again, too.

Giannis hands one to Tasos.

He hands one to Baba.

Then he hands one to Angeliki, and my mother, and finally he hands one to me, as well.

Outside, we hear the first explosions.

They come from the distance, from the south, near the sea, and perhaps even a bit west where we know there's an air base near the village of Maleme and we can also hear the buzzing sound of planes in the sky more clearly now.

We go outside, all of us, and we're not prepared for what we see.

The entire sky is filled with planes and what had once been the soft buzz of engines is quickly becoming a roar as they rapidly get closer, and there's more: little dots that come from the planes then fall down, down, down, towards our island, German paratroopers jumping and parachutes deploying as they glide and float and ultimately land.

Or at least some of them do.

There are so many that fall and then there's gunfire and some of them are hit, but there are many who aren't, and then there are more massive explosions over the noise of the gunfire, both near Maleme and the city of Chania itself.

Bombs.

Being dropped on our cities, and on our harbors.

Smoke begins to rise.

Not near us, though, or our village.

Near us the noise is getting louder and there are so many paratroopers that the sky in front of me looks nearly black. All the other villagers have come now, as well, and Giannis carries the duffel that still has more weapons in it as he passes out all that he has left, giving a rifle to Vassilis the baker, then Enfield revolvers to Chrisoula, my friend Ione, Anteros the cobbler, and his young son Philippos, who is the same age as Ikaros, and even Father Thiseas, as well, the priest, along with Doctor Papadakis and his wife who stands next to him. Elena, the wife of Anteros and mother of Philippos, has a Cretan dagger that must have been made by her husband and she's tied it to the end of a broomstick which she'll use as a spear. The rest of the villagers who don't have British rifles carry old, rusted muzzleloaders, left over from the Turkish wars several decades earlier, I'm sure.

I look at them.

Will their muzzleloaders even work?

If there's anything that's certain in all this, it's that we'll soon find out.

We are only old men, women, and young children, because all our soldiers or any men of fighting age are still on the mainland.

Where are the British, who promised they'd protect us?

Father Thiseas steps forward.

He stands in front of the gathered and raises his arms to bless us, to bless all of us that are here and he speaks his prayer over our village and the villagers who will try to protect it. "May the almighty polish the rust from these rifles and those who carry them," he says with a loud voice, meant to carry over the hum of engines that are nearly directly above us now. "And may he watch over all today who are on this island, and fight for this island, just the same as he watches over us here every day."

He makes the sign of the cross, and so do the rest of us.

Giannis turns.

"You don't have to do this," he says, very quietly, just to me.

"Yes, I do," I answer. "We all do."

"From the time that they're very young, boys are taught how to fight. It's in everything they do."

"I know. And like all other girls here, I was taught how to cook and sew. But that's not my fault."

"It's not your fault, but—"

"I'll just have to learn quickly."

Giannis pauses.

He looks past me, and to my father.

Baba waits for a moment, then nods, once, very small.

I'm sure he knows what it is he's doing and the consequences it might bring to his only child, but then there's no time for words or nods or anything else because the planes are to us and we look up as they fly overhead and for a moment they block the sun. We watch as German paratroopers jump from them and plunge down and straight towards us, straight towards our village and mountains and fields, then parachutes deploy and they glide through air rather than plunge, but they still come.

They get closer.

We all raise our weapons.

There's nothing they can do as we look up and then all of us who have rifles aim, or at least try to, and as soon as they're close enough we pull triggers and the air is shattered with explosions and smoke as our shots travel upwards and mine misses any mark, but there are several that do not.

Screams.

Death.

When I fired, the strength of the gun almost knocked me from my feet, and the sound of all the gunfire nearly shatters my eardrums.

I recover, though, and next to me I hear Giannis.

"Aim at their heels!" he yells, and I know why.

We need to aim below them so their momentum carries them into our bullets.

We aim and fire again.

I brace myself more fully this time, but the force is still immense, and so is the noise that comes with the bullets.

I see at least two German soldiers that are hit—one of them by my shot, or at least I think it's my shot—and I'm surprised again.

Also, some bullets miss the actual Germans, but still tear through their parachutes, and once they do, the soldiers attached to them begin to spin and fall even faster towards the ground.

One parachute rips apart altogether.

The soldier that was attached to it falls and crashes against the ground not far from where we stand, and I hear more screams from those near enough to witness the death and mutilation of a body that meets earth from hundreds of feet above.

Three of the Germans land safely on the ground.

They're about a hundred yards from where we stand—beyond the olives and the cypress, and caught between our group and another group of villagers—and once they do land, they try to shrug off their parachutes and immediately start firing. Giannis pushes us behind the house for cover, but not everyone is so fortunate, and one of their bullets hits Vassilis and his body collapses before Giannis, Anteros, Father Thiseas, and the others start firing back and hit one German, who falls near the bakery, then the other two who see they're outnumbered start to run.

One heads straight towards Father Thiseas, who raises his weapon.

The other runs towards us.

The one that runs towards Father Thiseas tries to fire at the priest as he sprints, but his shot misses, then Father Thiseas drops to a knee, takes aim, fires himself and his bullet rips into the German's chest and he falls, then Ione and Chrisoula run forward with Anteros to kick his rifle away and make sure he's disarmed.

The one that runs towards us can't get his backpack off, though.

Giannis moves us farther behind the house, and as the German gets closer, he still has his parachute tied to his back and it's preventing him from being able to run properly before it catches in his legs and he stumbles. He's about to fall, but then doesn't, regains his balance, and that's when Giannis rushes forward and tackles him to the ground. The German's rifle is knocked from his hands and skids across the dirt, and when he sees Giannis on top of him, he immediately reaches to his boot and pulls a knife.

When Giannis sees the blade, he rolls off the German, who scrambles to his feet.

Giannis gets to his feet, also, and stands away from him.

Tasos raises his rifle and points it at the German, and so do I, but Giannis holds both his hands out: one towards the German, and one towards us.

"Stop," he says. "Everyone."

He turns to the German.

"*Stoppen*," Giannis says to him, in his language.

The soldier hesitates, just for a moment, then finally speaks.

"*Nein*," he says before charging towards Giannis, swinging his knife, and before I or Tasos or anyone else can fire or do anything, the German's to him, the knife plunging down towards Giannis's chest and the German is too close for a shot now, but Giannis steps back and dodges the blow. The German swings again and misses, then swings once more, and when he swings wildly for a fourth time, and Giannis expertly dodges again, it's clear the German won't stop so Giannis then brings his own blade back around and plunges it into the German's chest.

The German stands there.

He looks down at the carved and ancient dagger protruding from him, and wielded by a man he didn't know is a Cretan knife-fighter, and he must be wondering where he's come to as he takes a last look at the big barrel-chested man that the ancient and carved dagger belongs to.

His own knife slips from his hand and falls.

Then he falls, too, his body crumpling in an exhausted heap.

Giannis goes to him and kneels, very slowly, and puts his hands back onto the carved handle and breathes in. He'll do this part quickly. He rips the dagger from the German's chest then plunges it into his neck, just where it meets his shoulder, and pushes down, between the bones and into the heart in what will be the quickest and most painless death for the man.

The German cries out, in pain and surprise.

Then after a moment, he doesn't, and lies still.

My hand is steady, where it holds my Enfield rifle, with my breathing quicker than normal, which is to be expected.

I'm surprised none of this seems to have affected me.

Why?

Is it because of my blood?

I don't know.

I do know there will be time for questions like these later, though, because right now it's time for something else and in the distance there's another German that got caught with his parachute in the branches of a cypress so he just dangles there, twisting, and decides to fire his rifle wildly as he spins. We all duck. He keeps spinning and firing until Elena sneaks beneath him and thrusts up with the broom with the dagger on the end of it. The dagger pierces his stomach, just above his waist, and he screams now, too. He tries to contort his body to fire down at her but she moves and stabs again, this time into his side, and he drops his rifle and it lands in the dirt at Elena's feet and she stabs again, and again, and then once more after that, until the German's still, though his body continues to swing and twist in the wind.

I turn back to Giannis.

His hands are covered in blood, and I realize even though I've known him since before I can remember, just how little I actually know him, which I suppose is a realization all children eventually make in regard to parents. It's clearly not the first time he's handled a knife. It's also clearly not the first time he's fought an enemy, or the first time he's taken a life.

What else has he done?

Who else has he been, and that I don't know about?

He wipes the blood from his hands on the German's uniform.

He starts to gather the German's weapons—the knife he used, rifle he dropped, and ammo he finds in the German's backpack—and once he does, he holds them out to Tasos.

"Take these back to the house," he tells him. "Hide them where we hid the others, then cover it."

Tasos stands for a moment longer, staring at his father, at the blood that stains Giannis's arms and sleeves and the knife that's tucked back at his waist that's brought this blood.

"*Hurry*," Giannis says, gently.

Tasos comes back to himself then nods and runs to do as Giannis has told him, as Giannis turns to us now.

He doesn't speak.

Neither do we.

Instead, he jerks his head towards where there are still gunshots being fired amongst the streets and houses of our village, so we all start to carefully go in that direction. The gunshots end, then we see other villagers, ones that are still alive, and we see the dead. There's the German that Father Thiseas killed, in a pool of blood in the streets of the village. There are two more Germans swinging from giant oak trees where their parachutes were caught, that have been shot in their chests, and then there's the third in a tree set apart from the others that was stabbed by Elena and her makeshift spear.

I look at them, all of them.

So does everyone else.

Overhead, planes still fly near the coast and there are still intermittent explosions from the areas around Chania and Maleme, and we all know what that means: that the invasion is still happening.

Anteros breaks the silence.

"Do we bury them?" he finally asks.

Stavros who owns the taverna opens his mouth to answer when the valley suddenly explodes again, and a bullet rips through his chest; he's lifted from his feet before he crashes back to the ground, paces from where he stood before.

"*DOWN!*" I yell to both no one in particular and also to everyone.

I'm surprised at my reaction and the speed of it as I grab Baba and Mana and pull them to the dirt and next to me Giannis does the same with Angeliki and Tasos, who's rejoined us now. Then more of the air explodes as Chrisoula and Ione both dive for cover, too, and we scramble across the dirt until we reach the safety of our house. Once we're behind the stone walls, we stand. I peek around the side and see a company of Germans coming from the hills, a group that must have landed farther south, higher in the mountains, and they're near the cypress now, heading towards the village.

"How many are there?" Baba asks.

"I don't know," I say, as I try to count. "More than ten."

But it doesn't matter exactly how many, because they're to us.

I raise my rifle and fire from the corner, and so do Tasos, Angeliki, Baba, and Giannis. I see some of the Germans stumble and fall, and while I'm confident it's not my shot that's hit them this time, someone's has, though they keep coming and they run now instead of picking their way carefully down the hill and through trees. They spill into the village and there looks to be more than a dozen, which is more than I thought. We fire again and I hit one this time, I'm the only one to do so, I think, then the other Germans see us and fire in return as we duck back behind the house and bullets bury into stone. We get off one more round, the Germans duck when they hear the shots, though one more of them is hit by a shot from Giannis and falls. The others come towards us now, and there will be too many to fight against so Baba grabs us and pushes us farther behind the house and then around it and towards the village on the other side.

"*Go!*" he yells.

And so we do.

He fires one more shot from the corner, then joins us and we retreat from the house and run towards the streets. There's even more gunfire, echoing between stone buildings that are our buildings and have heard gunfire and seen this type of fighting before, so it's here that we have the advantage, I know, because this is our village and it isn't theirs and they don't know it.

Baba takes a side street.

Giannis guards our retreat.

We make another turn, then Baba stops in the small alley behind Anteros's cobbler shop and kneels to hide behind a wagon and motions for us to hide behind it, too, and we do.

We wait.

We don't breathe.

We're silent, completely silent, then—

"Where's Tasos?" Angeliki whispers next to me.

I look around in panic as we realize he's not with us, then a group of three Germans walk past the opening to the alley and when we see this, we all stand and fire and while the others miss again, I don't, and one of the Germans falls. The second and third turn towards us and raise their rifles but Giannis and Baba fire again quickly and their bullets each find their mark and the Germans are lifted from their feet and fall, too. We slowly come from where we've been hidden and back towards the larger streets, and see that two of the Germans we shot aren't quite dead. They're still crawling on stone, trying to reach rifles they dropped when they fell and Giannis and Baba move their wives and me behind them then go to the Germans on the stone and put bullets in their skulls.

They lie still now.

I walk from my place behind my father and stare down at the German I shot, surprised at how many of them I've hit since this began.

Then I look up and search for Tasos.

I don't see him anywhere so I take the corner around Anteros's shop, on my own, and as soon as I do, I stop, because there's another German standing there at the other end of the alley with his rifle raised and pointed directly at me.

I have no time to do anything.

I see his finger start to squeeze the trigger.

A shot rings out.

The shot's not from him, though.

It comes from the roof and the German looks up and so do I and at the same time we see Tasos there above us, and the German whips his rifle around and fires but Tasos dives out of the way and the bullet misses him, then when the German turns back to me, my rifle is already raised and pointed at his chest.

I don't hesitate.

I fire.

The bullet covers the distance between us in less than a second and tears into his stomach and I've hit another one. The force of it knocks him over and he falls to the ground where he drops his rifle, reaches for it again, like the others did, but I run over and kick it away. Tasos jumps from the roof to the wagon, then the ground, to come stand next to me, and then Baba, Mana, Angeliki, and Giannis all come from the other end of the alley and do, too. Angeliki hugs Tasos and pulls him close. Baba and Giannis try to push me away from this German that's on the ground, holding his stomach now, blood pulsing between fingers that try to cover the bullet hole, but this time I don't let them. It will be me. I don't know why, or why it's important, but it is. I can feel that it is.

So I go forward.

I stand over the German who still holds his stomach as more blood comes and I can see the shadow my body casts across his face, his eyes, blocking him from the sun. He opens his mouth and I don't speak German and won't understand his words, but I still don't want to hear them, so I raise my rifle and once again I don't hesitate.

I squeeze the trigger.

Another shot echoes through the alley.

His head snaps back, then he lies still.

There are a few more shots in the distance, through the streets and village, then soon there aren't any more.

We all look at each other.

"Carefully," Giannis warns, and we understand.

We move as silently as possible, in a calculated and careful manner, back through the street and towards the center of the village. We see no more Germans. Then once we're close and finally get there, we see bodies in the town square and I recognize three of them: the first is Nikos, who also worked in the taverna, the second is Ismini, who was married to Stavros, who was already killed, and the third is Georgiana, the wife of a different man in the village named Giannis who is of the Daskalakis family and had been recruited to go to the mainland. We were all surprised when the letter arrived for him, because he was nearly fifty, but he'd just put away his fishing equipment, his wife had told us, reached for his boots, then kissed her and left with all the others.

Those are the only three Greek bodies I see.

There are other bodies around them, but these bodies I don't recognize, because the rest of them are German.

We stand there.

We all stand together, and we're silent.

Then Father Thiseas comes forward, his black robes torn and stained red and he walks through the square until he comes to something on the ground. He bends and picks it up, and as the light hits it, I realize it's the large gold cross he wears around his neck, only now the chain is snapped and broken. They must have grabbed for it and tried to rip it from him. He picks it up anyway, and holds it in one hand while the other makes the sign of the cross as he walks amongst the deceased and begins to chant a prayer, for all of them, both Greek and German alike, as next to us Anteros whispers.

"The women, too," he swallows. "My god, they killed the women, too."

There are more gunshots in the distance.

They echo, and in the way that they do, it tells us they come from the far side of the valley, and we all know what's there.

Elaionas.

"Ikaros," I whisper.

Then I start to run.

Tasos runs with me, and Mana and Baba call to us, but we don't listen, so they start to run, too, down the same path, and so do Giannis and Angeliki, but they're all old and Tasos and I are young, so we're in front of them and they follow behind.

They try to go faster, but they can't.

There's soon more and more distance between us and we slow as we get close to Elaionas, and see a similar sight to the one we just left: there are both Greek and German bodies, and amongst them, in the center, I see Anastasios Magarakis standing with two rifles crisscrossed on his back, more old muzzleloaders from the Turkish era. There is a group of men standing next to him; they're either older, like he is, or much too young to be doing this, like Tasos, and here it is, another village that's had to be protected by the old, and young, and women of Crete, since all fighting-age men are gone.

I turn to the dead.

I quickly scan their faces and don't see Ikaros amongst them.

I'm relieved, and then feel shame because of all the death in front of me, as I look up to the living and finally see him behind Anastasios and next to the girl I know is named Kyriaki, who's there with her older sisters, Efimia and Iona, as well as her younger brothers, Errikos and Kyriakos, both holding muzzleloaders, the same as their father.

Ikaros turns.

He sees us.

He swings his rifle across his back then runs through the village and all the people and embraces me, first, then Tasos, before he turns back and meets my eyes.

I know what they ask.

"They're fine," I tell him.

"All of them?"

Then as if in answer to his question, Mana, Baba, Giannis, and Angeliki appear from the distance, sweating and breathing heavily, but when they see Ikaros next to me everything else is forgotten and they're whole again, or at least almost whole, as they still have another son that's missing and hasn't yet returned home.

"Thank God," Angeliki breathes.

Ikaros goes past me and Tasos and hugs his parents, too, the same as he did us, then he hugs my parents, also.

There are more distant explosions.

We turn towards the noise, and that's then when we see them.

Soldiers.

A whole company of them.

They're to the south and east, coming from the soft and rolling hills at the base of the White Mountains, stepping over wired fences where the shepherds of Elaionas keep their flocks. They continue on and towards us. The soldiers are German, and there must be ten dozen that have landed then reformed and they're all armed to the teeth. I still have my rifle, and my family have their rifles, too, and Anastasios Magarakis and his sons and a few other men of Elaionas are armed with muzzleloaders, but there aren't many of those. Most carry Cretan daggers, some have kitchen knives, and I even see a man with a bow and arrow that would normally be used only for hunting in the mountains.

Primitive.

Everything we have is a toy compared to what they have, so if we fight, it will now be a massacre.

Anastasios and Giannis look at each other.

There are no words and I realize this might be the only thing in the history of their two families they've ever agreed on, and they don't even need to speak to agree on it, I realize, as Anastasios slowly slips the muzzleloaders from his shoulders.

Giannis does the same, taking his Enfield from where it's been strapped to his back.

A man from Elaionas pushes his way through the crowd.

I can see the anger in his eyes.

"What are you doing?" he asks Anastasios, with venom and poison. "We don't surrender. No one from Elaionas ever surrenders. We die on our feet, the same as our fathers did."

"No, Nikos," Anastasios answers. "We do die, but right now I'd prefer to live, because that's how we'll eventually kill our enemies, no matter how long it takes. And if we don't lay down our arms now, then no one in this valley will be able to do that. If we die here today, then we're conquered. If we stay alive, we never will be. Do you understand?"

There's a moment.

Anastasios has spoken loud enough for all to hear him, not just Nikos, who clearly doesn't agree, but the rest of us do.

We all do.

From the hills, the Germans shout.

They get closer and wave to us and shout more foreign words which we don't understand, but we know what they want, we all know what they want, and what they demand.

This is how fast our lives change.

Anastasios puts his rifle down.

Next to him, so does Giannis.

I put mine on the ground, and the rest of us do, too, my family and brothers and all the villagers of Elaionas drop what few rifles and pistols they have along with their bows, daggers, kitchen knives, and everything else they've used to defend themselves. Then they hold their hands out in front of them, palms upward, to show the advancing Germans what they've done.

They see our empty palms.

But then there's trouble and more talking amongst them as they get closer because they see the German soldiers that are dead in the middle of the village, and an argument breaks out between them. There are two leaders, both dressed the same way and with the same insignias on their lapels, which I know must mean they're of the same rank. It's clear what they each want. One wants to kill and punish us for what we've done, and he yells and points at the bodies. The other argues and keeps pointing south, towards Maleme and Chania. I understand. This isn't just one company, but two. The officer that wants to kill us finally pulls a pistol and points it at his counterpart's head, and I think that's how this will end, but then there's something else.

An explosion erupts fifty paces north of us.

There's one, then another, and then another after that.

I've never heard a grenade before, but I have no doubt this is what we've heard and what a grenade sounds like and we reach and cover our ears. Or at least I do. The Germans all whip around and we're not their focus anymore because this new threat is. They form up again and start to move towards it and as the smoke and dust and dirt clear, they see there's nothing there.

I see the same thing.

There's a moment of quiet, calm, as they inch forward.

Then there's more.

Elaionas is nestled on the far side of the valley and while bordered by the White Mountains to the south, it's bordered to the east by a dense forest of pine and oak, and it's those trees that now light with gunfire that tears into the Germans where they've gathered to examine the explosions that I now realize were just distractions.

Beautiful, brilliant distractions.

Is it the British?

It has to be the British, right, finally honoring their oaths and promises of protection, coming to deliver us from the Germans?

More shots follow.

The Germans try to return fire, then I see my father.

He's next to me.

I watch as he reaches into his trousers and takes one of the grenades that Giannis gave him, pulls the pin, then throws it directly into the middle of the German company.

It rolls against an ankle, and a soldier looks down.

Another does the same, and sees it, too.

Their eyes go wide, but it's too late.

The grenade explodes and Germans fly into the air and the ones that don't fly are cut down by bullets from the trees and bullets from us now, too, as we all reach back and take our rifles again and fire at our enemies—both modern and ancient weapons together now—and the Germans all fall, then there's silence.

We turn to the forest.

Soldiers start to come from the trees.

It's not the British, I see that immediately.

Then I see who it is.

I start to run.

Some that come go to the fallen Germans and shots ring out as they dispatch those not yet dead, but I don't pay attention to that anymore. Instead, I cover the distance faster than I've ever covered any distance before. Then when I'm there, I jump and I feel him, and I smell him, too, for the first time in so many months, and I smile wider than I've ever smiled before in my life because it's my Demetrios that's finally come back to us, with the rest of the 5th Division behind him, and still coming from the trees.

卐

I hold him, and he holds me.

Though Anastasios Magarakis and Giannis had agreed on the best course of action when the Germans first came, they don't agree now. Anastasios wants to continue to Chania and keep fighting. Giannis doesn't. He says we should stay in our villages to protect them from any more Germans that might come, and not go marching into a situation we don't know and trying to fight where our enemies are stronger and have the advantage. Let the British fight them in the cities, Giannis says. We'll fight them in the hills, and mountains, where *we* have the advantage. In the distance, more planes fly over the island and more paratroopers drop from them, but they're all near Chania now, where there are still more explosions yet. "But we have the 5th with us now!" Anastasios yells, waving his arms at all the young and armed men that have returned.

"No, you don't," Demetrios finally speaks.

"What?" Anastasios turns and raises an eyebrow. "What do you mean? Here you are."

"There is no more 5th," Demetrios tells him, very evenly. "Our unit was dissolved in the Peloponnesus, during our retreat, so we've come home simply as Cretans to return to our villages. We've earned that, and that's what we're going to do. We're no longer soldiers. We no longer take orders or answer to anyone but ourselves and our families."

"You're going to stop fighting?"

"Did I say that?" Demetrios answers, meeting the older man's eyes.

"You said there is no more 5th, but yet here you are in front of me, dressed as a soldier, armed as a soldier, and we—"

"The Greek army is finished, Anastasios," Demetrios cuts him off. "All that's left now are Greeks. That's *all* that we are, and it's also how we'll win this war. We'll win by fighting in the mountains and the hills, as my father has said, and fighting against them in our way. The ancient way, not the way of the army, which is the way of our enemy. That's what broke us on the mainland, and if we try it again, it's what will break us here, too."

I hold him even closer.

Tasos comes on the other side, and Demetrios reaches out and puts an arm around his youngest brother, also.

Anastasios isn't a man who likes to be embarrassed.

Since he has been, he's now a dangerous man.

Giannis holds Anastasios's eyes, and so does Demetrios, then after a moment and no further discussion, we all turn and leave. We head back down the path towards our village, and we walk as a family. We finally, once again, walk as an entire and complete family. We're only a few paces away, though, when Anastasios decides to speak once more, his words echoing between the hills, a warning, a threat. "And tell your other son, Giannis, never to return here to Elaionas," he says. "And tell him if he does," Anastasios continues, "or tries to talk to Kyriaki again, or seduce her with his lies, then I'll kill him myself. This will be his only warning."

Ikaros swallows.

Next to Anastasios, Kyriaki begins to cry as she looks back at Ikaros, who stands with us, then turns and runs to her house.

We stand there for a moment.

We all just stand there, for one more moment: our family and his family, facing each other again, in our valley.

Ikaros opens his mouth.

Demetrios shakes his head.

"*Oxi*," he says, knowing the only thing that can happen today is more harm.

Ikaros looks at his older brother and understands, and he listens to Demetrios; of all the people in the world, it's Demetrios he will listen to, so with nothing else left, we all turn once more, and continue on our way home. Behind us, the men who were once the Cretan 5th start to disband, everyone leaving and heading in separate directions towards their own villages. I see a young man named Elias and another named Stelios who are from ours, so they walk with us, and my heart sinks when I realize these are the only men who will be returning. My heart also sinks for them, and Stelios in particular, because I know what he will be returning to find. We continue to the far side of the valley, and when we get there, we see the Greek bodies in the town square have begun to be prepared for a funeral, with Father Thiseas still chanting Orthodox hymns. Then Stelios sees the body of his wife, Ione, and her mother, Chrisoula, and he runs and begins to sob as he kneels and takes his wife's pale and lifeless face in his hands. I can't imagine. I can't even imagine, to be so close, then to have this happen. We go to him. We all go to him, as a village, and hold him, and grieve with him. My friend Kore finds her husband Elias next to my husband Demetrios, and she runs to him as I ran to Demetrios in Elaionas, and they embrace and kiss and through her kisses I hear her ask where they've been, and what's happened to them, but I don't hear him answer.

Father Thiseas comes towards us.

He goes to Stelios and we move out of the way as the priest kneels next to him, his hand on Stelios's back, and we stand and move away to give him privacy and perhaps some comfort in the words that Father Thiseas will bring, though how much comfort, I don't know, because what words, even if they're from God, could possibly make sense of this? What words could possibly justify what's happened and what we've had to endure, and for what? What is in it for these Germans? What have they been told, and why have they come here, so far from their own land, to try and take ours?

I shake my head, as tears begin to come to my eyes, too.

I look at the bodies again.

I see the Germans have been prepared the same as Greeks, and Anteros notices me looking and tells us that Father Thiseas said he'll bring the bodies back to the Germans once the fighting has subsided. They all disagreed with him, but the priest said that men are men, and God is God, and they'll be granted the same rights by their own people as the rights that we give to ours, then no one had said anything further; if the priest wanted to bring them to the Germans, he could certainly do that, and we couldn't stop him, but he'd also surely be doing it on his own.

No one would help him.

Not after what's happened, and after what they've done.

The sun is beginning to die and the explosions near Maleme and Chania along the coast are now not only noise but also flickers and bursts of light and there are less and less of them as the sun sinks, and fewer planes fly overhead as the sun disappears behind the mountains and darkness starts to come.

We look at Stelios.

We want to go to him, but he's still with Father Thiseas, and there will be time for all the things we'd say and offer later, I know, so instead we turn and go back to the house.

We walk slowly.

None of us have eaten a single thing today, so Angeliki and Mana go to the kitchen and start to prepare something as Demetrios sits at the table and I sit next to him, then Giannis, Baba, and Tasos sit across from us.

We look around for Ikaros, and Demetrios sees him in the corner.

"Hey, Ikky," he says, a nickname only he uses.

Ikaros looks up.

He doesn't smile, as he normally does, and as he normally would, and we all know why. He comes from the corner, though, and takes his place with us, his family, and sits at the table next to Tasos who reaches over and puts his arm around his older brother. Ikaros also doesn't stop him like he normally would. He just sits there. His eyes look dead, and now that we're all together, Giannis asks Demetrios about everything that's happened since his last letter, and Demetrios tells us. He tells us how they fought in Albania, against the Italians, at the Kleisoura Pass and Trebeshina, and how they won there. Then the Germans came. They came from farther east, north of Thessaloniki, near the incomplete Metaxas Line, and when Greek soldiers were withdrawn from the Italian front to face the Germans, they knew it was the beginning of the end. I glance at Ikaros as Demetrios continues, but Ikaros stays staring at the table, with his brothers next to him. The Greeks were outnumbered four to one by the Italians, Demetrios explains, which were odds they'd beaten, but against the Germans, too, they were outnumbered by more than twenty to one, and those were odds that could not be defeated. So when the Germans broke through the Metaxas Line, that's when Demetrios and the 5th and the rest of the Greek army began their retreat.

They knew the Germans would try to get to Athens as quickly as possible, so that's what the 5th decided to do, as well; get to Athens before the Germans and find boats that could take them back to their island and their homes. There were men from Chania, Rethymno, Irakleio, and all the rest of the eastern villages with them, and when they got close to Athens and saw the true speed of *blitzkrieg* and that the Germans had beaten them, that's when there was a disagreement over the best way to proceed. In the end, the men of Chania and Rethymno decided to turn south and west and the other group, led by soldiers from Irakleio, decided to head east towards the port of Rafina where one of them had a cousin he said could help. Demetrios isn't sure what happened to them—if they made it or not—but he and the others decided to head to the Peloponnesus and as far south as they could go, then try to find boats that could take them the rest of the way home.

I can feel myself squeezing him as he tells his story.

My hand is still inside his, where it's been since he's returned, and I've moved as close to him as I possibly can as he tells of the small patrol of German paratroopers they fought near the Isthmus of Corinth, the narrow stretch that connects the Peloponnesus to the rest of the mainland. It was just an advance group that was supposed to hold the bridge and prevent any Greeks from passing, but they fought their way past the Germans and to the harbor and there was a large shipping boat there, transporting civilians, but before they got to it to see if there was any more room, a German plane dove and dropped a bomb and destroyed the boat with all the men, women, and children on it. There was nothing they could do, so as the boat sank and the lives were all lost, they turned and carried on. It was slow going because they had to travel on foot over unfamiliar and difficult terrain, carrying wounded with them, all while searching for food and water.

They eventually made it to the walled city of Monemvasia, near the southern tip of the Peloponnesus, and it's there they found more boats assembled: some left by the British, some from Greek fishermen, both local and not, and some no one seemed to know where they came from. Such things happen in war, Demetrios explained. The fishermen wanted to come with them, too, to escape the occupation that would surely ensue, so they did. They organized all the soldiers that had shown up, of which there were many, including Cypriots and Palestinians who had come with the Commonwealth troops, and they found boats and guides then began to sail. They sailed from the Peloponnesus into the Aegean and everything was calm at the beginning, when they first set out, then soon it wasn't. It was a familiar sound that approached, over the boats, and the soldiers all knew what was happening before it did. Like us, the Greek soldiers thought if there was an invasion of Crete, it would be by sea, like all previous invasions had been, but when they heard planes overhead, they knew exactly what was happening. The Greeks tried to make their boats go faster, but they couldn't, so the planes reached the shores of our island before our soldiers did.

They finally landed just west of Chania, where there were no bombs being dropped, but they ran into a group of Germans on their way to Maleme. That was the German goal, to try to capture the airfield, so they could actually land their planes on the island, rather than just fly overhead and drop bombs or paratroopers. Demetrios and the other men of the 5th fought the Germans and won. There was disagreement again on what should happen next, though: some wanted to help the British that were holding the airfields and cities, while others argued that helping the remaining British, who would soon be overwhelmed, was only delaying the inevitable, and they needed to get home to their families who were left unprotected without them, and that was their priority.

Ultimately, that's the group that won.

So they left the coast and Maleme and split as they continued into the hills towards the mountains; the men from Rethymno went east, and Demetrios and the rest continued south. They saw the large group of Germans that looked as if they'd landed just south of Elaionas, so they went to Elaionas first, rather than our village, then from there, we of course know the rest as they hid in the trees and planned their diversion and strategy to save us.

We're silent.

We're all silent.

Then Angeliki comes from the kitchen with Mana and I see they've made *kleftiko*, which has always been Demetrios's favorite, and I smile when I see they've made *sfakianes pites*, too, some with *mizithra* and some with honey, stacked on a plate next to the large bowl of *horiatiki* and olives harvested from our trees. I think of when we first met. I think of where we are now, and all that's happened. Then I put it from my mind because Demetrios asks Ikaros about Kyriaki, and everything that's led to this point while he's been gone, and for a few moments as we all sit and eat and begin to talk of things other than war—of just the simple and great moments of our hearts and lives—the world feels normal again. It won't last, I know, so I want to feel it while it does. I want to feel all of it, and I want to feel my husband.

We finish eating.

Angeliki and Mana begin to clear the dishes and Angeliki taps Ikaros and Tasos on the shoulders to help, and they do. Giannis waits another moment then stands, too, and Demetrios goes to do the same but Giannis stops him and tells him it's still not safe in the village or the hills, and he'll keep watch outside along with my parents and the boys, through the darkness and night, in case any more Germans come.

"I'll come with you," Demetrios says.

But Giannis shakes his head.

"*Oxi*," he says. "You've earned at least one night of rest," he smiles at his oldest son, then soon the dishes are done and after Demetrios's parents kiss his head they gather their weapons once more and leave and I, of course, know the real reason they're doing this, and so does Demetrios.

The house is quiet.

It's just me and Demetrios now, as I dreamed it would be again, as I dreamed so many times in our room not very far from where we now sit, in our bed that's only been my bed for much too long.

He turns to me.

"I'm sorry," he says, and his words are barely more than a whisper.

"Sorry?" I ask. "What could you possibly be sorry for?"

I look at him and now that the others have left, the walls have gone, the walls that men and soldiers make and I see the tears that come, on his cheek, the ones he wouldn't allow if his family were still here, or mine, or any of the others he fought with.

He will allow them with me, though.

I move closer to him.

I reach and wipe the tears from his cheek and when they're gone, and before any more come, I tilt my head towards his and my lips find his lips and even though we've just eaten, his mouth is hungry, it's so hungry, and so is mine.

He stands.

He gets up from the table and in the same motion reaches down and picks me up, too.

He carries me.

I hold him.

I bury myself against his chest.

He takes me to our room where I've slept and dreamed so many times of seeing him, and he kisses me again.

He gently lays me down on the bed.

It's dark but there's moonlight and with every minute that passes there somehow seems to be more, and I watch above me as he takes off his ripped and stained uniform. He takes off his shirt, next, that's under it, and I see scars on his chest, his side, reaching around and to his back, scars that weren't there when he left and I don't ask him about them. I don't want him to have to tell me. He reaches down and takes off his trousers, next, so he's naked and I look at his body again, tracing and retracing in my mind all that's so familiar and perfect then he lowers himself onto me and the bed and his lips find mine again. I don't want them anywhere else except where they are now. He helps me take off my clothes, too, and we lay there together and there's once again only moonlight between us and I feel him and remember what it's like to feel this and I close my eyes. We lay there together and feel each other again and we were two, only moments ago, but we're not now because now, once again, we're one.

My face is near his face, and my lips are near his ear.

"*Demetrios*," I whisper.

"*Maria*," he answers.

And I feel him. I still feel him, and I know he feels me, too.

Above us a plane flies overhead, then another, and still another after that, and I wonder: are they German planes? They must be, I know, but for this moment I ignore what that might mean and I live here, in this room, in this light, with the person who for me, and this moment, is the only other person in the entire world. I feel his breath, warm on my neck. His scent is once again in my nostrils, and with it, memories flood my mind; memories of when we were young, and things were simpler and different than they are now, and when he moves and lays next to me and holds me, just holds me now, I realize we were young once, but we also still are because this feels exactly the same as it did then. And now, after that thought and contentment, I feel nothing except the warmth of his skin next to my skin, and the promise of what we once were and are now again.

It's strange how quickly our lives can change, I think.

But it's also equally strange how quickly they can come back together.

7

MAY 21, 1941

We wake the next day and dress together, and when we do, Demetrios doesn't put on the uniform of the Greek army he's worn every day for the last six months, but rather the clothes of Crete: black trousers, a white shirt, simple cummerbund, and the stitched jacket that I wore when he was gone. After he puts the jacket on, I hand him the brown leather belt that he fastens his Cretan dagger to, then wraps and cinches around his waist. I dress, as well, in the same way I do every morning. When I'm finished, and he is, we leave our bedroom together and there's no one in the house, so we go outside. That's where we see them. They're all at the table near the olives and the cypress, rifles propped against the wood, mugs of steaming *malotira* in front of them. We go and sit at the table, too, and Angeliki pours *malotira* for us. My parents aren't there; it's just Angeliki, Giannis, Ikaros, and Tasos, which means my parents must have gone back to the farm. Demetrios asks if anything further happened in the night, or they've heard any other news, and Giannis tells him there were no more soldiers that had come or been seen in the mountains, but they've seen something else, he says, and it's not good.

"What?" Demetrios asks.

Giannis nods into the distance, to the north and west.

And that's when we see it, too.

We see the large German Junkers passenger planes coming from the north and they don't continue over the island now, as they did before, when they were dropping paratroopers. Instead, as soon as they cross the Sea of Crete and reach land, they begin a descent near the coast and I realize what this means: the Germans have taken the Maleme airfield, and they don't need to drop paratroopers anymore, so they just land and each one of the Junkers is carrying hundreds of Germans inside it, I know, an entire army of enemy soldiers that are now here and on our island.

There's silence.

It's clear what it means.

Then the silence is broken by a snapping twig from beyond the cypress trees, closer to the mountains, and we all whip around and while it's a soldier that's there, and coming towards us, we see it's a Greek soldier. I recognize him as one of the men I saw with Demetrios in Elaionas, and rather than calling him a man, boy might be more accurate, because he looks the same age as Ikaros. He doesn't have to shave. His skin is still smooth and young, and his body not yet filled out in the way it does with men as they age.

"What's wrong, Belen?" Demetrios asks, as he stands.

I wrinkle my nose at the unusual name, wondering how a boy from Crete came to be called something so Spanish.

"They're gone," he says, almost just a whisper.

"Who?"

There's a moment.

He meets Demetrios's eyes, then strangely, turns and meets mine, too.

"Everyone," he tells us.

I stand.

I go and take him by the shoulders, and so does Mana, and we sit him at the table with us and give him *malotira*, as well. There's nothing else we can think to do for this boy, this poor boy whose story is going to be so similar to so many that are just returning home and find they have no home, village, or family to return to. As we comfort Belen, Demetrios and Giannis move away from the table and begin to talk, and then after that, argue, and I know what it is they're arguing about: the same thing they'd both argued about with Anastasios Magarakis, just the day before. I hear their voices begin to rise so I turn to Belen to try to distract him and ask him about what I'd been wondering, the story of his unusual name, and he tells me.

He starts all the way at the beginning.

He explains how his father was from Sevilla, but his mother is from Zakynthos, and that's where he'd grown up. His mother had died in childbirth, he says, so even though his father had given him a Spanish name—to honor his Iberian heritage—he also honored the last promise he'd made to her, and raised their son on her island and in her village. Then things changed, though. When war became imminent, the islands between Greece and Italy seemed the most likely place for first conflict. Belen had wanted to enlist in the Greek army while he was on Zakynthos, but his father wouldn't let him; he'd wanted to send his son back to Spain, but Belen didn't know the language, and didn't want to leave Greece, so their compromise had been while his father would remain on Zakynthos to fight, Belen would go to Crete, and stay with his closest living relative which was his mother's sister who lived in the small mountain village of Topolia. Once he was there and no longer under his father's supervision, though, his father couldn't stop him from volunteering, which is what he promptly did and left for the mainland with Demetrios and all the others. He'd returned with them yesterday, and had gone back to Topolia, but when he'd gotten there, he found the Germans had landed in the mountains near the village and while the villagers had fought against them and won, like we did, the Germans had killed both his aunt and uncle so now there was nothing left for him, and it was time for him to go home.

"How?" I ask him.

"What?"

"How are you going to get back?"

"The boats that brought us here," he says, then nods towards where Demetrios still stands with Giannis. "We left them on the shore, where we landed."

"And you'll go by yourself?"

"It's not that far, only around the Peloponnesus," he says, then smiles at me, or at least he tries to. There's a hollowness to his eyes, which I think must be new, especially for one so young and I recognize parts of the same hollowness that's now in Demetrios's eyes.

War.

War, and the cost of it, and what it does to us.

The conversation between Demetrios and Giannis ends, and Demetrios returns to the table. Belen tells him what's happened, and what he's going to do, and when he does, Demetrios sits for a moment, looking back at him. Then after another moment, he stands and walks into the house and a few seconds later returns carrying two things: an Enfield revolver, taken from the stock of weapons that William gave to me, and one of the carved Cretan daggers Demetrios made when he was young.

"I already have one," Belen says, patting the pistol holstered at his hip.

"It's British and better than the Bulgarian shit they gave us at the front," Demetrios tells him. "And you don't have one of these," he adds, handing him the dagger. "It's made here, and while it's the best quality in the world, it's also more than that, too, and won't let you down."

"What do you mean more?"

"You'll see when you have to use it."

Belen sits there and looks back at Demetrios.

Then he finally nods.

He takes the pistol and dagger as he stands and Demetrios hugs him, while Giannis comes and pats him on the shoulder. He might have a disagreement with his son, but he doesn't with this boy. I nod to Belen and Ikaros does the same, while Tasos just watches us, then after one more moment, and one more look, Belen turns and continues on. He goes past our house then down the road that will lead past the farm, too, and the olives we tend and finally to the beach near the place where I found William, so many weeks ago.

It's only been a month, but it seems like a lifetime.

So much has changed, and so much more is about to, so that's what we all discuss next. The 5th has been disbanded and the British have seemingly left and given up the fight, as there are already reports of a mass evacuation from the southern coast of Crete, across the sea and to Egypt. I think of James Roosevelt, and I think of William, and all the others I saw on their way over the mountains. Why didn't they keep their promise? Why did they leave at the first sign of fighting, as they swore over and over they would never do? All I can think is that we betray each other. We always have it in our hearts to betray each other, but during war those betrayals seem so much greater because of course the consequences are so much greater. In essence, though, it simply leaves us in the same place on our island as we've always been: alone against an enemy that's come to try and take it from us.

And that, Demetrios tells me and all the rest of us, is why he is going to have to leave again.

So there it is.

This is what he was arguing about with his father. He won't be going far this time, though, he tells us—and me, specifically—meeting my eyes again. He will continue to fight, he says, but he'll do so from the hills and mountains, along with all the other men that are of fighting age. The Germans will regroup and soon be here once more, and this time they won't come as unorganized soldiers that have just landed from the sky; this time, the next time, they'll come as an army and they'll leave women alone, as well as the elderly, and young, as long as they don't resist, Demetrios tells us. But men of fighting age? All those men will be treated as combatants, because that's what they are. He wanted to be an architect when I first met him. He was a boy who wanted to create and make homes and buildings, not destroy them.

This is what war does.

I lost my husband once, only to have him return, and now I'm going to lose him again.

I think it will be too much.

But what, really, with all that's happened is too much?

"We'll settle into a rhythm," he tells me as he takes my hand and holds it. "You'll still see me, as often as possible, I just won't live here."

"Where in the mountains will you go?"

"The caves."

I know where he's talking about.

I've been there with him, many times, especially when we were young and I know it's a good idea because they're high amongst the peaks and it's where we went when we didn't want to be found by adults, siblings, parents, or anyone else but each other, and we never were.

"I'm going with you," Ikaros says and adjusts the rifle that's slung across his back so it rests even tighter against him.

Demetrios's eyes flick to Giannis.

Mine do, too.

But he's silent now. He's just silent.

I look to Angeliki.

She's silent as well, then after a moment shakes her head before turning and heading back into the house to start preparing food for them. It's the way we give parts of ourselves to those that we love. She looks broken, though. So does Giannis. I think I might be broken, also, but these are the times, I suppose, the great times for both breaking and unbreaking, and all we can do is still sing and tell our stories, the ones that go all the way back until when gods and goddesses walked this island, and miracles and magic existed as essential fact, and then become part of the stories ourselves, too.

"Are you alright, *Maria-mou*?" Demetrios asks, as he looks at me next to him.

His words are soft, quiet, only for me now.

"*Oxi*," I shake my head.

"I'm not either."

"So what do we do?"

"The only thing we can."

"And what's that?"

"We continue."

I push myself closer to him.

I know he's right even though I don't want him to be, and I imagine how our life will be now, and I don't want it. I want our life to be the same as it was. Such is the world, though, and maybe one day finally this island will be our island again, and the Germans will leave, the same as the Turks, Venetians, and all the others that have tried to conquer us have.

"I'll still see you," he says again. "It will just be in the mountains, or under cover of darkness."

I nod.

There's another tear on my cheek.

I can fight, too, I know I can, but this is how it'll be, at least for now, because without me and the women still in the village there would be no one to tend the olives, or sheep, and keep things going while the men leave and fight once more. So I wipe the tear before he can see it, and Angeliki comes from the kitchen with as much food as she can carry, in two of the buckets we use for the olives, and she hands one to Ikaros, then the other to Demetrios. We turn and walk to the village square together, as a family. We find Father Thiseas there, and Stelios, as well as Philippos who's standing with Anteros and Elena, his mother and father. He didn't fight with the 5th, but he fought when the Germans came here to our homes, and he'll fight again now.

When we get to them, Demetrios leans close to Ikaros.

"Don't worry, Ikky," he whispers. "Philippos is coming, also, so you won't be the only one without a wife."

For a moment Ikaros looks like he's going to explode, then he sees the smile on his brother's face and shakes his head and Demetrios messes up his hair as Ikaros used to do to Tasos, while Demetrios was gone, then Ikaros finally smiles, too. It's the first smile since Elaionas and the words of Anastasios Magarakis. He tries to hide it, he tries so hard to hide it.

But he can't.

"I forgot what it was like having a *malaka* in the house," he says instead.

"We keep fighting," Demetrios says in return, messing his younger brother's hair up once more. "We keep fighting, and in between, love will figure itself out, as it always does."

We all stand there.

Father Thiseas has changed out of his torn, blood-stained robes, and walks in front of the gathered group and says another prayer over all who have gathered in the center of our village, holding his golden cross in one hand and making the sign of the cross with the other.

When his blessing is finished, we all turn to each other, one more time.

Demetrios looks into my eyes, and I look into his.

I stand on my toes and kiss him.

"This won't be forever," he whispers.

"It's alright," I answer, whispering, too. "Because I know where you are now."

"I never left," he tells me, and I feel his words, also. "I never left, and never will, no matter where I am or where I go. Not when you remember me, and we remember who we are together."

I hold him.

I hold him for one more moment, then let go, and he goes to his parents next, then Tasos, and I go to hug Ikaros, and he hugs me back, and he hugs Tasos, also, before going to his parents, after Demetrios, then both of them turn. They join Stelios, who has no family left to say goodbye to, and Philippos, who's hugged his mother and father, then after one more brief moment, look, and nod, all four men turn and start to walk. They take the path that leads south and towards the White Mountains, because that's where they'll go. They'll go past the fields and pastures where I take the sheep with Baba, where we've been taking our sheep for centuries and generations, then they'll go higher. They'll go up towards the very highest villages that are impossible to get to except by those who know their way, and they'll go to the caves that are there, above even those villages. They say they were caves that belonged to the first men here on the first island in the world, and while I don't know if that's true, there are certainly things that have been carved and traced in them, and on the stone, very ancient things. I've seen them, the carved stories of great women and men that have come before us.

What will our story be?

What will we set into rock, and history?

That's what we'll now find out.

At a certain point, Demetrios pauses and turns and waves once more.

I see him and wave back, then he turns again, and they continue on.

They go even farther into the distance, the love of our entire village once again departing and walking with them, until very soon they become specks and then disappear altogether, on their way up and into the great and timeless mountains that watch over us all.

1942

8

JANUARY 8, 1942

After the Germans parachuted onto our island and bombed our cities into submission in the late spring of 1941, the fighting lasted another week before most all British and Commonwealth troops completed their evacuation and we were left on our own, exactly as they promised we wouldn't be. We fought back, while the British soldiers were still here, and it was a fair fight. Then, after the British left, and it wasn't fair, we still kept fighting anyway. We don't have many modern weapons. We don't have enough men of fighting age, either, though more continue to show up every day, returning from whatever distant place on the mainland they'd been trapped and they're joined by the few Allied troops that didn't make it to the south coast in time for the evacuation and so were left to fight with the rest of us. There are British among them, of course, and also Australians, New Zealanders, Cypriots, Palestinians, even some Maori. At first it seemed our resistance would be only among Cretans, but then as more and more made their way to the camps and gatherings in the mountains where the resistance was headquartered, it became a literal gathering of soldiers from around the world.

It was only fitting, I suppose, for an event that was being called a "world war."

After Demetrios left, I developed a new routine.

I know the place where both he and the other fighting-age men hide and live in the caves, and one night during the week I rise from my bed after the sun goes down and make the long trek into the mountains, to the village that's there called Skiafos, and that's where he meets me. I vary the night I choose so there is no pattern. Then, on the weekend, either Saturday or Sunday night, Demetrios, Ikaros, and the others come down to see us. No matter which direction we go, though, the visits are always under cover of darkness, and too short.

It's also not long after the initial fighting and open warfare on the island ends, that it turns to guerrilla resistance, and when it does, I go back to Chania for the first time. I see the destruction the Germans have caused: there are bombed and shelled buildings everywhere, including the movie theater near the Old Town where we used to go every Friday night and which is now completely caved in, the roof gone and only two crumbling walls still standing. I'm relieved when I get to Cassia's and see her building intact because it's one of the only ones that is. She's not there when I arrive, so I wait for her, and when she comes back, I hug her as soon as I see her. She hugs me, too, and answers all my questions and tells me how it's been since occupation. And then, instead of just telling me, she shows me, also. She takes my hand and leads me through the city. She shows me bullet holes in the stone from the fighting that took place in the streets. She shows me all the bombed-out and destroyed buildings, and the damage to the Yali Tzamisi Mosque, down by the water, the mosque of the Janissaries which is now missing its tall, defining, and once very-visible minaret. There's some irony, I think, that we let the minaret stand, even after all the brutal years of Turkish occupation, and it was their allies from the first great war who were the ones that finally destroyed what even we had allowed to remain.

We keep going and Cassia shows me the German officers who have now made their headquarters in the town hall where only a few months ago the British did, and we go to the exact spot near the fountain where we left William as he returned to his countrymen. Now, though, there are none of his countrymen here and the entire area is filled with Nazis in pressed uniforms and polished boots. There are a great many more Germans at Souda Bay, too, Cassia tells me, which was also heavily bombed during the invasion. The city is quieter. There are just soldiers, and those, like myself, who the soldiers think pose no threat to them and have business here because even though our island is now occupied, a certain part of life must go on and we all need to continue to eat, so I still sell our wares in the *agora*. Some are ashamed that I sell to Germans. I ignore those voices, though, because what they don't understand is that to sell to anyone in an occupied country, we must sell to everyone.

And it's a front and cover for something else, too.

Cassia still works at the nightclub and it's no secret how she makes enough money to afford the apartment she has in the best building in the nicest part of town, right next to the harbor. So now, instead of sleeping with British soldiers and officers, she sleeps with Germans. They treat her nicely and lavish gifts upon her, and they also do something else: they tell her secrets. They tell her of troop numbers and movements because they want her to know when they'll be leaving, then coming back, and able to see her again, and they tell her all sorts of other things in answer to the questions she asks. And then, after they tell her, she tells me, and I tell Demetrios on either the days I see him in our village, or up in the mountains, during the week, when I go there.

It's good information, too.

One time, we learned of troops leaving Chania and heading to Rethymno under the command of someone Cassia regularly saw, and Demetrios and his men were able to set a trap for them on the road. After they killed them, they took the German weapons and ammo from the *kubelwagen* jeeps, then drove them into the sea. In addition to the *kubelwagens*, the Germans also had a Zundapp KS 750 motorcycle with them that Demetrios managed to ride back to the mountains with the weapons and ammo, and that's how they were well-armed again, with more rifles and bullets for everyone, and a motorcycle, too.

There was poetry to it, I thought.

They'd now kill Germans with their own German weapons.

It was also around this time that Demetrios started to notice a change in Ikaros.

In the beginning of their time in the mountains, Ikaros was apprehensive, Demetrios told me, as many men are when they first experience battle. Very quickly, though, his apprehension turned into something else. He had learned he had a talent for shooting and killing—a steady hand and precise eye—and that led him to becoming quite bold, and then even bolder still, after he'd been with them for some months, and it was now to the point where his actions during the fighting and skirmishes against the Germans had become reckless. On one hand, he's beginning to live up to his name. On the other, he's unnecessarily risking a life, and a life that's needed, too, just the same as the original Ikaros did. We don't see any of this, though, me or his parents in the village, but I'm there when Demetrios comes on a Thursday night, which is unusual, and he comes without Ikaros, which is even more unusual. He asks to speak with Giannis and tells him everything that's been happening. Giannis listens, stone-faced, and after he hears all his oldest son has to say about his middle child, he simply stands and leaves. He doesn't say anything else, he just gets up from the table where they'd been sitting, takes his jacket to protect against the chill of the winter night, and begins to walk.

"Where's he going?" I ask Demetrios.

He doesn't answer.

Instead, Demetrios just gets up, and so do I, and we go to our bedroom.

I don't ask any more questions about Giannis because the limited time we have together is so precious, and I count every moment. So we go, and when we're there, and close the door behind us, I put my hands on his chest.

My lips find his.

I take off his jacket, his cummerbund, his shirt, and when I do, I see there are now more scars crisscrossed on his skin.

Fresh scars.

"What happened?" I ask, very softly.

"Nothing," he whispers, as my hands trace the angry lines as if my fingers could command them to reveal their mystery. He gently takes my hands from the scars and places them on his shoulders, then my thoughts begin to slow and turn to something else as we move to our bed. I didn't become pregnant in the first years we were married, leading up to Demetrios's deployment to the mainland, and I haven't become pregnant since he's been back, despite us continuing to try, though of course we try less now than we did before the war. It's something I always think about, however. Sometimes, I wonder if it's us; one of us, both of us, our biology. Other times, though, I wonder if it's God and his protection. Either way, we soon drift to sleep, together, holding each other, and when I wake, he's gone again, back to the mountains, and my bed is empty once more. I quietly dress and when I leave my bedroom, I see that Giannis has returned. He's sitting at the kitchen table, holding Angeliki's hand, as she sits across from him with her steaming mug of *malotira* and tears on her cheek.

"What is it?" I ask, looking between them. "What's happened?"

"It's time to prepare for a wedding," he tells me.

9

JANUARY 9, 1942

I don't know what Giannis said to Anastasios Magarakis.

In fact, no one does, and however often we might ask, I'm not sure anyone ever will; all any in our family or either village knows is that Giannis showed up in Elaionas that Thursday night, woke Anastasios from his sleep and after an entire night spent talking alone, the next morning they both agreed there would be a wedding. Are ancient and eternal things finished and undone just as simply as that? I guess the answer is sometimes they are, especially during war. Time will surely tell, but it seems if there isn't an outright peace, there's at least a truce, though it becomes clear after the announcement that the truce isn't an all-encompassing one, but rather a begrudging impasse reached for the happiness of children during these times where there is so little happiness. I don't know Kyriaki Magarakis, but I look forward to getting to know her as we become family. I've seen her, of course, but never spoken to her and I ask myself: what could she have possibly said or done to change the mind of her great and stubborn father? Because surely it was her, right, who changed his mind? In the end, it doesn't matter. If there's one good thing that's happened in the whole of the last year, it's this, and the entire valley will be able to share in the happiness of Ikaros and Kyriaki.

Happiness.

Joy.

Pure, unadulterated elation and love.

Giannis and Angeliki told Demetrios what Anastasios said before he left to go back to the mountains, so it's their oldest son who gets to tell their middle child this news, and I'm sorry I won't be there. I imagine it to be something like this, though: a scene where Ikaros tries to take off and run again, straight to Elaionas, and her arms, the same as he did when we heard the German planes, but Demetrios stops him. Demetrios grabs him and holds him so he can't run to the village where he might be seen by Germans, then tackles him to the ground and Ikaros starts to laugh, and so does Demetrios, who feels the same love and joy his brother now feels. I imagine there will be too much drinking among the men there in the mountains, and too much celebrating, and I keep smiling at all of this and all I imagine must be happening there.

I won't see any of it, though.

At least not until the wedding.

Giannis and Anastasios both agree the wedding needs to be sooner rather than later, while it's still winter, and it'll be in the mountains at the town of Skiafos. It's an area still covered with snow in January, and while the German patrols occasionally reach those heights in the summer, in winter, they rarely venture out of the cities. So while there will always be risk to having a wedding and large gathering, that's the calculated risk that will have to be taken. Since the fighting began and the Germans took our cities, they've flown planes over the entirety of the island and dropped leaflets in Greek that warn any villager who holds or owns a weapon will be treated as an enemy soldier, regardless of age, sex, ability, or anything else. And also, any village that harbors resistance fighters of any kind will pay the most severe price. So in the mountains, and protected by season and elements, is where and how the wedding will have to take place.

It's also decided, to minimize risk, that neither Ikaros nor any others will return to the village before the wedding.

I realize what that means.

The next time he sees Kyriaki, it will be on the day that will mark the beginning of their lives together.

How beautiful, I think, but it also leaves very little time to prepare.

It's normally the mother of the bride who would be in charge of food, wedding dress, and decorations, but Kyriaki's mother died many years ago—during the birth of her last sibling—so we split duties between all of us instead. My mother will handle the food, she enlists the help of the women of the village to assist her with it, and I walk to Elaionas with Angeliki to prepare the wedding dress. Kyriaki opts for traditional rather than modern and will wear the same dress her mother wore when she wed Anastasios, she tells us. So we'll tailor it to fit her, and since on our island a wedding dress is a map of a family's history, we'll also add her history to it, as well. It's the first time I've really met or spoken with her, or even seen her closely; she has jet-black hair and brown eyes set in a triangular face with sharp angles and features, rather than the soft and diminutive shape many men seem to prefer. I wouldn't describe her as beautiful in a traditional sense, but the more I'm with her, the more I find myself not able to turn away, and though her beauty isn't the type we've all been shown over and over, I see and understand what's so entranced Demetrios's middle brother.

Her mother's dress has been stored in a chest of cedar, made of wood from the trees that grow on the southern coast of the island, near Elafonisi, and when we take it out we see all the color, layers, textures, and images that have already been embroidered on it. These are images of her family's story, up until this point, and this is what they are: a *kaiki*, a sheep, a lion, a crescent moon, an olive tree, a dolphin jumping next to an island, and a gold coin. I don't ask her about them. Instead, I ask what she would like to add. Each successive bride that wears the dress usually adds one embroidered motif, but she tells me she wants to add two: a snow-capped mountain, and a Cretan dagger.

We look at her curiously, both Angeliki and I.

"It's where we met," Kyriaki says simply, "and it's also who we are."

I don't know how they met, but I suppose she's telling us it must have been in the mountains. However it happened, we have what we need, so we take the dress and begin the process of embroidery, as she's requested, which we'll do here, in Elaionas, and in her house so that the dress will remain with her and her people. Now that we've seen the colors, pattern, and fabric, Angeliki will weave and sew the headdress that will be made for Kyriaki, and that she'll be given on her wedding day and not before. I look down at the motifs once more. I still wonder about the mountains and what they mean. The dagger, of course, is in regard to the continuation of conflict we're all now part of. They will both be there now, in the story of her family, forever, which means it will now be in the story of our family, too. I suppose it's as it should be.

The next days go by quickly.

Every time I walk through the house, Angeliki is at the dining table sewing the headdress, and despite the circumstances and family into which Kyriaki was born, I can tell that Angeliki is ecstatic to finally have another daughter after a life of raising three wild boys. Giannis seems more reluctant, however. He seems apprehensive about the future and becoming part of the family that his family has been at odds with for more time than any can count, but things change, as the world has shown us, so many times now; things do indeed change, and this wedding, of course, will be proof of that.

The day soon arrives, and when it does, my mother loads all the food she's prepared onto a wagon that's pulled by our donkey and covered with hay and the tools we use to trim the olives to disguise what's really there.

Then she sends Tasos with it up to the village.

He needs to be there earlier than us, as he will stand as *koumbaro*, and the rest leave in pairs, or threes, and we don't all go at once but rather stagger our trips and we won't be gone long: our plan is to be back before the sun comes up tomorrow. Or at least most of us. I go with my mother and father, and it's hard for them to travel all the way to the highest parts of the island, though they try not to show it. They don't want to let me or anyone else see their struggle because it's such a joyous occasion and they don't want anything to take from that. The trip takes nearly half a day. We soon get to Skiafos, though, and begin to walk through the narrow and tiered streets of the ancient village, one that's seemingly hanging from peaks and clutching to the sides of the White Mountains around it. And as we walk through it, we see how the village has been decorated: there are blue and white banners, the colors of the Greek flag, strung between buildings, and there are also petals of white and blue flowers spread through the streets that lead to where the ceremony will take place in the small Orthodox chapel of *Agios Giorgos* on the bluff facing south. When we get to the chapel, I see Father Thiseas standing in filtered and dusty light, in front of the altar, and I see Ikaros next to him in full traditional Cretan dress which is the uniform of weddings, of everyday life, and also battle. He has new clothes, though, that are bright and colorful and freshly starched, and I see he has a new dagger, too. It's one that's been recently carved and made by Giannis, I realize, for this occasion, and it's strapped to his right hip. Next to Ikaros stands Tasos, also in full traditional dress, then I see that they've spurned tradition and Demetrios stands next to them, also, dressed the same way and as a second *koumbaro.* He sees me and shrugs very small and I just smile back at him. I smile at Ikaros, also, and what he's done, because I know he's right: a *koumbaro* is a best man, a godparent to future children, and a marital sponsor all rolled into one; a *koumbaro* is the person who will always be there for the couple, to help them, to be relied upon, and in these times, we need that help. We will all, certainly, with what is to come, need all the help there might be.

We take our seats.

Our family is in the front row on the right side of the chapel, the side on which Ikaros, Tasos, and Demetrios stand at the altar.

Everyone from our village also sits on the right.

Across from us, on the left, I look and see all the people who have come from Elaionas.

There are no rifles or pistols amongst them, or us, not anywhere in the chapel, so that if by chance we are found by Germans, we can claim innocence and perhaps be spared. There's another moment of silence and near-darkness, then the doors to the chapel open again and light pours in. We all turn to see Kyriaki in the dress woven by her ancestors and by us. She's holding the arm of her father, and her two sisters are there, Efimia and Iona, to stand as *koumbara*, as she's made the same decision as Ikaros, to have two siblings stand with her rather than just one. They walk down the aisle together. Kyriaki goes first, her father next to her, and she holds his arm as her sisters follow. When they pass where we sit, I see the finished embroidery we've added, then I see more, too. There's another image that's on the dress and I realize she must have done this one herself, after we left, or alone with her sisters, and I smile when I see what it is: a piece of string that's bent and twisted and tied into a complicated, unbreakable, and never-ending knot. I smile because I know what it is. It's us. It's our families, once separate, but now joined, forever joined in a way that's made to be enduring, unbreakable, and without end.

The ceremony is beautiful.

Tasos and Demetrios hand Father Thiseas the wedding rings.

He puts each ring on just the tip of Kyriaki and Ikaros's fingers, and he does this three times and blesses them each time he does it. Then Efimia and Iona come forward. They carry with them the *stefana*, the wedding crowns that have been woven out of branches of young olives, from both our trees and theirs, and decorated with flowers picked from a place between the two villages. Once the *stefanas* are placed on the head of the bride and groom, and joined by a single strand of string, Kyriaki and Ikaros are led around the altar three times, to symbolize the journey they're about to undertake together. When they stop and stand in front of each other, Father Thiseas blesses them one last time, removes the crowns, then they kiss as they're now joined for all eternity and we cheer. It's a muted cheer, though, especially from the Elaionas side of the aisle, as resentments, bitterness, and jealousies don't end simply because a wedding takes place. The only thing that can cure such things is time, I know, which is if such things can be cured at all.

Ikaros and Kyriaki turn and face us.

They leave the altar and begin to walk down the aisle as we mimic spitting at them, each three times, to bring the greatest amount of luck and good fortune, then we follow after them and back outside to the mountain streets.

And that's when we stop.

Demetrios is at my side now, and he's taller than me, and can see over the crowd, so it's him that stops first. I can see Ikaros and Kyriaki ahead of him, too, and when I look, I see the joy that was on their faces only moments before has now left and turned to something else.

Anger.

Fear.

Then I see why.

Soldiers.

They're German soldiers, an entire battalion coming from the mountains and down the narrow streets, armed with rifles that are pointed at us and after a quick count, I realize there are about twenty of them. I see Ikaros tense in front of us, his entire body on alert now as his hand reaches towards his Cretan dagger, but behind him, and next to me, Demetrios whispers into his brother's ear: "*Oxi*," he says, under his breath.

I of course know why.

There's another young man here, though, from Elaionas, who doesn't have an older brother to whisper to him and doesn't look to be more than sixteen, the same wild and uncontrollable age as Ikaros, and he breaks from us and starts to run in the opposite direction. One of the Germans raises his rifle. He aims, then a shot rings out. It echoes between the mountains, and after the boy stumbles and falls, there are screams that echo between the mountains now, too. The screams are all around us, and I want to scream, as well, but I don't. I don't let myself. I won't give them that. Some of the women run to the young man that's fallen, while some of the men instinctually reach for daggers or anything that could be used as a weapon, but the other men—Giannis, Anastasios Magarakis, and Demetrios among them—urge them to stop. They know what we have always known, and the reason why we have no rifles or pistols with us: we are no match against the Germans in open combat, and if we try to fight them as we are, it will be a bloodbath.

The soldiers approach.

They continue to walk slowly towards us.

We wait for them.

Giannis, Anastasios, and Demetrios go forward from our group, along with Anastasios's sons, Kyriakos and Errikos, then a leader steps forward from the German battalion to meet them.

There's silence.

The German commander surveys all of us, his eyes twitching and moving between each individual, as he takes us in, our purpose, and the reason we're here.

He opens his mouth and speaks in his language.

None of us understand, so he smiles, then tries again.

"My name is Klaus Gunter," he says, in German-accented English. "I'm an *Obergefreiter* in the Fuhrer's 5th Mountain Division, and there are men here of fighting age. Do you understand my words?"

"Yes," Anastasios answers, also in English. "I understand your words, but you're mistaken and there are no men here who have fought, against Germany or otherwise."

"You say you understand my words, and I understand yours, but do you really expect me to believe that?" Klaus raises an eyebrow and smiles even wider now.

Danger.

That's what he is.

Danger, and cruelty, just like all of them are.

"They're all either too old or young, or they're injured and unfit to serve," Anastasios answers, then waves towards all those gathered, as if to illustrate his point. "Also, we have no weapons, just as your papers told us. We have followed all your rules."

"A knife isn't a weapon?"

"It's part of our dress, for the wedding," Anastasios explains. "The daggers are tradition, nothing more. The messages you dropped from your planes said no firearms. That was the only rule. They said nothing about anything else."

"I'm aware what our messages said," Klaus responds, slowly now, as his eyes scan, and we wait. "What about him?" he finally asks, and I think he's pointing at me, at first.

Then I realize he's not.

He's pointing next to me, at Demetrios.

"What *about* him?" Anastasios asks.

"He looks like he can fight, and on this island, I've found that men that look like they can fight do."

"He was born with a twisted foot," Giannis says quickly, walking forward. "He can't run or march or anything else, much less fight. He can barely even walk."

"Who are you?" Klaus asks.

"His father."

There's a moment as Klaus's eyes flick from Demetrios to Giannis, next to him, to Anastasios, then back to Demetrios again, and me at his side.

"They're lying," he says, after a moment, to his men. "Bring them with us, every single man that's here."

"What?" Giannis yells. "These are kids!"

"Your son walked just fine coming from the church, and besides, what do kids do? They grow and become men, and men pick up rifles and fight. They all pick up rifles and fight, so we'll stop that from happening, and perhaps save some German lives in the process."

"You can't do that!" Giannis yells.

"You're a liar!" I scream, too.

Klaus turns to me now.

"What have I said here that's been a lie?" he asks. "I only speak truth, even if no one else will, even if it's truth you don't like or agree with. I would also suggest some prudence now, young lady, and old man, unless the rest of you wish to come with them and die, too."

He motions with his hand.

His soldiers come forward.

They start to roughly grab all the men that have come from the church, and when they get to Demetrios, I hold onto him because I've already lost him once. The German who tries to take him turns and roughly hits me in the arms until I let go and Demetrios yells at him in English, and shoves him, but the German shoves Demetrios back and then they're pulled apart.

He spoke to the German in English, but he turns and quickly speaks to me in Greek.

"We have to go with them," he says.

"They'll kill you," I answer, panic in my words.

"If we don't, they'll kill all of us," he says as he jerks his head towards where the soldiers are leading Ikaros away now, too, still in his wedding costume, along with my father, and Giannis, and they even come for Tasos, taking the Cretan daggers that all the men wear and throwing them away to the ground. Next to Tasos, they start to pull another young man from Elaionas away from his mother, but she holds onto him, and when they pull harder, she takes a dagger from her skirt and before she can swing, another shot rings out, there's another echo between the mountains, and she falls clutching a bloody leg as her son is hauled away with the Germans anyway and she screams in pain on the cobblestone street as her daughters run to her.

It's just women standing in front of the church now, and I find Demetrios's eyes, with the other men, and he tells me, one more time, in Greek.

"It'll be alright."

"No, it won't," I answer in the same language, our language.

He doesn't have any more words because what else could he possibly say?

He's turned and led away, with the others, through the narrow streets of the village, some of the Germans pointing their weapons at the men they take and some pointing their weapons behind them, at us, to make sure we don't try anything, to make sure we stay where we are and don't move.

They keep going.

Soon they're nearly gone, out of sight, and when they are, all that's left is terror.

Grief hasn't begun yet.

What should I do?

Is there still time to do anything, because doing something, even if it means death, is surely better than this, isn't it?

I look at my mother who stands there in shock, then I go to where the Cretan daggers are scattered and loose on the street and I find Demetrios's. I reach down and pick it up before turning back towards where the Germans went with my heart. I lift the hem of my skirt, and before I know what I'm doing, I begin to run, even as my mother tries to grab me and screams now, too.

"No, *Maria-mou!*" she cries. "*Oxi!*"

"They're going to kill them!" I yell back at her, and everyone else.

"If you go after them, they'll kill you, too!"

"Then this is my death, because without doing something, there is no life!"

I don't know exactly what I plan to do, but I know I have to do something, and I also know what I'm doing is selfish—that Mana and Angeliki will now lose more than just their husbands and sons, if they lose me, as well—but I don't care. For once in my life, I don't care, and I'll be selfish, because for once in my life I'm only thinking of myself, and I need this.

I keep running.

I'm just about to round a bend in the road, and that's when everything explodes.

The noise and force that comes with the explosions is so great it knocks me from my feet and to the ground. I land roughly on stone as the noise continues, and I recognize not the sound of rifles being fired, but automatic rounds from a machine gun. I've never seen a machine gun before, but this is what one must sound like, I realize, and the staccato of automatic fire is punctuated by loud and uneven blasts from multiple rifles, as well as detonating grenades, which I recognize.

The noise continues for another moment, then stops.

I slowly stand.

I look up, and still don't see anything through gathered smoke, so I begin to run again.

I fear the absolute worst—I fear I'm too late, and am going to come upon my husband, fathers, brothers, all dead in the street, the stone slick with their bright, proud, fresh blood that is my blood, too—and while the stones in front of me are indeed red and slick with blood, it's not proud or bright, and it's not ours, because when I look, I see our men still standing.

They're still there, and still alive.

Then I look farther and what I see just beyond them are saviors, and what has happened: there are about fifty dirty and exhausted Commonwealth fighters, holding rifles at the ready along with two machine guns, coming from behind the buildings where they've been hiding.

I see them, but I ignore them.

I run to Demetrios and into his arms.

I hold him.

He holds me.

The other women that have been by the church come running now, too, with Kyriaki in front and she reaches Ikaros, and Angeliki gets to Tasos, and Giannis, then my mother finds Baba and goes to him. After we're reunited, I turn and look at the British that are now walking through the streets towards where we all stand and hold each other. The faces I see are faces of all different colors and races: from the British islands and Australia, as well as from India, Palestine, the Maori from New Zealand, and so many more soldiers from the Commonwealth that are here and fighting against our common enemy. They're of all ages, too. I see one soldier that looks to be no more than sixteen, and another that looks to be fifty, minimum, and perhaps older. I keep looking amongst all the different and unfamiliar faces, then I'm surprised when I find one that's not. He limps, very slightly, on a leg that's healed from a wound that will never really heal, the remnant of an event and time that will always be with him and part of him no matter how many doctors he might see or days that might pass.

"*William*?" I breathe, just his name, barely a whisper.

But he hears, and turns.

When he does, I see his face is more gaunt, eyes more sunken, and it's not from lack of food or nourishment, it's simply war and what killing does to us and what it's done to him, in the last months.

"Maria," he looks back at me.

Then he sees my husband, next to me.

"Do you know each other?" Demetrios asks, looking between us.

"This is the British *palikari* I found."

"My goodness."

"You must be Demetrios," William says and extends his hand. "I used your crutches."

"Is that right?" Demetrios laughs.

"I'm afraid so."

"I can't believe the timing."

"What do you mean?"

"That you found us, just as they came."

"We've been tracking this group since they left Chania yesterday."

"Really?"

"We didn't know they were coming here," William tells us. "But we followed them, looking for a perfect spot for an ambush. Then when they got here and did what they did, we figured here would have to do."

"Well, however it happened, I'm certainly glad it did," Demetrios says.

"Me too," I add.

"And me as well," William looks at me, then Demetrios, then back to me once more as a smile starts to spread across his lips. "I'm certainly glad as well."

We decide the wedding will continue as planned.

It's less festive than it would have been, but it's the parents of the boy who was killed that suggest it should proceed. Their son, whose name was Ioannis, would have wanted it to, his mother tells us.

So it does.

The British and Commonwealth troops join.

They don't want to intrude, William tells us, but we insist, so they finally agree.

When Tasos sees William, he runs and gives him a hug, and Ikaros comes, too, and shakes William's hand, as William looks Ikaros up and down. "My goodness," William says, and then pauses. "My goodness," he says again. A warrior can tell another warrior, and that's what Ikaros is now. Not everyone is so happy and glad to see the new soldiers, though. Anastasios Magarakis, for one, has great distrust of the British for the betrayal they made both before the Germans came, then after, and Anastasios isn't alone, either, among us or on this island: the British said they would defend Crete if we sent the 5th to the mainland, then when the Germans came, the British fought for a moment, a brief moment, a little more than a week, then they left us to occupation and death and to carry out our own resistance. Some of the British, like those that have saved us, just didn't make it to the boats in time. That's good for our resistance, of course. But poor timing, Anastasios argues, isn't a substitute for lack of honor. Either way, they're still here, and so are we, and even though Anastasios might have no interest in being friends with them, we all share a common enemy, so there will be a type of peace amongst us.

The women of Skiafos go to their houses.

They retrieve mountain herbs and remedies that they bring back and put into the wound on the leg of the mother who was shot, who I learn is called Anthousa. Then soon after that, the eating begins. My mother always makes too much food, no matter the occasion, and in this instance, and perhaps this instance only, that turns out to be fortunate because it means there is enough for the unexpected guests. I can tell by their tired and weary eyes that they're grateful for the meal. And then after the eating, that's when the dancing begins. It's normally louder, more festive, and with much more cheering and clapping and laughing, but there hasn't been much of those things in these last months, especially now with one of our own dead, and the rest of our men nearly sharing the same fate. So instead of something more joyous, the first notes I hear are the slow and sad melodies of a *zeibekiko*, a deliberate and emotional dance of pain, love, longing, and desire. Gradually, a circle begins to form. It's the men that form the circle, and there are a few women who join, some standing and others kneeling and slowly clapping with the rhythm. I watch as Demetrios goes to the center. He slowly raises his arms on either side, from his waist to his shoulders, then finally above his head. He begins to dance. It's fitting, I think, as I watch him. It's fitting for us to dance our immortal dance of grief and loss tonight, in these mountains. Then I turn from the dancing and see William sitting with a small glass of *raki*. I wait for a moment, then another, before I finally stand and walk through the crowd towards him and sit next to where he sits.

In front of us, the music picks up.

Demetrios begins to jump and slap the sides of his feet as he dances, as he continues with his passion, his pain, his lament.

William nods in his direction.

"He dances well."

"Yes. But we all do here."

"You all do what?"

"Dance," I tell him. "As soon as we learn to walk, we also learn how to dance."

He smiles.

He takes another sip of *raki* and I notice he makes no face: he's used to it now, I realize, what it tastes like, how it burns, what to expect.

"What about you?" I ask him.

"What about me?"

"Do you dance?"

"I'm English," he laughs. "I think it's safe to say I'd probably rather die."

"You've been here nearly a year."

"Yes."

"So perhaps you're a little Greek now, too."

"Perhaps."

"So maybe you should try?"

"I don't think so. There are bridges that can be walked, and bridges that are too far, and dancing, my dear Maria, seems like it will most definitely be the latter of those two structures."

I turn back to the men and women, and the circle they've formed.

Demetrios leaves the center and Ikaros enters now, from the crowd, and the groom takes over. He's still dressed in his wedding outfit, and when he begins, I wonder if he's been practicing because he dances better than he normally does, and I wonder if it's practice or simply this moment, this time and place where blood and history have met and perhaps make us more than we are.

He jumps higher than his brother, which I've never seen.

He twists and sails through the air, contorts his body, leaps and slaps one foot, then the other, and when he returns to the ground, arches his back and bends lower, lower, lower still until the top of his head touches the ground.

Then he rises again.

"He seems different," William says, next to me.

"He is, I think."

"A man now."

"War does that to boys."

"Yes," he says, quieter. "But girls do that, too."

"Do what?"

"Make boys into men."

"I suppose you're right," I laugh. "I suppose we do that, too, as you've said."

"I come *bar-ring* a message."

I hear the words and look up to see Demetrios walking towards us, and he sits next to me with his own glass of *raki* that he sips as he wipes sweat from his brow even though it's winter, even though it's cold, and there's a very sharp chill in the air.

"*Bearing*," I say, correcting his English.

"Yes," he smiles. "Bearing, that's what I meant."

"What's the message?"

"It's not for you, *Maria-mou*," he says, then nods towards William. "It's for him."

"Me?" William raises his eyebrows.

"There's someone trying to get your attention."

"Who?"

But Demetrios doesn't answer, he just jerks his head and William looks in the direction Demetrios is gesturing, towards a woman I don't know. She must be from Skiafos. She's younger than I am, and wears black, the colorless outfit of one who has lost their husband.

"Her name is Myrine and she doesn't speak English."

"She's a widow?"

"Her husband fought with us on the mainland and died near Klisoura. I don't think she's looking for another husband, just perhaps a warm bed tonight," Demetrios says, then stands as he finishes his *raki*. "There, message delivered," he smiles. "That's all I can do."

He reaches for my hand.

I take it, and stand with him.

I look back down at William.

"Thank you," I tell him again. "For being here. For coming back."

"*Parakalo*," he smiles.

I smile, too, for one last moment, then Demetrios starts to walk and I go with him.

We go back through the party and towards where Ikaros finishes his *zeibekiko,* then pulls Tasos into the circle after him. Demetrios kisses each of his brothers on the head, then whispers something into Ikaros's ear, something only they two can hear. I watch, then when Demetrios moves away, I go and hug Ikaros and kiss him on the forehead, too, then turn and do the same to Kyriaki.

Demetrios leads us away from the wedding.

We go back through the now-dark streets of Skiafos.

When we're on the far side of the village, it begins to snow, and we don't hurry.

We take our time, walking through the soft and drifting flakes, then once we're past the village, we turn north and head farther up and into the mountains and it's not long until we come to the caves, and one cave in particular.

His.

I normally meet him in the village, when I've come before, but this is the first time I've gone higher.

We go inside.

It's wide and deep, and he takes a match and lights the candles he has placed in each corner so it's no longer dark. Then, when light comes, I see what else is in the cave: there are marks on the walls where those who came before us drew pictures, their stories, which I've already seen, when I was a child. And below them there's now an entire pile of both German and British rifles and ammunition. I know where these weapons have come from, and what they are, exactly what they are. New stories. They are new stories, our stories, now, next to the ancient ones etched above. I keep looking and also see the Zundapp KS 750 motorcycle Demetrios took from the Germans on the road to Rethymno, propped against the far wall, as well as a low, homemade bed he's recently constructed near a small table where I assume he takes his meals when he's alone.

He walks towards me, then stands in front of me, and I can smell him.

"What's the matter?" he asks.

"Nothing," I breathe. "Absolutely nothing."

I stand on my toes so my lips find his lips, then I reach and unbutton his jacket, which slides off.

I pull his shirt up and over his head.

My hands find the thin leather belt that holds his black trousers, and I uncinch it, then his pants fall and everything else is gone, too, and it's just us again.

I take my clothes off.

He doesn't help me.

He stands as close as he can and his eyes don't leave my eyes, which look back into his, and when I'm done, he moves even closer still so his skin touches my skin and I don't only smell him, I feel him, then he takes me and lays me down on his bed and moves so that he's on top of me. We will survive, like our ancestors did, and we will love like they did, as well, and maybe they survived *because* they loved, just the same as this, and perhaps even in this very cave. That's what I'm thinking as it begins. Then, once it does, all I think of is him. All I think of is this man I waited for my whole life, first once, then again, and now here he is, in my arms, in our cave of stories and flickering candles, casting their fractured light that dances across our naked and intertwined bodies, and fills our once-empty but now full-again souls.

10

JANUARY 17, 1942

After the wedding, the women all go back down to our two villages, the men of fighting age remain in the caves above Skiafos, and things for the most part return to what normal has been since the German invasion. Or perhaps more accurately, things return to normal for everyone but me. In the moments before the German paratroopers arrived, nine months ago, when I thought I had lost Demetrios, I felt a change in myself and both who I was and thought I should be. Once Demetrios returned, though, that faded and I went back to being a wife and fulfilling the role in my family that young wives fulfill. But if there's anything that's been made clear, it's that these times are not normal. The incident in the village and seeing the young widow wearing black has changed me, also. The men have all changed themselves into someone new, who they are during war, rather than peace. There's a new and different person I can turn myself into as well, isn't there?

Of course there is.

And I have a plan.

When we return, I make an excuse to go back down to Chania, telling Giannis and Angeliki I have more olives to sell. I tell my parents the same thing as I load olives into a cart that will be pulled by the donkey, then begin the trek north and to the coast. Giannis and Angeliki want to send Tasos with me, but I tell them it's more risk than anything else, and they know I'm right, so I'll go on my own.

I reach the town, but don't walk to the *agora*.

Instead, I go past the harbor, and *kastro*, and all the German soldiers standing on the streets, and walk straight to Cassia's apartment. I tie the donkey outside her building before going up the stairs, letting myself in, and when I go to her room, I find her still sleeping.

I don't wake her.

I sit down, pick up a newspaper that's on the table, and scan the headlines.

The German offensive in Russia—"*Operation Barbarossa,*" as it's been called—has failed, and the Russian counteroffensive has gained ground and the writer calls it the first Allied victory in the whole war. I smile wryly, not because of the paper itself, but because of course this isn't the first Allied victory in the war because that was in Greece, and won by my husband and so many others in the Albanian mountains, fighting against the Italians. Even though this British reporter is wrong, I'm still glad to see what we've done; I'm still glad to see the Greek resistance did indeed give Russia time to prepare their defense and deploy their ultimate weapon, the harshness of their winter. It's the only way they could've defeated the Germans, and so we're the reason, I realize, the reason the Allies are still fighting and not yet conquered, and we're the reason the world still has a chance to win and be free. I scan the paper further then smile even more, without any wryness this time, because there's another headline: the American president has pledged more supplies to the Allied cause, it says, and there's a picture of Franklin Roosevelt having just given a speech at his annual State of the Union address.

"*Maria*?" I hear. "What are you doing here?"

I look up to see Cassia coming from her room, rubbing sleep from her eyes.

"I need to ask you something."

I stand and put a pot of water on to boil.

When it does, I make two strong cups of *malotira* I've brought with me—*malotira* from our village, and our mountains—and then we sit on her balcony overlooking the harbor, each with a cup in our hand, and she smokes a cigarette. I tell her what happened, and what I've come to request and ask. I tell her I can pay, of course, but she just stares back at me when I say this, then tells me that even though she no longer lives there, it's of course still her village, and always will be, so she'll do what I ask for free.

And she'll be happy to do it.

She nods to the paper.

"What's going on outside this island?"

"Do you recognize him?" I ask, showing her the photo, then she smiles when she sees what I see: the familiar face of James Roosevelt standing near the president's left shoulder.

"I hope he's able to convince his father."

"I do, too. But his father is wise, and good, so I don't think it's his father he needs to convince."

"What do you mean?"

"It's his father that needs to convince the people who vote for him."

"They're so young," Cassia shakes her head, and it's her turn for a wry smile now. "They're so very young in America."

"They are, just as we were once."

"And so it goes."

"So it goes."

"Do you think it was simpler then?"

"I don't know," I tell her, then stand. "I don't think so, but I also don't know."

I thank her again, give her a hug, then I leave.

I go back down to the donkey and cart with the olives I've left outside her building.

I start walking and go to the small *kafeneio* that's just past the apartment, one of the many where the old men sit outside and drink coffee while twirling *komboloi*. There aren't as many men here as before the war, but there are still some, dressed in their suits and the way men dress in the city, not the way we dress in the village. I take a bucket that's near one of the tables and go back to the donkey. I pour the olives I brought into the bucket, then bring it back and set it on the table. They all look at me curiously as they spin their *komboloi*, expertly catching the beads in their palm, *clack clack*, *clack clack*, then spinning them again.

"On the house," I tell them.

Then I turn and go home.

11

FEBRUARY 7, 1942

A month passes and I make excuses to return to Chania again. Cassia told me she can come to the village once she finds what I've asked for, but I tell her if she does, then people will know how I've gotten the information, so I'll return to Chania instead, as it's better if information of this sort and where it's been procured from is kept secret.

It's better if it's kept very secret.

"What if I haven't been able to find out by the time you return?" she'd asked me.

"Then I'll come back as many times as it takes, until you have."

We needn't have wasted our words, though.

The next time I go she's already gotten what I need, then asks what will happen next.

"I'm not sure," I tell her.

"That's not true."

"You're right."

"It'll be blood, won't it?"

"It will."

"He's going to die?"

I pause for a moment, thinking.

"Yes," I nod slowly. "One way or the other, I suppose he's going to die."

"Good," she says.

I stand looking at her and I'm silent for another moment, then I nod again. "Yes," I tell her. "It will be. It certainly will be."

When I get back to the village, I don't tell anyone what I've learned.

Then the news I have is overshadowed by other, more joyous news.

Since the wedding, Ikaros has been borrowing Demetrios's motorcycle and coming from the mountains under cover of darkness, as a young groom might be expected to do, to spend as many nights as possible with his new bride. The longer the occupation has gone on, we've become more bold. Even though we take as many precautions as possible, our lives are still our lives, and they must be lived in the very short time they're ours and that we're here, right? We're all only here a very short time, so that's what Ikaros has done, with Kyriaki, and I'm surprised when I see him in daylight, walking towards our village with a rifle slung over his back. I'm even more surprised when I see Kyriaki with him, as well as the large figure of Anastasios Magarakis, behind his daughter, along with his other sons and daughters, her siblings.

They walk to our house.

Giannis and Angeliki come out to greet them.

Their eyes flick from their middle son to their new daughter-in-law, back to their son again, then the rest of the entire Magarakis family that's accompanied them.

"What is it?" Giannis asks. "What's happened?"

Kyriaki gently puts her hand over her stomach.

Ikaros looks very proud.

"I'm pregnant," she tells us.

And the news brings such joy.

Angeliki runs and kisses her new daughter, then her son, and Giannis does the same, too, and shakes hands with Anastasios. It's their first grandchild. For both of them, it's their very first grandchild, and as I watch them it's amazing how a blood feud that's lasted more than six hundred years can now truly and suddenly be a distant memory simply because of the pending arrival of a long-awaited child and the growth of a family.

But such is the way it is on our island, and amongst our people.

Even in war, such is the way it is.

Math comes to my mind, and I think of the date of the wedding, and the date of the announcement, and I'm sure now I know what Ikaros was doing on the nights he wasn't in his own bed in the barn, but they're married, so it doesn't matter and I'm sure everyone else can do the same math I can, but no one cares.

He's a young man.

She's a young woman.

They love each other, and it's as it should be.

It's as simple as that.

We don't celebrate the news until dark.

But then, when light departs, my parents come from the farm, and Demetrios comes from the mountains, and Angeliki has made another feast with my mother because not only will there be a new child coming, but also, this is the first time a Magarakis has eaten in this village in a hundred years, Anastasios says, as he toasts the future health of his grandchild as well as the unborn child's parents, and all those gathered, all those that are now family.

"That's right," Giannis looks back at him. "Not since your grandfather came and killed my grandfather, and tried to steal our sheep."

"And now it doesn't matter," Anastasios laughs, and I find it a strange time and reason to.

"Why?" Giannis asks.

"Because now all our sheep, whether mine or yours, at some point . . . they'll all be his," Anastasios says, and points to his daughter's stomach. "So there will be peace in this valley."

"Yes," Giannis finally nods, slowly. "There will, finally, be peace."

"Once we've killed the Germans," Ikaros adds.

"Of course," Anastasios nods. "We need to kill the Germans first."

"Of course."

"Of course."

I'm glad for Ikaros.

I'm so glad for him, and both of them.

"Can I take you somewhere?"

The words are whispered into my ear.

I turn to feel Demetrios behind me, watching me watch all this, as he puts his arms around my waist, his lips on my neck now.

"Where?" I ask, then turn to look at him.

He kisses me.

I kiss him in return.

That's my answer, he knows, so he takes my hand in his and we slip out and into the night, together.

We walk through moonlight.

The path is familiar and there's so much light from above, even though it's the middle of night, but even if there wasn't light, we'd still be able to find our way. We've taken this path so many times. We've taken it together more times than either of us can count, and we go north. We go down the road and towards our olives that will need to be trimmed soon, then continue on past them, and soon leave the main road. We take a smaller and more hidden path, one that can only be walked, and that Germans or anyone who isn't from this island would never know about. We were young here, though, and this is our island, so we do. We get closer to the city. I can see the light and outline of buildings in the distance, the tall ones that hug the *limani*, so there's a chance Germans could be near, but we don't go all the way to Chania. Instead, we turn west, and I smile when I see where he's taken us.

Chryssi Akti.

We walk towards the beach, and as we come from shadows, I look at the sand and sea and remember the exact spot I found William. I look at the place and remember what his body looked like lying there, and not knowing whether he was alive or dead. I'm glad. I'm glad he lived, because he saved us, and is that perhaps why I saved him? Is that why he was placed into my path, in the way that he was? I wonder. I wonder a little bit more, then nod, because then I'm sure. I look farther and see a boat in front of us, near the spot on the beach where I found him; it's a small *kaiki* and it's anchored in the shallows of the bay, bobbing gently on soft waves.

We go to it.

We wade into the water, which is freezing this time of year, and when we reach the boat, Demetrios helps me over the edge then jumps up himself on the edge as he swings a leg over, then the other, and climbs in next to me. He takes the oars that are in the boat and starts rowing, dipping them into the sea to push us over the small waves and towards the island at the entrance to the bay that blocks the larger waves. I smile as he rows. So many of those who are in love talk about first dates, which is different in a small village like ours than it is for most, and this was ours. I'd known Demetrios since we were young, and we'd played with other children, all together, often. Then when we were older, that's when he'd come to my family's farm to help build the barn where his father would keep the sheep my father would watch for him. Those were the long and hot days when we really began to notice each other, and began to grow closer. But the first time we did something that was away from our house and our families and their watchful eyes, we'd come here. We'd been to the beach many times as children, of course, but on one particularly hot afternoon when we were working together, he asked if I wanted to come with him the next day, which was a Saturday, down to the beach.

"Just the two of us?" I'd asked.

"Yes," he'd nodded.

I thought for a moment, realizing what he was asking.

Then I'd nodded my head, too.

"*Nai*," I'd told him. "I do."

The next day he came to my house and spoke with Baba, first, then after Demetrios nodded, and Baba nodded, we'd left together and gone to the beach. The other kids were already there. Normally we all played together, as a group. We didn't that day, though. Instead, that day, we went to a spot farther west and to where there are trees and some shade, and we'd sat there together. He'd packed us *spanakopita* that his mother made, along with some fresh mountain water mixed with honey to sweeten it. His mother's *spanakopita* wasn't as good as my mother's, but I smiled and didn't tell him as we ate it. I wondered if he'd asked her to make it. I wondered if he'd asked her to make it special for that day, and if he'd told her why. We sat there together as the other kids played, and we chewed and ate, and I couldn't help but wonder if he wanted to join them;

if he wanted to run and play with his friends in the waves, rather than this, and just sitting there and watching them.

So I'd asked him.

"*Oxi*," he'd said. "No."

"Really?"

"*Nai*."

I'd waited for a moment.

"Do you want to swim out to the island?"

He turned and looked at me.

"It's too far," he spoke slowly. "I don't think you'd make it."

"Can you?"

"Can I what?"

"Make it to the island."

"Of course," he'd said, as he sat a little taller.

"And you've done it before?"

"*Nai*."

"Then I can, too."

He kept looking at me.

Then I stood.

I'd walked to him, then leaned down and whispered a single word into his ear.

"*Ela*," I'd said. *Come on.*

I took off the loose-fitting shirt I was wearing so I was just in my bathing suit, walked down to the water, then into the waves. I began to swim. He watched for a moment, then stood and took his shirt off, too, so he was also in his bathing suit and ran to the beach and began to swim quickly after me. He started to swim faster. So did I. He tried to catch me, but I pushed and kicked even more and didn't let him. I eventually came to the rocky island and where it jutted up from the water, pulled myself up and onto it, as a few body lengths behind he then reached the same place, and did the same thing.

Eleven years have passed since that afternoon.

It's been eleven years, but we now make the exact journey again, together, but eleven years older, and in a boat.

We reach the island.

It's small, can be walked across in less than ten minutes, but near where we arrive, there's another cave. It's not nearly as tall or wide as the cave where Demetrios lives in the mountains; this is instead just more of an opening with a piece of rock hanging over to shield from the weather, and enough room for two of us to either sit or lay, but no more than that.

It's alright.

We don't need more.

We drop our anchor then climb from the boat to go sit there, just the same as we did when we were young, both that first time and so many other times after. I see he's already been out here because there are blankets and a jug of wine, and things to make a fire that are waiting. He crouches and sparks wood far enough inside and behind the rock it won't be seen on the mainland, then once it's lit and going, we warm ourselves next to it. Eleven years ago, this is where he'd kissed me for the first time, after we'd swum here. The bright and hot summer sun was setting in the distance, over our shoulders, and as we'd sat together in our bathing suits on the rocks, he'd leaned over and kissed me.

I'd kissed him back, my very first kiss.

Now we kiss again.

This time, we do more, though.

We take our clothes off because the fire is hot, it's very hot, and warms our skin that's filled with fire again now, and when we're done, we lay there next to the flames.

We lay there, and he holds me.

We don't move.

We stay, together, just like that.

It seems perfect except, of course, it isn't, and not only because this cave and this island are no longer our cave or our island, along with so much else.

There's another reason, too.

"*I'm sorry*," I whisper.

Anyone else would ask why, or what I'm sorry about, but since his soul is my soul, he doesn't need to. It's why we're here. We'd wanted to have a family, as everyone does, and from the moment we were married, we tried. We were very young and some told us to wait, but we couldn't think of a single reason to listen to them, and could think of a million reasons not to, so after the celebration in our village—after the dancing, music, food, and wine—we began to try, but even all these years later, there was still no child. It was easy to not think of it, when he was gone, and we weren't trying anymore because we couldn't. But he's back now, so we are, and while Ikaros and Kyriaki's news brings such joy, it also brings something else for me.

And he knows that.

"You're perfect," he says. "Don't be sorry, about anything, because you're perfect. You're absolutely perfect, and so are we."

I think of the blankets that are here, the things to make a fire.

"You already knew," I say, and it's not a question.

"He told me three days ago, in the mountains."

"Did you have a celebration?"

"We got him very drunk."

I smile.

My head's nestled between his shoulder and jaw, so above me, I can feel him smile, too.

Then we're silent again, staring at flames as they leap and crack.

"Why here?" I finally ask him, breaking the stillness.

"Do you remember the first time we came?"

"Of course. We talk about it often."

"I never told you how scared I was that day."

"You were?" I frown. "Of what?"

"That you wouldn't like me. I was scared you wouldn't care for me and everything would be over, and I wouldn't ever be able to talk to you again. You might think it a small thing, but you don't know how much I thought about you, how every waking moment of my life was about *you*, and if that had been taken from me? I'm not sure I could have gone on. I could have, of course, but not in any way I was interested in. Then when we were swimming, I was scared you weren't going to make it, and I was going to lose you."

"Really?"

"*Nai.*"

"Why?"

"Because I didn't realize then."

"Realize what?"

"How strong you are."

I turn now and look at him. He looks back at me.

Our faces are inches apart as we lay there together, my head on his chest.

"What do you mean?" I ask him. "How am I strong? I haven't fought, I haven't defended us, I haven't done anything at all."

"Because you haven't been allowed to. But just wait until you are, because then, that's when the Germans will really be in trouble," he smiles. "That's when the Germans won't stand a chance, and perhaps soon after that . . . well, perhaps that's then when our island will be ours once again."

I stay there and look at him.

What does he know?

Me. He knows me.

"And when you kissed me?" I ask him.

"What about it?"

"It was right here, in this very spot."

"*Nai.*"

"You remember?"

"How could I possibly forget."

Silence, for a moment, then—

"Do you know a Petros Varalakis?" I ask him.

"Of course. He's from Elaionas and served with us in the 5th. I know him well. What does any of this have to do with him, though?"

"He's the reason the Germans came to Skiafos."

"What?" Demetrios frowns, then turns to me, my head still on his chest.

"He gives them information in exchange for money."

"Are you sure?"

"I'm more than sure," I tell him, still staring ahead now, straight at the fire, and the light. "He's the one who betrayed us, and told them where we would be."

12

FEBRUARY 8, 1942

We rise together the next morning, when we're woken by light from the sun, and while we don't want to leave, we know we have to. The fire has burned to embers and ash, which we scatter and remove all other traces from the island that we'd ever been there. Then once it's back to the way it was, we walk together down to where our boat bobs at the rocky shore. The waves are less this morning, as they so often are at this time, and Demetrios helps me into the boat again then follows after himself. We head back the same way we came. We row towards the familiar beach that's our beach, and as we go, I notice something I didn't on the way over: below us, and beneath the clear azure water, there's the outline of a wrecked German bomber that's visible.

"Look," I say.

And he does.

Then he keeps rowing.

We get closer to the beach.

Last night, after I'd told him what I'd found, he'd asked how I knew, and who told me, so I explained the whole thing. I told him how Cassia slept with British soldiers in exchange for money, and he didn't react when I'd said that, but when I told him after the British left and the Germans came, she'd begun to sleep with German soldiers, too, I could feel his body tense next to me. So I told him the British still pay her, and there's one British soldier in particular that's still on the island working as a spy and he finds her every week and she tells him everything she's learned from the enemies who come to her bed.

When I'd gone down, I'd asked if she could find out one thing for me.

For us, actually, because she's still part of our village, as she reminded me, and so she did. One of the German officers had told her about Petros Varalakis, and how he'd come to them and informed them of the wedding in exchange for coins, and at first they thought it might be a setup, and Cretan plan for an ambush in some distant village in the mountains. Then they found out more about Petros, and that he'd loved Kyriaki Magarakis his entire life. What I didn't know is that while he was in the mountains of Albania, he'd written letters to her, and when he'd returned, he thought they would be married. She didn't share his feelings, though. He thought she had tried to respond to his letters and proposals, but the notes just didn't make it through the war. The reality was much simpler, though, and it was that she wasn't interested in him. She wasn't when they were young, in Elaionas, before he'd left, and she wasn't later, either. And then Petros found out why, or at least he thought he did.

There was someone else.

Ikaros.

He couldn't bear to think about them married, much less see them together, and happy, so he'd decided to do something about it if it couldn't be him with her, after he returned, and saw them, and went straight to the Germans.

"Are you sure?" Demetrios asks, a second time. "This is a man's life."

"I'm sure," I nod to him.

Then we're back to the beach.

We leave the boat where we collected it, and the fisherman it belongs to, another of Demetrios's friends from the war, from Galatas, comes to retrieve it and when he does Demetrios shakes his hand and I do, too. I thank him for letting us use his *kaiki*, then we leave Chryssi Akti and continue on and take the same path back towards our village. We soon return, and instead of going back to the house, we stop at the farm. As we get closer, I smell cinnamon and almond as the sun continues higher, and know my mother is making her *paximathia* again. Then when we get to the door and go inside, we see that she is. She hands me one and Demetrios three, and he smiles and says *efcharisto*. She tries to make us breakfast but he tells her he can't—that he needs to get back before the sun is fully up—and she asks if he can stay for a short *kafe* to go with the biscuits she's given him, but he just kisses her on the cheek, and that's his answer, I know, and tells her he hopes he'll be able to stay again one day soon.

I do, too.

I hope that, also; it's all that I hope.

Well, not all.

There's one other thing, one other thing that our time on the island has gotten me thinking about again, and I shake my head to try to push it from my mind because I don't want to think about it.

It's easier when I can ignore it, and have my excuses.

We leave the house and go to the barn and as we arrive, I see Tasos coming from the path that leads west, not the one that leads east. He doesn't see us, then does, and looks shocked at first, before embarrassed. I glance at Demetrios next to me and he shakes his head, very small, so only I can see, and I understand. Tasos gets closer and Demetrios smiles at him.

"Where have you been?" he asks.

"I had to go to the bathroom. What about you?"

"What about me?"

"Where have *you* been?"

"I'm older than you."

"So?"

"That means you don't get to ask that. Questions flow downward, from oldest to youngest, not the other way around," Demetrios smiles even wider and messes up Tasos's hair. Tasos pushes him away as we all turn and go to the barn together. Baba's already there. He's getting ready to take the sheep up to graze in the upper fields, and when we see him, I kiss him on the cheeks, Demetrios shakes his hand, and Baba looks over at Tasos.

"Where have you been?" he asks, too.

Tasos opens his mouth, but I'm quicker.

"He's going to help me with the olives today," I say, before he has to respond, and lie.

Baba nods.

Tasos looks grateful as he goes to collect the shears and pruning tools we'll need, and Demetrios walks to the far side of the barn where we've stacked bales of hay. He starts to move them to the side. Behind them, and under a bunch of loose straw that's been scattered over the top, I see his motorcycle, the one he keeps in the cave above Skiafos.

He takes it and wheels it out of the barn.

I go with him, just the two of us, and before he starts it, I reach my hand out and stop him.

"It was the same with his brother," I tell him.

"What was the same?"

"Leaving at night and sneaking back in the morning. It was the exact same, when he was going to see Kyriaki."

"It turned out alright for him, didn't it?"

"Yes," I nod.

"But?" he can sense my tone.

"It was a different time."

Demetrios looks back at me.

"It was," he nods, too. "But whatever time it is, Tasos is that age now, also, and can't stay a boy forever, as much as either of us or my parents would like him to. Nor should he, or have to. There are no more boys left on this island," Demetrios tells me as he starts the engine and it roars to life. He swings his leg over the motorcycle, and I go to him. I lean towards his mouth and kiss him and let my lips linger for just a little bit longer than they normally would, because he's going back to the mountains, and I don't know when I'll see him next.

"*S'agapo*," I tell him. "I love you."

"*S'agapo moro mou*," he answers.

We kiss again.

He's just about to leave, but before he does, there's one more thing; one last thing I need to tell him.

I lean close again. I whisper into his ear.

He pauses, then turns and looks at me, once he hears what I say.

"Are you sure?" he asks.

My eyes don't change, nor does my heart.

"Yes," I tell him, and my voice is strong.

He looks at me for another moment, then finally nods and starts to drive away, into the distance, up towards the great snow-capped mountains, and the story-filled cave that's in them, where he now makes his home.

卐

Once Demetrios is gone, I help Baba and Tasos load the rest of the pruning equipment into the wagon that the donkey will pull. Then Baba goes north with the sheep, and Tasos and I head south to the olives. When we get to the trees, we begin to silently unload our tools and go about our tasks, and it's warm. It's unseasonably warm, actually. Tasos takes his jacket off so he's just in his white shirt and black trousers, and he usually trims and prunes the branches closer to the ground, leaving the higher ones that need to be reached for me, and his older brother. But Ikaros of course isn't here anymore, it's just me, so I'm about to get the ladder to do those branches but Tasos gets to it first and takes the ladder and starts to do it himself.

I watch him.

I don't say anything.

He's gotten taller, his body stronger, and I can see the muscles in his arms and chest have grown and expanded from the work like this he's done both here amongst the trees, and also at home and the farm.

I look at his face.

He'll need to shave soon, I realize.

How had I missed it before?

Then, in the distance, we hear a noise.

It's the sound of engines, and they're coming towards us.

We both turn and look, me from my place on the ground, and Tasos from his new place on the ladder, and higher in the trees.

A *kubelwagen* appears around the bend.

After a moment, another appears, then another, and another still after that.

There are four German soldiers in each *kubelwagen*, and when they see us, they begin to slow on the road.

Then they stop.

They look at us.

They've seen us working here before so this isn't strange to them, or a surprise, to see a young woman and younger-than-fighting-age boy continuing to harvest their family's crop, and I'm glad they've seen us before, I realize. I'm glad because perhaps that means they won't notice the change that's now come to Tasos either.

I meet their eyes.

Tasos doesn't, and keeps his face obscured in the branches, which is good.

I'll have to talk to Demetrios about it.

I don't want Tasos to leave, and so many things will be harder once he does, but at some point, he'll have to join the men in the mountains, right?

Not yet, but soon.

That's what I'm thinking when the Germans arrive.

They can't know that, though.

They keep looking at us, then after a moment, the one who sits in the passenger side of the first *kubelwagen*, who must be their commander, nods.

"*Gut*," he says. "Good."

And they carry on.

I exhale because we've heard stories.

We've heard stories of the cruelty of the Germans, what they've done to entire villages they've found or suspected, even, to harbor resistance fighters either Cretan, British, or from any other nation. Sometimes they haven't found anything at all, we've heard, they just want to punish us for something, for continuing to fight, for continuing to struggle and persevere and resist their occupation.

Why did they think they would be different from any other enemies that have come here?

Who did they think we were?

Once they're gone, all that's left is a cloud of dust, and we turn back to our work.

Tasos continues to prune, and so do I.

I think of Demetrios, and the last thing I said to him, and I wonder: is this still me?

Am I still who I was, before all of this?

I'm not, I realize.

I'm not at all.

I want to be there, I'd whispered to him. *When you find him, and when it happens, I want to be there and it was my information, so promise me, Demetrios. Promise me this one thing.*

He'd waited a moment.

He'd waited, looked back at me, my eyes, deep into my eyes.

Then he'd nodded.

Entaxei, his eyes had said to mine, and after a moment, they'd said it again. *Entaxei, Maria-mou. Entaxei.*

13

MARCH 13, 1942

I think it will happen sooner, but things such as this take their own time, I learn, as winter turns to spring and it's many weeks until I see Demetrios again. I still work in the olives with Tasos, but our work is different now. We put the pruning shears away and mix buckets of slaked lime and water. With the changing seasons, it's time to paint the bottoms of the trees once more, to protect them from the insects that will soon hatch and destroy them if they aren't painted. We work in the sun, as days begin to get hotter, and I wonder more about Tasos, and where he goes at night and who he might see. I don't ask him, though. He saw how it turned out for his brother, so I'm sure he thinks and hopes it will turn out the same for him. I'll let him have that hope, as we all should have, and won't make him speak about it or anything else before he wishes to speak about it, or tell us.

Outside the olive groves, life in the village goes on pretty much as normal.

We see more of the Magarakis family as Kyriaki's belly grows, and she's begun to show now, too, in a way that no amount of clothing can hide. I continue traveling to Chania, also, and staying with Cassia. We don't have fresh olives this time of year, so instead I bring the wool I help my father sheer from our sheep and sell it to the weavers and tailors of the city that come looking for material to make shirts, bags, gloves, scarves, and all sorts of other things. We work during the week, all of us. Then we enjoy ourselves on Saturdays, and Sunday we go to the small church in the village to listen to Father Thiseas.

That becomes our routine.

I wonder about Petros Varalakis, because he hasn't been seen in Elaionas for some time now, even before I found out what he'd done, and his father Nikos hasn't been there for some time either. Before they'd left, though, Nikos had said they were going to Elounda, on the eastern side of the island, to help care for his uncle who lived there and was in poor health. No one in Elaionas knew he had an uncle, but they'd wished him and his son well, and a safe journey. They asked what Petros would do, as a fighting-age male who'd fought with the 5th and Nikos had said Petros would stay in the mountains outside the village, while he was with his uncle, and they'd make it work. After the information I brought to Demetrios, men from Elaionas had gone to Elounda and asked for Nikos Varalakis or anyone with the Varalakis name, but the people in Elounda said there was no one in their village called Varalakis, and they'd never heard of either Nikos or Petros. So the men from Elaionas went to Plaka and Agios Nikolaos, and no one in either village had heard of anyone named Varalakis, or seen them there, or in any other neighboring villages. It confirmed their guilt. It confirmed everything Cassia had found out about what Petros had done. The problem now, though, was where had they gone?

Demetrios, Giannis, Anastasios, and all the other men had asked everyone they knew—every relative and friend, spread across all the villages of the island—but no one had seen or heard of anyone that matched their description.

So we had to wait.

Then one night, while I slept, I heard a whisper.

"*Maria* . . ." I could hear Demetrios, softly, in our bedroom.

I knew it was him before I opened my eyes because the way he's always said my name, the "M" sounding deeper when he says it than when others do. And I could smell him, too.

I open my eyes.

"What is it?" I ask.

"Get dressed and follow me," he says, still quietly. "And put on something warm."

I stand and quickly dress in as many layers as I can find, as he waits, then when I'm done, we leave the bedroom together and go outside. We walk past the tall cypress at the edge of our yard, then go farther, and into darkness. There isn't much light from the moon tonight, so we move and walk by memory. Our feet find the path we know so well, the one that leads south, towards the mountains, and as we walk, his hand reaches and takes mine.

I look down at it.

We don't stop, though.

We keep going.

Soon we leave the path and begin to climb, straight up, needing to use our hands and feet to scale sheer rock faces that reach towards a bluff I know is there, above us, the highest point around and also the hardest to get to. "Just a little farther," he says, from his place beneath me, protecting me in case I slip or start to fall.

I won't.

Soon I get to the final rock, pull myself up, and then I'm there.

I look around as Demetrios pulls himself up after me, onto the top of the rocky bluff where we now stand, and I see all the others gathered: Giannis, Anastasios Magarakis and his sons, as well as Ikaros, and all the other fighting-age men from our village, and Baba, too. Even Father Thiseas is here with them. Across from them, I see more men from Elaionas, and one group of them holds Petros Varalakis. His lip is split and his face cut and smeared with blood. There's one eye that's swollen shut, and one that's still open and blazes in anger and defiance. Across from him, another group holds Nikos Varalakis, who seems to be more whole than his son, and less harmed.

They see us.

Petros Varalakis's lip turns into a sneer when he does.

"What is *she* doing here," he asks, when he sees me. "I would say she's a whore, but you're the one that's a whore, Magarakis," he spits. "Marrying your daughter to our enemy."

Ikaros walks forward with a raised fist.

He's about to hit Petros for what he's said, but Anastasios comes and stops him.

"Is that all?" Anastasios asks, turning from Ikaros back to Petros.

"What do you mean?"

"I thought you'd at least deny it, beg for your life, or offer some excuse or explanation."

"There is no Varalakis who begs."

"Very well, then," Anastasios says.

He turns and nods to Father Thiseas.

The priest comes forward and says a prayer for Petros Varalakis, raising his hand with three fingers together—his thumb, index, and middle finger of his right hand—then makes the sign of the cross three times over Petros's body. When he's done, he reaches into his robes and takes out a small vial of oil to wipe some across Petros's forehead, giving him last rights.

Then Father Thiseas turns.

He backs up, and returns to us.

"Is there anything you would like to say?" the priest asks him.

Petros glares back.

He looks at the priest, then Anastasios and Giannis, the power in our villages, then he looks at their sons, and especially Ikaros, the son from the hated village on the far side of the valley who married the girl that he loved.

And then, he finally turns, and looks at me.

He waits, just for a moment, and I wonder why.

Then he shakes his head.

"*Oxi*," he says.

Ikaros goes to walk forward again, but Anastasios stops him.

Next to me, Demetrios takes my hand.

"He insulted me, my wife, and my sister," Ikaros says, his eyes burning as he looks back at his father-in-law.

"This isn't revenge," Anastasios tells him.

"Then what is it?"

But Anastasios ignores him and moves him to the side, then goes forward himself and stands in front of Petros.

He takes a pistol from his belt.

It's Bulgarian, left over from the first war.

When Petros sees it, he shakes his head.

"At least give me the dagger," he spits through clenched teeth. "At least do it with something that's ours."

Anastasios pauses for a moment.

Then he puts the pistol away and takes his carved Cretan dagger from his hip.

He walks closer to Petros.

I can see Petros close his eyes as Anastasios leans his lips close to his ear and whispers: "You betrayed your ancestors and your village. I hope you find the salvation you're looking for."

Petros opens his eyes.

"You've stood in the way of love," he says, very loudly, so all can hear. "It's your salvation I'll pray for, Anastasios Magarakis. It's your salvation, as well as hers, and all the rest of you that stand in false judgment because I found what I was looking for, then had it taken."

There's a moment, one last moment.

Then Anastasios flexes and thrusts.

The dagger plunges into Petros's stomach and underneath his ribs and even though I'm not a doctor, I of course know all the vital organs that are there.

At first, there's nothing, just an inhalation of breath.

Then the blood starts to come and when it does Anastasios quickly pulls the dagger back, and even more comes, bright and red on Anastasios's arms, staining and covering his sleeves. But before there's a scream, or more pain, or anything else, Anastasios pushes Petros in the chest, once, very firmly, so he's shoved backward and falls from the side of the cliff.

His body tumbles and twists.

It flies through air and night until we hear the distant thud of it landing and breaking on the rocks that are below.

I don't look away.

I think I will, but I don't.

I've done this.

It's me that's made this happen, and I'm glad I have, because of what he did, and since it was me that took his life, shouldn't I also watch it be taken? I need to see what I've done. We all need to, always, and next to me as he holds my hand, I can feel that Demetrios understands that, too.

This is serious business.

This is the most serious business.

"And what of you?" Anastasios asks, turning now to Nikos.

"What of me?"

"Do you denounce your son's actions, and do you wish to remain part of the village?"

"My son is my flesh and blood, just as yours are. I denounce nothing except you. You're a traitor, Anastasios Magarakis, and while I honor my blood, you do the opposite and betray your own."

"How?"

"You heard my son. You know who she married."

"That's your final answer?"

He doesn't speak again.

He just stands and stares at Anastasios, his eyes burning, or at least trying to, as Anastasios then motions for the men holding Nikos to release him and move away, which they do.

"Would you like the pistol or the dagger?"

In response, Nikos Varalakis speaks his final words.

"May the Germans kill you all," he says.

Then he turns and starts to run, covering the space on the cliff and when he gets to the edge, he launches himself off.

His body begins to plummet.

Down, down.

He sails through night and darkness, just the same as his son did, until there's another thud as he lands on the rocks that have already broken one body, and now they break another, too.

There's silence.

For a moment, there's nothing but silence.

Anastasios turns to me.

"*Efcharisto*," he says.

I nod.

We all stand there, then there are more nods as Demetrios and Giannis go to Anastasios and shake his hand, and I go to Ikaros and embrace him and whisper into his ear.

"She's doing wonderful," I tell him.

"*Efcharisto*," he says, too, and I can feel him smile.

"She *is* wonderful."

"She is, isn't she?"

"She'll be the best mother."

"*Nai*."

"So stay alive, so that you see it."

"What do you mean?"

"No flying too close to the sun, like your namesake."

"That's just a story."

"And what are stories?"

"I don't know. What are they?"

"A future that's already happened."

He looks back at me, then nods, understanding.

"She goes to Chania to see the doctor tomorrow," he says, as he moves away and smiles even wider now. "Tell her I'll see her tomorrow night, and will be in Elaionas waiting when she gets back."

I look at the joy that's there in his face, the anticipation.

It's beautiful.

It's so beautiful, and so are they.

"Of course," I tell him. "Of course."

14

MARCH 14, 1942

Demetrios comes back with us to the village, but he leaves again before the sun comes up. I've spent the entire night with his arms wrapped tightly around me, holding me, and haven't closed my eyes since we returned because I want to feel and remember every moment he's here; the size of his hands and roughness of his palms, the way he smells and how he feels with my head resting between his chin and his shoulder, where I can smell so much of him. Sometime before dawn, though, his arms unwrap from around me and he stays like that, just for a moment, in the bed, then stands. Once he does, it's immediately cooler. I wrap the blanket tighter around my body as in front of me he begins to dress again: pulling on his trousers, his cummerbund, then his shirt from the place he has left it on the chair. His belt is last, with his Cretan dagger on one end, and a holster that holds a British pistol given to us by William on the other. He pulls the belt around his waist then tightens it, takes his jacket from the back of the chair, before finally reaching for the rifle propped in the corner, which he slings across his back.

He's ready.

I stand from the bed and dress quickly, too, before the cold comes.

He watches, and once I'm done, I adjust my dress into place, along with the jacket I wear over it, and go to him.

One more moment.

That's what I want: one more moment here with him.

I stand on my toes and tilt my head, and he holds me again, one hand on my waist, the other on my neck, and he guides my lips up and towards his.

They linger there.

So do his.

Then we hear a rooster and the moment's gone because the morning means it's time for him to leave, so I open the door and walk out to find the house empty. With such a late night, I'm guessing Giannis and Angeliki are still sleeping, so we walk quietly through the house and go outside.

Mist rises.

We walk through it, down towards the barn.

We get there before the sun really comes up and go to where Demetrios keeps his motorcycle, hidden behind the bales and under the loose straw.

When he gets there, though, he stops.

"What is it?" I ask.

"It's not here."

"What?"

"It's gone," he says, turning back to me.

I look over his shoulder and see where the motorcycle would be, where he always keeps it, but now nothing's there. Panic rises.

I turn and run from the barn and he calls after me, to wait, but I don't listen, so he follows. I run to the house and go inside. In the kitchen, my mother is putting freshly-made *dolmades* in a bag for Baba to take to the mountains for lunch. I turn and see Baba coming from their bedroom, adjusting his jacket over his shirt, then looking at me with surprise in his eyes.

"Maria? What's the matter?"

"Has anyone been in the barn?" I ask, with more urgency than I've ever asked anything before.

"I don't know, probably just me," Baba shrugs. "Why?"

"The motorcycle's gone."

And there it is.

I see the panic come to their eyes, too, knowing what this could mean, all the awful things it could mean then Baba pushes past me and we all follow him outside. We run towards the barn and he looks around, just as we did. Then he looks down at the ground. He's looking for tracks that might help solve or figure out what's happened, and I can't believe I didn't think of that. There's been too much coming and going, though, and anything that might have been in the dirt and straw has been stepped on too many times and won't be able to help us.

We look at each other.

Then I turn and look east towards where the sun is beginning to rise above the mountains, and the light that's soon to come.

"You need to get back," I say to Demetrios, very quietly.

"I'm not leaving," he says. "You could be in danger. There could be another traitor, or someone else that knows what was here, and has told them."

"Or it could be nothing."

"*Nothing?*" he says, louder now. "How could it be nothing?"

"Where's Tasos?" my mother asks, quietly, from behind us.

"What?" Demetrios turns to her.

"Where's your brother?" she asks, louder now. "Has anyone seen him?"

We stand there and all think back to the last time we saw him, or at least we try to.

Had he been in his bedroom when we left the house?

I don't know.

Then after I think of that, the same as I'm sure Demetrios is thinking, too, I then think of him coming home through the mist, early in the morning, after being out late at night and the panic rises again. This time it's Demetrios that begins to run.

He sprints up and towards his house, and I'm right behind him, and he runs inside and Giannis and Angeliki are up now and they see the look in their oldest son's eyes, the terror.

"You're still here?" Angeliki asks him.

"Have you seen Tasos?"

They look at each other as I go to his room and push the door open and I already know it's going to be empty before I look and see that it is, and that he didn't sleep here last night.

"What's happened?" Giannis turns back to Demetrios.

"My motorcycle's gone."

Angeliki puts her hands to her mouth.

"Oh my goodness," she breathes.

"Let me think," Giannis says. "Let me just think."

"He's been going to see someone at night," Demetrios tells them, giving away his brother's secret, but this isn't betrayal because it could be his life that now hangs in the balance.

"Who?" Giannis asks.

"I don't know. I'd guess a girl, maybe someone from his class, from before the war."

"Because of Ikaros," Giannis shakes his head now.

"No," Demetrios says firmly, "because he's a boy, and that's what boys do."

"And you *knew* about this? And did nothing?"

"I didn't see the harm."

"How could you possibly not?" Giannis practically yells at him, raising his voice.

"I didn't think he would steal my motorcycle!" Demetrios yells now, too. "As much as you might want, Baba, you can't keep your children alone here forever. Surely you must realize that by now. War or not, there's a whole world out there, there's a whole other world where—"

"*Enough!*" I hear my own voice.

I interrupt my husband, and they all turn to look at me.

"Enough," I say again, softer now. "We just need to find him."

"Where do we start?" Angeliki asks.

"Who was his last schoolteacher?"

"His name was Angelos Daskalakis, from Delphinos."

"That's where I'll start," I tell them. "I'll start with Mr. Daskalakis and see if I can get a list of classmates, or if he knows who he might be seeing."

"Good idea," Demetrios says, then starts towards the door.

But I stop him.

"Not you," I say.

"What?" he turns back, angrily.

"The sun's up."

"It doesn't matter."

"Yes, it does. We can't lose both of you."

He turns and looks outside, sees the light that's come now, that's all around.

It's almost as if he's forgotten about it, and where we are, with what's happening.

"I'll be careful. I'll be careful, and stay out of sight, and—"

Then I see Cassia running up the path, towards the village, which is a strange sight, and Demetrios sees her, too.

I go outside.

"What is it?" I ask as she reaches us.

She's out of breath.

"*Tasos*," she says. "They have him. The Germans."

"Where?" Demetrios asks, pushing past me.

"Chania," she tells us, still catching her breath.

And Demetrios doesn't wait for more, or anything further.

He starts to run.

I yell after him.

I tell him to stop, but he doesn't listen, so I have no choice.

I start to run, too.

I try to catch him the entire way to the city, and while I don't lose ground, I don't gain any, either.

We go past the olive trees that sit unattended and waiting to be trimmed.

We go past Chryssi Akti and the place where sand gives way to rock, then there's sand again, and we sprint around the point that reaches into the sea before we come to the *kastro* and the beginning of the Old Town.

A crowd has gathered.

Demetrios pushes his way through the people that are going the same direction as us, and I do, too, shouldering through the same people behind him, and trying to catch up.

I try.

But I don't.

He gets to the front of the crowd first, then when I do, what I see takes my breath away: the motorcycle is there on the ground, in front of Tasos, who's been stripped naked, his wrists bound in handcuffs and shackled to a large pole behind him so his body is stretched and pulled.

His eyes are barely open.

I don't know how long he's been there.

He has large red welts across his chest, arms, and legs where he's been whipped.

There's a German officer that stands in front of him, holding the leather whip that's done this, and he speaks to the crowd. "This boy was caught in possession of a German motorcycle! A sacred instrument of our war. He will not say where he found it, and it's a crime to harbor resistance members who kill German soldiers and take our vehicles, so this boy will pay with his life unless he, or any of you, tells me where it came from!"

The German looks around.

No one answers.

"Anyone?" he yells again. "Does anyone want to help this boy and spare his life?"

Silence.

Then someone yells.

"Let him go! He's just a kid!"

"Children can be traitors, too, and he's old enough to know that," the German says, then turns back to Tasos. "Tell me now where you got the motorcycle, and this will all be over."

Tasos looks back at him, through swollen eyes.

But he doesn't answer.

He stays defiant and keeps his lips closed, and even though the pain and embarrassment he must be feeling is immense, he still won't say anything about the motorcycle, or where he's from, or anything else.

Not to a German.

Not to an enemy.

That's why I panic, because I know who will tell them these things, and I try to reach in front of me, between all the people who are gathered and who are shouting now at the Germans to let the poor boy go because he is just a boy, after all.

But I'm too late.

Demetrios gets to the front, ahead of where I can reach, and calls in a loud, clear, and defiant voice.

"The motorcycle's mine!"

The German turns and sees him, as Demetrios pushes his way through the last of the crowd.

"Is it now?" he asks.

"Yes," Demetrios nods. "I've never seen that boy in my life. He must have stolen it from me, but he's not the one who took it from you," he says, then offers the German his hands to be cuffed.

"Because it was you who did that?"

"Yes."

"Very well, then," the German nods.

Then he pulls a pistol from his waist and shoots Demetrios in the head.

It happens that quickly.

I open my mouth to scream but nothing comes and the screams and noise I hear are from all those that are gathered and dive for cover at the sound of the gunshot piercing the air.

People fall to the ground.

I do, too, then crawl through and over them.

Demetrios's body collapses, then the German pushes it off the stone of the harbor and into the shallow water. I reach the feet of the German then scramble past him and to the edge to reach and pull my husband out and back up onto the *limani*.

I do.

I pull him from the water, but as I hold his head in my lap, I look down, and I can see he's already gone.

The bullet passed straight through his temple.

There will be no last words, no final moment.

I open my mouth again.

Above me, I can hear Tasos yelling, crying, struggling against the bonds that hold him stretched and upright.

Still no words come.

The tears do, though.

They pour down my face as I hold Demetrios and beg for this not to be real.

But it is.

Then I hear German above me, and look up to see another officer point at me, and my heart sinks when I recognize him.

It's the German that was in the *kubelwagens* that passed where I worked in the olives.

He speaks with the officer that killed Demetrios and points south, and a little west, in the direction of our village, and my heart sinks even more because I know what he's telling him.

"*Oxi!*" I yell. "*No!*"

I try to stand, but other German soldiers come and grab me.

The officer turns to the crowd and speaks once more.

"You've been warned that harboring enemies of Germany will result in death, yet still you do!" he pauses, and looks around. "Let this be a lesson to all of you, both what's happened here in Chania today, and also what will now happen to the village that gave shelter to enemy combatants who killed the Fuhrer's soldiers, and stole our possessions. Tell your family. Tell your friends. Tell all of them, every single one. Tell them that this is what being an enemy of Germany brings," he spits. "It's so much easier not to be. It's so much easier to be our friend, then we can all live here together, in peace. Tell them that, too."

I glare up at him with the blood of my husband staining my arms, my clothes, and I hope it's a sight that will live with him for the rest of his life; I hope it's something that will haunt his soul, for the rest of his days, though I doubt it.

"What, you would like to curse me, is that it?" he asks, speaking to me now, only me.

"You're already cursed," I tell him through my tears.

He spits again in disgust.

I can see it in his eyes, and why?

This is our home he's come to; this is our island he's invaded.

The spit lands next to me and he waves his hand, towards Tasos, and soldiers untie him from where he's been strung, then grab me, too, and pull me from Demetrios. I try to hold onto him but they rip me away and carry me and Tasos together across the rest of the *limani*. I struggle against them and try to push my way back to my husband, who lies dead and alone now, behind us, but I don't win.

I'm not strong enough.

Not alone, and against all of them.

I continue to struggle. So does Tasos.

They pull us both along with them, though, then the *limani* turns into the Old Town, but we don't go there; instead, we're brought to the town hall that's the German headquarters. They carry us inside. We go past more Germans and they all turn to look and see the bloody and crying wife, and naked boy, both still fighting, being carried past them. I'm sure it's not a sight they see every day. The soldiers take us to a cell where they open the door then roughly shove us inside, as we both trip, and fall to the ground.

They close the door behind us and lock it.

On the other side of the bars, one of the German soldiers takes an old pair of clothes and tosses them through the bars for Tasos.

We lay there.

We both lay there.

Tasos slowly pulls himself towards the pants and carefully, gently, pulls them on over his bruises and cuts, through his tears, wincing in pain as the fabric touches places where there's raw skin because he's been whipped.

We lay there.

"I'm sorry," he finally says. "I'm so sorry."

I move closer to him.

I hold his head in my lap now, as he cries, we both cry.

"I'm so sorry, Maria," he says again.

"It's not your fault."

"Yes, it is."

"No, it's not," I whisper, my heart completely broken, my soul shattered, no longer whole, once again unmade, and I also know now it never will be whole again.

"If I hadn't—"

"*Oxi*, *Tasos-mou*," I interrupt him, as strongly as I can in this moment. "No. If *they* hadn't."

"But I—"

"It's not your fault. He knew that, too. It's not your fault," I tell him, then I tell him once more. "It's not your fault."

Silence.

Tears.

We both lay there in blood and grief.

"What are we going to do?" he asks.

"I don't know."

"What's going to happen to them?"

I know who he's talking about, of course.

The village.

Our parents, our friends, everyone that we know.

"I don't know," I say again.

But I do.

I know.

So does he.

What else can we do, though?

What else can we do in situations that are beyond what we've been made to be able to endure?

I don't know. I don't know.

Next to me, Tasos closes his eyes, then soon I do, too.

It doesn't stop the tears, though.

It doesn't fill the hole, or ease any of the unbearable pain.

15

MARCH 15, 1942

I don't sleep. How could I?

How could I, or anyone, possibly sleep?

Tasos doesn't, either.

I don't want to close my eyes because I know I'll see his again, staring blankly up at me from where I cradle his head in my lap after I pulled him from the water.

I try not to think.

I can't.

There's the jingle of keys and I look up to see a German soldier at the entrance to the cell.

He uses the keys to unlock the door. He swings it open and says something to us in German.

I don't understand the words.

I understand what he's telling us, though.

We're free to go.

How?

I don't know, but I painfully stand, and so does Tasos, next to me, looking with questions in his eyes I can't answer and we walk out of the cell and past all the other Germans that are in their headquarters, that was once the headquarters for the British, but before that was ours.

The center of our town, our city.

We keep walking.

We go past them, then outside.

And once we do, I understand.

I see Cassia waiting for us on the street.

I glance to the side and see an unfamiliar German officer standing by the old Venetian fountain and when he sees us walk out, he tips his hat, very small, to Cassia, before he turns and starts to walk down Zampeliou Street, towards the Old Town.

I go to Cassia.

"Do you have him?" I ask her, very quietly.

"Yes," she nods.

I nod, too.

Then I start to run.

I hear her call after me to stop and be careful and to wait for her, but I don't, and then before I'm too far away, I hear her tell Tasos to run after me, and he does.

He runs.

But he doesn't catch me.

I sprint along the familiar path, through town where I dodge vendors, soldiers, and Cretan men dressed in suits spinning their *komboloi* that *clack clack* together, then past the *kastro*, the craggy point in the sea to where there's sand, then rocks, then sand once more at Chryssi Akti.

I keep going.

I go past the olives.

And then, that's when I begin to see smoke.

The Germans have dropped fliers since the beginning of the invasion, telling us what they'll do to villagers who harbor Greek resistance or enemy combatants, and we've heard rumors they've done similar things and destroyed other villages.

As I get closer to the farm, I see they've destroyed ours, too.

The sheep are scattered because the barn has been burned, so they wander the hills and across the path and graze on any grass that's there.

They look at me curiously as I run towards them, then I slow, and walk.

Behind me, Tasos catches up, and he slows, too, when I do.

I go to the house.

That's where I find them.

They're together on the ground, so that's something at least, that they didn't face this alone and they're halfway between their bedroom and the kitchen and I wonder if it was quick, or if they saw their murderers coming and knew what had happened and what their fates would be before it came.

Tasos reaches out.

He takes my hand.

There are no words.

There's us.

There's just us now.

We continue.

We go up and towards the village and our other house and there's smoke there, too.

There's so much more smoke because the entire village has been burned, decimated, anything of value pillaged and stolen, and the rest simply destroyed for the sake of destruction, and a warning, of course.

We approach the house.

We don't need to go in, though.

Unlike my parents, Giannis and Angeliki are outside, near the overturned table where we all shared so many meals together.

Behind them, the house still burns.

So do the ancient olives and tall cypress across from where the bodies now rest.

Tasos falls to his knees.

I keep walking through the rest of the village and I see no one, I don't see a single other person as my feet lead me through smoke and ash, then I come to the middle of the village, and that's where they are.

They're not here anymore, though.

They're bodies.

They're just bodies.

They all lie where they fell, and I see Doctor Papadakis first, with his wife next to him.

I see Vassilis the baker.

I see my friend Chrisoula, and her mother Ione.

I see Anteros the cobbler, and his wife Elena, then I look even farther and see Father Thiseas, his body alone, the white collar and his black robes stained red again with spilled blood.

I see others, too.

I see the bodies of all those I grew with, who helped raise me, and I'm unmade once more.

There's still one, though.

There's still one person that's not accounted for.

Ikaros.

I turn and see smoke rising at the far end of the valley, also, and then hear his last words to me again: *tell her I'll see her tomorrow night, and will be there waiting when she gets back.*

My heart sinks once more.

I need to know, though.

I need to be sure.

I turn and begin to make my way through the narrow valley towards Elaionas, and when I get closer, I choke on the smoke that's there, too, swirling and being blown straight at me by the wind that's begun to pick up.

I don't go to the Magarakis house.

I don't need to.

As I get closer, I hear the soft sound of grief and crying, through smoke and wind, and I walk towards it.

It takes me to the center of the village.

The bodies aren't laid out nicely here, like they were in my village, but rather all piled on top of each other in a giant heap and I see Kyriaki on top of the pile and next to her are the bodies of her father, her brothers, and there's one that she holds even closer to her, though, she holds the body as close as she can to her pregnant stomach as she cries and cries and rocks them both back and forth.

I don't need to go any closer to know who it is.

They're gone.

They're all gone.

I fall to my knees now.

Why?

Why me?

Why have I been chosen to stay, when this is what's happened to every single person I love?

Because I don't want to, I realize.

I don't want to stay, not anymore.

I fall farther, all the way to the ground.

I fall to the ground, and I don't get up.

16

JUNE 8, 1942

The next days are weeks, and the next weeks are months.

I barely eat, and while I don't sleep at all, I'm not sure I'm awake, either.

After I return to the ruins of our village, I find Tasos still on the ground next to his parents, and Cassia next to him, hugging him, holding him, the donkey behind them that she'd led all the way from Chania pulling a cart, and in the cart the body of my dead husband.

There's no one else to help us.

They're all dead now, so Cassia, Tasos, Kyriaki, and I bury all the dead in her village, first, then we come and bury all of the dead in ours.

We do the best we can.

We say a prayer over every grave we dig.

When we get to my family, we choose to bury them close to where they fell, which is of course also where they lived, and had made their own.

I choose a spot in the field next to our house, near where the sheep graze, wild now.

For his parents and brothers, Tasos picks a spot underneath one of the cypress that's still standing. Most of the trees are burnt and charred from the fire that's consumed them and the house, but after a few days, he spots a small bit of new growth under one of them, a fresh blade of grass next to the promise of an *akanthos* flower that will soon come. He takes it as a sign. These trees and this place were once beautiful and this, he says, is a sign it could be again.

Will it?

If we can make it.

If.

I don't have the strength, though.

After the graves have been dug and prayers have been spoken, I go to the ruins of what had once been the house where we'd lived, I find the remnants of what had been the bed I'd shared with my husband, and I sleep.

I eat only when Cassia brings me food.

I get up only to go to the bathroom.

I have to close my eyes even though I don't want to, and at first, I see the lifeless features of Demetrios staring up at me and replay the final moments of his life over and over again, thinking of what I could have done differently because that's the thing about final moments: we so often don't realize they're final until then they are.

I wish I could do it over again.

I wish I could go back and do so much differently, and I wish I'd known the moments we had were actually the great moments of my life, the only great moments that I'll have.

Then something happens.

My dreams change.

The face of my dead husband and all the moments I wish I'd enjoyed more, and held closer, and want to change, begin to fade, and they're replaced with something else.

Eyes.

More eyes, different ones, and two separate pairs of them.

The eyes of the German soldier I'd seen on the road, who gave me away to his superior.

Then the eyes of that superior.

The eyes of the German officer who killed Demetrios, and ordered our villages to be burned and every man, woman, and child killed as retribution for a stolen motorcycle.

It violates every law of warfare.

It violates every law of humanity, and goodness.

But those that have lost humanity and goodness don't care, and there's only one thing that can cure them of what they don't have.

Death.

They need to be removed from this world.

Suddenly, like an arrow piercing my soul, I feel purpose again as my eyes snap open and I know what I'll do.

I rise.

Slowly, I rise.

I don't tell Cassia, Tasos, or Kyriaki anything about what I'm going to plan, I just tell them we need to go, so we do, and we all walk down to Chania together. Our village is gone, and so is Kyriaki's, and our families are gone, too. We're all that we each have left in this world now, and we need to remember that.

That's what I tell them, and nothing else.

I tell them nothing of what's now in my heart.

As we get closer to the city, I wrap a scarf around my head and face.

Even though the Germans let me go, I don't want anyone to recognize me and end up changing their mind, but none do, and most pay me no attention at all as I walk past them because I'm a woman, and so is Kyriaki, and Cassia. They give Tasos a few looks, but I hurry him along the narrow streets and towards the harbor. Kyriaki tells us one of her cousins owns a hotel near the *limani* where Cassia has her apartment, and she can stay there.

That's good, I tell her, as we continue to walk.

That's very good.

I go to the bank at the corner of Zampeliou Street and Chalidon.

I tell Tasos to wait at the Venetian fountain with Cassia and Kyriaki, then I go inside.

I look around.

It's completely empty; there are no tellers, no bankers, no managers, no ways to withdraw any money at all.

Of course.

Because of the war.

My father had deposited a small sum here for emergencies, and that's what I want to use to try to pay for lodging for Tasos, to be able to stay here, in the city, away from the fighting and everything else, but how?

How will I be able to do that now?

"He can stay with me," I hear from behind my shoulder.

I turn to see Cassia has opened the door and she sees there's no one inside, too, no one else but me, and I shake my head.

"I can't ask that of you."

"You haven't. I've offered. Kyriaki has a place to stay at her cousin's hotel, and Tasos can stay at my apartment."

"You can't have him around all the time."

"It'll be fine. Good, even."

"Are you sure?"

"I'm more than sure. Are you going to tell me where you're going?"

"No."

"Why?"

"So if anyone asks, you can be honest."

She swallows.

"You're not going to tell him, either?"

"No."

"He'll want to come."

"I know, which is why he can't know."

"Alright," she nods.

"You're the best friend in the world."

"So are you, Maria. And I'm so sorry."

"So am I."

"What else can I do?"

"The only thing you can, the only thing we all can, and must."

"And what's that?"

"Survive."

She looks at me. I look back at her.

"So that's where you're going? To survive?"

"Yes."

She continues to look at me there in the pseudodarkness, nothing between us but drifting dust and shafts of light from the windows. Then she finally nods, understanding, and takes my hand, or I take hers, I'm not sure, and we turn and walk out from the empty bank and back into the city, together.

卐

We set up Tasos's bed in Cassia's living room.

He asks where I'm going to sleep, and I tell him in Cassia's bed with her, in her bedroom that looks out over the *limani* and lighthouse and all the German soldiers coming and going. It's strange. It's strange to be so close to our enemies, so close to those that have taken so much, taken everything, and to do nothing to them in return.

That won't be forever, though.

It certainly won't be forever at all.

Cassia and I make dinner.

It's a simple meal because simple is all that's left on an island that's been at war for over a year now, so we prepare a traditional *horiatiki,* some fresh *tzatziki,* and buy a small loaf of bread from Fotis's bakery on Zampeliou Street, even though he's not there, and it's sold to us by someone I don't know.

After the meal, we go to bed, but I don't sleep.

I don't even close my eyes.

I lay on Cassia's bed with her while Tasos sleeps in the living room, exhausted, and I wait until the noise on the street below starts to dissipate, then disappear altogether, and that's when I rise. I lean over and kiss Cassia on the cheek, then I go to the living room.

I look down at Tasos.

I think about how young he is and the experiences he should have had in this life, the experiences that his parents had, that I did, and his brothers, too, in all of our much too short lives.

He's had all that taken from him.

It's been replaced, I know, by guilt because of what happened.

I wish I could heal him.

I wish I could give him what he deserves.

But to be able to help heal him, I have to heal myself, first, and this is how I'll do it.

I bend down.

I kiss him on top of his head, as well, pull his blanket a little closer around him to protect from the chill that comes to our island with darkness, then after one more look, I turn and leave.

He'll be upset when he wakes.

That's alright, though.

He can be.

I walk through the city.

There's no one on the streets anymore so I don't bother to cover my face, and I leave the city the same way I'm so familiar with, and head back towards what was once my village, one last time.

I go past the olives that are untrimmed and unpainted.

I go past the farm where I grew and where my parents are now buried and our sheep still graze, wild amongst the ruins of what was once the barn.

I finally come to where my husband and I lived together with his family, and I go into the remnants of the house first, back to the bedroom we shared, where not as much fire has reached, and the dresser where he still has some clothes.

I stand there for a moment, breathing in.

Then I take some of his clothes, leave the bedroom, and walk to the kitchen.

The fire may have destroyed the structure of the house, but it didn't destroy what's hidden underneath it, so I push rubble and debris away and open the door to the space that's there, the hole underneath the boards, and I take what's inside.

I leave and go back out to the yard.

I go to his grave beneath the cypress, and I stand in front of it.

I want to speak but no words come, only tears, and I don't need the words anyway because they couldn't possibly explain all that's in my heart and if it's in my heart, it's in his, too, right?

I wait for another moment.

Then I take off my clothes.

I take off the embroidered and colored jacket I wear, then my white blouse, and finally my skirt, so I stand completely naked in the moonlight in my village that's no longer either a village, or mine.

I stand there a little bit longer.

Then I reach down and take the clothes I've brought from our bedroom, Demetrios's clothes, and begin to put them on: his trousers first, then his loose white shirt, cummerbund, and finally his vest. I take his thin leather belt with his carved dagger on one end and string my father's on the other. I put a British pistol into it, too, before cinching it around my waist that's smaller than his waist so I have to wrap the loose end of the belt up and over and tuck it between the leather and my body. I take two British rifles and strap them across my back, crisscrossed and touching each other, and I take Giannis's dagger, also, and tuck it into one of my pockets for safekeeping.

Am I ready?

No.

Will I be?

I won't ever.

That doesn't matter, though, because none of us are ever ready for the great times and moments of our life when they come. I stand there a little bit longer, silhouetted under the trees and in the moonlight and I don't hope they can hear. I know they can. I know they can see me, too, and what I'll do next, and that will be enough. That's what I hope. I hope it will be enough, both for them, and for me, then just the same as my husband once did, I turn and I leave. I head south, into the distance, following the same path he took, the one that leads up and towards the great White Mountains that rise above us, our village, above everything, just the same as they always have, and just the same as they always will.

17

JULY 14, 1942

The day after I leave the village is the first truly hot day of the year, and every day since has been near unbearable. It doesn't matter, though, because armed as I am and with what I carry, I only travel at night now. It does matter for the Germans, however, who patrol less and less in the heat and don't wander as far from the cities, or sea, and the higher I climb in the mountains, the cooler it becomes, too. Once I'm high enough and amongst the peaks and small villages that are there, I don't bother travelling at night at all. These are places even other Cretans don't often go, or perhaps even know about. These are villages, higher in the mountains, that have never been ruled, never been subjugated or conquered: not by the Venetians, not by the Turks, and certainly not by these Germans.

And that's why I'm here.

I travel east and each place I stop, I tell the villagers who I'm looking for, and ask if they've seen them.

They look at me strangely.

It's because of my clothes, I know, and how I'm dressed.

When they hear my question, most just shake their heads.

They don't trust outsiders, even ones who speak Greek with the same accent they speak, and are from the same island they're from.

And they don't trust a woman dressed in men's clothing.

I continue.

There's finally one old man I meet sitting at a *kafeneio* and spinning his *komboloi.*

"The British?" he asks, when he hears my question. "That's who you're looking for?"

"*Nai.*"

He spits on the ground.

Then he stops twirling his beads, and looks me in the eyes.

"I haven't seen them, and even if I had, I'd shoot them myself."

"What do you mean?" I frown. "They're fighting with us."

"They're cowards and the reason the Germans are still here. If they had fought longer than a day, as they'd promised, they would have driven our enemies away and into the sea, and we'd still be free."

"They fought longer than a day."

"How much longer?" he asks. "An hour? Another day? They promised they'd fight until the end, and they didn't."

"Some are still here. Some are still fighting."

He doesn't say anything further, though.

He simply stands and walks towards me, and I see he's shorter than I am, so he tilts his head up to meet my eyes again. "I don't know why you're dressed the way you're dressed," he speaks slowly. "Or how you've come to have the weapons that you have. But my advice, young lady? If you see them, use one of your fancy rifles to put a bullet in their skull, because it's what they've done to us."

He holds my eyes.

Then he spits on the ground, once more, before he turns and leaves.

I watch as he walks into the distance.

Then I carry on, and it's not much farther, and in a village not far from the one I've just left, when I ask a woman on the street the same question and she doesn't answer, she just walks away; there's a boy sitting in a doorway nearby listening, though, and after the lady leaves, he stands.

He comes towards me.

I look at him as he gets to where I wait, and he tells me he knows who I'm looking for, and to follow him.

So I do.

We go even farther into the mountains.

We go up past where the trees stop, up towards the snow that's still there, even in summer; we climb through fields where we see goats perched precariously, grazing on the side of rocky cliffs, and then we go even farther.

Soon I hear voices.

I smell a fire, too.

We walk towards a specific peak that's hidden between the others and as we get nearer to it, I hear the voices are speaking English. Then I see the men who are speaking, and most are British, but there are some others here, also. They all have drinks and are sitting by the fire, and there are tents set up behind them. When they see us, they stop talking, and one of them speaks.

"Who is this, Philippos?" the man asks.

They don't recognize me.

I recognize them, though, and I'm glad I do because it means I've come to the right place. I look around and past them and that's where I see the hunched figure I'm looking for, sitting on a stool outside his tent, checking his ammo, reloading his weapons. I ignore the others and walk towards him. I get closer, and when I do, he turns. He sees me. He sees me and then stands and does so slowly, on a leg that's been wounded and allowed to set and heal, but the wound's still there because it will never heal, not really, and while he walks better than he did before, he's still not whole.

That's alright. Neither am I.

"Maria?" William asks, his blue eyes finding my dark ones. "What are you doing here?"

1943

18

APRIL 26, 1943

When I first arrive in the mountains, at the British camp, William tells me I can't stay with them, and that being in the mountains and amongst the men who fight there is no place for a woman. I simply shake my head, though, and refuse. At first, I don't tell him what's happened to the village, and my family. Then, when I finally do, I see the look in his eyes, the disbelief, and after I tell him what happened, he doesn't say I have to leave anymore. He must tell the same to the others, too, because they don't say anything more to me about leaving, either. I know they also think the mountains are no place for a woman, but that's not who I am. Or at least that's not all of who I am now. I'm proud. I'm strong. I'm Greek, and I'm Cretan; that's the blood that's in my veins, and the legacy and history I carry.

There used to be many in my village who carried it with me, but now I carry it alone.

For my family, even if I do nothing else, I will carry it.

After the men get over their initial feelings, they're all soon glad to have a Cretan amongst them that knows the island and speaks both

Greek and English. I'm able to guide them and help with the locals, some of whom are more forward-thinking and receptive to them, and some, like the man I encountered before, who are not. Such is the way of the world, I suppose. Some Cretans blame each British soldier for the orders of their superiors, even though these soldiers are the ones that are still here, still fighting, and still killing Germans with us. And that's all their lives are dedicated to now, just like ours. They wait for German convoys and supply chains in the narrowest parts of valleys and mountains, and that's where they attack them, when the land can help their numbers. They also tell me how they gain supplies by doing this, and pass along intelligence, too, back to what William calls the SOE and which I learn stands for Special Operations Executive.

This means the British haven't completely abandoned us, I realize.

I ask them how it's done.

They won't explain and instead say I can see for myself, if I show them the quickest way to Balos Beach. They won't take me on any trips where they expect to fight, but they'll take me on this one, they say, because the point of this trip is to *avoid* the Germans.

I nod.

I know exactly how to get to Balos, of course, and it's not too far from our camp and we leave as the sun is sinking so once we're no longer in the mountains, which are ours, and safe, we'll be travelling under cover of darkness. I lead them west. I lead them past where Chania would be if we went just a few kilometers north, then I show them the way out of the mountains. We skirt the Maleme airfield that of course belongs to the Germans, and we keep going. We pass the town of Kissamos, and it's just on the other side of Kissamos that the main road ends. We still continue, though, even when it does. It's just a small path that we'll take, one that only I know, or perhaps another local, and the British and Germans don't. The path takes us even farther west and a bit north, out onto the narrow Gramvousas Peninsula that juts up into the Sea of Crete. That's where we are when the sun begins to rise. It's alright, though; there won't be any Germans here because vehicles won't be able to cross the rough, rocky, and mountainous terrain once the road ends, and they wouldn't know where they were going anyway. There are no signs, or markers, or anything else on this path. We see wild goats, looking curiously from their places perched on sides of cliffs around us that descend down into the sea. I look into the distance and towards the water and see the sharp-peaked island that's there, and that's how I know we've reached the place I've been trying to reach.

There's another path I show them.

It takes us precariously down the side of a cliff, where we climb carefully, then when we reach the beach and sand below, that's when the light finally comes.

I see them take it all in, the sand giving way to the translucent azure of the Cretan waters, the sun reflecting off it.

It's perfect.

It's a perfect beach and even more than that, it's completely secluded from the outside world and only reachable by boat except to those, like me, who know exactly how to find it.

It's paradise.

Well, normally it's paradise, but now it's something else.

Until this is over, there is no paradise here anymore.

The heat begins to come, too, when we reach the beach and the sun climbs even higher and we have to wait until darkness again, they tell me, so as it gets hotter and hotter, the men strip off clothes, down to their shorts, and go into the water.

I sit on the beach with William and watch them.

Peter.

Walter.

Evelyn.

Charles.

Owain.

Abdel.

Tane.

They laugh and dive, jumping over waves, wrestling, throwing water at each other. Abdel, who is from Palestine, and Tane, who is Maori, have darker skin than their more pale English and Welsh counterparts, who will easily burn in this sun if they're not careful, and as I watch them, I can feel William watching me.

In another life, it could be a perfect day.

But it's not another life.

It's this one.

We sit in silence until the others come back and William turns from me as they lay on the sand in front of us, the ones with paler skin letting themselves dry in the sun for just a few moments. They dry in no time at all, of course, then dress once more and we eat some dried and canned food we've brought, then wait in the nearby caves above the beach where the others smoke cigarette after cigarette, until soon it's dark once more.

When it is, they put their cigarettes out, and keep their eyes peeled.

It's not long until we see it: a small, flashing light in the distance, in the water.

Once the light flashes, they stand and run down to the beach and I follow after as Peter takes a flashlight from his pocket and turns it on. He cups his hand over the top of it, obscuring the light it brings, then letting it shine, covering it, letting it shine, and it's creating specific patterns of long and short intervals.

"What's he doing?" I whisper, asking William next to me.

"Morse code," William answers.

I turn back.

After the message is sent, Peter turns off the light for good, then I realize what I've been seeing, and what's been answering him: there's a submarine that's out there in the shallow bay.

The sea is still.

Then it's not, as I see the ripple of waves where there should be none and realize the waves aren't being made by wind or current, but something else.

The submarine comes closer.

It comes close enough that it's nearly to the sand, then the top opens and two British soldiers poke their heads through the opening before they climb out and jump into the waist-deep water and walk the rest of the way towards us.

"What have you got for us today, Your Royal Highness?" Evelyn asks with a grin.

"Everything you asked for, Mr. Shakespeare. Perhaps even just a little bit more, too."

"Oh goodie," Walter rubs his hands together.

This new British soldier is tall with high cheekbones, sharp blue eyes, bright blond hair, and takes a cigarette from Owain then leans close as Owain strikes a match and lights it for him. Beyond us, Peter, Evelyn, Abdel, and Tane walk towards the submarine. When they get closer, up to their chests in the water, there are more British soldiers still inside that start handing them zipped duffels to bring back to the beach, carrying them above the water and on shoulders to keep them dry.

"And who is this newest addition?" I hear, then turn back to the blond soldier with the bright eyes.

"Maria," William answers.

"*Geia sas, Kyria Maria*," the soldier says in perfectly accented Greek.

I look back at him, wondering who he is and how he speaks our language the way he does.

"*Geia sas*," I answer.

William takes a piece of folded paper from his pocket and hands it to him.

"There are less troops in Chania now, and more in Rethymno," William tells him. "We still don't have a number for Irakleio or Knossos, but that's where most of them are. It's all written out there, along with how frequently we've seen movement on the roads between cities."

"What about the mountains?"

"The mountains are still ours."

"And the south coast?"

"Just a few patrols that make their way once or twice a month, no garrisons or anything permanent, so the south coast is still very much wild, and contested."

"Very good," the blond soldier says as he hands William a piece of paper in return. "Very good, indeed, Ryder, and there's something else in there to make sure it stays that way."

"Much appreciated, as always," William nods.

"We'll see you again just then," the blue-eyed soldier winks at me before finishing his cigarette, dropping it in the sand, then shaking William's hand and mine before he turns and starts to walk back out into the water and towards the submarine. He gets there and climbs up onto it, then he and the other British go back inside and lower the door and seal it as the vessel starts to submerge again. Within a few seconds, they're completely gone, just that quickly, as if they were never there, leaving not even the smallest wake on the surface or anything else to give away where they've been.

I look out, for one more moment.

Then I turn and look at what they've brought us.

Fifteen stuffed and zipped duffels.

"What's in them?" I ask.

"A bit of this and that," Owain answers.

"A bit of everything, really," Tane nods, agreeing.

"Everything . . . like what?"

"Weapons," Peter says as he counts on his fingers, "food, intelligence, and liquor of course."

"They better have sent the bloody good stuff this time," Evelyn adds. "I can't abide the shit from Liverpool, from the last visit."

"And even some correspondences from home," Peter smiles.

"Is that right?"

"As fun as we might seem," Evelyn winks at me, "it's not unmarried men that you're looking at."

"Some of us are!" Charles laughs.

"Yes, and that's why you don't get any letters," Walter pushes him, and Charles pushes him back, and they both laugh.

"We still do get letters," Abdel adds. "It's just they're from our mothers, mostly."

"So don't listen to them," Charles speaks to me and Abdel now. "Because they're just jealous of all the fun we have, and that we're able to do whatever we please."

"Oh, yes," Owain waves his hand. "All the fun, alone and high up in the mountains."

"We need to get going," William cuts them all off. "We need enough darkness to get home."

"Of course, of course," Peter nods, the leader of the group.

They all grab duffels, each man carrying two, and Tane goes to grab a third, but I take it from him.

"No," he shakes his head, not letting me.

"I can carry it."

He looks at me for a moment.

Then he looks at William, who nods, very small, and once he does, Tane finally lets me take the duffel. I sling it over my shoulder and we all begin back the way we came. The others lead and go first, knowing the way up the cliff now, and across the desolate, rocky, and uninhabited Gramvousas Peninsula. Behind them, I walk with William, and as we do, I turn to look at him.

"Those are some strange nicknames," I finally say.

"Which ones?"

"Mr. Shakespeare?"

"Evelyn's a bit of a writer."

"What type of writer?"

"A novelist. And quite successful, too. Peter's a writer, also, and so is his brother, so the Mr. Shakespeare name is actually quite general in this group, rather than being specific."

"Peter has a brother?"

"Yes, Ian."

"He's not stationed here, though?"

"He's in intelligence back in London, or at least that's where he is as far as we know. But as it's intelligence, and all very secretive, he wouldn't be as good as he is if we knew more than that, or really anything at all."

"And the soldier?"

"Which one?"

"You called him Your Royal Highness. He spoke Greek well. Is he a writer, too?"

"No, he's not a writer."

"Where did his nickname come from?"

"It's not a nickname. That was Prince Philip of Greece."

I pause and look over at William, my eyebrows raising in surprise.

"*What*?" I ask him. "Are you serious?"

"Indeed," he nods.

"Strange," I say, as we keep walking.

"It's not, really. He's the fifth child of a seventh child, so in line to inherit nothing. He's not an heir, so I'm sure they're not too worried about the succession, if anything happens to him."

But that's not what I'm talking about.

What's strange is I've gone my whole life without ever meeting, seeing, or being near a single member of any royal family and now I've met two, in the course of as many years. But that's what war does, I suppose, and the war here on our island has brought together so many to fight against evil, both royal and common alike. We soon leave the Gramvousas Peninsula and once we do, and come back to the main road again, we're silent, so that no one that might be near will hear our voices. We speak again when we reach the mountains, then when we're to our camp, we'll each go to our tents to sleep the day away and regain the rest we've lost by marching through the night. Before we do, though, we sit around a small fire and the men take out the contents of the duffels: red wine, scotch, and brandy, first, followed by dried beef, cans and tins of coffee, and cartons of cigarettes, as well as piles of grenades and more bullets for the weapons we already have. Then come the letters. The men all start to read them as they drink and laugh and share news from home as the sun rises. I feel something soft, light, and wet that lands on my cheek. I look up to see snowflakes slowly starting to fall from the clouds above. It's unusual for April, in the mountains, but of course still not unheard of.

I look down.

I look at William, through the snow that's started to fall.

I notice there are no letters that arrive for him, and he sits by himself.

He has his secrets, I suppose, and that's alright because I have mine, too, and I haven't told him or anyone else the real reason why I'm here, sleeping in a tent on the ground and sharing all the pathways and mysteries of my island.

They will know.

They will know soon enough.

But not yet. Not yet.

19

MAY 4, 1943

Friedrich-Wilhelm Muller and Hannes Koch.

These are the two names that haunt my dreams.

Koch is the soldier who recognized me, and Muller is the officer who killed my husband and ordered our village destroyed. Those are the two men I'm now searching for, and I'll stop at nothing until I find them and make them pay for what they've done. It's the only way there might be peace for me. I'm still not sure there ever will be, even when retribution comes, but it's the only thing I can think of to try to search for at least some peace, so I will. It's what men do, right? And does it work for them? I don't know, but perhaps it will work for me. I ask Cassia to use the connections she has amongst the Germans in Chania, and she's the reason I know their names. She's also the reason I know they've been sent away from Chania. Since I know their faces, of course the others in the city do, too, and saw or heard what they did, and that's the reason they've been transferred: so as not to incentivize revolts among the locals who know what they've done. And while Cassia finds out they've been sent away, she doesn't, however, find where they've been sent. It's something too dangerous to ask and risk any Germans wondering *why* she asks, and what she might do with the information. She's bought a lot of goodwill with the Germans she now lives amongst, and needs to keep it that way.

So I've decided to start the search on my own.

That's why I'm here, in the mountains.

William and the men I've taken up with tell me I still can't join them on trips from the camp where they expect there will be combat, and instead, when those mornings come, to stay at camp and cook for them while they're gone, and I tell them I will not.

"Why?" Peter asks.

"Because that sounds like a job for a wife."

"And what are you?"

"A *palikari* now, just the same as anyone else. Just the same as we all are."

They just smile and shake their heads and I can tell they still don't take me seriously, not even William, until one trip when they leave to intercept a German convoy bringing supplies from Irakleio to the garrison at Rethymno, along the northern coast. The plan is to eliminate the Germans before they get to Rethymno, and the British don't know the best way to the coast without being seen on the main roads. So they tell me they need me, just this one time, and I lead them east through the mountains until we come to the Arkadi Monastery, nestled on a soft plateau high amongst the peaks. I know the monks there will give us shelter and food, because it's what they've always done for those who fight for freedom, for many hundreds of years. When we arrive, I speak to the monks in Greek, telling them who we are, and they welcome us inside and as we go past them, and walk through the monastery, I can see the others taking it all in: the beauty, the size, the history. I tell them how this monastery has been a symbol of Cretan resistance for years, and how during the Turkish Wars nearly a thousand men, women, and children—though it was mostly women and children—had left their villages and hid here. Then when the Turks came and laid siege to the monastery, they fought against them. They fought and fought, but when it became clear the resistance of so few against so many would end in defeat, they made other plans, and when the Turks finally breached the walls and flooded inside they lit all their barrels of gunpowder and munitions at once, creating a massive explosion that killed them and destroyed parts of the walls and buildings, but destroyed the Turks, too. I show them the exact spot; I show them where the remnants of the explosion can still be seen, near the walls and chapel, and they take it in. I show them the inscriptions that commemorate it, in the crypt where the gunpowder was kept and lit and I read them the words that are there, the ancient words of the Archbishop of Crete Timotheos Veneris of Rethymno, from 1933:

> The flames which lit the depths of this crypt
> Were a godly flame in which
> The Cretans perished for freedom.

William looks at me in darkness, as we go back up and leave the crypt, back into the light, and the courtyard.

"None of this is really new for any of you, is it?" he asks.

"No," I tell him, and shake my head. "Unfortunately it's not."

We go through the cloisters and past the chapel and I cross myself when we walk in front of the chapel door, and I do so in the Orthodox way, the ancient way, to my right shoulder first, then left. I then walk out the gate of the monastery and they follow after and I show them the memorial that was erected for the dead, near the cliff on the northern side of the plateau, opposite the route we took to get here. I read them the inscription that's there, too.

Nothing is more noble or glorious than dying for one's country.

It's short, simple.

It's also the reason all of us are here, isn't it?

We stand for another moment, taking it in, each with our own thoughts that are probably the same thoughts, or near enough. Then the light fades and the monks don't have spare rooms, so they allow us to sleep in the chapel amid the icons and stained glass. As we get there and settle in, I think about the lives that have visited this place and been a part of its stories and history.

Now we are, too.

None of us sleep very much, and near dawn we rise and leave again before the sun comes. Before we go, though, Tane walks to the edge of the plateau—towards the graveyard where all the past leaders of the monastery are buried—and as the sun just begins to crest the mountains, he does a traditional Maori *haka* dance. We stand and watch him. There are so many that think it's a war dance, what he does, but it's not. It's a dance to honor guests, or commemorate great achievements, moments, and sacrifices, so that's why he does it here. When he's finished, we say our farewells to the monks, who come and line the monastery walls to see us off and give us their blessing one last time, then we start to walk again.

It's not long until we come down from the mountains to the sea, being careful not to be seen, and when we're near the main road that hugs the coast between Irakleio and Rethymno, William spots a shepherd. The shepherd's young, not more than fourteen years old, and while William, Peter, and the others had a plan at the beginning of the day, they now might have a different one. The shepherd tells us his name is Theodoros, but he goes by Theos, and when William tells the young boy who we are, he's more than happy to help. He moves his sheep, as William asks him so that instead of grazing on the side of the hill and cliffs that sink straight to the waves below, they're on the road and block anyone that might come in a vehicle.

And soon enough, some do.

We all sit together, I'm next to William and Evelyn, and while we wait, I ask Evelyn what it's like to be a writer, and a famous one, too. He looks at me and doesn't answer at first, and I can tell it's perhaps something he's not comfortable with, something he doesn't like talking about. Then he's saved from having to say anything by the low rumbling of German *kubelwagen*s. The rumbling gets louder as they get closer, and there will be no more words now. When the *kubelwagens* round the corner and see the sheep blocking their path, they begin to slow, then when they see it's just a boy with the sheep they stop altogether. One of the Germans gets out of the lead *kubelwagen* and starts yelling at Theos, but his words are in German, which of course the boy doesn't understand. Theos simply shrugs towards the animals in the universal sign to say, *I'm trying, I'm trying.* The other Germans get out of the *kubelwagens,* too, once it looks like this will take a while; one lights a cigarette, another goes to the bluff to relieve himself and piss off the side as Theos moves his sheep from the road. Then once the sheep and the Greek boy are far enough away, and enough of the Germans are out of their *kubelwagens* and the protection that the vehicles give, that's when we open fire. The men had made me stay hidden behind the rocks while they snuck down and spaced themselves across the length of the road, hiding behind bushes in the narrow ditch, then jumped up and the sound of their gunfire exploded between the hills and the sea.

Germans fall.

So many of them fall as bullets rip through bodies, and Theos covers his ears and his sheep scatter as soon as the shooting begins. Some of the Germans that don't fall in the initial attack return fire, but so do we, and so do I. They told me not to, but I do anyway. I pick out one of the Germans in the driver's side of a *kubelwagen,* carefully aim, then squeeze the trigger on my rifle and am surprised when the bullet smashes through the window and ends his life. Soon there's only one German left. He's barricaded himself behind one of the *kubelwagens* and while William and the others shoot at him, all they do is waste ammunition because he's protected by the steel of the vehicle. They don't have the angle they need to hit him. I do, though. So I line up another shot with the British rifle that William gave me a lifetime ago then squeeze the trigger and the bullet whizzes through air and buries itself in the German's chest. The others run towards him to kick his rifle away, but there's no need. He's dead.

I come from my hiding place behind the rocks as in the distance another man runs towards us, having heard the gunshots, and we raise our weapons when we see him, but Theos jumps between us and shouts "*Oxi!*" because it's just his father. We gather all the supplies from the *kubelwagens*—all the food, ammunition, and liquor—and as Theos and his father begin the process of rounding up the sheep that have scattered because of the noise and commotion, I come and translate and tell them we'll leave some of the food if Theos can help us carry what we've taken back to the mountains. They both nod and accept. They would have accepted even if we'd offered nothing, I know, but Cretans are proud so I wanted to make it fair because while Cretans have always been proud, during this war they've also been very hungry. So we take the food and anything else we can carry, push the *kubelwagens* off the cliff so they crash against stone below and will be useless to the Germans, then Theos comes to the mountains with us. When we return to camp, we find Philippos waiting, the other boy who originally showed me the way from the village. We cook a feast and all the men get drunk and Theos drinks with them and gets drunk, too, for what might be the first time, I realize, though I don't want to embarrass him and ask. I watch as they all drink, Theos and Philippos near each other, who are close to the same age, and realize what I've discovered today: that contrary to what I thought when the Germans first came, I have a talent for marksmanship and shooting. Also, it will now be impossible for William and the others to leave me behind or not allow me to go with them when they know they'll be killing Germans. So when we receive more intelligence from the SOE about movement we need to stop and not let happen, it isn't a question of if I'll be able to join or not; at this point, I'm integral, and not just because of my knowledge of Crete, the language, and island, but something else, too.

Something ancient, and embedded deep in my blood.

Have I been denying it, all these years?

No.

No, I haven't.

It's just that, like so many other women, both here and elsewhere, I hadn't yet been given a chance.

20

MAY 13, 1943

The Germans control all the major cities on the northern side of the island, which is by far the most populated side, but the southern coast is still wild, and still ours. We need to keep it that way. We need to keep a part that's just for us, and more importantly, we need access to the sea. The ports on the southern coast aren't large but it's where reinforcements could arrive, potentially, if they were to be sent, as well as supplies. The rugged, arid, and mountainous terrain means there are fewer people without farming or agriculture, and it also means it's a place that's much more difficult to conquer. Still, though, it seems the Germans will try. We all sit in our camp together after receiving the latest dispatch from the SOE, and Peter unrolls a large, detailed, topographic map of the entire island. There's a convoy of armed Germans that will be heading to the southern coast to try to kill any resistance and terrorize the locals into giving up information about where other resistance might be found, and it's our job to stop them. I show Peter, William, and the others how there's only one road from

Chania that goes to the southern coast, and it's a road that traverses a valley with steep mountains on either side, for many miles.

It'll be perfect for us.

That's where we can ambush them, much the same as we did the convoy on the road between Irakleio and Rethymno. So without wasting any more time, and after we've slept off the journey to the coast and beach at Falasarna to retrieve this intelligence, we once again leave our camp under cover of darkness and head west. I know where we'll go, too; just beyond the small mountain village of Topolia there's the sacred cave of Agia Sofia that's secluded and hidden and has panoramic views of the entire valley and road running through it. We'll be able to see any convoy that comes from there. We walk through the night and reach Topolia at dawn, just as the sun begins to rise, and as we head along the narrow street that runs through the heart of the village, the people we pass look at us warily. They look at the rifles on our backs, the pistols at our waists, the two Cretan daggers I wear, one on each hip. They're mostly women, children, and the elderly, as are most in any village on this island, with men of fighting age either dead, or in the mountains. I remember what Belen said, and how a squadron of paratroopers had blown off course in the initial attack the year before and landed near here and killed his family. So it's of course easy to understand the distrust of foreign soldiers in these parts, and in these villages.

But I'm not.

I'm not foreign, I'm one of them.

And I need to make sure they know that.

The first man I see amongst the women and children looks middle-aged, with greying hair near his temples, and a bald spot on the top of his head. He comes forward and introduces himself as Eugenios Pateraki, and tells me he's the *dimarchos* of Topolia.

I tell him who we are and what we're doing, where we want to go and why, and he offers us rooms in town, instead. I tell him we'll go to the cave because we don't want to put them in any danger by having resistance amongst them. He protests further, saying it'd be a great honor, despite the leaflets dropped by the Germans, but then finally relents, and as we keep walking through town, and before we're gone, he has one last thing to say.

"What about you?" he asks.

"What about me?" I respond, turning back.

"You speak our language. You're clearly from here," he says, then nods to the two daggers at my hips. "But how did you end up with those, and dressed like a *palikari*?"

I look back at him.

I wonder what he sees in my eyes.

"I'm not dressed like one."

"What?"

"I am a *palikari*," I tell him, and won't say more.

He understands.

He doesn't know specifics, of course, but tragedy is now a part of all of us, so he simply puts his hand on his heart and nods to me.

"*Efcharisto*," he says.

"What's he saying?" William asks.

"Nothing," I turn to him. "I'm just telling him we're going to the cave, and we won't be staying in the city."

William looks from Eugenios, back to me, and I'm not sure he believes me as it's clear we've said more, but he doesn't speak Greek so we continue on through the town and then not far after Topolia, I show them where to leave the road. I show them the stairs carved into the side of the mountain, and how to start climbing. The beginning is hidden by trees and bushes, so will be missed by those who don't know where to look, but as I push them aside, and we go past and begin to climb, the stairs become much more defined until soon we get higher, much higher, then reach the top and the sacred cave that's there.

There's a landing, carved into the mountain.

And then, outside the entrance to the cave, there's a bell tower built onto the side of the landing with a large brass bell, used to alert all those in the valley when there's danger near.

There is. There is danger.

But we won't use the bell, at least not yet.

We walk past it and go inside.

The opening to the cave is so large we don't have to duck and can all walk in together. Once we do, we're immediately greeted by damp air and muskiness, and the sound of *drip drip drip* coming from the ceiling and forming a small puddle of water on the stone near our feet. I watch as they look around and take in the rock formations above and below us, the unique stalagmites and stalactites protruding from the ground in unordered columns and hanging from the ceiling in the same way. The stalactites on the ceiling are small, but the stalagmites protruding up from the floor in the shape of fingers clawing and reaching are unique and stunning, and unlike stalagmites anywhere else in the world, or at least anywhere else I've heard about. The cave has been converted to an Orthodox shrine, for veneration of all Orthodox saints, but it hasn't always been. Before Christianity came to this island, this cave was still important, and ancient weapons can be found in some of the deeper and less explored areas of it and there are etchings on the walls, too, stories and pictures from before history. Now, though, it's a cave dedicated to the worship of our Christian God, and his wisdom, and many pilgrims come every year to pray and be healed. One such famous pilgrim is St. George, and I show the others the hoof-shaped mark on the stone floor with the puddle of water gathered in it where it's said his horse stepped when he visited.

"I didn't realize St. George came to Greece," Owain says, looking down at the imprint that does indeed look like a hoofprint.

"You may have taken his standard as your flag, and adopted him as the symbol of your country," I tell them. "But he's not British. He was Greek."

"Surely that can't be right."

"It is," Abdel tells him. "We worship him in Islam, too. It's said he's buried in Mosul, where he was tortured and killed. The dragon he fought was at Ashkelon, not very far from my own village."

"Didn't he live there, though?" Charles asks. "In Palestine? Wasn't he St. George of Lydda?"

"*Nai.*"

"So how is he Greek?"

"Not all Greeks live in Greece," I tell them. "Alexandros conquered the world, so there were many of us there, too, out in the world, spanning from the Middle East as far as Afghanistan and India, and all corners of what was once his great empire."

"Interesting," Evelyn adds.

"Who is this St. George?" Tane asks, still looking down at the hoofprint.

"He was a member of the Praetorian Guard in the Roman army," Peter tells him. "He became a Christian and refused to renounce his faith, so was tortured and killed. He's the patron saint of England, as well as the saint of soldiers everywhere."

"So," Tane smiles. "It seems like we've come to the right cave, then."

"It seems like we have," William smiles, too, then looks at me. "It seems like we most definitely have."

Then we hear something.

We all grab our rifles and sneak back towards the entrance, but exhale when we get there and see that coming from the stairs leading up to the cave is Eugenios and some of the villagers. It's women and children that are with him, we see, and they carry things in baskets: bread, olive oil, mizithra cheese, *raki*, and jugs of red wine. Then behind the villagers, there's one man, a priest dressed in the black robes of Orthodox clergy with a long beard of dark and gray and he carries a box of candles. When the women and children reach us, they hand us all they've brought, and the British who don't speak Greek nod and say *thank you, thank you*, or *efcharisto*, one of the few words they do know, over and over. The priest comes forward, after the villagers, and gives the candles to Peter, who is middle-aged and the oldest amongst us, and probably looks the most like our leader, too, which he is.

Then the priest backs up.

He speaks to all of us now, in accented English.

"You will need them, for light, here in darkness," he speaks slowly, and meets our eyes. "Every time you light one, say a prayer, in this cave of wisdom, so that when you fight, the light stays, it always stays, and the darkness remains in the cave."

"Of course," Peter nods, answering for all of us.

The priest nods in return, then turns to the mayor.

Eugenios comes forward and takes a leather belt with a carved Cretan dagger on it.

He holds it up so we all can see.

"For . . . fighting," Eugenios says, in broken English. "For Cretan . . . *palikari*?" he turns to me for the word in English.

"Warriors," I nod, translating.

"For Cretan . . . *warriors*," he says, then comes forward.

He ties the first belt around William's waist, cinching it tight so it doesn't move and the dagger hangs at his hip. Then he takes another leather belt with a dagger and does the same for Evelyn, then Abdel, and all the rest of us, too, except me because I already wear my husband's dagger on one hip, and my father's on the other.

When Eugenios is done, he takes two steps back.

"*Bravo*," he nods. "Cretan warriors now. *Palikari*."

"We can't—" Owain begins.

But the priest cuts him off.

We all know where the daggers have come from: from the fathers and husbands and sons of this village, who have been killed and are not coming back.

"*Axios*," he says, in his loud and commanding voice.

Owain and the others turn to look at me.

They don't understand the word, or significance.

"You're worthy," I tell them, translating again.

They look back to the priest who walks to the imprint made by the horse of St. George of Lydda. He bends down and scoops some of the water that's collected into his left palm, then walks to each of us in turn and with the fingers on his right hand, dips them into the water, wipes some across our forehead, as if he's baptizing us again, then makes the sign of the cross before moving on to the next person. He comes to me last, next to William, and stops. He holds my eyes then nods, very small, and slowly rubs the water across my forehead and makes the sign of the cross over my body.

Then he backs up.

"*Axios*," he says again, even louder. "May the spirit and presence of the warrior saint guide and protect you," he finishes as one of the children from the village hands him a thurible filled with lit incense which he shakes in our direction and the familiar scented smoke comes and passes over us, filling our nostrils, filling the cave, gathering in a cloud that hovers and stays.

"*Efcharisto*," William says again, and so do all the rest of the men.

"*Oxi*," the priest shakes his head. "It is we, the people of Topolia, and this island, who thank you."

Then with nothing more, Eugenios and the priest and all the rest of the villagers turn and leave, filing out of the cave the same way they came, back down the mountain, and we're alone again. The sun's beginning to sink so we walk from the cave, too, towards the bell tower with the view of the valley. We sit there and eat some of the food they brought, tearing pieces of bread to go with olive oil and mizithra, as well as tins of bully beef from the supplies we've received from the British SOE, and we drink the Cretan wine.

When we finish the food, then comes the *raki*.

William pours large amounts into tin cups and starts to pass them out, but Evelyn tries to keep his wine glass.

"I'm fine with the red," he says.

"Sorry," William shakes his head. "It's not an option. This is what they do here after a meal."

"And how would you know that, Mr. Ryder?"

"Because not too long ago, I was part of a village, even if it was only for one night, and the kind folk that took me in taught me."

"Did they now," Owain laughs.

"They did," William says as he glances at me and smiles. "They taught me that *philoxenia* is everywhere on this island, and this is part of it, which means we are now, too."

I of course remember the night he's talking about, the one with my whole family around the table outside our house with Giannis, Angeliki, my father, my mother, and the boys talking to him about *philoxenia* as we ate and drank and they smoked their pipes.

We were all there.

All of us except Demetrios.

Now how many are left?

It's just me and Tasos.

William still smiles, but I don't.

He knows why.

"We have something similar in Palestine," Abdel says. "It's called *arak,* and we drink it after meals, and offer it to guests in our home."

"Is it this strong?" Charles makes a face as he sips.

"Of course," Abdel says, as the *raki* catches in his throat, too, but he doesn't make a face. "Because why not, right? We are all here for a short time, so why not eat, drink, and live as much as possible while we are?"

The sun sinks further and we sit for a few more moments without words, as the light begins to fade and change, and there's silence as we take in the majesty that's in front of us.

I've seen this many times.

I know they haven't, though, and while I'm sure their island is very beautiful, this is a different type of beauty, isn't it; a more ancient one, and perhaps a more cursed one, too.

They sip their *raki.*

I sip mine.

"I think I'd like to come back here in another life," Peter finally says, very softly. "I think, in another life, this is where I'd like to live."

"Another life when there's not war, you mean?" Tane asks.

"Exactly," Peter nods. "Another life once we've finished this war, won and gone home, then can come back again."

"There's always war here," I tell them.

"Surely there are moments, though, right?" Peter turns to look at me. "Surely there are moments in-between?"

I don't answer. I just stand and go back inside the cave.

I pass the threshold where the air immediately cools and instead of going to the right, where the hoofprint of St. George's horse is embedded in the rock, I turn left. There's a shrine there on the far side of the cave; it's a small area sectioned off by tall Orthodox depictions of various saints and icons painted onto pieces of wood that create a makeshift wall with a small door. I duck through the doorway, past the saints and icons, and go into the heart of the shrine, near the altar. There are burned and unlit candles plunged into sand, and names carved into the rock behind the candles. I look at the names. I look at all those that have come before me looking and searching for miracles, and is that what I search for, too? I see faces. I see all their faces. I'm not searching for physical health: cancer to be cured, a leg to be healed, a heart to lose its disease, or anything similar to what they came for. Instead, I'm searching for peace, and that's its own type of miracle, isn't it?

I find an unlit candle.

I take it from its place beneath the altar, and there are matches next to it, so I strike one against rock where matches have been struck by the faithful since before history, then reach out and bring fire to the candle I've chosen.

One more time.

I see their faces, one more time, my entire family, and I especially see his.

I see him the way we were when we were young, when he was working on the barn at my house, when we both felt for the first time all the things we hadn't felt before and were fortunate enough to still feel every day after, too, and not have fade, not ever.

Why?

Why did it have to end like this?

I don't know.

I'll spend the entirety of the rest of my life asking that question and perhaps just asking, because is it something I'll ever find, no matter how hard I search, and is it something I'll ever understand?

I don't think so.

So I'll just search, instead, and this is how I'll begin.

I place the candle in the sand, and with it, my prayer.

I make the sign of the cross after my prayer, and then stand there. I just stand there. I can hear them still out by the bell tower drinking *raki* and speaking louder and louder, the more they drink, which doesn't surprise me as all the British I've met, since they've been here, seem to drink a lot more than we do.

Is it because there's a war?

I don't know. I just know they do.

"Are you alright?" I hear, then turn to see William behind me.

He's ducking his head through the entrance to the shrine, then he stands there in front of me, his body illuminated by the flickering light of the candle I've just lit. I look back at him. I don't know what to say, which he must see in my eyes, so I just look at him.

"Sorry," he says.

"For what?"

"I know it's a silly question."

"It's fine."

I sit down near the bedroll I've brought to both keep me warm at night and also protect at least a little bit from the rocky surfaces upon which we've slept. I don't say anything further so he comes and sits next to me, too, and looks around at the small shrine: he sees the altar, then the polished, golden stand filled with sand where I lit and placed my candle. Then beyond that, and carved into the stone, he sees the names written in Greek.

"What does it say?" he asks, not able to read it.

"It doesn't say anything," I tell him. "It's names."

"Names of who?"

"People who have come here and been healed."

He keeps reading and then touches them, the letters carved deep into stone.

"So, kind of like Lourdes?"

"Yes, I suppose a bit like Lourdes."

He looks at all the items now that have been brought and left: the crutches, glasses, and leg braces, as well as splints, gloves, and stuffed animals with fur that's beginning to age and turn yellow. He reaches up and gently touches these things, thinking, I'm sure, about who they belonged to, what ailed them, and what cure they found. "Do you think this is a place where miracles happen?" he finally speaks again, his voice softer now, too, and I know why.

"I don't know."

"You don't?"

"I hope it is."

"Why?"

He turns and looks at me and while I don't say the words, I know he knows them, and can feel them. *Because I need one, William. I need to be healed, too. I brought us here because I also need a miracle.* It might not look it, because my wounds are not visible to the eye, but I still need to be healed just as much as a boy with a broken leg, a father fighting cancer, a grandparent with an inoperable tumor and only days to live.

He looks at me for another moment.

Then he nods and begins to settle himself across the shrine from me on the cold rock.

Outside, I can still hear the others, voices, words, getting louder as they drink even more *raki*.

"What are you doing?" I ask.

"Going to sleep."

"Right there?"

"Yes."

"Why?"

"So that you know I'm here," he answers, then takes his jacket off and makes a pillow from it.

He lays his head down, then closes his eyes.

I look at him for another moment.

I look at him lying there, his arms crossed over his body for warmth.

Then I shake my head and stand and walk to where we dropped the spare bedrolls we brought, in the main part of the cave, and I already have mine, so I get one for him. I come back into the shrine and lay it over his body, like a blanket. He pulls it closer around him once he feels it, but doesn't open his eyes, doesn't move or say anything further, so I go to my corner and lay down, pulling my bedroll over my body like a blanket, too, close my eyes, and it's not long until we're both fast asleep.

21

MAY 16, 1943

We wait in the cave for three days, then the Germans finally come. We learn they're approaching through the valley when a young girl who looks like she's maybe eight or nine years old comes running up the steps. Evelyn is outside shaving, using a razor to cut the stubble from his chin and cheeks, then cleaning the razor in a small bowl of water he gathered and calls for me when he sees her because he doesn't speak Greek. When I come from the cave, she tells me the Germans have been spotted heading this way and as soon as her message is delivered, she turns and starts running back down the stone steps again and towards Topolia.

I call to the others.

They're all going about various morning routines, but as soon as they hear my words, they drop everything and grab rifles to sling across backs, grenades to tuck into pockets, pistols to holster at hips, and now Cretan daggers to tie at waists. And once everyone's ready, we begin to make our way down the steps, the same way the young girl came and then went.

The road is right there, at the end of the stairs that lead up to the cave.

But that's not where we'll meet them.

We hurry farther south to a place where there's a bend in the road that we chose when we first arrived because of the cover it will provide, and the element of surprise we'll be able to preserve until the very last moment. We jog together and when we get there, Peter picks a medium-sized stone from the hillside and places it in the middle of the road near the bend.

He makes sure we all see it, then we take our places.

Peter, Evelyn, Tane, and Abdel are on one side.

I'm on the other with Owain, Charles, Walter, and William, who takes me gently by the elbow and leads me near his hiding place so I'm there, too, and next to him.

"May St. George watch over us," Evelyn says, so we all hear. "Just the same as he has."

We nod, agreeing.

Then we're silent.

We won't speak again until we see them, but we feel them, first, the soft rumbling of the ground caused by heavy vehicles travelling on the same road at the same time, and it feels like a small earthquake, which is of course something we're no strangers to on this island, either.

We take the rifles from our backs.

We hold them ready and in front of us, one in my hand and another loaded and propped against the rock next to me.

The rumble of their engines gets louder, closer.

"*Stay near*," William whispers, next to me, into my ear.

A few seconds later, we finally see them, coming around the bend and straight towards the part of the road where we wait. They keep coming as we grip our rifles tighter, and when they finally get to the medium-sized stone Peter's placed in the middle of the road, we all rise as one and begin to shoot.

The valley explodes.

The sound of gunfire echoes everywhere and it's nearly too much for our ears.

Half of us aim for the tires of the *kubelwagens* while the other half aim towards the windows and the men driving both the *kubelwagens* and the motorcycles, and we fire once, then again, and when I hear the *pop pop* of the tires that are hit and explode, I know the day will be ours.

They won't be able to get away.

A bullet pierces the front tire of the lead *kubelwagen* and it causes the vehicle to veer to the right. The driver tries to correct the swerve but overcorrects, and the *kubelwagen* skids and flips over and onto its side in a shower of dirt and there's yelling from inside as bodies are tossed this way and that.

Behind, the other *kubelwagens* try to slow, but they can't.

They crash into the first and there's a massive pile of twisted metal and broken bodies.

Some of the Germans on the motorcycles fire at us and their bullets bounce harmlessly off rocks as we duck back behind them, then rise once more and return fire and cut those soldiers down, too, and they fall near their bikes and don't rise again.

Soldiers crawl from the *kubelwagens*.

They aim and fire at us and we fire back at them, and our bullets find flesh and then they lie still and the few others that are left drop their weapons and raise their hands into the air.

They call to us.

It's a single word.

I don't speak German and neither do any with us, but then one of the Germans speaks in a different language.

"*Surrender!*" he yells in English.

He's older than the others, a bookish-looking man with glasses who looks like he'd be more suited to a classroom and teaching schoolchildren rather than here on our island fighting and trying to conquer us. But here he is, and here I am, and it didn't have to be this way but it is, so I come forward from my place behind the rocks.

The others do, too.

They go to the Germans and kick their weapons away, but I don't go to the Germans that they go to, I go to the other one, the older man who spoke English and said "surrender."

I kneel next to him.

He looks back at me and I think I'm going to see surprise in his eyes, at who I am, and how I'm dressed, and that I'm a woman.

But I don't.

"*Danke*," he says instead. "Thank you."

"Friedrich-Wilhelm Muller and Hannes Koch."

"What?"

"Where are they?"

"I don't know. I don't know who —"

Before he can finish, I take my father's dagger from my hip and plunge it deep into his thigh and leave it there.

He screams.

He yells in pain.

I yell now, too.

"WHERE ARE THEY!"

"I DON'T KNOW!"

I reach down and twist the dagger.

"RETHYMNO!" he says. "MULLER IS IN RETHYMNO!"

"AND KOCH?"

"I DON'T KNOW."

I take the other dagger, Demetrios's, and raise it in my hand but William runs and grabs me by the arms and pulls me from the German.

I shake free of him.

I run back to the man and slam my husband's dagger into his other leg.

He screams again.

"WHERE IS KOCH?"

"I DON'T KNOW! I SWEAR!"

William grabs me once more and some of the others come, too, and pull me from the German and I struggle against them but they hold me tighter this time, then I begin to stop struggling and feel their grips begin to relax.

I turn to look at them.

"What are you doing?" William asks, his eyes finding mine, and I see horror in them. "Who the hell are Koch and Muller?"

"They're the men that killed my family."

"How do you know?"

"Because I do. Does it matter how?"

"Is that what all this has been about? Is that why you came to us, and the mountains?"

I don't need to answer, because it's clear.

"Let's start binding the rest of them up," Peter finally says, and the others nod, agreeing.

William goes to the German with the two Cretan daggers in his legs and I watch as he bends down, about to figure how to pull the knives back out as painlessly as he can.

"What do you mean *bind them up*?" I ask.

"Take them prisoner," Peter answers.

"And where exactly are you going to hold them?"

"I suppose we'll have to figure that out, won't we."

"How?"

"I don't know."

"They murdered my entire family."

"I'm very sorry to hear that, Maria. But in war there are rules, and we follow them."

"They murdered everyone in my village, too, and the village next to ours. Old men, women, children, literally *everyone,* then they burned the buildings all to the ground. Every single one, built by our grandfathers, and great-grandfathers, and great-great-grandfathers before that. They've tried to completely erase us from the world. We were women, children, old men beyond fighting age, and even a priest. So tell me, Peter, and all the rest of you that would agree with him . . . tell me, what rule of war is that?"

Silence.

"They did . . . all of that?" Peter finally manages.

"They did that and more, and my village wasn't the only one where they did this, and they will certainly continue. There will certainly be many more villages who suffer the same fate, because this is who they are, how they fight, and you'd stand here and tell me about rules of war and that you must take them prisoner?"

Peter looks at me for one more moment, then turns.

He looks at the others now, while the Germans in the dirt watch, unaware of the English words being spoken, and what they mean.

One German understands, though.

"Please . . ." the older man whispers, through the pain of my family's daggers in his legs. "Please, it wasn't us. It wasn't any of us."

"Quiet," Peter motions towards him.

"I don't want to say she's right," Evelyn finally says. "But I can't say she's wrong, either."

"It's how we would do it at home," Tane weighs in.

"And my home, too," Abdel nods. "It's not an eye for an eye, it wouldn't even be close to that. But it's at least some form of justice."

"I'm not sure we'd do it at home," Owain says.

"No, I don't think we would," Peter turns to him.

"But perhaps we *should*," Owain adds.

So now they have that to think about, too.

"You could shoot every single one of them in the head," I tell them. "If you did that, it'd still be more merciful than what they've done to my family. If you want to see the graves, they're not far from here. I can show you where I dug them, alone, because everyone else was executed."

There's another moment.

Then William finally turns to me.

Everyone pauses, waiting to hear what he's going to say.

He opens his mouth, about to say one thing, then seems to change his mind and say something else.

"Revenge is a very dangerous thing," are the words that finally come.

"This isn't revenge. It isn't even reciprocity."

"Reciprocity?"

"That's the word, in English, isn't it? An equal action? Well, this isn't equal."

"Then what is it?"

"If you'd seen what I've seen, and have happen what I've had happen to me, then you'd understand. But perhaps you can close your eyes and still imagine it. You sat at our table. You knew them, my family, my village, you knew all of them."

He pauses again.

Everyone still looks at him.

"I did."

"So then do this with me."

"One question first."

"What?"

"If I do, when does it end?"

"What do you mean?" I frown. "It ends whenever they choose. This is a war that came to our shores, not the other way around. If they stop there will be no more fighting. If we stop, then there will be no more Crete."

"So if the war ended tomorrow, and the two men you're trying to find went back to Germany, you'd have peace?"

"What do you mean?"

"If the war ended, but they lived, would you have peace?"

I open my mouth.

But just like with William, the words don't come, so I close my mouth and just look back at him.

The answer is obvious.

No.

I still would not have peace if the war ended but the men who took so much from me went free, so is this who I am now? Not long ago I asked to be someone else, and I now am, I very much am, but is it who I want to be? And is it someone who's good?

"I say we kill them," Charles breaks the silence. "I don't have to imagine anything, I know what they've done, not just here, but everywhere."

"Was it these men that did that?" William turns to him.

"Does it matter?"

"I think it does."

"I agree with Charles," Abdel adds.

"Me too," Tane says.

William then turns to Peter and Evelyn.

"And what about you?" he asks the pair. "What do you think?"

"She's right about one thing," Peter swallows. "We can't hold them. We can't bring them to our camp."

"We could for just a few days," Evelyn answers. "Until we can get them to a submarine, and off the island."

"The submarines can't hold that many with our men in them, too, and when's the next coming?"

"I don't know," Evelyn shakes his head. "Perhaps they could make more than one trip?"

"What if one of us died on the way there. Or waiting for the submarine to come back? Could you forgive yourself?"

"That's not the question, is it," Evelyn speaks quietly, but so all can hear. "The question is if we do this, will we be able to forgive *ourselves*, when this is all over?"

"No one will know a single German that died here surrendered, and didn't die fighting."

"They won't," Evelyn turns and meets Peter's eyes. "But we will, won't we?"

"I'm fine with that," Charles answers.

"Me too," Owain says again.

"And me," Tane nods.

"There is no shame," Abdel adds his support.

So all eyes turn back to Peter and Evelyn.

It will be Peter's decision, and he finally nods.

"So be it," he sighs.

It's only Evelyn left.

He stands there for a moment with eyes turned down, then looks up, and I'm surprised when he looks directly at me. "You asked me once what it was like to be a famous writer."

"I did."

"The first thing you learn is that we both write, and we also are written."

"What does that mean?"

But he doesn't answer, he just turns to William.

"She shouldn't be here for this," he says.

"Why?" I ask.

"Because even if it has to be done, it shouldn't be enjoyed."

I look back at him.

He's finished, though, and turns from me as he pulls the pistol at his waist and starts back towards where the Germans wait on the ground.

"Let's go," William says and takes me by the shoulders to turn me away from them.

Before he does, though, I see the looks on the German faces and think I can feel their thoughts, too; I see the looks on the faces of all those that lie there in the dirt and the surprise and shock at what they know will now happen as all the rest pull their weapons, and I don't know if they're the ones that burned my village, and killed my family, but they've done awful things. I know they've done many awful things and they've done such things for so long it's been as if they were fighting one war, with one set of rules, and we who are their enemies were fighting another.

But they've come to a different place.

And perhaps they realize, here and on this island, that we're all fighting the same war now.

"Come on," William says.

"Where are we going?"

"Away."

"My daggers."

"The others will get them."

"They're important."

"They know. Trust me, they know."

He pushes me in front of him and makes sure I keep walking south, so I don't see what happens, but after we go a few paces, I hear it. We both do.

A gunshot.

Then another.

There's another after that, then more, the staccato noise piercing the stillness of the valley and echoing between the mountains on both sides of us.

Then, nothing.

Quiet.

William closes his eyes.

I do not.

Then after a moment he opens them, pushes me in front of him once more, on the path that heads south, and we keep walking.

卐

We walk in silence, together, for a long time and I wonder when it will end. It doesn't seem like he will break it, though, so I decide to.

"Where are we going?" I ask again.

"I don't know."

"We're just walking?"

"Yes."

"It seemed like you had a plan."

"I don't."

"Then we should go this way," I say, and point.

"What?" he asks, as he finally turns and looks at me.

We're at a spot where the road forks and changes, from where it winds along the valley and side of the mountains and continues on to the south and west. But there's a path that goes just south, instead, and through the valley towards a small village that's there in the distance.

"Do you know that road?"

"Of course."

"How?"

"My family used to come here every year."

"Here? Where's *here*?"

"I'll show you."

"Tell me."

"Trust me, it's better if I show you."

"*Trust* you?"

He looks back at me.

I don't answer, I just stare impassively back at him.

We stay like that for a moment, neither of us flinching, neither blinking, then he finally nods and motions for me to lead the way so we take the road I've pointed to that goes towards the village called Elos. We soon get there, and when we do, I go into a familiar shop to buy a dozen *kalitsounakia* and he follows after me and watches as the old baker wraps them in newspaper with shaking fingers. I'm sad when I see this, then he glances at Demetrios's clothes and sees the blood on my shirt from the German I stabbed and who told me where to find Friedrich-Wilhelm Muller, and he doesn't react. He just turns back and hands me the package of *kalitsounakia*. I try to pay him but he shakes his head and won't hear of it, so I tell him *efcharisto* then walk back outside and we continue on. We go over a stone bridge that spans the small river that runs through the village, then come to the Byzantine dome and bell tower of the Agios Ioannis church. We walk in front of it, and when we do, I pause and make the sign of the cross over my body and once I do this, William looks at me then does the same thing, only not in the same way.

"We do it to the right first," I tell him.

"The right?" he frowns. "What do you mean?"

"How you're crossing yourself," I say, then show him.

I put my thumb, index, and middle fingers together, then to my forehead, my navel, my right shoulder first, then my left.

"Really?"

"Yes."

"Why?"

"I don't know."

"First the wedding rings, now this?"

I don't say anything further, though, and we just continue.

We're soon past the village, and once we are, the mountains that were on either side of us recede. The climate begins to change, too; it's more arid, dry, and everything's brown compared to the lush greenness brought by vegetation in the mountainous middle of the island where it's more fertile. I put one foot in front of another. So does he. We keep walking, and we go the rest of the way in silence again.

When we finally reach the coast, we stand on rock overlooking the beach, and he takes in all that's there. Directly below where we stand there are low, dotted shrubberies that give way to scattered palms. Then there's the sea beyond that, gently lapping against sand, and in the sea, nearly connected to the beach, there's an island with another beach surrounding it and I breathe sharply when I see it because the lighthouse that used to stand on the island has been destroyed.

"What is it?" he asks, next to me.

"Germans," I tell him, and nod to the remnants.

"What is this place?"

"The best beach on Crete. Maybe even the best in the entire world."

"What's it called?"

"Elafonisi," I tell him, then start to walk again.

He looks both ways as we're about to lose the cover of the hills, then follows me down and towards the beach. We pick our way between shrubberies that drop sharp seeds that litter the path and we crush under our boots. We soon come to the palm trees. We walk between them, then to the sand, and that's when I point down towards it, to show him, as we get close to the water.

"Look," I say.

"What?"

He looks at our feet, first, where there's just normal sand.

Then his eyes travel farther, towards where I point, and I see them go wide.

The water is shallow and very clear and at the place where it gently laps against the shore the sand is a bright shade of pink. I haven't been many places in the world, but this is the only place I know where there's pink sand like this, and by the look on William's face, I can tell it's the only place he knows, too.

"That's amazing," he says. "What causes it?"

"I have no idea. It's just always been that way."

He looks at me for a moment as I uncinch my belt and hang it over my shoulder along with the bag I've been carrying with the *kalitsounakia*, then he does the same, uncinching the belt that holds his pistol and hanging it from his shoulder.

I bend down and pull my boots off.

He does, too.

We leave our boots there, side by side in the sand, and he follows as I walk out and into the sea.

The water's not very deep.

It stays shallow between the beach and island, and while at lowest tide the water would be at our ankles, it only comes to our waists now as we walk, which is why I've taken off my belt because the only things I don't want to get wet are our firearms; my rifles crisscrossed on my back, and the pistol now hanging from my shoulder. I'm not worried about my clothes. This close to summer, they'll dry in less than five minutes in the sun. The water gets a little deeper, then shallower, then we're there. We walk up onto the sand and rocks, then farther, though not much, as the entire island is very small and can be covered in the single throw of a stone and I show him where the lighthouse used to be. It's just ruins now, though, a pile of broken and scattered rocks, which is sort of like us, too, right? I reach down and touch one, letting my skin feel the heat that comes from it, the sun and light that's been absorbed.

We keep walking.

As we do, I tell him the history of this beach, and island.

I tell him about the shipwrecks that have happened here, off the coast of Elafonisi, but most of all I tell him how during our war against the Turks, there was a large group of Greek refugees—mostly women, children, and the elderly—and they were with a small group of soldiers fleeing the Ottomans, and they hid on this island, in the exact spot we're now standing. The Turks pursued them but lost sight and made camp on the beach we've just come from, giving up the chase. Then just as they were about to leave, one of their horses wandered across the shallows and the Turk who owned the horse came to the island to retrieve it, and that's when and how the Greeks were discovered, and after they were, most of them were massacred.

"Most?" he asks.

"Just the soldiers and elderly."

"What happened to the women and children?"

I turn and point across the sea in front of us, to the south and in the opposite direction we just came. "If you sail that way, it won't be long until you're to Africa," I tell him. "The same way your people went when they left, heading back to Libya, and Egypt, and that's where they took the women and children and sold them into slavery. I'm sure they raped them first, of course, and did many other awful things to them, just the same as the Germans are doing again."

He's silent for a moment.

"I had no idea," he finally says, still looking south, beyond the waves.

"All this might be new for you, William, but it's not for us. I know you fight one way, and believe in a specific version of the world, but that's your version, and based on your history. Your family, your country, and your memories. But these are ours. Are you beginning to understand?"

He still stares out at the horizon.

Then he turns and looks at me, his eyes meeting my eyes.

"I think I might be starting to."

"This isn't the first time our villages have been burned. This isn't the first time those who said they would help protect us have broken their promise and sailed away. Yet still we endure. This is *how* we endure. It's the only way we have, and the only way we can."

"You know this beach and its history well."

"My father took us here every summer when we were growing up. We used to stop in Elos, where Baba said they had the best *kalitsounakia* in all of Crete, and he would buy a bunch and bring them for a picnic."

"Is that right?"

"Try one," I tell him as I reach into the bag and hand him a pie.

He looks at the pastry, then bites into it.

"What do you think?" I ask as he chews.

"It's good."

"Just good?"

"It's *really* good," he says, though half-heartedly and I realize perhaps it's the memories that go along with the *kalitsounakia* that make it taste a certain way as I take one and bite into it myself.

Does he have such memories, too?

Does he have tastes and smells that remind him of times like the ones I had with my family on this beach?

I don't know.

He finishes eating, and so do I, then we sit in silence for a moment longer, the sun beginning its descent now to our left and orange light spilling across sea and soft waves.

"Are we going to go back now?" I ask him.

"No," he shakes his head.

"Why?"

"Because you need to make a decision. That's why we came here."

"What decision?"

"You can still survive this, Maria," he says, and his voice is different now, strained, almost pleading.

"So can you."

"Not in the way I'm talking about."

"What do you mean?"

"If you want to kill these men, these two very specific men, then I'll help you and convince the others to help, also."

"But?"

"Know that it will change you."

"What do you mean? Change me how?"

"It will keep you here, in this time, and in this place, forever."

Water gently laps against sand, in front of us, and the sun sinks further.

I keep looking at him, next to me, and see the orange splashed across his face and features and for the first time I notice the pain that's there: the extraordinary emotion, and burden.

And what of me?

Am I marked in the same way, or will I be, as he says, if I continue?

"That used to be something I wrestled with and thought about all the time," I finally tell him.

"What?"

"The type of person I wanted to be."

"And now?"

"I realize it's a choice that was taken from me."

"Is that really what you believe? Because it wasn't. This could all end. You know that."

"No, it can't, William."

He sighs.

"So that's your answer?"

"Yes."

"What do you think they would have said?"

I know who he means, of course: Baba, Mana, Giannis, Angeliki, Ikaros, and Demetrios. They're all my thoughts are, and they're never far from me.

"They would want justice."

"But not like this. Not from you."

"You sound so sure."

"I'm not."

"Neither am I, but it's all I have. So will you help me?"

The color is splashed across our faces and eyes and the breeze picks up and I taste salt. We don't move, neither of us move, and we stay like that. Then he finally stands and reaches out and I take his hand and we go back to the water together and that's his answer, I realize. I put my belt over my shoulder, he does the same, and we wade into the waves. We walk back and the water's lower, the sun sinking further, and the tide's going out and doesn't even reach our waists now. Soon we're to the other side and the pink sand that sticks between our toes. We go to our boots, pull them back on, then keep walking.

He follows me.

We go past the shrubberies again, the ones with the seeds that fall to the ground, then we're to the path we came on.

I lead him past it, though, and towards the hills.

"What's up here?" he asks.

"A cave."

"Another one?" he raises his eyes. "How many are there on this island?"

"A lot."

We keep walking.

He smiles now. I still can't.

We climb, then come to it: it seems secret and hidden, but every child on this island knows about it and used to come here during days at the beach to hide from parents and be alone with boys, and there are even still a few empty *raki* bottles on the ground from the older children in nearby villages that I'm sure brought the girls they loved here and made promises about the lives they'd live and share as they drank and dreamed and looked at the moon and stars.

Those were different times, though.

There clearly hasn't been anyone here in a while.

The boys who looked at the moon and stars and dreamed with the girls they loved, where are they now?

I know.

They're gone.

I start to gather twigs and leaves, and some larger branches, too, and William does the same. When we've gathered enough, we push them into a small pile and he takes flint from his pocket and strikes it and soon a spark catches and begins to spread, and a fire builds.

I sit next to it.

So does he.

In front of us the sun disappears, and even though it's gone, there's still light, it's just coming from a different place now, the fire that's between us, the one we've just made, and that helps make a cold night just a little bit warmer.

22

MAY 17, 1943

When we leave Elafonisi the next morning, we walk back to our camp, and it takes most of the day. It's alright to travel while the sun is up in the southern part of the island, as there are no regular German patrols here like there are on the northern coast where their *kubelwagens* and motorcycles easily drive and navigate the coastal roads between cities. So we leave the cave as the sun comes up and walk in silence, each with our own thoughts, but there's something different both on the island and between us, and I can feel it; there's been a change in the war we're fighting—not the larger one, against Germans and Italians, but the one inside us, inside each of us, in our heart and souls—and there's been a change in each other, too, and perhaps that's not a bad thing? He knows about me now, and how I feel.

But what about him?

I don't know. There's so much about him I still don't know.

"What are you thinking?" he asks as we walk, breaking the silence.

"Do you really want to know?"

"Yes."

"I was thinking about the last thing Demetrios said to me, before he left to go fight on the mainland."

"And what was that?"

"Don't look for me in the sunsets, look for me in the sea."

"Is that right?"

"I looked, every single day, just as he told me. Only it wasn't him that I found."

"What was it?"

"It was you."

He looks at me after I say this and I think it makes him uncomfortable, so he swallows, then neither of us speak again until we're back to the mountains. The sun is setting when we return and Evelyn gets up from his place by the fire when he sees us, where he's been eating with the others, and walks towards me. He stands in front of me, then reaches to his belt where he takes my two Cretan daggers—the one made by my husband, and the other by my father—and gives them back to me.

I look down at them, in my hand once more, cleaned and polished.

Then I look up and meet Evelyn's eyes.

"*Efcharisto*," I tell him.

"*Parakalo*," he nods.

Then he turns and goes back to the fire and his meal.

I uncinch my belt and string the daggers back onto it, where they belong, before putting the belt back on, then William and I go to the fire, too. We sit with the others and I see a pot of *giouvetsi* that's been made; stewed tomatoes and pasta with spices and pieces of beef in it, and I also see it's still steaming hot. Tane sees me looking and finds a metal bowl and puts some of the *giouvetsi* into it, hands it to me, and I taste it.

It's good.

Better than I expected.

I'm sure they can all read the surprise in my eyes, because we all know they can't cook, and they especially can't cook Greek food, and Abdel smiles.

"Theos brought it to us," he says. "His mother made it."

That makes sense.

I turn to look behind us as William comes and sits next to me, and Tane hands him a bowl, also, and he starts to eat, too. I see Theos there with an axe away from the fire and Philippos is with him and they're splitting wood together then stacking it in neat piles alongside our tents.

"He came back?" I ask.

"He was waiting for us when we returned, with his mother."

"What happened?"

I ask the question, but then realize I don't need to.

I know what a boy and his mother showing up on our doorstep means: the same as it did when I showed up here.

"His father took some of them with him," Owain tells me. "Or at least that's what his mother told us. She stood here with the *giouvetsi* and asked if we could take him in and if he could join us, because it wasn't safe for him anymore, because he'd killed some of them, too."

"So he's one of us now," I say.

"Yes, it would appear that way," Owain nods.

I finish my *giouvetsi* then stand.

I take my bowl and rinse it in the water that's there, then put it out to dry before walking towards Theos and can feel William watching me as I go. Theos lowers his axe when he sees me, and when I get there, I go to him and embrace him. I simply hug him and hold him to hopefully let him know he's not alone, and I stay like that for a moment, as he hugs me back, his head between my shoulder and chin.

We're the same now, he and I.

We're the same, and there's too many of us, too many that have lost and been irrevocably damaged and had holes torn and scars made that will never be able to heal or be made whole.

But we'll try. We'll still try.

If there's one thing that's certain, it's that we will try.

23

MAY 18, 1943

When I rise the next morning, I expect to go to each member of our group and see if they want to join in what I'll now do next, but I'm surprised that William has already spoken to them. They'd all nodded when he told them what he had agreed to help me do, and they said they would help, also.

We need to wait, though.

We need to put a plan together, they all agree, and do reconnaissance and scouting to see how we might be able to get to a well-guarded officer of the Reich, which is of course no easy task. We also need another submarine to arrive with supplies from the SOE and more ammunition, which won't come for a few weeks, because after all the bullets we used on the road outside Topolia, we're starting to run low. Abdel takes Theos under his wing, and we see them together every day. William and I hunt and forage for food together, and he's surprised when I tell him there are no deer here on our island for us to hunt.

"Really?" he asks. "I thought they were everywhere in Europe."

"There used to be," I tell him. "But not for a long time now."

"How long?"

"I don't know. There are only fossils left, so quite some time."

"What do you hunt, then?" he asks, and I show him how we trap rabbits and hares, and can find goats and sheep that are wild and don't belong to anyone. I explain to him that since it's an island we're on, we don't have the same animals they do on the continent, like deer, because they can't migrate across the sea. We have tons of smaller things to catch, though, since the sea means there are no natural predators on the island, either—there are no wolves, or foxes, or bears, or anything similar—so the smaller animals here flourish. There were wildcats once, I tell him, but no one sees them anymore, and they're either gone and extinct, or nearly.

"What about boar?" he asks.

"Still no," I shake my head.

"So I suppose rabbit it is, then."

I nod and show him how to make traps out of sticks and string, the way my father did when his sheep were grazing in the mountains, and as weeks pass and the weather turns warmer, we begin to wander farther and farther from camp searching for food, setting our traps at greater distances, though we always stay in the mountains and away from the Germans.

We get looks from the locals, the two of us together.

In the villages, we most certainly get looks, and I of course know why.

I don't care, though.

If I've learned anything in my life it's how short it is and how quickly it can be taken, so more than anything, I don't care what these villagers think, or say, or believe, or gossip.

I care about me.

We don't talk much of important things when we go farther into the mountains in search of food, we just do the same thing, over and over, but then one afternoon when we've gone farther than we ever have before, farther to the east and south, I ask if he wants to keep going.

"Is there another place you had in mind?"

"There might be."

He smiles, and nods. So we continue.

We keep walking and leave the area around Chania, heading east, before we turn farther south. The paths here are not familiar to me like they are near my village and city, and I know the direction we need to go, but not the exact route. I make a best guess and walk until we eventually start to come down from the mountains, carrying a few rabbits we've caught slung over our shoulders, and as the hills get softer, we can then see the sea in the far distance and taste salt on the breeze again, and that's when I know we've arrived.

We walk the short distance across the green and fertile plain that's there when the mountains end, then come to the ruins.

They're perched on a plateau.

We climb the ancient path up the side, then get to the top.

Once we're there, he looks at the remnants of the city and fortress spread in front of us: the stairs, streets, houses, temples, and tall pillars, many of which have crumbled and are on the ground, but some of which still stand or partially stand, proud and tall against weather, elements, and passing time.

"What is this place?" he finally asks.

"It's called Phaistos," I tell him. "It was built by the Minoans. I would have taken you to Knossos, but the Germans have their command set up there, so I thought this would have to do."

"It's amazing. How old is it?"

"How come men always ask such things? It's old, old enough to participate in the Trojan War. Who knows exactly how old, though."

"Really?"

"Homer mentions the Phaestians in his *Iliad*, so it was a city founded even earlier than that, and by King Minos himself."

"The man with the labyrinth?"

"The same."

He opens his mouth to ask another question, but then we hear something in the distance, and I freeze.

An explosion.

But then we realize it's not the Germans: it's only thunder.

I look back to the north and west and see dark clouds gathering and beginning to head this way, and it's only a few more moments before the sky opens and rain starts to pour.

We're quickly drenched.

"Do you know any more caves?" he asks and laughs.

"Not here," I tell him, shaking my head.

We look around, scanning the area, then he sees something.

"There," he says.

And he takes my hand.

We run through the streets of the ancient city and I see what we run towards: the ruins of the many-chambered palace, and part of it that still has walls and a roof that we run under and out of the rain.

We stand there and look out.

Drops fall heavy and splash on stone and grass.

We watch the rain for one more moment, then turn back to what we've found: there's a worn and faded mosaic under our feet, and it shows the sea, and a dolphin, and a boy riding the dolphin, then we look beyond to see there are more rooms connected to the one where we stand.

William drops the rabbits we've caught at the entrance, and we begin to walk.

The rain continues to fall in staccato rhythm on the stone above, creating a soothing noise.

I see a doorway.

We bend down to walk through it because people four thousand years ago weren't as tall as we are now, and he goes first, I follow, and before my eyes adjust to the semi-darkness, I see him point.

"Look," he says.

There are carvings in the stone.

There are words, names, and painted scenes that all tell a story: a story of heroism, gods and demigods, and those that they loved and favored on this island.

"What is it?" he asks, not able to read Greek, either ancient or modern.

But I can.

So I tell him.

I tell him it's a story about a boy from Gortyna, who loved a girl from Phaistos, only they couldn't be together because their cities and families were enemies and had waged war against each other for longer than either side could remember.

He reaches up to point and ask about another scene, and as he does, our hands brush against each other.

I look at him.

We stand in front of the great stories of those who came here before us, and I meet his eyes, just for a moment.

Then I look away.

I translate a bit more for him, then turn and head back towards the entrance and even though the rain is still coming, I see it's slowed a bit.

I sit near the doorway.

He sits next to me.

It's cold now with the breeze and the sun and light gone, but there won't be any wood dry enough to make a fire so we just sit there on the mosaic and stare out at the rain, and valley, and sea beyond.

"You've heard the story of Minos's labyrinth, and the Minotaur?" I ask him.

He turns to look at me.

"Of course."

"So you know of Ikaros and Daedalus, too?"

He nods.

"I was there when they named Demetrios's brother. Angeliki had just given birth and the whole village came to see the new baby, and my father was working for Giannis by then, so we went, too, to pay our respects. Demetrios was thirteen, I was twelve. He had a broken arm from something, climbing a tree and falling out, maybe, or trying to jump from a running horse into the river. Anyway, as we were all there looking at this new baby, going through names of aunts and uncles, *theos* and *theas* on both sides, Angeliki was tired from all she'd gone through and just smiled and said whatever they decided, she hoped he was a boy who didn't fly too close to sun, like her oldest so often did. Everyone laughed except me, then there were words that came from my mouth and I don't know who put them there because they weren't mine. I had never really spoken to Giannis and Angeliki at that point, or at least any more than a child would, and I was scared of them."

William looks back at me, his brow furrowed.

"What did you say?" he finally asks.

"I hope he does," I tell him, then I'm silent.

He takes that in.

Then he realizes.

"*Ikaros*," he says.

"Yes."

"Why are you telling me this?"

"I don't know. I think perhaps I'm telling myself."

"So that you don't forget?"

"I could never forget. But sometimes we need to remember, too, which isn't always the same thing."

"I don't understand."

"I feel so guilty."

"You have nothing to feel guilty about."

"Yes, I do."

"What?" he asks.

Then I lean in and kiss him.

It seems to surprise him at first, because he's a man, and then it doesn't, for the same reason.

He moves away from me.

I watch as he swallows, hesitates, and I try to read what's in his eyes.

"Are you alright?" I ask him.

"No," he says.

Then he leans and kisses me, too.

I reach for his cheeks. He reaches for mine.

Then my hands go farther, to his wet shirt, and I lift it up and over his head before I pull my own shirt up and over my head, too, and press my body against his so that my skin touches his skin.

We continue. There's more.

He takes off his trousers and I take off mine, and we come back together, and for a moment we're one.

I think of Demetrios who was mine, when he was here.

Now he isn't.

He would want me to live, though, right?

And isn't this part of being alive?

I know what the world says, that I should wear the black and never allow love in my life again, but I know what my heart says, too, and which should we listen to: the world, or our heart?

I've made my choice.

So has he.

When it's finished, our bodies still wet from the rain, we lay there together, me leaning back against his chest and his chin on top of my head, his arms wrapped tightly around me. He still wears the ring on his left hand, after switching it when we left my village. I reach out and touch it. I feel it. I trace my fingers along the lines of the crest that's there, and he's silent, his chest rising and falling. I can feel his heart pressed against me, and I don't think he's going to say anything. But then he does.

"It was my mother's," he finally tells me.

"She gave it to you?"

"Yes."

"You sound sad."

"I am."

"Why?"

"Because she's gone."

I turn and look at him.

He stares out at the rain, watching as it slows, but still falls and pools on the ancient stone not far from where we lay.

"I'm sorry."

"So am I."

"What about your father?"

"My mother was everything that was good, and pure, and beautiful. My father is the exact opposite of all those things."

I'm silent.

I still feel him, his heart.

"Fathers can be that way sometimes."

"Before she died, I was engaged. There was a girl in my own village I grew up with and loved very deeply, and I proposed to her and she said yes."

"But you're not married."

"No."

"What happened?"

"My mother supported it, of course. My father forbade it. He was from an old and distinguished family that had fallen on hard times after the war. He had land and estates, but couldn't pay the upkeep on it all. So he found me someone else, a girl from London who was born common, but whose father aspired to be more than that. They had money. My father had titles. They arranged the match then told us about it afterward, and the place it would happen, and when."

"What did you do?"

"We fought, at first, my father and I. Then mother got sick, so we didn't anymore, for her. Eventually the date got closer and closer, but before it happened, mother died. When she was on her deathbed, she called for me, pulled me down close to her and whispered in my ear. *Everything is more beautiful because we're doomed,* she said. *You will never be more beautiful than you are now, and we will never be this way again.*"

"Homer," I say, recognizing the passage.

"Yes."

"Perhaps we're not so different, your people and mine."

"Perhaps."

"So you married the girl from the village, the one you'd loved your entire life?"

"When she'd seen my engagement in the paper, she wasted no time in finding someone else. He was nearly the same as I was in every way: the same age, from a family of the same sort, he even looked similar. I realized then it wasn't me that she loved, but what she would be if she married me."

"I'm sorry."

"I was, too."

"And that's how you left things?"

"The day after I found out about her engagement, I booked a ticket to London, walked into a recruiter's office, and joined the war."

"I thought everyone your age had to join?"

"Many do. But not if your father knows the right people."

"I'm sure that went over well."

"I don't know how it went over."

"Why?"

"Because I haven't spoken to him since."

I'm silent.

I move closer to him.

My hand is still in his and now my fingers trace and retrace the lines of the crest on his ring once more, as it rests there on his finger, and in my palm.

"So this . . . reminds you of her."

He finally looks down at me.

I can feel him and his sea-blue eyes that search for mine.

"It reminds me of my heart," he eventually says. "Which I suppose is another way of saying the same thing, and reminds me to follow it."

I think of his story, and what he's just told me.

"You're a Lord."

"My father is."

"So you will be when he dies."

He almost laughs.

"Not if he disinherits me."

"I'm sure he won't."

"I hope he does."

"Why?"

"Because life is so much simpler when it's just your heart, then everything else."

"Like it has been since you've left?"

"Yes. Exactly like that."

We sit there another moment, together, me in his arms, leaning back against his chest, then he begins to slowly unwrap his arms from around me, and he stands.

"What are you doing?"

"It's going to be cold without a fire, and we'll be hungry with no way to cook our friends over there," he nods to the rabbits we've caught.

"All the wood's drenched."

"I'm sure there's some that's not," he says, then picks up his shirt.

He doesn't put it on, though.

Instead, he bends down and softly kisses me, then walks out into the rain, completely naked and without bothering to dress.

I watch him.

I watch as he walks through ancient ruins, and then on, beyond them and towards the countryside.

I think of everything he just told me.

I think of his mother, and her last words: the ancient ones from the most famous of Greek poets.

Everything is more beautiful because we're doomed.

Has a single sentence more accurately summed up an island, or people, or time?

I reach towards my own trousers and belt and pull my husband's dagger from where it's sheathed. I take the rabbits from where William set them when we first came to the palace, when the rain started, and I begin to skin them. I start at the legs and cut around them, then pull the skin back and away, and as I do, I look at the dagger that I work with, and I think of him again.

I think of Demetrios.

What would he feel, if he could see me?

What would he say, if he could speak?

I don't know.

I've only ever been in his arms before in my life, and had always intended that to be the case and my future, but now I've been with another, and one that I'm not married to, also.

The world changes, doesn't it?

The world changes in so many ways, and perhaps it should, too, and it's us that are going to change it.

It's always us.

Those of us that are still young, and feel, and dream of ways this can all be different, and better.

Will I ever lose that?

I don't know.

I don't want to, but I don't know, because so many do, don't they.

I look up and see William coming back; his beautiful, slender, naked figure walking through the rain with his slight limp and clear blue eyes that are sunken into his now-tanned skin, from his time in the Mediterranean, on our island and in our sun.

His eyes are the color of the rain, the sea.

The sea that brought him to me.

The sea that will eventually take him away again.

He carries sticks of all sizes wrapped in his shirt to keep them dry, and when I ask how he was able to find them, he said he gathered a few from places under stones, trees, and bushes, where there wasn't much water. He drops them in a pile then takes the flint from his pants and strikes it again. It takes a bit longer this time, but eventually there's a spark, then flames that spread and burn. I skewer the rabbits on another stick and we hold them over the flames until they're cooked then eat together in silence, and when we're done, my eyes look and find his again, and he comes to me.

We lay there, next to the flames.

I lay there in his arms.

It's different with him than it was with Demetrios, and after a moment, I realize why; with Demetrios, we were both young, and exploring, full of passion, optimism, and hope, and all that was reflected in our love and in each other. With William, we no longer have any of those things. Well, none except passion. We're two people that have been broken and we're the same because that's the language we speak, and share: the too-often experienced language of shattered and broken hearts. I can feel him begin to drift to sleep, his chest rising and falling in equal intervals, his head to the side and between my neck and shoulder.

I feel him, the warmth from his body, the heat.

I look at the fire in front of us as it continues to burn, lower, the wood he found being consumed and the light it brings dancing across everything; our skin, the stones of the mosaic on which we sleep, the walls that surround this place and protect us and give us shelter from what we know we'll soon have to face again when we leave.

The world.

The world, and what it does.

But not now.

Not tonight, and not yet.

So instead I lay there, I just lay there with him next to me, and I feel my lips begin to twist and move, and for the first time since my husband and family were killed, I realize, for the first time since then, and through all the darkness that's come, I finally smile once more.

24

MAY 21, 1943

We stay amongst the ruins of Phaistos for another two days, and the only person we see is a shepherd, who comes down from the hills. He just nods when he sees us, at the way we're dressed, and who we are, then continues farther east and across the plains to where the mountains begin again. We hunt and fish and cook, and we take our clothes off and swim in the sea together before coming back to lay and dry in the sun, on the sand and amongst the rocks.

It's beauty, and it's peace.

We both know it can't last, though.

On the third day, after we've eaten and slept in the palace one final time, and gone to the sea, we return to the ruins. We dress in our Cretan clothes. Once we're dressed, we turn and leave. It takes us a whole day again to walk from the sea back to the mountains above Chania, and we check the traps we left on our way. We return with a few more rabbits to be cooked and eaten, and when the others see, they take the food from us and start to prepare it.

Once we're all together again, they tell us they received the visit we've been waiting for from the SOE. They don't ask where we've been or why we've been gone so long. Instead, they just bring duffels and open them and show us the ammunition, rifles, pistols, alcohol, and letters from home. And there are even grenades this time, too, some that were left over from the fighting south of us and across the Mediterranean in North Africa.

So that means only one thing.

It's time.

After we're done eating, I stand and rinse my plate, then turn and go back to my tent, and William does the same thing.

He doesn't go to his tent, though.

He comes to mine.

The others see, of course.

Once again, they don't say anything.

When he walks in after me, I nod towards the cot that's pushed against the far side of the space.

"It's small," I tell him.

"That's alright," he answers.

Then begins to take his clothes off.

After a moment, I do, too.

Is this how quickly lives begin again?

I suppose it must be.

He climbs onto the cot, so do I, then he wraps his arms around me and we're tired because of how much we've walked and how far we've travelled, so we're both asleep in no time and when I rise the next day, before the sun, as I always do, I unwrap his arms from around me, stand, and begin to dress. He opens his eyes when I get up and he watches me. When I'm done, he stands from the cot, too, and gets dressed, then we're ready.

We're about to go outside, but he stops me.

His eyes meet my eyes.

"What is it?" I ask him.

"*Kalimera*," he finally says.

I nod.

It's strange, this moment, and sharing it with him.

It's strange, but is it right?

"*Kalimera*," I tell him in return.

Then he pushes the flap open and we walk out, together.

The others are there, already dressed, and ready, too.

We walk towards them.

I stand in front of them, with William next to me, and I try to meet as many of their eyes as I can.

"Are you sure?" I ask, one more time.

They know what I'm asking, of course.

"No," Evelyn speaks for all of them. "But what in war is?"

I look back at him, at all of them.

Then I nod, so does he, and we all start to walk.

I lead them east through the mountains and back towards Arkadi, but we won't go there this time. Theos joins us now, too, keeping pace next to Tane. Instead of taking the southern route that would bring us to Arkadi, I opt to take the route farther north and lower in the mountains so we can find a place nearer the city to make camp, and this is where I take them: it's the remnants of another village that was destroyed by the Germans for harboring resistors, or something similar, and it's still in the mountains, though not as high as our camp. It's situated at the end of a long gorge with a river running through it and thick forests on each side which will be a perfect position for us; we'll be able to tell if Germans are coming because there's only one way into the gorge from the north, and we can flee to the south if we hear them, or see them.

The others walk together, in front of us.

Behind them, William walks next to me.

He looks down at my hand next to his as we walk, and I think he's going to reach out and take it.

Also, I feel myself wanting him to.

But he doesn't.

We start to come farther down from the mountains and have to loop around to enter the gorge from the north end, which we do, then hike back up it and farther south. We get to the point where vehicles can no longer travel on the road—not *kubelwagens,* or motorcycles, or anything—then we go just a little bit farther. After we've walked what Peter deems to be an appropriate distance, we leave the road and head into the forest.

This is the place from where we'll stake out Rethymno, in search of Friedrich-Wilhelm Muller.

Once our camp is set, we leave the gorge, and go to the hills above the city.

We remain in the hills where we can't be seen, but we can see them, coming and going, and make note of the military vehicles we see, and their movements. After a few days of observing habits, behaviors, and timing of patrols, we guess as to what patrol Muller might be part of and the best way to intercept him and make him pay for what he did.

We have to be sure, though.

So we move closer to the village.

The patrol leaves and we watch it from behind trees and rocks in the hills, though when it passes below us, we can't tell if he's in any of the *kubelwagens* or not, so I start to take the rifles from my back—first one, then the other—and put them on the ground next to William. Then I take the pistol from my belt and put it there, too.

He looks at my weapons, in the grass, then back up at me.

"What are you doing?"

"I'm going down there."

"Why?"

"I'm going to find him."

"Don't be mad," Peter turns when he hears this.

"I'm not," I tell him. "I'm a woman. They have no reason to suspect I'm anything but that."

"And you're, what . . . just going to ask someone?"

"Maybe."

I've removed all my firearms and now I reach down and take the two daggers that hang from my belt and flip them so they hang *inside* my trousers, and can't be seen.

"Maria," William begins.

But I just start to walk.

He tries to reach for me but I dodge his hand and move away from the cover to where I can now be seen by anyone watching, which the men can't do, and I start to walk down the hill.

I can hear them talking behind me, whispering urgently.

Then someone else breaks from cover, and I turn to see it's Theos.

"You're too old now," I tell him. "We can't take the chance they'll think so, too."

He reaches down.

He takes the cuffs of his pants and begins to roll them so they become shorts, reaches to his waist and tucks his shirt in, before he turns to look at me again.

"There," he says. "Just a schoolboy, out for a walk with his older sister."

I look at him as we keep walking, then just shake my head.

It'll be risky, but he does look younger and I can tell he has no intention of turning back, so I suppose there's no use arguing further.

I smile and run my hand through his hair to mess it up.

He smiles, too, and we walk in silence until we get closer to the city and enter from the western side. We go all the way to the sea, then take the road that winds between the water and *kastro* that they still call *Fortezza*, having kept its Venetian name through the years, even amongst the locals. It's the most impressive defensive structure in all of Crete, and I see the Germans have discovered that, too, as a whole line of *kubelwagens* drive through the narrow gate and up towards the top.

We don't go to the *Fortezza*, though.

We keep walking.

The path leads us around the side of the acropolis and into their Old Town where the streets are very narrow, the same as ours, too, then we go to the *limani*, their harbor. It's not quite as large as ours and we see their lighthouse at the end that's not quite as impressive as our lighthouse. We keep walking and go past the Rimondi Fountain, where women fill jugs with fresh water that comes from the holes between the carved Italian columns of marble, and there are a lot of people here; there are women coming and going with their daughters, and the *kafeneios* are filled with German soldiers of all ages who watch the women as they sip coffees and talk amongst themselves. Besides the Germans and the women, there are only children and the elderly, anywhere we look, as the men are of course either in the hills, or already dead. We hurry past the *kafeneios* and towards their agora, where vendors on either side shout and sell their wares, then in front of us, at the end of the road, there's the *megali porta*, which some of the locals still call by its other name, the Guora Gate, named for one of the Venetian rectors that ruled the city a long time ago when it was still walled and fortified. The gate itself is the only piece left of the old walls of the city, and it's also the only way into and out of Old Town by vehicle. So we know this is where the caravan of Germans we saw leave this morning will return.

We pass the time.

We walk amongst the vendors and feign interest in their wares before carrying on and to the next one. After some time, I hear a rumble in the distance, coming from the south, and can even feel a little bit, too, under my feet.

I tap Theos on the shoulder.

He hears and feels it, also.

We walk closer to the gate, to get the best view possible, then see the *kubelwagens* as they start to return and we stand next to a pillar, as discreetly as possible and out of view, and watch them.

First one comes, then another.

Then there's another still after that.

All told there are nine *kubelwagens* that have come back from whatever dark business they've gone about on the island, and they slow as pedestrians move to get out of their way, which gives me time to look inside each of them.

I don't find who I'm looking for.

"Is he there?" Theos asks, as the last one rumbles past and on towards the Rimondi Fountain, the way we just came.

They don't get there, though.

They turn to the right, before the fountain, and head towards the Mikrasiaton Square in the middle of the city. The streets are a bit wider there, and that's also where they park, I'm guessing, in the open area of the square and more modern part of the city under the towering minarets of the Neratze Mosque, a remnant of when the Turks controlled this city and that's been allowed to remain and continue, just like the mosques in Chania.

I sigh.

It won't be as easy as I'd thought, or hoped.

"Let's go back," I tell Theos.

He nods and we start to walk again.

We head back down the street, away from the *megali porta* and towards the Venetian fountain, and I glance to the right at where the *kubelwagens* are being unloaded near the mosque. Then we turn left. We're not quite to the ruins and that's when I see him; there are a row of *kafeneios* on the street, where we're walking, leading towards the fountain, and he sits at one of them.

My breath catches.

Theos feels this, next to me, then follows my eyes.

"Is that him?" he whispers.

I don't answer.

I don't need to, because it's clear what the answer is.

He sits in uniform with a woman about the same age as me, and she's Greek, so he speaks to her in English as they both smoke cigarettes, then he says something I can't hear and she throws her head back and laughs and I can hear her laugh from where I stand in the street with Theos.

I pull him to the side.

There's an alley nearby with a small restaurant and tables on the street that have a view of the *kafeneio* where Muller sits with his Greek girlfriend. I take the seat with my back to them, so they don't see me, Theos sits across from me, and when the woman who owns the restaurant comes, I order *bougatsa*. She nods and it's not long before she returns with the baked pastry and we pick at it, each eating small bites to make it last as long as possible, and when I see a slight change in Theos's eyes, I know it's time. I put a few coins down on the table, we take our last bites, then we stand. Behind us, Muller does the same as he finishes his coffee, puts his cigarette out next to the coins he leaves, then starts to walk through the streets along with the Greek woman.

We follow after them.

We stay far enough back that they don't see or notice us.

They take the narrow streets through the Old Town, the same way we came earlier in the day, and on towards the *Fortezza*. But then, instead of taking the road that leads around it, they walk towards the walls, then through the ancient gate that's there, the large wooden doors that are propped open, and I begin to follow after them.

Theos tries to grab my arm, to stop me, but I ignore him.

I shake myself free and keep going.

He can't protest too much, or do much else to stop me because of the scene it would make, so with no other choice, he starts to walk with me.

We go up the steep hill.

We're soon inside the massive fortress on top of the acropolis, and head down the main street. We go past the giant amphitheater to our left, which looks south towards the mountains. Then we continue, and see what they've done: there are *kubelwagens*, motorcycles, and giant pieces of artillery, shells, and all other tools of war that rest or are parked in neat and ordered rows on the grass between the buildings that are here, and I glance towards the Ibrahim Han Mosque. There's more artillery and ammunition stored there, then I see beyond it the old Venetian prison at the far northern side of the fortress. I look even closer and see the Germans have started using it again, and there are Greek men and women locked in the prison and behind the bars.

How do they decide?

How do they decide who they're going to arrest, and who they're just going to kill in the streets, or the middle of their village?

I shake my head.

We keep following and soon Muller ducks his head and goes into one of the houses, and the woman ducks her head, as well, and follows him inside.

I stand there, for a moment, with Theos.

Then he tugs on my hand.

"Let's go," he whispers.

This time I listen.

We turn and head back the way we came, past the Ibrahim Han mosque, and amphitheater, then through the large wooden doors set in the stone walls and down towards the city.

When we get there, we don't leave, though.

There's a *kafeneio* near the entrance to the *Fortezza* and we sit there and I order coffee for myself and water for Theos which he thirstily drinks after how much we've walked, and climbed, and the sun's even brighter and stronger now, too, so it's hot.

We wait.

He wants to know what I'm waiting for, what I'm going to do, but I don't tell him and we just continue to sit there and I order another coffee and put a few coins on the table as I sip it.

Then she comes back down.

I stand when I see her.

"Wait here," I say to Theos.

Then I begin to walk towards her.

There's a bunch of people on the street, and as I get closer, I pretend to try to squeeze past some men going in the opposite direction and I bump into her.

"Watch where you're going!" she yells, as she stumbles.

"*Signomi, signomi,*" I say, as I reach out to make sure she's alright.

"Could you not see me?"

I stand there and look at her; I pretend to feign recognition.

"Do I know you?" I ask her.

She looks back at me.

"I don't think so," she says, then shakes her head and goes to leave, but I reach out and stop her.

"No, no, I'm sure I'm right. Didn't I see you at the *kafeneio* earlier?"

"Which one?"

"By the Rimondi Fountain."

She narrows her eyes.

"Maybe," she speaks slowly now.

"Who was that you were with? He was handsome."

"Have you been *following* me?" she looks back at me then shakes her head again. "You're just like all the others, and you can save your judgment, *malaka*."

She turns and starts walking again.

I wasn't expecting this.

I was expecting her to have gone with him and been there against her will, and be open to helping me; I hadn't considered she was doing this on her own, and free of coercion.

I still need more information, though, so I hurry after her.

"You're with him? The German?"

"What is it to you?"

"I'm just curious."

"Yes, I am."

"Why?"

"He's a man. I'm a woman. There's a war, and he takes care of me. What if it's that simple?"

"I would say it's not."

"Because he's German."

"Yes."

"Which means what?"

"I don't understand."

"It means he's *here*. It means he's in Rethymno, in my city, living and taking care of me while all the other men that used to live here are gone, either dead or soon to be."

"What do you mean? He doesn't leave the city?"

"He commands the entire *Fortezza*. Why would he leave?"

"I don't know."

She stops now and turns to me, others passing us in the street, her eyes flashing with anger.

"Your jealousy is unbecoming, you know. All of you and your jealousy for what I have."

"Some would call it loyalty."

"*Loyalty*?" she asks, then laughs. "Loyalty to who? The British who've abandoned us? The Americans who refuse to come at all? They're all the same, all these men that rule over us. How can you not see that? How can you live your life based on some notion that nobility and honor still exist. A Greek husband? Sure. A German one? That's fine, too. Men are men, women are women, no matter what country they're from or fighting for or what language they speak, and we can't exist in this world without them. You're old enough. Surely you've learned that by now."

I don't answer, I just look back at her.

"You will," she says. "Soon enough, if you haven't, you will, as we all do."

Then she spits at my feet, her curse, and continues on through the city.

I watch for a moment as she disappears amongst the people coming and going, and when she's gone, lost again amongst them, I turn and go back to where Theos is waiting. When he sees me, he stands and we start walking to the road we took to get here—the one that winds in front of the *Fortezza*, between the giant castle and the sea—and that heads back south to the forests and where the rest are waiting.

"Did you speak to her?" Theos asks.

"Yes."

"What did she say?"

We keep going a few more paces as I look into the distance, the sun beginning to set, a breeze picking up from the opposite direction and bringing with it the taste of salt and the smell of fresh lavender from the mountains.

"Exactly what I needed her to," I tell him.

When we get back, I share with the others what I've learned.

They're skeptical.

Peter in particular, along with Evelyn, thinks that with only one way up the *Fortezza* it would be suicide to try to abduct or kill Muller, and would certainly result in all the rest of us getting killed, too.

"How many guards are at the gate?"

"A dozen," I say. "Maybe more."

"Madness," Peter shakes his head. "Madness, and impossible."

"So we wait until he leaves, and take him in the streets."

"What?" Peter looks back at me incredulously.

"He doesn't stay in the *Fortezza* all the time, and that's where I first saw him, in the streets. He was at a *kafeneio* by the Rimondi Fountain. So we wait and take him when he leaves. He doesn't stay up there every waking moment, he just doesn't leave the city, or go on any patrols."

"Why?" Tane asks.

"Because too many on this island know what he did, and are searching for him, for the same reason we are, I assume."

"Trying to take him in the city is also madness," Peter tells us. "Complete recklessness, and impossible."

"Why?"

"Because as soon as we do, every German in Rethymno will be upon us!" he yells. "And not just the ones at the *Fortezza,* all of them that are in Rethymno, and in case you've forgotten, we stand out. We don't blend in like you do, and Theos, or speak Greek, so we'd be fired upon in the streets before we even got to him."

I pause.

I think of the woman Muller sleeps with, and what she said to me, and I think of the streets and all who are there: the women, children, elderly.

"There's more than one entrance."

The voice comes from next to me, and I turn to see it's Theos that's spoken.

"What do you mean?" Peter asks, turning to the boy now.

"There's more than one entrance to the *Fortezza*."

"I only saw one way up and one way down," Owain says.

"When were you there?" Evelyn frowns.

"Before the Germans came. I was stationed in Rethymno."

"There are two other entrances," Theos says. "One's on the north side, that goes down to the sea, and one's on the west that leads out of town and back up to the mountains and forests here."

"And the Germans know about these, too?"

"Of course."

Everyone pauses.

"There are prisoners up there, also," I break the silence.

"*Prisoners*?" Peter turns back to me.

"They've started using the old Venetian prison, and there are prisoners being held who I assume would love to be able to fight again against their captors."

Everyone looks at each other. This could change things.

Abdel speaks up.

"So what would the plan be?" he asks.

"We sneak to the *Fortezza*," I tell them. "We go up the path on the west side, that Theos knows about. We release the prisoners, arm them with the weapons they're storing in the Ibrahim Han Mosque, then find Muller."

"When we do, the other Germans will still come," Peter says.

"And we'll fight them. We'll kill as many as we can, then leave the same way we got there."

There's silence.

There are looks between all the men and the boy that's amongst us, then finally small nods, and it's William now that turns back to Theos.

"And you can find this secret entrance?" he asks him.

"It's not secret. It's just hidden. And it's my city."

"What does that mean?"

"Of course I can find it."

"If anyone doesn't want to come," I speak slowly, and to everyone. "If anyone thinks it too much, just to kill one man, then you can stay behind."

There are no more words. There are only nods.

"We'll sleep tomorrow," Peter says. "Then we'll go the day after that."

25

MAY 23, 1943

We wait two days for everyone to get ready and outfit themselves, then once final preparations are made, and it's dark, we leave the forest and begin to head towards the sea. We go to a place west of Rethymno, where Germans won't find us, and that's where we'll wait until later in the night when they'll be least expecting anything and more of them will be asleep; all except the guards, who will only be awake because they have to be.

We're guided by the moon.

I show the others the way, then when we get there, we sit amongst the rocks as the sea gently laps against sand.

I hear a noise.

We all turn with weapons ready, then lower them when we see it's only Philippos with a rifle slung across his back and carrying a large basket as he carefully climbs down the same way we've just come.

He opens his basket.

It's fresh *spanakopita* his mother's made that he passes out to all of us, and I take two from him, look to William, and we walk down the beach together and sit on one of the rocks. I give him one of the pastries, keep the second for myself, then we both begin to eat.

Moonlight cascades over sea and stone.

It touches his face, too, casting it half in light, and half in shadow.

We chew in silence, then swallow.

There's a noise out in the sea, and I point to it.

"Look," I whisper.

"What?" he asks.

"Dolphins," I tell him, then watch as he squints and looks closer.

There's a ripple in the waves about a hundred yards from shore as a pod breaks the surface then dives again. They swim silently at night, and there looks to be about a dozen in the pod. I watch him as he watches them.

"Amazing," he breathes, quietly.

"They're the symbol of this city."

"Of Rethymno?"

"Yes."

"Why Rethymno and nowhere else on the coast?"

"I don't know," I tell him.

He reaches out and takes my hand.

I look down at it, his lighter skin juxtaposed against mine that's darker, then I turn and look back towards the sea.

"Are you alright?" he asks.

How can I tell him what I'm thinking, and what I'm feeling?

How can I tell him, without breaking his heart?

"I'm fine," I say instead, then we're silent again.

In front of us, the dolphins keep swimming, heading farther east like we soon will, too, then they're beyond a piece of rocky coast that juts into the sea and out of sight.

More time passes.

We sit there together as moonlight shifts and changes, and I look over at the others: most are sitting alone, after they've eaten their *spanakopita*, alone with thoughts and silent preparations for what will soon come, all except Theos and Philippos, who sit together and whisper in the darkness.

I can't hear what they say.

I can guess, though, as I watch Theos show Philippos the dagger he wears that belonged to his father, and Philippos shows him the dagger at his own waist that I can only assume he made himself.

Even more time passes.

I look up, gauging the position of the moon.

Then I squeeze William's hand.

He knows what that means.

We both stand from the rock where we've been with our thoughts, and each other, and start to walk back to the others. When they see us they stand, too, because they know what it means, seeing us, and Theos and Philippos stand, as well, and walk to join and take their place with us.

Peter sees them and shakes his head.

"No."

"We're coming with you," Theos says.

"We don't need to get any children killed," he tells them.

Theos opens his mouth to respond, but the words that come next come from me. "There are no more children on this island," I say, echoing the words I've of course heard before.

Peter turns to look at me. So do the others.

He recognizes the truth of what I've said, though, so just shakes his head then reaches down to pick up his rifle, and I turn to the boys.

"Watch out for each other," I tell them. "Stay close to each other, and don't take any unnecessary risks."

Theos nods.

So does Philippos.

"We will," he says.

"*Nai*," Theos agrees.

William pats them each on the back to give them courage and strength, then we turn and start down the beach, into the distance, guided only by instinct and memory, and the fading light of the once-bright moon.

卐

It's not long until we're there.

We walk most of the way near the sea, and when we get closer to the city and can see the giant shadow of the *Fortezza* in the distance on the massive point that juts out into the water, we climb the rocks back up towards the road.

We walk carefully now, and silently.

We hear something, a noise, an engine.

We scramble for cover in the bushes on the side of the road, but then the noise goes in the opposite direction, away from us, and then is gone altogether.

We come out from our hiding places.

We keep walking.

Soon we come to the base of the *Fortezza* without hearing or seeing anything else, and Theos shows us the path up the side that's obscured by bushes and dirt, so we sling the rifles we've been holding over our backs once more, and begin to climb again.

Theos goes first.

We follow after him.

Soon we reach the top and push aside a few more branches that Theos ducks under, and that's where he shows us the small door that's in the wall, there on the western side, just like he said it was, which is really just a gap in the stone wall with nothing to cover it.

I nod to him.

"*Efcharisto*," I whisper.

"This is far enough, lad," Peter whispers, also, trying one more time. "Take Philippos with you and meet us back by the beach."

"You shouldn't forget," Theos tells him.

"I shouldn't forget what?"

"They killed my father, too."

I see Peter look back at him, and his eyes: the flashing, brave eyes of this young Greek boy, this young Greek boy who is now a *palikari,* like all boys here are, and can he see it? Can he see the entire history of this island in this one look and this one boy? All the death, and blood, and sons avenging fathers, and burden that all of us carry because of who we are?

I don't know.

Peter doesn't say anything more.

He just looks at Theos, and Philippos next to him, then pushes past them and towards the door.

He silently climbs through.

There are *kubelwagens*, heavy artillery, and wooden carts for carrying food and ammunition that are blocking the way, to obscure the opening from the other side, so Peter climbs underneath these things first, then I follow after, and William follows after me, then Evelyn and the others, with the two Greek boys bringing up the rear.

Soon we're all there, on the other side.

Everything's quiet.

I point to the northeastern part of the plateau and cells beneath the walls there.

"That's the prison," I tell them.

"And the weapons?"

"In the mosque next to it, just there to the right," I whisper and point towards the large structure that's directly east of us and south of the prison.

"What about the German?"

"There," I say, and point now towards the house in the very middle of the fortress that I saw him enter with the Greek woman who sleeps with him.

Peter nods again.

"You'll go on our move and not before," he tells us, very quietly.

"Of course."

"Good," he says, then makes a signal and Tane, Owain, and Evelyn all begin to hurry and sneak through the long shadows of the night, but I make a soft whistle to stop them.

"What?"

"Take the boys," I tell him.

"No," he frowns.

"They speak Greek. The prisoners need to know who you are, and what you need them to do."

He looks at me for one more moment.

Then he finally nods, reluctantly, and I nod to Theos and Philippos and they go with Peter and the others, hugging against the wall, making their way towards the prison on the far side of the fortress.

I watch for a moment, then start to move, too.

I sneak from our hiding place near the wall to behind another building, William and Abdel following after me, doing the same thing with less cover in the middle of the fortress.

I wait.

There are no noises.

So we sneak once more across the distance to the next building, and we do this until we're finally to the house where Muller sleeps, this man who destroyed my entire world. These are ancient houses, built during the time of the Venetians and used by Greeks, Turks, and all sorts of others that the walls have protected.

Now, they protect a Nazi.

Not for long, though. Not for long.

I look over and see Peter and the others reach the prison.

There's no guard there, though, there's only the cells which means there's no key to open them, either, so they'll have to shoot the locks off. I see the prisoners start to stand, when they see these new soldiers in the darkness, and I see Theos and Philippos whispering to them before they back up.

Peter takes a pistol from his waist.

He turns to look at us. He nods.

So do we.

He puts the barrel of the pistol into the keyhole of the lock.

There's one more moment, all of us inhaling, holding our collective breath.

Then the shot rings out.

The bullet smashes into metal, but I see that the lock holds, and doesn't break.

People start to shout.

Peter raises his pistol again, but Tane pushes him aside.

He picks up a large rock and brings it down with all his strength, smashing it against the lock.

It still doesn't budge, so he strikes it again, and again.

Germans run from their houses now, to see what's happening.

"Come on," William says, grabbing my arm as we run into Muller's house.

Abdel stays behind to guard the door.

I follow William and my eyes begin to adjust to this place where there's no moonlight, just darkness, and the house isn't very big so as soon as we walk in, I see him.

I see her, too.

He goes to jump from the bed where they lay together, then he sees us and William's pistol pointed at him, so he raises his hands in the universal sign of surrender.

The Greek woman looks at me, recognition in her eyes.

"You?" she asks, but I ignore her.

Outside, I hear gunshots, which is of course because of the other Germans who have found their weapons and we're fighting back against them.

Have we freed the Greeks?

I hope so.

It's how we'll survive. It's the only way we'll survive.

"We need to hurry!" I hear Abdel call to us, from outside the house.

I take the dagger from my left hip, the one that belonged to my father, and I walk towards them near the bed and I hold it so he can see what it is that's now in my hand.

Muller sits there, in front of me, the sheet wrapped around him.

"Do you remember me?" I ask.

"Should I?"

"This is my father's dagger. You ordered his entire village burned and looted, and everyone killed, and now—"

I want him to know who I am.

I want him to know why I'm here, and to remember what he's done and who it is that's about to take his life, but before I can finish, he jumps from the bed, completely naked, and runs towards a chair in the corner where his own pistol hangs from a belt and William fires, but Muller ducks, and the bullet misses.

I swing my father's dagger.

I aim for his chest, but he jumps backward so the dagger misses his chest and pierces the flesh of his leg, in his upper thigh.

He doesn't cry out.

He grabs his pistol and spins to fire again.

William ducks and Muller's bullet also misses.

I rip my dagger out and that's when I hear him cry in pain as he turns back and swings a fist that catches me in the jaw, and I fall to the ground.

Behind me, the Greek woman screams, and she doesn't stop.

Then in a blur, I see William rush past me and tackle Muller.

He's on top of him.

He gets in a blow to the German's face, then another, then another still.

Muller drops his pistol.

William takes it and stands.

He aims both weapons down at Muller who lays panting on the ground, blood gushing from his nose, mouth, and the wound on his leg.

I grip my dagger tighter as I stand.

I can taste blood in my mouth, too.

I walk towards him and begin to raise my dagger again, about to bring it down squarely into his chest and end his life, but before I can, another shot rings out and his head snaps back.

It's William that's fired.

It's William that's killed him.

I open my mouth but he grabs me by the elbow, instead.

"We have to go," he says, but I shake loose of him.

I look down at Muller and the blood spilling from his head across the floor, because I want to remember this.

I will.

I will remember it, and will there be peace?

I don't know.

I can hope. I can only hope.

William tries to grab me again but I shake loose once more and go to where the Greek woman's clothes are neatly folded on the dresser, and I take them, then turn and walk back to the bed where she's still naked under the sheets.

"There are things in this world that are easy," I tell her. "And there are also things in this world that are not, but are right. Perhaps you'll choose differently next time."

There's fear in her eyes. There's terror.

Good.

There should be.

There should be for what she's done and she nods, very small, and I hand her clothes to her before turning and following William towards Abdel and before we get there, and to the door, I unsling the rifle from my back, and so does he.

We duck and go outside.

There's a firefight in the *Fortezza*, bullets flying in every direction.

I look across from where we stand, towards the prison.

I see the Greek captives that have been released and are now fighting along with the rest of us, and they've fought their way to the Ibrahim Han mosque and killed the guards there so they can take the weapons stored in the mosque: the pistols, rifles, and grenades.

Some of the Greeks fall.

Some of the Germans that come from the gate and their houses fall, too.

I hear Peter yell.

"*Fall back!*" he shouts, as loudly as he can. "*This way, fall back!*"

William touches me on the arm again.

We start to run across the distance, William in front and leading us, me in the middle, then Abdel behind and bringing up the rear, until all of a sudden there's a German officer in front of us.

He rushes from his house, only half dressed.

William crashes into him and they both fall heavily to the ground.

The German officer holds onto his pistol.

William loses his grip on his rifle, and drops it in the grass.

The German raises his pistol, about to fire, but I bring my rifle around and he's so close I don't even bother to aim, I just fire, and a bullet explodes then rips into the German's chest and he's lifted from his feet and from William and is thrown to the ground again.

This time, he lies still.

He doesn't move, and he won't.

I run over and grab William's hand and pull him to his feet and he reaches down and grabs the German's pistol before we keep running, along with Abdel, and soon we're back to the western edge of the fortress and the small, hidden gap where we entered not very long ago.

We take cover behind the *kubelwagens* that are there.

We fire into darkness and across the distance as the rest of our group makes it back, then does the same, and the Greek prisoners come, too.

There's not much death now.

The Germans have cover behind the buildings.

We have our own cover behind their *kubelwagens* that have been parked and put here to try to cover and hide what will now be our escape.

I see Theos and Philippos.

Philippos has a large bruise across his face, and a bloodied lip, but they're alive, they're both alive.

I see the others, too.

I breathe a sigh of relief.

Peter waves for some of us to start heading down and away while the rest of us cover, and I stay above with my rifle and since they know my marksmanship skills, they let me.

I fire.

I fire again.

My shots don't hit anything but they keep Germans pinned where they are behind the buildings, as bullets bury into stone that has seen so much war, pain, death, and suffering.

Tonight is no different. We are no different.

It's soon time and Peter makes another motion with his hand and after a few more shots, we sling our rifles across our backs then turn and hurry down towards the road below.

We get there.

The others are waiting.

We hear noises in the distance again, the sound of engines roaring to life, so we begin to run.

Theos leads us and we leave the road and head south.

Then we begin to climb.

That's what we do because the terrain is rocky, and that's why we chose this path because it's terrain that's impassable to anyone who doesn't know their way; but Theos, the son of a shepherd, brought his flock here every day to graze, so he knows every inch of this land.

We climb and climb.

We go first, and the Greek prisoners we've freed follow after us.

At one point, I turn and look back in the direction we came and see a caravan of lights on the road we've just left.

Kubelwagens.

An army of Germans looking for us.

They won't find us, though, where their vehicles can't travel and where we're hidden in darkness.

We continue on.

We continue on through that darkness, up and away from those who would try to kill us, on our own island, in our own land, as the sun starts to rise in the distance, and a new day finally begins.

26

JUNE 2, 1943

There are nineteen Greeks that have survived and been freed, and come to join us in the mountains. I learn the man who became their leader in prison and then after, too, is named Antonis and most of them don't speak English, so I translate, when we first arrive back at camp, but then realize they have Theos and Philippos, and they can translate, too, so I leave and go to my tent.

William watches as I go.

Then he follows after me.

I go to the cot we normally share as outside all the Greeks, British, and everyone else start to open bottles of wine and pour *raki* and drink to being free, and making it back from Rethymno alive, and killing Germans and all else that's happened.

But I feel no such joy or satisfaction.

William comes to the cot.

He goes to lay on it with me, like he normally does, but this time I push him away.

He knows why. He looks down at me.

"It was a gift," he says.

"What?" I answer, frowning.

"Once day you'll realize it was a gift, and the greatest one you could ever possibly receive," he tells me, then turns and leaves the tent.

He doesn't come back.

I don't know where he goes but I sleep the entire next day and night, and when he returns the morning after that to change his clothes, I reach and grab him and pull him down to me.

I push my lips against his lips.

I pull his body into mine, too.

I've been somewhere else, but I slowly start to return, then I leave while William's still sleeping and go to check the traps we set before we left. The nineteen Greeks that have been added to our camp are of course welcome company and eager to help kill Germans, but it'll be harder to feed everyone now. So I walk through the mountains and check the traps, which takes me until about midday, when the sun is high and bright, and I only find a single rabbit that I pick up by its legs and carry with me.

I head back towards our camp.

I walk through the part of the forest where I know there's a lake not very far away, and that's when I hear the voices, young voices, and they're whispering, laughing, speaking in Greek to each other.

I pause.

I can't make out what the voices say so I walk towards them and that's when I see Theos and Philippos on the stones together next to the water in just their shorts, their arms over their heads and elbows and touching as the sun beats down and tans their already tanned skin.

I open my mouth.

I'm about to call to them, then Philippos stands, and I don't.

He reaches down and helps Theos to his feet, and they both take their shorts off and run and jump into the lake together with a loud splash.

They wrestle.

They play-fight and struggle against each other, in the water, then stop, and they don't.

Their faces are inches apart.

They breathe.

I breathe, too.

Even at this distance, I can see their chests rising and falling in the water, in unison, next to each other.

Philippos is slightly taller than Theos and he's the one that leans down, closer, and as soon as their faces are nearly together, their lips almost touching, I turn away.

I know what comes next.

I don't wish to intrude, though.

This is their moment and their love, and that's exactly what it should be, theirs and only theirs and not the world's, too, so I turn and go back the way I came before they see me and feel they have to explain themselves, or anything else, because they don't need to.

I think the sight of this, of love, and their love, will ease some of the darkness I feel.

It doesn't.

Instead, it makes me question the world in which we live in that these two boys who have done absolutely nothing wrong, and so much right, have to retreat to the forest and hide amongst trees and lakes to be who they are and as they were made, and experience love with the person they've found that makes them feel that. Once, when I'd first started dating Demetrios, he'd told me something his father had said to him and that had been told to him by his own father, after the Turkish wars. He said he fought for all the young people of the world, because that's who the world would belong to, and so it was their job to then take the world and shape it and mold it in their own image: one of youth, and beauty, and also one that's better than what they were left by those who came before them.

I keep walking.

I return to the mountains and our camp and I go back to the tent where William lays on the cot with his shirt off because of the heat, and reads a book. I go to him and lay on the cot, too, and kiss him, and he puts the book down and holds me as we lay there together.

He just holds me.

I want to stay there like that, in his arms and with my skin pressed against his skin and sticking together as our sweat mixes, then I hear something.

My name.

I pause.

I hear it again.

I recognize Peter's voice, but don't know why he'd be calling me, so I give William a look as I stand from the cot and walk outside.

Once I do, I stop.

I see Cassia standing there, along with Tasos, who looks like he's aged ten years in as many months, and I run to them and hug Tasos first, then Cassia, and look past them and see that Kyriaki has come, too.

And I see what she's holding.

A young child, a baby.

Her son. Ikaros's son.

I look to the others, to Cassia, then Tasos, searching for answers as to why they're here, but Tasos has no eyes for me. Instead, I follow his eyes as they move and look behind me, to where William is coming from the same tent I've just come from, putting his shirt on and buttoning it as he walks forward and towards us.

1944

27

APRIL 13, 1944

When they arrive in the mountains, the first thing I ask about is the baby, and Kyriaki tells me she named him after Ikaros, Ikaros's father, and hers, so his name is Ikaros Anastasios Giannis. I glance at William when I hear this, but he just smiles as he stands there next to me. I think of the last night I saw Ikaros, the last time I saw him alive, when he promised he'd come to visit her after her doctor's appointment, and what I'd whispered to him in response.

She's doing wonderful, I'd said.

She is wonderful, he'd answered, *and she'll be the best mother.*

If only he was here to see.

I then ask them how they found us, and why they came, and the answer to how is the same way that I did: they walked to the mountains and went to all the villages and instead of asking where to find the British, they asked where they could find a single female *palikari* from the valley south of Chania, and it wasn't very hard from there. The why turns out to be different than what I expected, and strangely because of us, and what we've done. After our attack on the *Fortezza* and murder of Friedrich-Wilhelm Muller, all the Germans in the rest of the major cities—in Chania, and Rethymno, and Irakleio—they were all put on high alert and have become even more strict. They stop any man or boy they see now, regardless of age, and oftentimes take them straight to prison. They stop women, too, and the elderly, so when rumors started to spread, then Cassia saw it herself, in the form of a boy about the same age as Tasos who was beaten on the *limani* simply for trying to sell fish, they knew they had to go.

When Cassia tells me all this, I watch Tasos, who stands there with his eyes turned down.

Then when she finishes, he immediately spins on his heels and walks away.

He's upset.

Of course I know why.

I will not apologize, not to him, or anyone, but I understand, so I let a few days pass as he begins to adjust to life in the camp. He becomes friends with Philippos and Theos, who are the only other boys his age, and they give him a pistol to carry from some of the many they've taken for themselves and show him where their traps are in the forest and bring him with them when they go to check the traps. They show him these parts of the mountains he doesn't yet know well. Then, one day, when Tasos is back and sitting on a log by himself with one of the rabbits they've caught, using a kitchen knife to skin it and get it ready to make *kouneli stifado*, a rabbit stew, I go and sit next to him.

He doesn't say anything, just keeps skinning the rabbit.

I lean closer, so that our shoulders touch.

"When did you get taller than me?" I ask.

"I don't know," he answers, still not looking up. "Probably a while ago."

"You should use this," I say, then take Giannis's dagger and hand it to him. I took it from the burned remains of the house where his father both lived and died, and I took it and kept it amongst my things for this moment.

He looks down at it, recognizing it, what I have and am giving to him.

He sits there looking at the dagger, then finally reaches out and slowly takes it and looks down at it in his hand, too, feeling it, turning it over, and perhaps feeling his father again, and his mother, and his past and the tragedy that's defined it.

He still doesn't look up, or at me.

"My father's dagger has the blood of the man who killed him on it," I tell him.

He's silent for another moment.

"Is that why you went to the *Fortezza*?" he finally asks.

"Yes."

"What about this one? What blood does it have?"

"This one will be yours now, so it will have only what you give it."

He still doesn't look at me, just down at the dagger, at the log where we sit, at the grass, anywhere but meeting my eyes so I reach over and gently put my hand on his cheek.

I turn his face so that it looks at mine, so his eyes meet my eyes.

"I know why you're upset, Tasos, but you're my family. Nothing changes that. You, that boy, and Kyriaki are the only family any of us have left. Do you understand?"

I keep looking at him.

There are tears in his eyes.

He doesn't want them to come, but they do, and he nods then finally wipes at them.

"Yes," he says.

"Good," I tell him. "So don't be upset for too long, alright?"

I put my hand on his back, for a moment, so he can feel me, so he can feel that I'm there with and for him, and always will be.

Then I stand and walk away.

A few days later, I wake to find William gone before the sun.

When I get up and walk through camp, I find that Tasos is gone, too.

They're away for three days together and neither say anything to me before they leave, they just disappear, then one day I see them returning together, as well. I stand at the top of the mountain and watch as they climb the path back up and towards us, the unmistakable silhouette of William walking with the slight limp he'll never get rid of and the tall boy next to him who is no longer a boy at all.

They see me standing there.

They reach me.

Tasos doesn't say anything, just simply gives me a hug, then walks past and back to the camp and I look at William.

He kisses me.

I kiss him back.

I don't ask where he took Tasos, or what he said to him, and I won't; I won't ask either of them. But from that point forward, Tasos seems to change and accept us, and we settle into a new life. We get bread from the village to eat with the *kouneli stifado* that Cassia and Kyriaki help prepare, then after the bread starts to get tough, we use it to make *dakos* which Antonis and the rest of the Greek soldiers devour, and the British, too, which is of course the national dish of this island and made from the hard rusks of bread drizzled with olive oil and topped with diced tomatoes, salty mizithra cheese, and some *rigani* sprinkled over it all that we pick from the hills where it grows wild and fresh near our camp.

We also continue to look for Hannes Koch.

We travel the length and breadth of the island in search of him.

William and Tasos come with me, and we go to Chania, and Irakleio, and Malia, and Agios Nikolaos, and even as far away as Sitia, in the east where the soldiers that hold the city aren't German, but Italians. We don't go into any of the cities themselves and instead meet with people in the villages outside the cities, in the mountains, and they help us; they tell us what they've seen, or they go into their cities and ask those that still live there what they've seen, and if anyone knows or has heard of Hannes Koch.

We get nowhere. We find nothing.

Even Cassia helps, going to Chania to meet with other girls she knows, ones that travel between cities, too, and sleep with German officers everywhere on the island, and they can't seem to find him, either.

Tasos and I have been family for a long time now.

But it's during these weeks and days we become a new type of family, the two of us, together, with William, too.

We travel the length and breadth of the island, as I've said, but it's the small moments between the travel that stand out; it's the moments when we stop and make camp, and before we've eaten when William takes Tasos away to a field to teach him how to shoot a rifle. He shows him how to hold the butt steady against his shoulder and a great many other things that I can only assume are things about war that men need to know and would normally be told to him by his father and brothers. Tasos listens and solemnly nods, internalizing each lesson, waiting until his day will come to fight, too, and help defend his island.

The days are peaceful.

They're so peaceful I almost forget what we're doing, and that we've failed, especially when we return from a long trip with still no signs of Koch. We get back to our camp and find Peter and Evelyn have gone to Balos to meet another submarine from the SOE, to get more supplies. So we spend our days with little Ikaros, and Cassia and I go for walks amongst the hills, in the spring sun, and one time we even leave Ikaros with William and Tasos and invite Kyriaki to come with us, just the three of us while the boys watch the baby. When we return, though, they tell us with wide eyes that we can never leave the baby alone with them again and we just smile and laugh and take Ikaros back and comfort him and begin to prepare our evening meal as William and Tasos take their shirts off and go for a jog amongst the peaks, which is something else they've started doing together.

I ask William about this one night, when we're alone in the tent.

He says that Tasos runs faster and faster, and can go for longer distances, the muscles in his legs beginning to swell and grow and he has long strides. He can't yet beat William, though, either in speed or distance, even with his limp. He's close, William says, and I feel him smile against my skin, his lips pressed against my back and neck, and I think it's pride I feel him smile with, pride in the boy he's helped and begun to think of as his own brother, or son, or perhaps a mix between those two things.

The other thing I do during these days, along with Kyriaki, is sew a backpack.

We start a small garden near the camp where we grow vegetables and some herbs that don't grow wild near us, like the *vasilikos* and *anithos* that Cassia in particular loves, that grow naturally at lower elevations. So we pick some and bring it up to the mountains with us to grow in our own garden and we make the backpack to hold Ikaros, and Tasos wears it on his back with Ikaros strapped in as he bounces up and down near where we pick and prune and water the herbs, singing a lullaby to the baby to try to get him to sleep.

He doesn't sleep.

He sees his mother, though, so he doesn't cry either.

He just watches as we work.

It's nearly *Pascha* so while I work in the garden with Cassia, Kyriaki, and the baby, Theos and Philippos, along with most of the men, construct an *epitaphios,* which is a large structure representing Christ's tomb that houses within it an icon of the dead body of Christ, waiting to be resurrected, decorated with fresh flowers of purple, white, and yellow that they've picked from the hills near us. William helps them and they explain to him and the rest of the British what it is, and that after it's completed, it will be paraded through the village at midnight.

Or in this case, just through our camp, because we're not in a village.

And that's when they return.

They've been gone for a few days, and I see Tasos look first—with Ikaros on his back laughing as Tasos bounces his nephew up and down—then raise his arm in greeting as Peter, Evelyn, Owain, and Tane climb the path back towards us.

They carry duffels full of supplies and weapons.

I expect them to go to their tents, to put the supplies away and store everything safely, but they don't.

Instead, they come straight to me.

Peter stands there, right in front of where I stand.

He meets my eyes.

"What is it?" I ask.

He hands me a note, a piece of paper.

I look down at it and see a name, and location.

"We found him," he says.

28

APRIL 14, 1944

Easter will go on as planned.

Then once it's finished, we'll all head east, because that's where Hannes Koch is and it's the SOE that have found him, not us. He's committed more crimes than just what he's done to my village, which is no surprise, so it turns out he's wanted by a great deal more than just us, and the SOE themselves want him to be eliminated now, too, which makes our job even more clear and not just revenge, but following orders, as well.

I'm surprised when I see the location, where the Germans have stationed him.

He's holed up in a villa outside of Knossos, just south of Irakleio, and near the ruins of the ancient Minoan city. And while at first I was surprised, after I think about it further, I'm not. If he's committed so many atrocities even the British are after him, that means he can't show his face in the cities, but there, in Knossos, he's still close enough to the capital and main garrison to give orders through intermediaries and stay informed of everything that's happening on the island.

It makes sense.

Since we can't go to any of the nearby villages for *Pascha*, for fear of being seen or found by the Germans, especially on a holiday like this when they're sure to be looking for us, the villagers instead come to us on Friday night. They come in pairs and families, and we all stand together as the flaps to Philippos's tent open and he comes out carrying the *epitaphios,* along with Theos, Tasos, and three other teenage boys from nearby villages. They walk through our camp that with so many people now has begun to feel like a village. We follow behind them. The night ends and the next day comes and a priest comes and joins us, too, and darkness soon falls again and the villagers pass out the *lambades* that they've brought—colored and decorated candles they've made and brought for all of us—then midnight arrives and the priest leads us in his chant and we turn to the person next to us and say *Christos Anesti*, and they answer by saying *Alithos Anesti*, then we all go and have a big feast, lit by the light from our *lambades* that we don't let go out.

After we've eaten and drank, William and I go back to our tent.

I carry our candles and tell him how we can't put them out, because the light they carry is blessed and holy light, so when we get inside, I prop them in the corner then stand and face him. He gently reaches out and slips the corner of my dress from one shoulder first, then the other, so that soon I stand naked in the flickering light of the resurrection. I pull his shirt up and over his head. Then I uncinch his belt, and let his trousers fall, and he steps out of them so that he's naked, too, and I move closer so our skin touches, inches away from the flames that leap and jump and cast shadows across the linen walls, and across us.

We go to the cot.

He lays down and I move so I'm on top of him, and when our love begins, I realize it's different now, not like it was at Phaistos, when it was the love of discovery, and beginnings.

It's still beautiful.

But it's different, and we both recognize it, I think, there in the flickering darkness with nothing else between us but skin and light, and all we've been through together, all that we've become.

After it's over, we hold each other and I think about what the next day will bring.

I think about the eggs that are already being dyed red, the smell of incense that will wake us in the morning, and the three young lambs that the villagers brought that they'll kill and show the British how to roast on a spit over an open fire, and then I think about what will happen after.

I think about Knossos, and I think about Hannes Koch.

This will be the last thing.

This will be the last, and final thing.

29

APRIL 21, 1944

We get everything ready at camp, then begin to head east towards Knossos.

Cassia and Kyriaki stay with the baby, and in a perfect world I would have liked for Tasos, or Theos and Philippos, or at least some of the others to have stayed with them, too, but this world is not perfect. Neither Tasos, Theos, nor Philippos will hear talk of any of them staying behind, so they come with us. Tasos especially will not hear anything about not fighting as I'm sure he thought for a long time it might be too late for him to do his part, but the war has lasted long enough that he's pleased he'll get to fight as well, just like his brothers did. It's strange, but I'm pleased he will, also. It will help him. I would be a hypocrite if I didn't think so, right? I've thought and hoped it will help me, when all this is finished and done, so I think it will help him, too, and in the same way.

Or at least I hope it does, and what else is there anymore?

I don't guide us this time.

Our number has swelled and there are more Greeks and locals, too, and more from this area where we'll now go—east of Chania, which is less familiar to me—so Theos and Philippos help, and so does Antonis, and the other Greeks from Rethymno that have stayed and go with us. We go past their own city and villages, just east of Chania, then on towards the one that houses the man that the SOE, at least, has dubbed "the Butcher of Crete."

How many others?

How many other villages has he destroyed, and innocent men, women, and children has he killed to earn that name?

I don't know.

But it will end.

Now, it will all end for him.

The other thing I learn is that while there were weapons and ammunitions in the duffels that Peter and Evelyn and the others brought from the SOE, there was also something else: German field uniforms. The others say this will make what we have to do easier, but I realize what it actually means, and how dangerous this will be, and how close to the Germans we'll have to get in order to pull this off and get to Koch who must be extremely well hidden and protected.

We will, though.

We will, or we'll die trying.

We pass the hills above Rethymno around midday, not too far from where we made our previous camp, and as we walk, William's hand brushes against mine and I think it's just an accident. Then I realize it's not, when it does again, and he reaches out. It's just a finger that intertwines with my finger, at first, as we walk, then his entire hand takes mine in his, and we continue like that. It's strange, but somehow still feels natural. I'm surprised that it does. Nobody looks at us or pays any attention to us and what we do, not even Tasos, who's next to Theos and Philippos and a few other boys who have come from Rethymno and it must be hard for them; it must be hard to be this close to their city, and families, and not be able to go to them.

One day they'll be able to.

Hopefully, that day will be soon.

We keep walking through the mountains and they begin to thin and soften, as we get closer to Irakleio, until they become flat and there's a plateau and field of flowers we have to go through before coming to the next set of hills that will provide us with some cover, and we stop.

"This is where we become Nazis," Peter says.

We understand.

He starts passing out German uniforms and the men all begin to change, putting their Greek clothes into the duffels and I'm the only woman that's there, so William and I find uniforms that will fit, then he takes my hand again and leads me away past some trees and towards a stream, and we stand there together.

He changes into the German uniform.

I change into one, too, and he helps me with the jacket, buttoning the shirt underneath it, his face close to my face.

He leans even closer.

We kiss.

He laughs because it's so strange, what we're wearing, both of us in German clothes now.

I laugh, too.

We put the hats on that go with the uniform and that will help obscure our faces, to any who might see from a distance, then I smile and we turn and start to jog back towards the others, but they've already started to walk again, so we keep jogging across the field of flowers that reach above our knees until we finally rejoin them. Tane is at the back, walking next to one of the Greeks from Rethymno, and they turn to look at us when we get there, and nod to us.

We nod, too.

William's hand finds mine once more and we continue.

There are a few more hills then soon we come from them and to the valley south of Knossos and Irakleio. We meet a local shepherd with his flock on one of the roads that crisscross between still-snowcapped peaks. We ask him about shelter, and he tells us about a system of caves above the village of Kastamonitsa, not far from Knossos, and that's where we decide to go. He tells us it's an area heavy with Greek resistance, so when we arrive, we go to Kastamonitsa first, speaking Greek words loudly as we come so they know who we are, and we buy food and supplies. None of the men, women, or children blink when they meet us nor do they hesitate in selling us anything we need, even though if it's found out, it will result in their deaths. They don't care, though. We ask them about the caves and they point into the distance and at one peak in particular, called Afendis, and that's where we go. It's not hard to find them. I'm stunned there's enough room for all of us if we pair off, or go in threes, and William and I take some of the *kalitsounia* we bought in the village and they're not as good as the *kalitsounia* from the baker on the road to Elafonisi, but it's nice to have warm food after the cured beef from a can and tins of vegetables we've eaten from the British rations during this journey.

We build a fire.

In front of us, the sun sinks and we finish eating the *kalitsounia,* then just sit there, with the fire we've made, and the setting sun in front of us.

Silence.

We're both still dressed as Germans, and what a strange sight it must be, if there was anyone else here to see it.

But there's not. There's just us.

"There was a time when this island was the center of the world," I speak very quietly.

"What?" he asks, turning to me.

"Even Athens paid tribute. Even Aegeus and the great heroes of the mainland paid us tribute and sent gold and slaves to this island, this place of minotaurs, labyrinths, and great myths of gold and wings."

"Perhaps it still is."

"Still is what?"

"The center of the world. At least for this moment, and in this war."

"And perhaps that's who we all still are, too, all of us who are here. Princes and princesses, just like in the stories, struggling to find our way through an unknowable labyrinth and avoiding the beast at the end of it, the only way we know how."

"And how's that?"

"Through love, of course."

He thinks about that for a moment.

Then he speaks again, turning to look at me now, and not the setting sun and brilliant display of colors in front of us.

"It's not about avoiding the beast."

"What?"

"It's about *killing* the beast, isn't it? Ariadne's love for Theseus is what helped him to do that, with the weapon she gave him, and string to find his way back out of the labyrinth again."

"Then what happens?"

"What do you mean?"

"He goes to take her back to Athens, but before they reach the city, he decides to leave her on Naxos."

"Really?"

"Yes."

"I didn't know that part. That's awful."

"But only too common, I'm afraid. The earliest versions of the story say after she was abducted, then abandoned, she hung herself in grief."

"And Theseus?"

"He sailed home to Athens but forgot to change the color of his sails, so when his father saw the boats returning, he thought his son had died and threw himself off a cliff into the sea."

"The Aegean?"

"That's how it got its name, from Aegeus, the King of Athens who jumped from the rocks and to his death in it."

"What was it called before that?"

"I don't know. Something else, I suppose, but now it bears the name of the grief-stricken father and serves as our reminder of those two things that have never left us, and never will."

"Grief and tragedy."

"Yes."

"Just like your stories."

"That's right."

"So change it."

"What?" I turn to look at him now.

"You told me the early version of what happened to Ariadne. That means there must be another one, too, right?"

"Yes."

"What happens in that version?"

"She marries a god."

"So change the story. We might all be lost in a labyrinth in this world, struggling to kill the beast that haunts us and find our way back out again, which means there's still time to escape, as there always is. There's still time to change the story, and turn it into our own."

I look back at him.

He looks at me.

Now it's my turn to lean over and kiss him, and he kisses me back, then we move apart and just sit there again. We sit there as the fire keeps burning, lower and lower, bringing us closer to the hour and day when I'll be able to change my story, just like Ariadne, another daughter of this ancient island, though unlike her, I am not alone.

30

APRIL 27, 1944

We learn that the villa where Hannes Koch is staying is named Villa Ariadne, and I smile wryly when I hear this. So does William. We spend the next days after we arrive in the caves above Kastamonitsa scouting the hills closer and closer to the villa, then one afternoon, we even go to the ruins at Knossos themselves and find them empty and abandoned and are able to walk amongst the tall columns that are there and into the throne room that's still standing. We all look at it in awe, taking in everything, feeling the history, but can't stay for too long, so we continue beyond the ruins, towards the villa, to a place we can watch who comes and goes, and how, and at what times.

We discover a pattern.

Koch leaves the villa every day at noon, and while we don't yet know where he goes, his car leaves and is followed by two others as well as a number of *kubelwagens* with heavily armed soldiers in them. We watch as they drive past where we hide in the hills, and we wait and watch as they come back, too, towards the luxury villa where the general has been staying and giving his commands for the control, subjugation, and torture of our island.

Not for much longer, though.

Not for much longer now at all.

We start to return to the caves, each with our own thoughts of how best to move forward from here: a full-on assault against the well-protected villa would certainly lead to more loss of life than we're willing to endure, and it would give Koch a chance to escape during the fighting, which we can't accept. Attacking his car on the road brings problems, also, because he only leaves the villa during the day. We'd have the element of surprise, if we attacked him on the road, but the Germans in his convoy would outnumber us and who knows how many more would come once the noise of battle echoes between the hills since this area is so full of Germans, being so close to Irakleio and their main headquarters.

Darkness is what we need.

But how do we get him in the open, and at night?

That's what we debate as we walk back, making calculations and assessing risk, and we're walking through the field of knee-high flowers again when we see a group of soldiers in the distance.

Peter raises his hand.

He motions to us and we quickly dive to the ground before the soldiers see us and I lay next to William. Ahead of me, I see Tasos with Theos and Philippos, breathing heavily. While this won't be the first action for Theos and Philippos, it will be for Tasos, and it looks as if it will be soon, too, because the soldiers aren't following the road; they're walking through the field instead, the same as we have, heading straight towards where we hide.

I look around, gripping my rifle a little bit tighter as I ready myself but Peter, at the front of our lines, seems to notice something as they get closer.

Then he speaks, loud enough that they'll hear.

"There's three dozen of us here, and we're about to stand from the grass!" he calls.

In front of us, all the enemy soldiers go on high alert, whipping rifles around, searching for where this voice just came from.

"What?" their leader calls. "Who the bloody hell are you?"

When I hear those words and accent, I smile.

They're British.

"We're going to look like Germans," Peter says in return, because we're still wearing the uniforms. "But we're not."

"Why should we think that!"

"Have you ever heard a Nazi speak English this well?"

"A million times. The king's own brother is a Nazi!"

Peter and Evelyn and the rest of the British all stifle laughs at that, then Peter continues.

"I suppose you'll just have to trust us, then, and that we could have killed you before I spoke. We're coming out, alright?"

A moment.

The British leader, in front of us, looks at his men, who just shrug, then he nods.

"Alright," he finally says.

Peter leaves his rifle on the ground, then slowly stands amongst the flowers with his arms raised.

He faces the new soldiers across from him, all their rifles pointed at his chest.

"Where are you from?" the leader asks.

"London."

"I hate blokes from London."

"We only lived there because my father was an MP for Henley."

The leader looks back at Peter, narrowing his eyes, then starts to lower his rifle.

Behind him, all the others do, too.

Then the rest of us begin to stand.

I look across and see there's about a dozen British soldiers, their leader walks closer, and once he reaches Peter, he sticks out his hand.

"Arnold Lawrence," he says.

"Peter Fleming."

And they shake.

"So are you going to tell me, Mr. Peter Fleming, why you're all dressed as Nazis?"

Peter nods and proceeds to tell them what brought us here, and they do the same and tell us how they've been operating on the eastern side of the island, just as we've been operating on the western side, and they're returning from a mission against the Italian troops stationed near Sitia. They tell us they lost contact with the SOE some months ago, though, so we then tell them what our mission is and eyes go wide when we tell them Hannes Koch is staying in the Villa Ariadne, near the ruins at Knossos.

"The Butcher?" Arnold asks, incredulous.

"The very same," Peter nods.

"How can we help?"

Peter explains what our deliberations have been and how we've been trying to decide the best way to get to him, with minimal loss of life, and as he does, Arnold interrupts and tells us that taking his convoy at night is of course the best option, and knows how we can do it, also.

"How?" Peter asks.

"We have a spy inside the villa."

"You must be joking."

"I'm not. It's the cousin of one of the Greeks we've met in Kounavi, and she was brought there as a maid, along with some other Greek women from her village."

So we finally have our plan.

We tell them where to find us in the caves before they continue west and north to Kounavi to deliver the message of what we need, then two days later they meet us at the caves. They tell us they've spoken with the woman who works in the villa and there are two dates in Koch's diary in which he has evening engagements he'll be leaving the villa for, after dark.

May 3rd.

May 6th.

I think it's the first one we'll choose, because why wait another three days, so I'm surprised when Peter tells them it'll be May 6th.

I ask him about this. He's firm, though.

It must be May 6th, and doesn't give a reason why.

It doesn't matter, though, because I've waited this long, so what are a few more days? They're nothing because retribution is finally coming for the Butcher, it's coming soon, and just as I've wanted, it's me that's going to bring it.

31

MAY 6, 1944

The day quickly arrives.

We force ourselves to sleep while the sun is up, because it will of course be a very long night, and while I lay in the cave with William next to me, sleep doesn't come. It does for him, though, as I feel his body next to mine and chest gently rising and falling in steady rhythm. Then as darkness returns, I eventually stand. I once thought my life would be a love story. Could it still be one again? I look down at William sleeping in our cave and he looks younger to me when he's asleep, laying there like he is. Is it because he's vulnerable when he's like this? I don't know. And I realize I don't even know how old he is. Does it matter? No, it doesn't, of course it doesn't. If I've learned anything from war, it's all that matters is the moment in which we're alive, and perhaps shouldn't that always be what matters, and the only thing that matters.

I don't know.

Maybe there will still be time to find out.

Maybe there will still be time for second and third and fourth lives, after this life of revenge, rather than love. There's only one way to find out, though, and only one path to whatever life will come after this one, so I gently wake William and when he's up and dressed, we silently leave the cave together to search for that path. With the new British soldiers, we number around fifty, so near enough to how many Germans we anticipate we'll face, but even with the weapons from the SOE, the Germans will still be better armed and equipped, and they have vehicles, too, and the roads.

We're about to leave, but then we stop.

We see Tane in front of us, in his cave, facing towards the last rays of departing light and he does another *haka*, his Maori dance, and we all stand and watch and I feel something. I can tell William, next to me, and Tasos, who comes and stands on the other side of us and who hasn't seen this before feel something, too, then when the dance is over, Tane joins us, and we all leave.

We walk back through the field of flowers.

I look at Tasos as he goes in front of us, dressed in his loose-fitting German uniform, head bowed as he walks and he looks young; he looks so very young, and for the first time in a long time, a wave of sadness crashes over me.

This is a child.

Is it, though?

I once repeated that there were no children left on Crete, but was I correct?

I shake my head because there'll be time for thoughts like this later, I know, thoughts of the lives we could have had, but those lives have been taken, and that's why we're here.

"What is it?" William whispers next to me.

I shake my head, not wanting to talk about it; not now, and not tonight.

He doesn't press me.

We skirt around Archanes, and we're sure to give the village a wide berth because of all the Germans there, then come to the road that's on the south side of it, between Archanes and Irakleio. In Koch's diary, it said his appointment was to meet a group of other high-ranking Germans officers in Irakleio for a dinner engagement, so this is the route we think he'll take, and the place we'll take him before he gets there.

There isn't much cover.

We come up with a plan anyway, though, and one that takes into account the landscape: while most of us will hide in the ditches, Tasos and some younger Greeks, wearing German uniforms, will be walking in the middle of the road and when the caravan sees them and stops to ask what their business is, thinking it's their own soldiers, that's when we'll take them. It's as good a plan as any, so I don't fight it, even though it will be dangerous for Tasos. I simply go to him and take his head in my hands and look deeply into his eyes and speak to him with every ounce of soul I can find. "Do not be reckless with your life today," I tell him. "As soon as their cars stop, run as fast as you can, and get out of the way of the bullets."

I'm surprised when he tells me the same.

"I've already lost two brothers," he says, meeting my eyes with his own, his soul rising in them, also. "I can't afford to lose a sister, too, and my last sibling on this earth."

We normally speak in Greek.

He's switched to English, though, and I know why, as behind me William comes and Tasos hugs me first, then William, then all three of us together and we stay there like that, like some sort of makeshift family that's been born and made out of all this blood and death and war. Then we move apart and take our places. Tasos and the other young men stand in the middle of the road, while William and I hide in the ditch on the eastern side with those that have come with us, and Arnold and the soldiers that have marched with him go to the ditch on the western side.

We wait.

The light's completely gone, and there's now nothing but darkness.

I think we'll have to wait for a while, as we've done during so many of the previous ambushes we've orchestrated, but we don't, and it's not long until we hear the hum of engines heading towards us from Archanes.

Then not soon after that, we see lights.

They go around one corner, then another.

They get closer.

In front of us, the lead *kubelwagen* comes around the last bend then begins to slow when the driver sees the soldiers he thinks are countrymen.

The *kubelwagen* comes to a stop.

So do the other vehicles behind it.

One of the Germans leans out and calls to the boys, and they don't answer, don't turn around, don't do anything.

This is it.

This is the moment.

I tense.

Before the German can realize what's going on, the boys scatter and I see the discovery and realization come to the eyes of the Germans as they have one last moment to recognize what's about to happen.

We rise first.

We rise and fire as one and a dozen Germans die, then we duck back into the ditch as the British soldiers on the other side rise and fire while we reload, and even more Germans die.

It looks to be half of them in the initial volleys.

The other half duck back behind the cover of their *kubelwagens* and pour out of them now and fire back at us as the entire valley echoes with gunshots because we fire again, too, at hands and feet and eyes that peer around and try to get more shots off, and some even do, and one of the Greeks on our side is hit with a bullet in his shoulder, but we still fire.

More Germans fall in the road.

We concentrate on the *kubelwagens* that are both in front of and behind the car where we know Koch rides, between the *kubelwagens* that escort him.

Gunfire comes from the car.

We return fire but are careful only to aim for the front seat, where the driver is, and not the back and the passenger that's there.

Soon gunfire starts to dissipate.

I move closer towards the car, and Koch, and catch glimpses of the back seat.

Polished boots, a pressed uniform, an iron cross.

They're familiar.

I see them again, the same as on that day at the harbor in Chania, and I see them once more in front of me.

So there's only one thing for me to do.

I jump from my hiding place in the ditch.

"*Maria!*" William yells.

But I don't listen to him.

I carefully pick my way between drifting smoke on the road and the lights from the *kubelwagens,* and bullets explode around me as I run to the car.

"*Maria, stop!*" William yells again.

He's too late, though.

I get closer.

I'm to the side of the car and see a man coughing, trying to catch his breath, and I see his slicked blond hair, cruel blue eyes, and the Knight's Cross that hangs at his neck.

I sling my rifle over my back.

I take my pistol from my belt.

Behind me, I turn to see William trying to make his way from the ditch and through the chaos of the battle, but he won't.

Not before I do this.

Around me, there's still intermittent gunfire.

I ignore it.

What can it do?

It can do nothing, it can't kill me, because I'm already dead.

I reach for the handle of the car door but as soon as I touch it, I'm shoved aside and Peter, Evelyn, and Arnold Lawrence are there and reach in and grab Koch, who's still coughing, and he struggles against them.

Koch blindly tries to reach for his pistol.

Evelyn rips the weapon away.

He still struggles, so Peter punches him in the jaw once, then again, and his body finally starts to slacken and they're able to pull him out and onto the road.

I look down at him.

He's at my feet.

He looks up and meets my eyes and I'm devastated when I find there's no recognition in them; no moment of regret for what he's done, and that now he'll pay for his crimes against me and my family, and I realize it's because he's done it so often and to so many that how could he be expected to remember a single woman and her family when he's destroyed and torn apart so many?

It doesn't matter.

I take Demetrios's dagger from my waist.

He sees it.

Light glints and reflects off the blade, as it's caught in the headlights from the *kubelwagens* that illuminate this road and crisscross our faces in jagged patterns of shadow and light.

I bend down on top of him.

He opens his mouth, about to say something, but then I'm grabbed from behind and roughly hauled up and away. I expect it to be William who's grabbed me, but it's not; he's some paces away with Tasos, who fights and struggles against a German in hand-to-hand combat, and just as the German gets the upper hand on the younger, lighter, and less experienced Tasos, William sprints and tackles the German to the ground. They both quickly stand, but William is faster and raises his rifle then crashes the butt of it down against the German's head, and the German falls again.

But then there's another.

He comes from the darkness and grabs William from behind, choking him and moving his hand upward to start gouging at his eyes, and as soon as he does, Tasos pulls his father's dagger and he plunges it into the small of the German's back.

He stays there like that, for a moment.

Then the German screams and falls to the ground, next to the other.

And that's also when I turn.

I see it's Peter that's grabbed me, and Evelyn, as Arnold hauls Koch to his feet and then Tane and Abdel come, too, and they all stand there and hold Koch between them.

"Tie him up," Peter says.

"What the hell are you doing?" I yell at them. "We came here to kill him!"

"We're taking him alive."

I understand now.

I understand why Peter wanted to wait until the later date and not tell me, rather than take him earlier, when we easily could have.

There's a rendezvous.

Where?

It doesn't matter.

"You know what he did," I say to Peter, pushing myself through the others and to his side.

"I do," he nods.

"So let me kill him."

"He's worth more to us alive, with what he can give and tell us. Either way, he won't survive this war. He'll never be free again."

"As long as we get him to the beach in time," Arnold adds.

"That's right," Peter nods. "As long as we get him to the beach, and off this island."

"The beach?"

"Yes."

I look between them.

I look to where Koch stands and doesn't struggle anymore, just glares back at us, his captors, and I realize he doesn't speak English and doesn't know what we're saying, but since he's still alive, I'm sure he understands the gist of it. Behind me, Tasos takes his pistol and silhouetted by the light from the *kubelwagens*, points the barrel down at the German he's stabbed with his father's dagger.

"*Danke*," I hear the wounded German whisper.

Then Tasos fires.

The pistol recoils in his hand.

The German is gone.

A boy's now gone, too.

William comes to stand next to me as Tasos takes his dagger back from the dead German's body, and I look at William as he takes in Koch, and realizes what's happening.

"You knew," I say to him, and it's an accusation.

"No," William shakes his head. "But it will be for the best. In so many ways, it will be for the best."

"Not if we don't get him to the coast," Evelyn interrupts us. "If we don't get him to the beach, then it will all be for nothing because we'll be dead, and he'll be free again."

"So this is where we leave you, then," Arnold nods.

"What?" I turn back to him, not understanding any of this.

"We all know every Nazi in Irakleio and on this island is going to come looking for this bloke," Arnold tells us. "Especially after the racket we've just made here. You're going south, right? So we'll take the vehicles and go north, and make them think that's where he's gone, too, and where we've taken him."

We all look back at him.

It's an unbelievable sacrifice.

"I'll go with you," I hear, and turn to see Owain limping towards us, one hand over a wound in his side where he's been shot and is losing blood. "I won't be able to make it south."

"I'll go, too," Tane says.

"Me as well," Abdel nods.

I look around, between all of them.

Peter nods.

So does Evelyn, and Arnold.

"So it will be," Arnold says.

They go to the *kubelwagens* to start getting them ready to drive again, and I think while they'll take most of them to the north, we'll take one south, but we don't.

Peter tells us we'll walk instead.

"No lights in the darkness," he says. "No way for them to find us, just as they haven't."

"Where are we meeting the SOE?"

"Near Rodakino. There's a beach just west of the village, and they'll be there at dawn."

I'm silent.

It's a long journey, but we can make it if we walk quickly, through the entire night.

And if Koch cooperates.

I turn to look at him.

He doesn't look back at me, just stares out and at no one in particular as his lips are turned up very slightly and there's a blank look on his face and it's the look of one incapable of emotion, I realize.

"I know what you're feeling," I hear Arnold's voice, next to me. "Don't ever let it control you, but don't ever forget it, either, or let it fade."

I turn to look at him.

"What do you mean?" I ask.

"There are too many that feel nothing. Never be one of them. But harness the wind, Maria. Harness the wind, and once you do, bend it to your will in the way that only you'll know how."

His words are soft, meant only for me.

I nod.

"Someone very close to me once wrote that all men dream," he continues. "They just don't dream equally."

"Was he from Oxfordshire, too?"

"Yes, but he travelled very far and did a great many wonderful things in the war before this one."

"What does he do now?"

"He's gone. I ask myself why every day, why the world would take my brother and in the way that it did, but even though he's gone, and I'll never get over the anger or injustice, his words are still with me, and they're with you now, too. Such is their power, right?"

I nod again.

I look back at him, and understand what he's telling me, or at least I think I do.

"*Efcharisto*," I tell him.

"*Parakalo*," he smiles, then turns to the others.

"So this is it," Peter says to him.

"Perhaps a tea in Oxfordshire, or something stronger, when all this is over?"

"Of course," Peter nods. "When all this is over."

"Send an invite my way, also," Evelyn adds. "I know you like the countryside, but London's not too far."

"Indeed," Arnold smiles, then tips his cap. "Until then, chaps."

Then without anything further, he turns and walks to the lead *kubelwagen* and gets inside.

Abdel helps Owain limp towards the same *kubelwagen* and get in the back seat, and Tane goes with them, too, and all the rest of the British that came with Arnold and that we met amongst hills and flowers.

We watch them.

They all get in the *kubelwagens* and car that Koch was in, then I look back towards the lead vehicle.

It's about to start driving.

Tane hangs his head out the window, and so does Abdel.

They raise their hands, in farewell.

So do we.

There are no words, because what words could there possibly be for all we've done together, and all we've endured? So we say nothing with our mouths, only our eyes and our hearts, and I hear Arnold put the vehicle into gear and start to drive, and the others follow. We stand and watch as they go, towards the lights of Irakleio in the distance, but they won't go all the way to the city, rather turn somewhere before it with as much noise as they can so Germans will come and follow them, and then what will happen?

In front of us, all that's left is a dull noise.

Then that disappears, too.

We all know what will happen, and it will do us no good to think of it now, or further, so we don't.

Instead, we turn.

"Ready?" Peter asks.

"Ready," we all nod, then begin to walk, in the opposite direction, heading south and through the dark night, on and towards the opposite coast and the justice that will wait there when dawn arrives.

32

MAY 7, 1944

I'm surprised that Koch doesn't resist.

In fact, he doesn't struggle at all, but rather walks along with us as if he doesn't have a care in the world, and I wonder why. Is it because he knows he's been taken prisoner, but thinks Germany will win the war, and he'll be freed? Does he think his soldiers will get to him before we reach the coast, and he'll be saved in that way? Or is he just one of those men, as Arnold alluded to, that feels no emotion at all, one that simply exists and whether it's kindness or cruelty he inflicts, it all feels the same, and that's how his life is defined.

A perfect criminal.

A perfect soldier, for those who don't care about rules, honor, or goodness.

But we do.

Here, on this island, those are three of the things that most greatly define our lives.

We continue to walk.

Once again, I don't lead us because I don't know this part of the island as well as the men from Rethymno, and we head west towards their city, first, then south to the coast, and I walk with my rifle slung over my back while William, next to me, holds his close and ready, in case any enemies might appear.

We walk in silence.

Ahead of us, Tasos picks at the hem of his shirt that's stained with crusted blood, trying to wipe it clean.

The blood stays, though, just as blood always does.

"What are you thinking?" I hear next to me.

I turn to look at William as we walk.

"Nothing."

"I'm sure that's not true."

"I'm thinking about what he said to me."

"Who? Koch?"

"No, Arnold. The words he gave me from his brother that made it seem as if he understood us, and this island. I wonder who he was."

"His brother?"

"*Nai*."

"You don't know? His brother was T. E. Lawrence."

I look back at him.

I just shrug, because the name means nothing to me.

William smiles.

"He was one of the heroes of the first war."

"What did he do?"

"He helped unite all the Arab forces in the Middle East to fight against the Ottomans, and they eventually won, small against large."

"It sounds like he would fit in here on this island."

It's William's turn to raise his eyes now.

"We like anyone that fights against Ottomans," I tell him.

He smiles wider, and laughs. We keep walking.

"And he died there?" I ask.

"No," William shakes his head. "He died years later, in England."

"How?"

"A motorcycle accident on an empty country road, if you can believe it."

I take that in.

I shake my head.

"He goes through everything he goes through, does all that he does, survives so much danger, and everything else, just to die like that?"

"There's a great deal of lessons in there, for all of us, I'm sure. About life, and fragility, and each day we're alive."

"*Nai*," I nod.

Tasos slows his pace and falls back to walk near us.

I look at him then reach out to put my arm around his shoulders.

"Are you alright, *Tasos-mou*?" I ask.

"*Oxi*," he says as he walks, and I'm surprised at this.

I'm surprised at his honesty.

"No?"

"I'm not, and haven't been for some time," he says, then turns to look at me. "It's taken me awhile to admit that, but it's the truth."

"I know. It's hard sometimes, and sometimes it's hardest to admit to ourselves."

"I will be, though, I think. Eventually, I will be."

"When this is finished."

"*Nai*," he says. "When this is finished, and then maybe a little bit longer after that."

"Longer?"

"The time it takes for things to fade, and new things to come."

"*Nai*."

"*Nai*."

We keep walking.

William slings his rifle over his back now, the same as mine is, then reaches out and takes my hand, the one that's not around Tasos's shoulder.

There are words not spoken.

If this is ever finished. If new things ever come.

Ahead of us walks the man that destroyed my entire village, killed my parents, and Tasos's, too, and most everyone we grew with and ever knew.

Yet here we are.

Here we still are.

And as we walk and I have my left arm around Tasos, and my right hand in William's, I realize that even though our family's been taken, here we are, and we're a family again.

There is evil in the world, and it's never very far.

There is good, too, and love, and it is much closer.

I squeeze William's hand.

Soon we begin to come down out of the mountains, one more time, and it's not long after until we can see the sea in the distance.

We walk towards it.

We get to the beach.

We all stand there together as in front of us the sun just starts to rise and the color and light it brings silhouettes us, just solitary figures in the much larger scheme of all that's happened on this island, on this continent, in this world, and this is our piece of it; this is our not-insignificant piece that we've done and contributed to the greater whole, I realize, as I look at the Nazi commander who stands in front of us, the man that's been called the Butcher of Crete.

He deserves death.

His fate will be something more important, though.

They will question him and hopefully the information he can provide will help save others, so perhaps that will be my revenge, that others might live and more families might be saved because of my mercy and that this will all be over sooner than it otherwise might be, and can I hope all of that?

I can.

Just as Arnold told me, we all hope, though unequally, and if nothing else, I will be one that hopes more than others.

What will it amount to?

I don't know.

That's what we'll find out, surely.

In all the days I have remaining, whether one, a thousand, ten thousand, or even more, that's surely what I'll now find out.

The water ripples.

It looks the same is it did when we saw the dolphins near Rethymno, before we went to the *Fortezza*, but this disturbance in the sea isn't from a dolphin or any other animal, I know, and so do the rest of us and we all stand there together as a submarine slowly rises and appears in the shallow waters.

The hatch on the top spins, then opens.

There are British soldiers that come from it, sailors, men of the SOE.

Peter turns to Hannes Koch.

The two face each other, then Peter reaches up and roughly pulls the Knight's Cross that Koch wears from his neck, ripping the collar of his shirt in the process, and for the first time since we've taken him, Koch reacts.

He flinches, visibly recoils, almost as if he's in pain.

Peter puts the cross in his pocket.

His dark eyes meet Koch's, which are light and cruel.

"I know you don't understand my words," Peter tells him, in level and unemotional English. "But what I want to say is that no matter what happens after this, I will never see you again. I will see all that stand here with me, and that fight for us, and I'll even see some again that fight for your side, but not you. There is no room for men like you in this world, who are not men at all. Before you die, you'll realize that and it will be your curse. That, and all that comes next, in both this world, and the one after."

Koch stares back at him.

Then he spits into the sand, at Peter's feet.

I walk forward now.

William watches me, but doesn't move, doesn't go to stop me, and I stand in front of Koch.

Tasos comes and stands next to me, as one, survivors of a village and family that is no longer of this earth, or this island.

I meet Koch's eyes.

He cocks his head to the side as he looks back at me, and I know what he must be wondering: who is this female *palikari,* here amongst all the other Greek and British soldiers?

"I don't forgive you," I tell him, my voice pitched low and strong. "I wish not to think of you at all, because you are nothing, but I still do. One day, I hope I won't. Killing you won't change that, or change me, which is why you're alive. Let these words be truth, and may you never forget what you've done, because we certainly never will, the same as we never forget anything on this island."

I back up.

So does Tasos.

My eyes don't leave Koch's.

"May you burn forever," Tasos adds.

Then Evelyn comes forward and takes Koch by the arm, and with a few of the other soldiers, begins to lead him out into the sea. The water is only up to their knees, then their waists, and soon they're to the submarine and the British sailors reach down and take Koch by the arms and pull him up and to the hatch then push him down and through it.

I'm surprised again.

I'm surprised he doesn't resist more.

The sailors turn back to us, we who stand together on the beach, and raise their arms and salute us for what we've done; what we've just given them, and the Allies, the great gift the information Koch has will be to our cause, and the great blow it will be to the Germans, as the sun continues to rise and bring light once more.

The soldiers follow Koch down the hatch.

After it twists and seals behind them, the submarine starts to submerge again, below the soft Mediterranean waves until soon it disappears, before it turns and heads south to deliver its cargo and prisoner to the SOE office in Egypt.

We all stand there, together, for one more moment.

Everything is calm now.

I turn and look around.

I look north, towards the hills behind us, then east towards Rodakino, the village that's there.

There's no one.

There's no one else here: no farmers, shepherds, fishermen, or anyone else to see who we are, and what we've done, and how the world has just shifted, moved, changed, and so have we.

It doesn't matter.

It will be known.

We turn and start back north, towards the mountains and our camp, and even if nothing else, I know what we've done has mattered: it has mattered a great deal, and will be remembered.

So will we.

We will be remembered, and we will remember, too.

There is nothing else.

As the sun rises even higher, into the clearness of the great island sky, we keep going, all of us.

Onward.

Together.

One last time.

33

JUNE 10, 1944

It surprised me how quickly it all began, when the Germans first came, and it surprises me how quickly it all ends, too. One moment I'd been planning for the revenge I would take on Koch, and the next we've abducted him in the middle of the night, marched him to the southern shore, then he's gone, under the waves, never to return to Crete or butcher anyone ever again. There's a whole lot more that goes into the abduction and the end, though, of course, and a whole lot more sacrifices that are made. Two days after we return from the coast and get back to our camp, Abdel and Tane return, also, and tell us what happened after they left; they tell us how they'd driven to a beach between Irakleio and Rethymno and left the *kubelwagens* and car there, to try to throw the Germans that chased them off the scent, and continued on foot and that's when they ran into more Germans on the road. They fought them. Three British soldiers from Arnold's unit died, and so did Owain, but not by any new gunfire, rather from the wounds he sustained on the road outside the Villa Ariadne. They tell us they buried them in marked and shallow graves they hope to be able to return to when this is all over, and bury them properly.

And Abdel and Tane show us something else, too.

They show us a piece of paper an old man gave them in a small village not far from Rethymno, that the Germans dropped via plane with a picture of Koch on it and threatening severe reprisal unless he's returned within three days. He of course won't be, and true to their word, the Germans butcher another entire village, this one called Hydros, and kill every single villager that's there, burn every house, kill every animal, and set fire to their olive trees. Similar things happen all over the island in retribution; sometimes the Germans kill the villagers, sometimes they just destroy the village and let those who once lived there have their lives. But do they? What do they do after everything they've ever known is gone? I don't know. There is so much I don't know. Was it worth it, what we did? In the end, we didn't take him for my revenge, but on orders from the SOE, and if I knew what would happen after, would we still do the same thing? Was one man's life, even if he was the Butcher of Crete, worth so many more lives and so much destruction? He must pay for what he did, surely. But what about what's happened because of it?

I don't know. I don't know.

All I know is that surely there are things in this world beyond what we've been made to be able to endure, and yet still we do.

In the days following Koch's departure, in addition to the destruction of villages and massacre of more Cretans, there's a great many German patrols on the roads and in the hills, so we stay high in the mountains, for the most part, until things begin to calm again. Tasos spends a lot of time away from camp, hunting I suppose, and being on his own. Kyriaki is occupied with the baby, and Cassia helps her though she leaves sometimes, too, which I understand, as we've all been here and together for so long. I take

William to places in the mountains I haven't taken him before. I show him the ruins of Rizinia, the ancient city that's unique on this island because in addition to the Minoan ruins and carvings, and statues of gods and goddesses still standing, there have been ancient Egyptian statues found there, too.

"Really?" William asks, as we look around.

The view is immense, mist rising between peaks, and around us.

"It's not so far-fetched," I tell him. "Egypt is very close, and Greeks have been living there and trading with them since there were Greeks at all."

He smiles. So do I.

Then I take him to the small village of Meskla nearby, and buy some bread, olives, and a wedge of graviera cheese then show him a waterfall I used to come to with my friends in the summer before Demetrios and I started to fall in love. It's exactly the same as I remember and the snow that's beginning to melt higher in the mountains has swollen the stream that plunges down from the peaks and forms a small, deep pool between mossy rocks. We sit on the rocks, in the sun, and we eat. We rip chunks of cheese to go with our bread, as it's a cheese firmer than feta, or mizithra, which crumbles, and we have olives after and with it while we're still chewing. Then when we're done eating, and the sun is even stronger, we lay down our rifles, unstrap our belts, take off our clothes, and go into the water. We go under the waterfall. He holds me, kisses me, and I kiss him back. We lay there in the sun as the heat dries the water from our skin, and then when we're dry, and the sun begins to sink, we make a small fire and sleep there. We wake early. We walk south again before the sun is up, and I take him to the village of Vouves and show him the olive tree that's there; it's the oldest olive tree in the world, and it's here on our island. It's more than four thousand years old, the scientists say, and still produces olives. It was here when Christ walked the earth, and Alexandros, and even Minos, Odysseus, and Achilleus, too. We stop and marvel at it, staring up, reaching out to touch the ancient and gnarled bark of the trunk, and the lower-hanging branches.

I breathe.

So does he.

This is history.

So are we, though, too.

We're history now, also, aren't we?

We can't stay in one place too long, even a small village such as this in the mountains, so we continue and there's one more thing I want to show him, on our island, and it's the Minoan ruins at Aptera, just east of Souda Bay, and we go to see them very early the next day because this is one place that is dangerously close to the German garrison that's still there in Souda.

We get there before the sun.

We walk through the ancient stone, nothing around us but darkness and mist.

I show him the ancient theater, the modern monastery, sites built upon sites at the same location, generations and lives stacked upon each other, and we stand in the middle of it all and kiss as the sun rises behind us to the east.

Then as soon as it does, and light begins to come, we hear engines.

We know what that means.

So we shoulder our rifles and start heading back south, back into the mountains, and I nod to the Izzedin Fortress on the way. It's down on a point that juts out into the water, with large, high walls around it that make it look like a medieval castle used to guard and defend the bay, which is exactly what it used to be; it was built by the Turks to defend against naval attacks, then converted into a prison by the new Cretan government after the Turks had been expelled.

Now, it stands empty.

We keep walking.

When we return to camp, we find Kyriaki and the baby and she tells us Tasos is gone, and so is Cassia, and Peter and Evelyn left a few days before them, too, and still aren't back yet.

We nod.

We go to our tent and take a nap, then when we wake, we go back outside and I see that Tasos has returned. He's dropped the rabbits he's caught and picked up his nephew and holds Ikaros, bouncing him in his arms as he talks to him, quietly whispering into his ear. He smiles when he sees me. So does Ikaros, and he laughs, too. Shortly after that, Cassia returns from a nearby village where she's gone to trade some of the other rabbits Tasos caught the day before for vegetables and bread, and she begins to make a stew that will be ready for dinner. Peter and Evelyn come back not long after that. They don't say much or anything about where they've been, or what they've done, but we're surprised when they tell us the Germans will be leaving soon.

"How?" I ask.

"By boat, I assume," Evelyn answers.

And now I know where they've been, and that they've received more orders and information from the SOE. They tell us the Americans landed in France a few days ago, and have begun to push the Germans back and have opened another front in the war. What does this mean for us? It means Hitler has begun to recall most of his troops that are abroad to come home and join the fighting in the West, against the Americans, and in the East, against the Russians. He's even recalled all his forces from Italy, too, we learn, not just Greece, with the Americans having taken Rome two days before they landed in France.

So these last forays of cruelness had been just that.

Cruelty and death, simply for the sake of it.

I shake my head.

A wave of sadness washes over me I can't describe, and can't articulate, even as Peter, Evelyn, William and the others break out the wine the SOE has sent and the *raki* we've gotten from the village, and the wine goes mostly untouched as they all pour small glasses of *raki* and toast to the destruction of the Führer and the Reich. Tasos drinks with them now, and looks natural amongst them, the way he smiles, speaks, moves his hands, pats them on the back, or makes a joke. He was forced to become a man too soon, but now it feels like he actually is one. I sit with William and think of the first time we had *raki* together. I think of the smiles. I think of what it smelled like, what it felt like, sitting under the cypress and next to our olives as the sun sank and left behind its lingering warmth and colors, but mostly I think of their smiles. All of them. So this is it. This is where my sadness has come from. It becomes too much so I slip away back to the tent I share with William, and I can still hear them. I can hear them drinking and talking, which soon becomes shouting, then I hear someone start to play a bouzouki for the first time since we've been here because they're no longer scared of being heard. It should be joy I'm feeling, the same as they are. It's not, though. It's sadness; deep, profound sadness. Soon sleep comes and sometime in the night I feel William return and pull our fur blanket back and get onto the cot next to me. The warmth of his body is familiar now, and I move and press myself closer to him. It comforts me, at least a little bit. Then sometime near dawn, I wake just before the sun comes, as I always do, but when I turn to look in the cot next to me, to tell him *kalimera*, I see that he's already gone.

34

JUNE 12, 1944

He returns two days later.

I ask the others where he went, but they just shake their heads and say they don't know. When he finally does come back, though, he finds where I stand with Kyriaki and Ikaros, holding him, bouncing him up and down, and tells me there's something he needs to show me.

"What?" I ask him.

"It's a surprise," he smiles.

And so it will be, because I have no idea what he might be thinking, or have planned.

I hand Ikaros back to his mother, and go with him.

We walk from the mountains, taking a path that doesn't bring us near my village, but around it, so we come to the sea by a different road. Then from there we start to head towards Chania. I ask him if it's safe, and he tells me all the Germans are officially gone from Chania. Some are still in Irakleio and Rethymno, he says, but the ones that were here left, mostly by boat, heading north and east towards some of the Dodecanese Islands where I can only assume they'll try to find a way back to Germany that's not blocked by the Americans.

We keep walking.

We come to Chryssi Akti, where I found William more than three years ago now, and I think back to all that's changed since then, and he must know my thoughts and the darkness in them because he reaches out and takes my hand in his as we walk past the beach then to the place where there are rocks, then sand again, and then rocks once more before we finally reach the *kastro* and the city. The *limani* is quiet, almost as if people don't quite believe the news yet, and then I realize it's not that at all, it's just there aren't many people still left. So many have been killed. So many have been killed and for such pointless reasons, and as we walk around the crescent-shaped harbor and come to the Venetian fountain in the middle of town, William tells me to wait by the fountain as he goes to a taverna and I hear him say *kalispera*, then *nai, nai*, and finally *efcharisto* as he's handed a basket and I realize how much Greek he's learned since he's been here. I smile. I can't help it, and it feels good, the way my lips turn and the feeling of wanting to laugh again. He comes back and takes my hand and we keep walking. We pass the old Turkish baths, then turn back towards the southern end of the Old Town and go down a small side street before all of a sudden it washes over me, and I realize where we're going, and where he's taking me.

We duck inside a small doorway.

I look up to see the roof of the building has been completely blown off by the German bombing, I assume, probably when they first came and destroyed so much of the city. There's still a small hole high in the wall that's behind us, though, and an improvised white screen that spans the length and height of the stage in front of us in what is left of the theater I used to come to with my family every Friday to watch movies from America.

I can't believe he's remembered.

There are no more seats in the building so he takes a blanket that's there and waiting and spreads it on the floor. We bend down, then lay there on it and eat together, the food he got from the taverna, in the basket, and drink as the sun goes down. Then when it does, and it's dark, he gives a thumbs-up, to somewhere above us, and I hear a whirring sound. There's a projector that's still behind the wall, behind the small hole, and as it starts and film is fed through, the white screen is white no longer, and images begin. The old man who's started it and I don't recognize comes down and William stands and goes to him and presses something into his hand, then comes back to the blanket and me and sits again and we're alone now.

The movie starts.

"They didn't have any Barbara Stanwyck, so Clark Gable will have to do," he whispers.

And I see the title.

Gone With the Wind.

I've already seen it, but I don't tell him, because I know I've seen all the films that would be stuck here in the projector room that they weren't able to send back to Athens because a war broke out, and there was no one to send them back to. The images flood over us, and we let them, as we lay there and his arm is around me and my head is on his chest. We watch all four hours of the movie with previews and credits, without ever moving, then when it's done, and I can hear the loose end of film flapping against the projector, he stands and goes up to the projector room himself and shuts it off, then comes back.

He lays down again.

We're in the exact same position, his arm around me, my head on his chest, only now there's no light; only now, there's no love story in front of us, or images flashing on the screen, no more lives that are both more similar and familiar than the first time I saw them because my life has now also been defined by the same two great things their lives were defined by: love and war.

I feel his chest rising and falling, then I feel him hold his breath.

He opens his mouth, but nothing comes.

"What is it?" I ask.

He waits another moment, then finally finds the words.

"That night on the beach," he says, "outside of Rethymno, in the moonlight."

"Yes."

"What were you thinking?"

"You already asked me that."

"I'm asking again."

I'm silent.

He knows.

He already knows, I'm sure of it, but I realize he wants to be sure, too.

I can't say it.

So he saves me, one more time, and it's him that says it, very softly, his words barely more than a whisper.

"You were thinking that you don't love me, weren't you."

I close my eyes.

A single tear leaks out.

"I do love you, William."

I stop. I don't know how to say it.

"Just not like him," he finishes for me.

And I'm silent.

I'm silent because that's exactly right.

I don't want it to be.

I want to love William in the same way I loved Demetrios, and continue with our lives in the way that Demetrios and I had done before war and had planned to do after, but we can't command our bodies, and we certainly can't command our hearts, either.

Does he feel the same?

"Perhaps we're only meant to love one person," he finally says, his voice even softer, and distant, and there are tears on his cheek now, also.

"I don't know."

"I don't either."

"Are you angry?"

"How could I be angry?" he says, louder now, and with a sad laugh. "Truth is truth, Maria, and love is of course love. Neither can be what they aren't, or forced, only found."

I'm not sure what that means.

I do love him, I love being with him.

But it's not the same.

Will it be with anyone else?

I don't know.

I don't think so, but the truth is, I don't know.

"I'm sorry," I say again.

"If only we could command our souls, right?" he says, and I feel him smile as he brushes tears from his cheek, first, then mine.

"We can try. We can only try."

"Maybe it's better that way."

"What way?"

"That we don't control our hearts and souls, only the world does, and other forces beyond what we know and understand."

"Maybe."

"Maybe."

"I do love you, William. I want you to know that."

"I love you, too, Maria."

"And I'm glad you came. I'm so glad that I found you."

"I'm glad, too. I'm so very glad, for both."

And then we lay there.

I hold him as I look at the projector screen in front of us and I think of all the times I came here with my family, my family who is no longer with me, then I look up at the roof of the theater that's no longer there, also, torn from the building by this war that has taken so much from us, and I look at the moon.

It's big, bright, whole.

Sometime while staring at it, and feeling him next to me, I fall asleep, a deep and peaceful sleep, and when I wake, just before dawn, as I usually do, I look next to me and see that once again he's no longer there. I sit alone for a moment, then stand, before brushing one last tear away, then I leave the ruined theater.

I don't look for him in the city. I know he's not there.

So instead, I leave Chania, taking the familiar path west to the place where there's sand, then rocks, then sand again, at the beach where I found him and I stop there and look out at the sea. I reach down and pick up some of the sand, that's once again our sand, and let it run through my fingers.

I think of Demetrios's words once more.

When I'm gone, don't look for me in the sunsets, look for me in the sea.

I've looked.

I'll keep looking.

I don't know if I've done the right thing and there is so much of me that's now filled with doubt and lost hope, and I just don't know. All I know is how I feel, right now, in this moment, and that's what we should perhaps be honest about most of all.

I sigh, then keep walking.

I go past the path that leads to our village and on to the one which brings me to the mountains, and when I get back, Cassia is there, and Tasos, and Kyriaki, and baby Ikaros, and they tell me the British have all gone. I already know, of course. They tell me Peter and Evelyn said that was the message received in their last visit from the SOE, that the Germans were in retreat and leaving Crete, and going back to their country, but the war was not yet finished so they were going to Egypt, first, and from there would be sent to Asia where there was still fighting against the Japanese. I swallow as I look back at them and they know I left with William, but didn't return with him, so Cassia hugs me, and so does Tasos, and Kyriaki, and even little Ikaros seems to know what's happening and wraps one of his little arms around my neck and I smile as we stay like that for a moment, the only people we have left.

Then I go past them and into the tent I shared with William.

I look around as it already feels more empty, and I'm just about to go to the cot to lay down, to take a nap, to think about all that's happened in the last hours, days, months, years, and that's when I see it.

We have a small chest in the corner.

It's where we keep our clothes, and the old German uniforms we wore outside Knossos and the Villa Ariadne, and I walk closer and see what it is that's there.

It's the ring he always wears.

The one from his mother, from his family.

He's left it. He's left it for me.

I look down at it then pick it up, turning it over and running my fingers back and forth across the surface, the crest, feeling all the history and emotion and love that's still there with it, and all of him that's still with it, too, and it's the first time I've ever seen it not on his hand, because now it's in mine.

1945

35

MARCH 13, 1945

After all the British leave, we go east with Antonis and the rest of the Greeks from Rethymno to their city, with the intention to keep fighting, but we find the Germans have left there, too. There are still some in Irakleio, we hear, but they've gathered near the *limani* and *kastro* and soon they'll be gone, also, in their planes and boats, and then our entire island will be ours once more.

That doesn't mean the fighting stops, though.

True to who we are, nearly as soon as the Germans leave, Greece divides itself into factions, left and right, Communists and Nationalists, and civil war brews, then erupts. I will have no part of it, though. Athens is liberated from the Germans in October, and I've fought on our island and done my part as my father and my mother would have wanted, and their mother and father, too, and on and on, back and back, but I want no part of this new battle, the one where countrymen will kill countrymen.

I don't think they would either.

I also discover that I'm pregnant.

As women, we're so conditioned to think that if children don't come after a certain amount of time, then the fault lies with us, and our bodies, and so I thought that, too, for so long, and made no effort to prevent such a thing from happening with William.

But then, very shortly after he leaves, I find that it has.

Without a village to return to, we all go back to Chania and Cassia's apartment, and when we get there, we see the lock's been ripped from the door and there had been German soldiers living inside. And just as quickly as they came, after Cassia and Tasos left, they also departed again and there is still food that's begun to rot, and we find there are weapons, too—a pistol and two rifles, carefully stored in a closet—such was the haste with which they departed. We spend three days cleaning it, all together, then Kyriaki uses some of the savings left by her father in the bank that's reopened to rent another apartment in the building next to Cassia's, still in the Old Town, and on the *limani*, and I search for a job myself, to be able to rent another apartment for me and Tasos. I find one selling bread for Fotis the baker in the *agora*, who knew me from when I used to stand next to him and sell our olives and wool, and when Cassia and I used to come into his shop. He's lost a leg. It happened in the initial invasion, he tells me, when Germans dropped bombs on our city and he was in his bakery early in the morning, ran outside and saw the planes coming over the sea, and when he went back in, to grab his rifle, that's when the bakery was hit and the roof caved in. A large piece of wood landed on his leg and trapped him there for two days. When he was finally freed, the leg was so badly mangled and infected it had to be amputated, he tells me, and he can no longer stand for any amount of time to sell the bread he makes, or wheel it to the *agora*. His son who would normally have done it died fighting with the resistance, he tells me, somewhere near Kissamos, in the first year of the war against the Germans.

So, he needs help.

He'll stay in the bakery, and he hires me to go to the *agora*.

After two weeks, I save enough to rent an apartment in Cassia's building, and even on the same floor, so we're not far from each other and can help each other, support each other, cook dinner together, watch Ikaros for Kyriaki when she needs to go to the *agora* or run an errand, and all other things that families used to do before the Germans came.

And this is us.

This is our family now.

My belly begins to grow and then show, and men and women I pass in the street give me looks because my husband isn't with me. If any ask, though, I tell them my husband was killed during the war, which is of course not a lie. And the reason they ask is because Greeks in the villages and cities have begun retaliating against women who took up with Germans during the occupation. We hear stories of women in Irakleio being pulled from their homes and having their heads shaved in the middle of the street, or near the Morosini Fountain, where all can see and witness their shame. A group of young men try the same thing in Chania, one day, and they grab a woman by the hair who's shopping in the *agora* and pull her towards the middle of the market. One of them forces her to her knees, as the other rips her dress, and the third takes a knife and is about to cut her hair when I walk from where I'm selling bread, take the pistol I carry at my hip, underneath my jacket, and hold it pointed at the one with the knife.

They tell me I'm making a mistake.

I tell them that of course it's them who are making a mistake, and jealousy is no substitute for truth, and I can see they know who I am and have heard of my reputation so they know I have no problem taking lives that deserve to be taken. They eventually lower the knife, and all shuffle away. I know I'll see them again, and when I do, a few days later, instead of there being a problem, they nod to me with respect and the one who held the knife and I threatened even comes and buys two loaves of bread and tells me he loves strong, beautiful women. I tell him he's a liar and I've already seen what he thinks of women, but he doesn't give up. He comes every day to buy a loaf of bread, until eventually one day he stops, and a few weeks later I see him walking near the *limani* with a girl half my age who looks as if she's just arrived in the city from one of the villages.

I shake my head. There's nothing I can do.

Tasos finds a job, too.

He's grown another two inches and the muscles in his chest and arms have started to expand, as well, then they do even more after he starts working at the docks helping to load and unload the boats that now come. He insists on using his wages to pay for part of the rent of the apartment. The dockmaster originally recruits him not because of his size, but because he heard there was a boy who spoke English and he needed that now the British had returned, and the Americans, too. Once the Germans left, there were more Greeks coming, from the mainland, and American and British, also, going between Athens and their armies in Egypt, where our government was, as well, and they'd stop for supplies, or to purchase firearms and ammunition that the Germans left behind, and a great many other things. Tasos would eagerly meet them and ask who they were and where they were going, and would load and unload anything they might have, or need, and show them around Chania. The only people he refused to help were the ones he suspected of being Communists. I worry about him. I worry he's going to run off and join the fighting that's begun again, but he doesn't. Instead, when I ask him what he wants to do, hoping he'll give some answer

I can pursue and distract him from thoughts of more war, I'm surprised when he tells me he wants to be an architect. Just like his older brother. The school in Irakleio that Demetrios wanted to go to isn't yet open again, but I'm able to track down one of the professors who taught there and contact him and he agrees to take Tasos on as a private student. Part of me thinks he'll be resistant to leaving Chania, but even though there are several girls here I know are interested in him, and take their lunches down by the docks on purpose so they can see him as he works, he hasn't shown an interest in any of them. So there's nothing keeping him in Chania in that respect. I ask Fotis if there's more I can do to make more money, and when he asks what the money's for, I tell him, and he tries to just give it to me. I refuse to take it. Then he tells me it's not charity, but an investment, and when I ask in what, he says his only condition is that when Tasos graduates, after the school eventually opens again, that he return to Chania and fix the roof that was destroyed by the Germans, and has still not been repaired.

I smile. I nod.

"He will," I tell Fotis.

"Good," he says. "*Efcharisto.*"

I work up to the date of my delivery, then when I feel the signs the baby is coming, I go back to the apartment and Cassia calls the midwife who comes and since the only small hospital we once had in Chania has been destroyed, the birth happens there in the apartment, on the *limani*, near the water.

Perhaps that's as it should be.

Cassia's there with me and the midwife, and Kyriaki, too, as Tasos watches Ikaros in our apartment next door.

When it's done, the midwife cleans the baby and wraps him in a small blanket.

She hands him to me and I look down and into his new eyes.

Then Tasos comes from next door, and hands Ikaros back to Kyriaki, and sits next to me and I hand him the baby.

He looks down into his young eyes, too.

Then he looks back up and at mine.

"What's his name?" he asks.

"Demetrios," I tell him.

36

SEPTEMBER 6, 1945

I thought I'd never hear Hannes Koch's name again, but then I see his face on a newspaper I pick up and read, and that's how I find out what's happened to him since I last saw him on the beach at Rodakino; he was taken to Egypt first, then Canada, so he could be questioned without any German troops trying to come and rescue him, then Wales, before he was finally brought back to Athens and killed by firing squad in Syntagma Square by the Communists. I think I'll feel something when I hear this, but I'm surprised I don't. I don't feel anything at all when I see his face or read about his fate. I think of Tasos, and how to keep him safe in all this, in this next war that is now here and will surely come again to this island, and I want to go to Irakleio with him, to meet the teacher I've written to and help him find an apartment to rent in the city, but it would be too difficult with Demetrios. So Cassia says she'll go, instead, and help him find a place and get settled. I stand there with them at the fountain in the middle of the city and give him as much money as I can to find his new place and he tries to refuse, because he's been working at the docks, but I insist, and he finally takes it then hugs and kisses me and takes Demetrios and kisses him gently on the forehead, too, before turning with Cassia and walking to the bus station just south of the Old Town. The bus has begun to run again from Chania to Rethymno, then on to Irakleio, and I think about the road it will take, and only a few short months ago all the things that happened on that road.

All the things that I did.

All the things that they did to us.

I shake my head.

It's no use going backward, we can only go forward, and that's what this is, that's who Tasos is, and Demetrios, and Ikaros, too; they're the future, and they're our future, exactly what I once was, as well, but am no longer, I realize. But perhaps it's as it should be, so I stand there at the fountain until they're gone and out of sight, with Tasos turning to wave one last time.

Time passes.

Time passes, and so do we, along with it, whether we want to or not.

I sigh and walk home.

1948

37

APRIL 27, 1948

A year after the war ends, and even in the midst of a civil war, the university at Irakleio opens again and Tasos enrolls as an architecture student and graduates with honors. When he comes home, we have a party for him, but before the others arrive, he tells me he needs to speak with me. I nod and we sit together in our living room, with little Demetrios on his lap, and he tells me he loves Cassia, she loves him, and they want to marry each other. This takes me by surprise, at first. Then, after I think about it, I realize it doesn't. I think of all the time they spent together, in the apartment next to the one that's now ours, when I first went to the mountains. I think of all we've been through together, all of us, and is there anything that brings us closer than shared experience? When we experience things beyond what we're made to be able to endure, is there anyone that we become closer to than those who have endured it with us?

I suppose there isn't.

"I'm so happy for you," I tell him.

"I know you might think she's too old," he begins.

"Too old?" I smile at him. "How could I think that? She's the same age as I am."

"But the age difference . . ."

"It's ten years, Tasos. It's the blink of an eye."

"Is it?"

"It is, trust me."

"I love her very much."

I look back at him.

Then I nod, still smiling, and stand and walk over to bend down and kiss him on the forehead.

"So do I," I tell him.

Later, after the others come for the party and Cassia's there along with Kyriaki and Ikaros, who plays with his younger cousin on the floor, Cassia takes me aside so it's only the two of us.

"Are you angry?" she asks.

"No," I smile, my lips trying to convince her of my heart, as much as my words.

"Are you sure?"

"Love is love, Cassia, and I'm so glad you've found it. I'm so glad he has, too."

"I am, also."

"How did it happen?"

"Slowly, I suppose. Then all at once."

"When you were here together?"

"No," she shakes her head. "He was just a boy then."

"When he went to Irakleio?"

"Then, and just before."

I understand now.

I understand why he ignored the girls that would come to see him at the docks, and I understand why Cassia volunteered to take him to the city to help him find his own apartment, and how she'd leave some weekends, and not tell us where she was going.

We stand there together.

We watch Ikaros as he tries to pick Demetrios up, then Tasos goes and helps him and he sits on the couch with both of his nephews, Demetrios on his lap, and Ikaros next to him.

"Have you told him?" Cassia asks me, looking at Demetrios.

"I've thought about it."

"And decided not to?"

"I was going to try to send a letter, but I didn't know what company he was assigned to, or even where in Asia he'd been deployed. Then the war was over. Now I wouldn't know how to find him, even if I wanted to."

"You think it's better this way," she says, and it's not a question.

I think back to our last conversation, some of the last words between us, and how he wondered if there was only one person in the world meant for each of us and all I can think about is: what if he's found his person? I found mine, a long time ago, and what if he's now found his, then a child shows up on his doorstep?

It would end all that for him.

I know how men feel about sons.

I also know the situation it could cause him—that we both could cause him—and I want him to have the happiness and chance at happiness that I had, so I made up my mind when Demetrios first came that I'd raise him here on my own and wouldn't try to track down his father.

Is it the right decision?

I don't know.

It's mine.

I see Tasos glance at us, and smile, and he looks like a boy again even though he isn't anymore, and I think of the olive trees. I think of trimming and pruning them and painting water and slaked lime on trunks, me and Ikaros standing on the ladders to get to the highest branches because he wasn't tall enough. I think about the sun, and what it felt like, and what I felt like then, and how now the trees sit wild and untended.

I shake my head.

The party ends and Kyriaki and Cassia leave, and I go to my bedroom, and Tasos goes to his. I lay in my bed thinking about everything that's happened until sleep comes, though not much, and I rise earlier than I normally do, an hour or two before there will be the hint of the sun or light. I quietly dress, to not disturb him. I leave the apartment with Demetrios. The harbor is quiet and I walk next to it, carrying my son, as I look across and see the silhouette of the mosque and think about all the lives that have been here and all the times this city has seen, all the ancient things that are quickly becoming modern, and I can't think about it for too long because the ache comes again so I don't, and carry on. I turn at the fountain to go down Zampeliou Street towards the bakery in the Old Town, and when I go a couple more paces, that's when I see him. Tasos wasn't sleeping after all, but already here, standing on a ladder and taking measurements for the new roof I promised in exchange for his education, all those years ago.

1955

38

APRIL 13, 1955

Tasos and Cassia don't have a traditional wedding. Instead, they go to the church a few weeks after they tell me of their intention and ask the priest to perform a private ceremony with no one else present except me, Kyriaki, Ikaros, and Demetrios. I know part of it is they're eager to get on with their lives; another part, of course, is we have no family left, and very few friends, so who would we invite? A city, as we've come to learn, is not a village. Once they're married, Tasos moves into Cassia's apartment, but they don't stay there very long. He tells me there aren't many opportunities for him to work in Chania, so they decide to move to Athens. I help them pack. I help them clean out the apartment and take all the furniture they leave behind, then go with them down to the harbor along with Kyriaki and our children and we hug them and kiss them and cry and then watch as they sail away.

I go back home.

Next to us, new neighbors are already moving in, a young couple from a village near Sitia on the far eastern end of the island and I smile to them and say *kalispera* when I see them on the stairs and they smile and say *kalispera*, too.

Once I go back inside, I walk out to the balcony.

I look behind me, at the apartment, then out at the city, at the *limani* where my husband was killed, and the lighthouse, the *kastro*, even the great mosque that stands there on the other end of the harbor and has been rebuilt from the damage it sustained during the bombing and I realize this is no longer my city, and this apartment is no longer my home.

It hits me that quickly.

So I make my decision.

Kyriaki tries to persuade me against it, but she can't, so I pack all my things, which isn't very much, even with what we've gotten from Tasos and Cassia, and return to our village.

Everything there was destroyed.

It doesn't matter, though.

Things that have been destroyed can be rebuilt, so that's what I do, and while it used to be a village of many, it will now be a village of two.

I go to my parents' house first, the one I grew up in, and I start with a single room, then continue on to all the others, fixing the stone and wood as Demetrios, who every day grows taller and stronger, helps me repair the place he never knew, but now will.

For the first months, I continue working for Fotis at the bakery.

Then, as soon as I've saved enough money, I buy a few sheep of our own and keep them in the barn I've begun to fix, also, and milk them and sheer them and bring the milk and wool to sell in the *agora* in a stall next to where Fotis's grandson now sells his bread and Demetrios runs and plays with the other children. He has blond hair and blue eyes which isn't unheard of for the boys on our island, but it makes him stand out amongst the children with dark hair, dark-colored eyes, and tanned olive skin, which is the same color as mine and most everyone else's.

He begins school, too, a couple villages over.

After I fix our house well enough to live in and fall into a routine with the sheep, along with Demetrios, who helps me with them, I return to the olive trees. I'll never be able to tend as many as we did before the war, but I do what I can, and bring some of them back by pruning them, coaxing the olives to return, painting their trunks with slaked lime and water to protect from the insects that hatch in the spring, and when Demetrios isn't in school, he runs through the rows and helps me with them. When he is in school, I tend them alone, and he joins me in the afternoon. It's one such afternoon when he's eleven that he finds me there and he doesn't run, as he normally does, and when I see his face and swollen eye, I ask him what happened. I think he's not going to tell me, as boys so often do, but he does. He tells me how some of the other kids told him his father was a German and a Nazi, so he got into a fight with them. I tell him he shouldn't fight, but it's only a half-hearted attempt, which I think he understands, too, and just nods and goes to get the bucket of lime and helps me paint the trunks of the trees near the far end of the rows where he found me. When the sun begins to set, we return to the house, and I make dinner and we eat together and when we're done, and still at the table, he asks me who his father really is.

I haven't told him the whole truth.

He knows I was married to Demetrios, who died during the war, and I've done nothing to dissuade him from thinking this is both his father, and his namesake. My husband was only one of those things, though, of course, and I think Demetrios can feel that, that he's different than those around him, though he doesn't quite know how, but he deserves to, and so I tell him.

I can't lie.

Not to him.

So I don't.

I tell him his father wasn't German, but British, and we fought against the Germans together and he was family, too, part of the family we created during the war, and when I'm done, he comes to me, hugs me, tells me *efcharisto*, then goes to his room and doesn't bring it up again.

1960

39

OCTOBER 3, 1960

I'm haunted by what I did.

I felt nothing when I saw Koch's face in the newspaper and read about his fate in front of the firing squad, but I can't stop thinking about the villages that were burned and villagers killed in reprisal for him being taken. For what we did. For what I did. We didn't know that's what would happen, but it still did. Was it worth it? The villages don't return, and the Greek government erects a monument to their destruction and the slaughter of all villagers, both those that were killed after Koch was taken, and those that were killed, like mine, before.

And I suppose that's the answer, isn't it?

Evil is evil, and how are we supposed to understand?

We can't.

All we can do is fight against it, and I suppose if nothing else, I'm glad I have.

I'm still haunted, though, just as William said I would be, that day on the beach.

I wonder: are they haunted, too?

I wonder: do they have the same sleepless nights I have, hear the same voices, see the same faces and eyes in the darkness?

I don't know. I don't know.

I begin to see Tasos and Cassia less and less, as well as all those who knew me when I was young and myself. When they first move to Athens, they make a point to come back every year at *Pascha* to celebrate with us in Chania, standing outside the Presentation of the Virgin Mary in the town square, just a stone's throw from the Venetian fountain. Then after the service, we come back up to the house to eat. I can smell Mana's cooking when I'm in our kitchen, with her skill in that department something I still haven't inherited, but I suppose I was given other gifts. After we eat, Tasos helps around the farm with minor repairs and adjustments to what I've done myself and tells me how many new buildings are being built in Athens. He tells me how the skyline's changing, and how it's him that's helping it change, and grow, and I smile and nod even though it's something that makes me sad, rather than happy. I'm still friends with Cassia, but we're more distant, too. It's not because she's married Tasos, but because they've moved to the city, and they've become the city, and that's what they think about. The village is slow. The city is fast. They start having children, also, as soon as they're married and first a girl comes, then another, and another still after that, so with each passing year their visits become shorter and shorter until they stop altogether and simply become letters, then cards, and finally just money. I still go to the *agora* to sell wool, milk, and olives now, too, and when I walk down from the mountains and take the path near the sea, I'm reminded how much everything's changed. There are cars now on the road near the beach, and when I get to the city, all the men I pass wear suits in the Western style, not just those who are not from here and years go by without seeing anyone dressed the way we used to dress in the villages and the way I still dress when I'm at home. I sometimes wonder what's happened to the others, how they feel, how they're coping. After the war, they built a cemetery at Souda Bay for the British and Commonwealth dead, and when it opened, I went and saw someone had come and moved Owain there, and made a grave for him, the same as they'd done for all the other Allied soldiers that had been buried in villages and beside roads and in the mountains and hills. Did the others I fought with all survive the rest of the war? If so, what are they doing now? I suppose I'll never know. I go every year and lay a wreath on Owain's grave.

When Demetrios is fifteen, his class takes a field trip to Rethymno.

The teacher asks for chaperones and I volunteer to go with them in one of the buses that leaves from the same station in Chania, just south of the Old Town, where Tasos once left for school in Irakleio, and after walking around the city and the teacher telling them about the architecture, and history, they have free time and most of the kids go off with their friends. Demetrios has a lot of friends, but I'm glad he seems different than them, and doesn't say *malaka* every other word like they do. When they head into the city, he doesn't go, though. I see him hesitate. The other boys all whisper and laugh as they leave, but he stays with a girl I notice has been watching him. They speak nervously to each other, so I go to them and give him some *drachmae* and suggest he take her for a gelato at one of the tavernas that circle the *limani*. He smiles and I know this isn't something he's going to want his mother around for any more than this, so as they leave together, I go to wander through the city myself. I take the road past the entrance to the *Fortezza* and there's no one that lives there anymore and I smile when I see an attendant at the gate collecting admission fees and that it's now become a museum. I keep walking and go past the

Rimondi Fountain where men, women, and children still come to fill bottles and buckets with water to bring back to their houses, and I look at the *kafeneio* where I saw Friedrich-Wilhelm Muller and where men in suits now spin their *kolomboi* and I continue walking. I'm almost to their *agora*, near the Guora Gate, and I see there's a new bookstore that's there. I'm just about to go inside when I hear someone call my name and I turn to see Theos. He's aged, of course, his body filled out and there are lines under his eyes, and he's grown a beard. I'd still recognize him anywhere, though. There's a woman who walks with him pushing a stroller and they come over and I hug him and he introduces me to his wife and their young daughter that he tells me they've named Melia. After they take her out and show her to me, he asks his wife to carry on with their errands, says he'll catch up with them in a moment, then we're alone together on the street.

"I'm so glad you're happy, Theos," I tell him.

"Thank you."

"Of course."

"No, I want to *thank you*," he says, and he says the words differently.

"For what?"

"I know you saw us. We heard something and turned, and when we did, we saw your back, leaving, and were scared you would say something. But you never did."

I look back at him.

I don't know what to say.

"Have you heard from him?"

"Not since the war ended."

"What happened?"

"He joined the Nationalists, and kept fighting."

"Do you think he's alive?"

"I know he is."

"How?"

He smiles then takes something from his pocket and hands it to me.

I look in my palm and see it's a small and carved wooden dolphin, and I want to ask him what it is, and what it means, but it seems like it's something just for them, and sometimes things are better kept that way, so I don't.

Instead, I hand it back, then look up to meet his eyes.

I think of something William once told me: *life is so much simpler when it's just your heart, then everything else.*

I'm sad Theos hasn't experienced this.

I'm sad this isn't the way he's been able to live in this world.

"You should find him."

"And then what?"

I open my mouth.

No words come, and I reach up and wipe a tear away.

He does, too, then turns his head so hopefully no one sees. There's war, then it ends, but it also doesn't, does it?

"It helps," he finally says.

"What does?" I ask.

"To be able to talk to someone about it. Someone who knew him, and us. There's no one else who knows."

I look back at him.

Then I hear Demetrios's voice behind me.

"Mana!" he calls.

And he runs towards me and when he gets to me, he looks at me first, then the stranger I'm talking to, and I know he's probably come because he's run out of *drachmae* and needs more, but now there are other questions in his eyes.

"This is my friend Theos," I tell him.

"How do you know each other?"

"We fought together, in the war."

"Good to meet you," he says.

"And what's your name?" Theos asks him.

"Demetrios," he says, as he moves to stand next to me, his shoulder brushing and touching against mine. I watch Theos's eyes as they go from Demetrios, to me, back to Demetrios again, and I nod very slightly to confirm what is the most obvious thing in the world to anyone who knew him: that this is William's son, because the older he's gotten, the more he's become the image of his father.

Theos clears his throat.

"Your mother's being kind," he tells Demetrios.

"What? How?"

"We didn't fight together, not really. I was there, but it was her who fought and taught me everything I ended up knowing about fighting, and even sometimes let me come along with her."

"*Really?*" Demetrios frowns, then looks at me next to him.

"Indeed," Theos nods. "Even right here, in this city, not very far from this spot when I was just a boy, maybe even younger than you are now."

"You came with me on your own," I tell him, smiling. "I tried to stop you, if you remember, but you wouldn't listen."

"Boys that age, right?" Theos says, then winks at Demetrios who smiles now.

I do, too.

So does he.

"I should be going."

"It was good to see you, Theos."

He looks at us one more time, then nods and leaves to go back to his wife and young daughter. I watch as he picks her up from her pram and spins her in the air, then turn back to Demetrios who's still looking at me with a million questions now, I know, about his mother and who I am, but I look past him.

I look at the bookstore.

In the window I see Evelyn's latest book and it's a novel of the war and a soldier, not very unlike him, who leaves England and travels to Africa, Crete, then Asia, and the first novel he wrote after the war was a massive bestseller, so every other he's written has always been accompanied by window displays and tours and fanfare on different continents, and literary celebrity.

I think of him.

I remember what he once said to me, and I think of it again now.

We both write, and we are written.

We have been written, here on this island, even if there's no novel of our exploits.

I have been written, too.

I've been written in how I've lived, and I've been written in so many others who both are and were here, who my life has touched, and I've been written in him, too, this boy who stands next to me.

There is nothing else, no other way to live, or be in this world.

"Are you going to buy it?" he asks me.

"No," I tell him, and shake my head.

Then I turn and start to head back towards the rest of the group, and the buses that will take us home.

He goes with me.

He's taller than me, I realize, as we walk.

When did that happen?

I once thought the same thing of Ikaros, then Tasos, and now I think the same of my own son.

Time, time, and what it does to us.

Another tear comes, and I keep walking.

Will it ever stop?

Can we ever slow it down?

1963

40

JUNE 10, 1963

Demetrios graduates in the spring, and he hasn't told me what he wants to do after school, and I haven't pushed him. I know he's a boy who's also a young man now, and he won't be one to stay on our farm, where he was raised, to stay in a village that is no longer a village, with his mother and the ghosts of what was once here and who we once were. I'm comfortable with these ghosts and memories, because they're mine, but I want things to be different for him. I *need* things to be different for him, but he still helps me paint the olive trees with lime for another season, and doesn't spend time with his friends anymore, all the boys who say *malaka* too often and for no reason at all. Instead, he wakes early and goes to the *agora* with me to sell wool, olives, milk, and the soft mizithra cheese I've begun to make. Then one afternoon, when we sit outside, under the sinking sun and beneath the great mountains, he asks about his father again, for the first time since I told him who he was.

"That man, that we met in Rethymno. He knew him, too, didn't he?"

"Yes."

"I could see it in his eyes."

"You look like him, you see."

"Will you start at the beginning?"

"I told you how he ended up here, and how I met him."

"No," he says. "Before that. All the way at the beginning."

I look back at him.

I realize he knows what he's asking, and how difficult this is, the pain it'll bring.

But it's important.

It's important to both of us.

So I nod, and I tell him.

I tell him about my parents, and Demetrios, his namesake, and Giannis and Angeliki, and the village where we lived. I tell him about Elaionas and the history of this valley, and the Magarakis family who lived on the other end of it and how they felt about us. He finds this strange because he of course knows Kyriaki and only knows love when he sees her, but I tell him things don't always stay as they were, and change and progress are our great obligations in this world. I continue and tell him about my life with Demetrios, then how Demetrios left with the 5th, and how I met his father. Then I tell him how Demetrios came back. I spare no detail. I give him even the most gruesome parts, because they happened, so he should know. When we don't speak truth, even if it's pain, that's the disservice, not shielding him from something that is part of this world and part of him and his family, and our story, and that he needs to know because he's part of this world and story, too. I tell him about the war, and I tell him about Demetrios's death. I can see the tears in his eyes when he hears this, then I tell him about my life after Demetrios, my life with William, in the mountains. The sun sinks as we talk and it becomes dark but we don't move and I tell him everything. I tell him, you see, because who will be here to remember when I'm gone? Who will be here to know who we were, and what we did, if not him? Tasos and Cassia have left and no longer come back, and after Ikaros graduated two years before Demetrios, he decided he wanted to live up to his namesake, so against my wishes, but with his mother's blessing, he joined the army and moved to Athens, too. Kyriaki also left and moved to the city, to be closer to him, so there is no more of my blood here anymore. There's only us. Paths turn to roads, villages become cities, and the way we once lived vanishes in front of my eyes, never to return. I've never been opposed to progress, as I've said, but I have been opposed to forgetting what came before us, and pretending we have no maps.

"Is he alive?" Demetrios asks, very quietly, when I finish my story.

"I don't know," I tell him. "And I understand if you're angry with me for not telling him, or trying to find him, or for not telling you."

"I'm not angry."

"I wasn't sure then if what I did was right. I'm still not sure. But I've done the best I could."

"I understand," he nods, then looks up and meets my eyes.

I know what he wants. I know what he's asking me.

"You want to look for him," I say, and it's not a question.

He's my son, and he's his, too, so of course he does.

"Do you have any way to start, any way to try to begin?"

"I have one," I tell him.

Then I get up and go into the house.

I go to the drawer in my closet and put my hand underneath all my clothes and feel it there, the familiar touch of the cold metal, then take it and look at it as it sits in my palm. It hasn't changed at all. It hasn't aged, or tarnished, and I remember the first time I saw it on his finger.

I walk back outside to our son, and hand it to him.

He takes it.

He turns the ring over and over in his hand, studying the lines, the shape, the crest etched into it.

He touches it gently.

"It was his?" he asks.

"It was his mother's, and it's her crest that's on it, the mark of her family. It was his most prized possession and he never took it off."

"Until he left."

"*Nai.*"

"And he left it here, with you."

"*Nai.*"

I think he's beginning to understand.

I think he's beginning to understand what we meant to each other even though we didn't stay together after the war because of what life does, what it does to all of us, and he'll figure that out on his own at some point in the future, too. We talk for a little while longer, then the next day he walks down to Chania and uses the money that Tasos and Cassia send every year at Christmas to book a ticket for a ferry that will take him to Piraeus, first, then on to London three days after that. He'll stay with Tasos and Cassia and his cousins in Athens for the two days he'll be there, then leave from Athens to go to another island, one on the other side of this great continent, to search for the father he's never met.

What will he find?

I don't know.

Will he find his father happily married and living in a castle, or will he be in the city, or perhaps a quaint cottage in the countryside, and does he have children besides just Demetrios?

Does my son have brothers and sisters he doesn't know?

Does he have another mother, and what is she like?

I hope for these things.

I hope he'll have all these things and that they're waiting for him on the island I've never been to, but where he will now go, because I understand that he must; he has to go and find this, and I won't stop him, or stand in his way.

I can't.

How could I?

And besides, what an adventure for a young man. What an adventure for anyone.

He packs a suitcase and I put fresh *spanakopita* in it for the boat along with some dried stems and leaves picked from the mountains above our house for him to make *malotira* because he'll need it in the rain and under the clouds and won't be able to get any there in England, or on the journey to get there. They drink tea in England, of course, but their tea doesn't heal like ours does. It might nourish the body, but it doesn't touch the soul, or at least not in the same way. When he's ready and packed I go down to the *limani* with him one last time. We get there early and then when it's finally time for his ferry, I hug him for the hundredth time that day. I cry and so does he as I look down at the ring he now wears on his left hand, his father's ring, and I push a fistful of *drachmae* I've been saving into his palm to help him on the great adventure of his life. When I do, I'm surprised at what I say, and the last thing I tell him which is to forget this place. I tell him to forget this place and island and to go find his future, the same as everyone has and does, or should do, then he cries even more, and so do I, and he tells me he'll never forget anything—not anything, ever, not in his whole life—but I tell him he needs to and I can see he doesn't know why I say this, or understand, and why I say it now, and I don't tell him.

I've told him everything . . . everything, except this.

I still need to have one last secret.

I know he wants to ask more but then it's time to go and he gets onto the boat and sails away, and north, on the same great sea that brought me his father, the same sea named for the ancient and grieving king who thought he lost his son to tragedy and war, too, and he wonders why I tell him to leave?

Who we have been.

Who we still are.

There are ghosts everywhere.

I go back home.

I walk in to the empty and quiet house, and when I do, I see a note sitting on the kitchen table that he must have put there when I wasn't looking, before we left, and I walk towards it.

I stand there for a moment, then reach for it.

I open it and see his familiar handwriting and hear his voice as I read it.

I couldn't possibly thank you for all that you've given me, it begins, *and all that you've sacrificed so I could be here in this world and be who I am. And I couldn't possibly thank you enough for knowing why I need to do this, and why I need to go looking for him. I also know you've watched me and know me more than anyone on this earth knows me, and even though you haven't asked, I know you've wondered what my future holds, and what I wish to do, and be. Well, this is it. I want to be a writer. This is the first time I've told anyone, and I wanted to make sure you were the first to know. I'm not sure if you'll be proud, or scared, or think me better suited to something else, but it's my heart and so I thank you for sharing yours and telling me all the stories of us, and who we are, and our village and island and family. There's just one story left, though, for me, and that's what I go to search for. Before I can tell the stories of others, I need to know my own, and who he is, so that I also know who I am. I love you forever. I wouldn't change anything, not a single thing, and I love you forever. Demetrios.*

I cry.

I cry as I read it, and I can't stop, and I haven't told him about the cancer that's in my body, and this is why, because he needs to do this.

He needs to live and have his life, and if I'd told him, then he wouldn't.

Then his life would be my life, and disease, so as I held him one hundred times and then watched him sail away, I knew it would be the last time I touched him, the last time I saw him, the last time I smelled him and looked into his young and brave eyes and it's too much for me to bear.

I love him.

I love him so very much, and I envy him, too.

I envy everything he'll do, and see, and feel, and I envy his youth and strength and how I know he feels at this age and point in his life even just walking down the street or thinking of the future and next day because I was once that age, and I felt the same things he does.

I don't feel them now.

Time.

Time, and what it does to us, and I know what he's doing and why he wants to find his father. I also know why he wants to be a writer, and it's because he wishes to speak to the dead, and I understand that, too, because I also wish to speak with them. Days pass, then weeks, and the pain in my stomach gets worse and the doctor in Chania tells me he thinks it won't be long now, so I find a lawyer in a small office in the new part of town, south of the *limani* and the *agora*, and I walk into his office and see him dressed in a suit and give him my last and final wishes. I tell him I want Tasos to be in charge of my affairs, and for everything I own to go to Demetrios, including the dagger I take from my waist and hand to him to put into his safe, the dagger that belonged to my father. Then and most importantly I give him very specific instructions on where I want to be buried, and how. He writes all this down and I sign the paper and he keeps one copy of this, my first and last will, in his office, to be unsealed when I die, sends one copy to Tasos in Athens, and I keep a copy for myself, to bring back with me to the house.

I almost don't make it.

I remember when I used to run on this path where I now have to move off to the side when cars come barreling by, kicking up dirt and stones, and instead of running, I can barely make it from the beach to my house at all. But I do. Then I go higher. I go to where his house used to be and the rest of our village, and I go to the place under the olive and cypress trees at the foot of the mountains where I buried him and I mark the spot where I want to be buried, too, next to where he is. Then I slowly go back down to my own house and more days pass and the pain becomes even greater until I can barely eat, barely go outside, barely do anything at all and I know that means it'll be soon now. I don't tell anyone. I want to be alone, I want to face this alone, this last and final thing, the same as all the others.

I think of my son, and where he's at, on another island so very far away.

Then I think of this island, our island, and I think of who we are and who we've been and I think not only of him now, but all the others, too: Tasos, and Cassia, and Kyriaki and her son, and those who are no longer with us, as well; Giannis and Angeliki, and Ikaros, and my mother and father, and of course Demetrios, and I think of this place where we've all together lived a thousand lives and loved a thousand loves, and as I think of this, I realize that perhaps our country isn't our country but rather our memories, our collected memories that are made, told, repeated, and passed down, our memories I've given to him now, too, to my son, and that become our stories which are more real than anything else and that will become *his* stories now. His stories that he'll tell. This is an island, a cursed and blessed island of both ghosts and dreams, but the stories? They're eternal, they can never be killed or conquered, like so many have thought we could be, and they're ours. They're all of ours, and no matter where we are, no matter how far and wide we might go and travel, they will go with us because they rush through our blood and spread through our souls until perhaps they *are* our souls, aren't they, and have they always been? Of course they have. And they always will be. They always, always will be.

Was my life a good one?

I don't know.

It was mine, and that will have to be enough.

There's one memory left.

I take the letter my son wrote in one hand and the dagger that belonged to my husband in the other and that I've kept through all these years, and I crawl outside so I'm in the light and I think again of that first summer we were together when he came to help build the barn that was a stone's throw from where I lay now in the grass. I think of the *skifanes pites* my mother used to make and the way the honey tasted on our skin as we sat there together under the exact same sun and ate them. I think of how I felt then and I think of my son again and I'm so glad his life and his struggles will be his own, and that they won't be mine, and I think of my husband and everything that could have been if there was no such thing as war. And then I see him, too. I look at the great mountains behind me and then turn towards the sea in front of where I lay, and can taste the salt on the breeze that comes from it, and I see him walking back up the path towards me, just like he said he would, all those years ago, and he keeps walking. He gets closer. Then, soon, he's almost to me. I smile. So does he. I have so much to tell him. I know this is where they'll find me, and how, clutching the note in one hand, and dagger in the other, and I smile.

Demetrios, I whisper, speaking to both of them.

Demetrios, I whisper.

AUTHOR'S NOTE

First and foremost, I'd like to thank the many people of Chania, one of the great cities of the world, and the surrounding areas of Crete who welcomed me into their homes and lives and shared with me so many of the stories that formed the foundation and basis of this novel. When the Italians invaded Greece on October 28, 1940, the fighting and resistance that occurred on the mainland would go on to change the course of the war and lead to the eventual Allied victory. The fighting didn't end, though, when the Greek mainland fell to the Germans, and as depicted in this novel, most all Cretan men of fighting age were either killed or stuck there on the mainland, so when the Germans invaded Crete, the Greeks that were fighting alongside the British and Commonwealth troops were mostly women, children, and the elderly. You can still hear those who lived through it talk about what it was like to see the sky black with paratroopers, and the unexpected fierceness, unity, and duration of the Cretan and Greek resistance made sure the invasion of Crete was both the first and last time a paratrooper-based invasion by Germany was ever attempted in the entirety of the war.

We so often commemorate things in an effort to forget them, and in true response to that idea, every German paratrooper that participated in the Battle of Crete received an Iron Cross.

There was also a confluence of so many influential and notable people in one place on Crete during these years, and I've tried to represent some of them here, and in this story, and while this is a work of fiction and the words, thoughts, and actions given to them are mine, here is who they are: Father Angelo, who Maria sees in the harbor at Chania is based on Angelo Roncalli, a Catholic cardinal who came to Crete ahead of the Germans and provided Jewish children and families with baptism certificates that said they were Catholic and his actions saved countless Jews from the death camps and Holocaust. After the war, he was elected pope, choosing the name John XXIII, was later canonized a saint, and is known today as "The Good Pope." James Roosevelt, the son of Franklin Roosevelt, was also on Crete both before and during the German invasion, as a clandestine representative for his father, assuring leaders and soldiers alike across the world that the United States stood with them morally and would engage with troops rather than just supplies and weapons as soon as it was politically possible because of the pressures at home to not engage in any foreign wars, no matter what, no matter the global consequences or level of evil. Prince Philip, born on Corfu as Prince Philippos of Greece and Denmark, and who would later go on to become the Duke of Edinburgh and husband of the late Queen Elizabeth II, was part of the Greek royal family and stationed on a British Royal Navy ship off the coast of Crete for at least part of the war, and King George of Greece really did evacuate to Crete from Athens, then once the threat of the Germans coming to Crete increased, travelled across the island on donkeys and mules, over the mountains and to the southern coast where he was carried on to Egypt by boat. There are still those near Chania who will tell you, if you ask them, of the night the king came and stayed in their village on his way.

After the island fell to the Germans, and the British troops evacuated, some British and Commonwealth soldiers really were left, stayed, or came back, and they really were brought information and supplies via submarine and boat by the SOE that they shared with their partners in the Greek resistance. Of those in this story, Peter is based on the writer Peter Fleming who fought on Crete and was the real-life brother of Ian Fleming, who would later go on to create James Bond, though Peter was a celebrated writer in his own right, too, with his novel *Brazilian Adventure* about his trip up the Amazon in search of the missing Colonel Percy Fawcett considered even at the time to be a classic of travel literature. Evelyn is based on Evelyn Waugh, who also fought on Crete and in many other areas during the war and achieved international fame and celebrity later with the publication of his seminal novel *Brideshead Revisited*, though the connection of the backstory of his protagonist Charles Ryder to William's own backstory and surname is purely my invention. The British commander A. W. Lawrence, brother of T. E. Lawrence, who is more commonly known as "Lawrence of Arabia," also fought on Crete, carrying on his brother's legacy from the first world war into the second, and I'm proud to be able to include some of his brother's words and sentiments from *Seven Pillars of Wisdom* in this story, also, which of course would be all too similar and familiar, to both of them.

Friedrich-Willhelm Muller is inspired by the German officer of the same name, who became known as "the Butcher of Crete," and Hannes Koch is loosely based on Heinrich Kreipe, the German commander who would eventually replace Muller and who was abducted outside the Villa Ariadne, near Knossos, by a group of British commandos, SOE officers, and Greek resistance fighters who brought him to the beach at Rodakino to be evacuated via SOE boat to Egypt and questioned. A plaque still stands on the beach commemorating the event to this day.

My debut novel, *Once We Were Here*, is a love story between three friends set on mainland Greece spanning from the fall of 1940 to the spring of 1941, during the initial Greek resistance of Italian and German invasion and the events that would ultimately lead to the Allies winning the war (and the events that William, who was a minor character in that novel, escapes from in the prologue of this book). Before the novel came out, a major publication wrote in its review that readers "who don't mind black-and-white WWII adventures" would enjoy it.

The story of a boy who stole a motorcycle being stripped naked and beaten in the town square, that I give to Tasos in this novel, is based on something that actually happened. More than that, I purposefully don't give a surname to Maria's family or a name to the village they're from that eventually gets destroyed and every single member massacred and killed and left to rot in the sun, because the same thing happened to more villages and innocent men, women, and children on Crete than can be counted, from the massacre of Kondomari and razing of Kandanos, to the Holocaust of Kedros, where all the inhabitants of nine separate villages in the Amari Valley were rounded up and killed by firing squad and their bodies covered in gasoline and lit on fire. Many of these Cretan villages, like Maria's, were never rebuilt after they were destroyed and the villagers massacred, and have been wiped off the face of the planet completely and forever.

We don't only tell stories so that we remember. We also tell stories so that we don't forget, and while I can't speak for all who fought, and sacrificed, and gave absolutely everything that could possibly be given, I can try to speak for some.

Time allows history and actions to fade and change, and when history fades and changes, that's when it happens again.

This is a story of the past.

It also at the same time isn't, and my greatest hope is that stories, and stories such as this one—stories of goodness in the face of evil, and of love in the face of all that would come and try to destroy love—can perhaps help guide us towards a better future built on decency, empathy, kindness, and understanding of all peoples; their lives, their struggles, their hearts, and their beauty.

As always, I thank you so very much for joining me on that journey.

Every time you read, share, tell a friend, or even think about this novel and story and so many others like it, I thank you so very much for helping to try to build that future alongside me.

Indeed, it's the greatest hope I have.

Christopher Cosmos
Grand Rapids, Michigan